STOLEN

WATERS

Love · Wisdom
May you be blessed with both!

SHAUN MACKELPRANG

April 2021

for Linda, who was patient (mostly)

TABLE OF CONTENTS

Prologue.
Blood Child.

A girl runs through the temple orchard. She clutches handfuls of her robe, pulling the bottom hem up to free her legs. Her dark, cropped hair flutters.

At the edge of the orchard, near the wall, she crouches next to a tree and traces her finger along a frosted spike of withered grass, melting the hoary crystals. In the bitter-cold air, her exhalations transform into smoke, and when she closes her mouth and breathes in deeply, she feels the moisture freezing in her nostrils. She relishes the sensation.

Other children crunch across the frosted, winter-beige grass, chasing each other quietly, only letting out little shrieks and bits of laughter now and then. They do not want to draw the gentle ire of their ever-present temple mothers, and they know it is right to be respectful in the House of Esana, even if they are not inside. The orchard is part of the temple complex; everything within the complex belongs to God.

The sun emerges from behind a cloud, and the orchard brightens. An icy drizzle the night before has encased the trees in a crystalline skin, and the branches and boles sparkle with rainbow sheens and icy-white glints. The girl strolls among the trees, looking up through the frozen branches at the winter-blue sky. In a few months, the ice will be gone; the trees will become supple, and leaves and blossoms will emerge, followed by fruits.

A group of children stands near one of the *sluiva* trees.

The girl walks over and sees they are playing the blood game. She smirks. The boy they are daring is uncertain; he is afraid. He carefully examines the thorns on the trunk of the tree; the girl thinks he is stalling. His blood must be weak.

"My blood is stronger," she says, rescuing him and humiliating him at once. She carelessly plucks one of the long spiny thorns from the *sluiva* tree. Ice crackles and snaps off the branch. "Watch."

The other children watch in awe and delighted horror as she drives the thorn deep into the pad of her thumb. She does not cry out, but she draws in a short, sharp breath, quickened by pain. Blood seeps up around the thorn, and she pulls it loose, already feeling the power of her body. A dark bead forms—almost black against her pale flesh— and then it slides over the edge of her thumb and falls to the ground, leaving a scarlet trail on her skin.

The drop is bright red on the withered grass.

But then the girl rubs away the blood, grins broadly, and displays her triumph to the other children. The bleeding has stopped; the tiny wound is gone; her body has been made whole by her regenerative blood.

"See," she says, full of defiant joy. "My blood is strong." And she looks from one child to the next, her thumb moving back and forth, pointing at one child and then another.

But the other children are silent, their mouths frozen open, their eyes wide. The girl does not see that she has been seen. A moment later, her temple mother parts the little group of children and takes hold of her hand from behind. The girl's triumph wilts.

"Come," her temple mother says, and she leads the girl away.

In the common room, standing by the wash basins, the old woman watches as the girl rinses away the residue of blood. The room is large, paved with smooth stones, and full of long wooden tables. The temple children eat and study there every day, but it is empty during the play hour, and the girl looks around with large eyes, glancing at doorways, alert. She wants to go back outside.

"You must not put your faith in the hand of the flesh," her temple mother says quietly, leaning toward her. A lock of her white hair has fallen down over one eye, and the girl thinks it looks pretty; she would like to have white hair. "You must not. No matter how strong you think it might be, it will fail you."

The girl nods. She dries her hands on one of the soft towels hanging beside the basin and turns to face her temple mother.

A man enters the room. He is not one of the priests; he wears a heavy cloak, and he holds gloves in one hand. His smooth, hard face marks him; he is a descendant of Yinock, a leader of one of the great houses.

"Is she made whole?" he asks.

"She is, my Lord." The temple mother closes her eyes as she dips her chin.

The man stares at the girl for several seconds. "She is very young." His voice betrays unspoken doubts.

"She is not yet of the age of accountability."

"I see. Well." The man stares at the girl a moment longer. Then he puts a finger beneath her chin and tilts her head up.

She offers no resistance. She is small, and he is big. Obedience to temple mothers and the priests and elders is an unchanging aspect of her days. His face is stern, but only the temple mothers ever smile at the girl, so she feels no concern.

He speaks with calm authority, his eyes divining. "The blood of our ancient father might flow in your veins, child. Be worthy of it."

The girl nods. The words flow over her without changing her; she has heard such words before, many times. She is thinking about the other children still playing in the orchard.

The man releases her chin and turns away. "When she is assigned, I want her assigned to my House, but to one of the lesser branches."

The temple mother nods in submission.

When the man leaves, the girl's temple mother takes her by the hand and kneels beside her. The old woman's dark eyes look into the eyes of the little girl. Her face is old and wrinkled, a map of many years; her eyes are compassionate.

"No woman should put her faith in the hand of the flesh, child. You must always remember that. Always. And when you are a little older—when you reach the age of accountability—you must put away childish things. The blood of Yinock is not a plaything, it is a sacred blessing. But some would use it for their own ends. So you must hold it secret in your heart, where thieves cannot break in and steal it."

"Yes, mother." The girl says the words, but inwardly she is wondering if she will be allowed to return to the orchard.

"I will give you to a good house," her temple mother says, and she glances toward the door where the man exited. "Now go back out and play."

That makes the girl happy.

CHAPTER ONE.

WATER WOMAN.

Sarana gave in to temptation and looked at her hands. The smooth perfection of her skin enticed her to speculate, to dream. But her lineage was shrouded—she did not know her parents—and the pride she felt when she looked at the clean, precise lines of her fingers was a childish impulse, a persistent vanity. It was true what her old temple mother had been so fond of saying: *Humility is harder to trap than water.*

She picked up her empty jars and went back to work.

It was nearly midday, and the women at the well were numerous. Sarana stepped deliberately among them, careful not to jostle their jars. She joined one of the orderly lines leading down the long, broad steps to the Pool of Geb.

At the water's edge, the gossip quieted, and the sacred muttering of the Line of *Es* rose from the lips of the women. The individual words overlapped and repeated, joining into a soft, lilting whisper of the ancient prayer of her servitude.

Chay on peya ikola bo on zheya. Over and over. And over again. *When he drinks, he will ever thirst. When he drinks . . . When he drinks . . . he will ever thirst.* Unceasing. Each woman who drew from the well repeated the line.

Sarana knelt on the bottom step and pushed up her sleeves. Down the length of the pool, other women knelt and drew water. But at its western end, where the long Pool of Geb emerged through the arched doorway of the well house, there were men instead of women. Guards. And beyond them, the cool interior of the well house, where pumps of ancient manufacture drew the waters of Geb out of the depths of the earth.

This was her place. The unending task of drawing water enfolded her, and she lived each day along similar lines—a dust-colored thread in a rug of repeating patterns. She dipped her own jars beneath the cool, rippling surface of the water.

"When he drinks, he will ever thirst," she said.

She took up her brimming jars and went back up the broad steps. One more trip, she decided, and then she would return home and rest a bit and eat. She had already made a dozen trips to the well that morning, and on her last trip home, she had smelled fresh bread coming out of the ovens. The other women of the house would have the midday meal ready soon, and she would sit with them in the courtyard and trade tales. This brought a smile as she worked her way home through the crowded streets of the lower city.

But her little smile faded when she reached the Stair Market and heard an unwelcome voice calling out an invitation.

"Come. Come and see."

He was not calling to her—not directly; he was calling to all passersby, hoping to lure them into his house of levity. Obviously rich, his hands gleamed with precious metals, and his red, silken shirt invited touch. Even his shoes, with their pointed, curled-up toes seemed to suggest ease. She glanced away and down, ashamed. His colorful clothing drew the eye, his words drew the mind.

Her temple mother had warned her against such men, her words frank. *Purveyors of flesh are abominable to God. That is what these men of levity are. They snare the foolish with promises of wealth and freedom, but their promises are false.*

The warning had not been enough, though, to keep her from wondering—to keep her from looking, just once.

Sarana lengthened her stride and hurried up the old, stone steps to the upper city. She kept her eyes away from him, but his voice conjured images of the wantons who entertained strange men in dim chambers.

At the top of the stairs, she turned to the right, passing by the homes of wealthy merchants and lesser branches of the great houses. A few of the houses were walled enclaves, like the house of her master. The streets grew less crowded, quieter. But even so, there was no stillness—servants, laden; stewards, hurrying; and rich young masters, walking with their friends or riding jaunty horses.

Inside her master's gates, one of the watchmen, Ganon, greeted her with a raised hand. He and Tobin were engaged in a game of stones, and they barely looked up as she passed. Still, she noticed Tobin glance at her again as she got just beyond him. Some patterns did not alter.

She crossed the courtyard and descended into the cool interior of the cistern. She emptied her jars into one of the dark pools. The ripples slowly flattened, and the surface of the water transformed into a gently undulating slate. A few water bugs skittered across the surface, their feet dimpling the water. Pelem would have to clean them out soon. They were harmless, but if they became too numerous, they drew other creatures.

She glanced toward the doorway, confirming she was alone. She removed her shawl and dipped a hand into the water. Her eyes closed as she rubbed the back of her neck with cool water.

One more trip, she thought. She let out a pent-up breath without opening her mouth, and a soft moan, drawn out and creaky toward the end, worked its way up her throat. *One more trip. And then I can rest a bit.*

But when she returned to the well, she had to abandon her secret plan. The steps at the water's edge had overflowed—she had arrived at one of those unpredictable moments when the multitude swelled and threatened to exceed the well's capacity.

She eased herself into the sea of women and looked for a spot to sit, preferring to wait rather than contend with the throng. She turned when a familiar voice called her name. A young woman waved her over.

"*Hala*, Tera," Sarana said, as she drew closer.

Tera smiled and made room for Sarana on one of the smooth white stones scattered about the place of water. The women sitting next to her adjusted themselves to make room. Some squawked, but they were good-natured squawks. The women of the well were accustomed to the constant shifting of women and jars, and some of these women knew Sarana well. They greeted her with nodding heads.

"So what do you think it means?" Tera asked.

Sarana was still settling her jars at her feet, and she looked up. "What what means?"

"The sign."

"I don't know—" Sarana shook her head, seeing that Tera was wide eyed, eager to share something. "What are you talking about?"

"You didn't hear?" Excitement warmed Tera's words.

"No. Nothing new. Not this morning."

Tera paused and glanced around at some of the other women. A few of them heard the exchange and looked on, their faces brightening with anticipation. Tera focused on Sarana's face and held up both hands.

"It's the Wayfarer," she said. "It's fallen from heaven."

"What?" The words were impossible and, thus, incomprehensible.

"The Wayfarer." Tera said. "It fell. It fell from heaven."

Sarana did not understand what Tera could mean. "It fell?"

"Yes, it fell."

"But how can that be?" Sarana looked from one woman to another.

"Everyone's been talking about it since I got here," Tera said, impatient.

"It's true, child," said one of the old women. "They say it tumbled across the skies of hari-Hrusk, shooting out flames. All the way to the Southern Sea. It passed over Shal-Gashun and went down somewhere far to the south. Just a few weeks ago—maybe three weeks."

"Shal-Gashun," Sarana said softly. A place so far off in her imagination she hardly believed it existed. And, yet, she knew her master had traveled there. He sent caravans there in the spring and fall.

"People say it's a sign," Tera said. "They say it burned in the night sky."

Sarana turned the words over in her mind and tried to imagine it. The Wayfarer falling from the sky. The dim, wandering star straying from its age-old path across the night sky. And falling. She could not remember when she last had looked for it.

The old woman spoke again. "A great fiery orb, they say. Burning and throwing off flames and sparks. It crossed the sky from one horizon to another—much slower than a shooting star. They say it must have come down in the sea."

"But how?" Sarana asked. "How could it fall?"

"It is a sign," said the old woman. "God has not forgotten us."

"But what does it mean?" Sarana's consternation left her mouth partly open. The thought of the Wayfarer falling from heaven, the thought of it burning up, could hardly be conceived.

"It means the forerunner has come," Tera said. "The prophet at the river." She looked around quickly. "At least that's what some people are saying."

Sarana smiled at Tera, a little indulgently; she, too, had heard the tales about the so-called prophet who had taken to preaching by the river, down in the valley.

"That's what his followers would have you think," said the old woman, shaking her head. "They want everyone to accept his teachings."

"Or it could mean God is done with us," said another old woman. "And that's why he finally took his watcher from the sky." Her voice was grim.

"I know someone who's been to see him," said a middle-aged woman. "And I think there must be a connection. It was two weeks ago he came—when he started preaching at the river. The Wayfarer fell from the heavens about the same time." She paused briefly. "I think he might be the Wayfarer, come back to aid us in this time of need."

Sarana shook her head unconsciously; that made no sense.

"The Wayfarer is a star," Tera said. "And it wasn't the same time, anyway. He's been down there barely two weeks. We just heard about this today, and everyone says it happened weeks ago."

"I heard a man say it was five or six weeks ago," the middle-aged woman said.

"No, that can't be right." The first woman was shaking her head. "We would have heard of it sooner if it happened six weeks ago. The caravans are rolling in already, and several have already arrived from the South. News has been pouring in for days and days. It could not have happened so long ago."

Sarana nodded. She had seen the wagons weaving through the city, creaking and trailing dust. And like her many sisters at the well, she greedily gathered the tales as each caravan unraveled and divulged its wares and people. Dark-skinned Hruskans—beautiful men bedecked with golden jewelry and colorful clothes—often rode as guards, clutching the long, curved swords common in Hrusk. It was said they wore magical trinkets to protect themselves in the empty wastes, where only beasts and robbers dwelled.

Two women stood suddenly, startling Sarana out of her thoughts. The crowd at the water's edge was beginning to thin.

"I'd better go," Tera said, and she stood, too. "But I'll talk to you later. Maybe tomorrow."

"All right," Sarana said. But she did not stand. Any thought of finishing quickly and returning home had fled.

The Wayfarer has fallen. It was a thought she could barely fathom. It was impossible. Yinock had placed the Wayfarer in the heavens to watch over his children. To comfort them. *How could it fall?* She thought back again, sorting through her evenings, but she could not remember when she had last gazed up at the night sky and searched for it.

The other women continued their talk, and newcomers picked up the threads of the conversation, repeating and embellishing the tale. Some of them, like Sarana, had not heard of the Wayfarer's fall.

Sarana closed her eyes and leaned back, listening to their voices, a familiar ebb and flow. But she gained no comfort. No one knew what it meant. No one could. The Wayfarer had fallen. Unrest in the South.

A prophet preaching against the priests and elders of the Great City. A sign. Stories of unrest were common enough, but the Wayfarer's fall—the sign—made the women uneasy and kept them searching for some assurance of safety.

And could this man down at the river be connected to the Wayfarer? Sarana opened her eyes and glanced at the chattering women. Some of them were wrinkled with age, bent and worn. A familiar pride crept into her thoughts.

Such women could not carry the pure blood of Yinock in their veins. *They are mongrels. My blood is strong.* Sarana regretted her thoughts immediately and berated herself silently. These were her sisters. And then, as she recalled the seamed and aged face of her kindly temple mother, her shame grew and blossomed, twining through her mind like a night-flowering vine.

Forgive me, Abasha, she thought, invoking her memory. She had loved her temple mother; but Abasha, too, had been a child of two worlds—a daughter of Yinock whose bloodline had been lost.

Sarana traced her fingertips over the stone where she and the others perched; she felt the soft thrumming of the stone's inexhaustible, internal energy. Like the ancient pumps in the well house, which had been scavenged from the abandoned water works of the Great City of Old, the stones were of ancient manufacture, remnants of a lost technology. They had come from the ancient city itself—in the moment of its transfiguration and departure into the heavens.

Though sorrowful, the tale of how the Great City fled was one of her favorite stories. The city had been taken up into the heavens with its righteous people, and the unworthy had been left behind. But as God had taken the transfigured city up, a giant section had broken away from its foundation and tumbled to the ground, scattering and breaking into hundreds of pieces. It was written,

Even as Yinock abandoned those who rebelled against him, God found it good to bless the remnant with an everlasting reminder of their destiny.

So said the Lines of the Law. And when the Children of Yinock left that forsaken place, they gathered up the fallen stones and used them to lay the foundation of a new city.

Sarana's fingertip came to a stop. A tentative thought ascended from the depths of her mind.

The Wayfarer fell from heaven, too. Like these stones. She felt a tingling thrill go through her body. No one had thought about that—or at least none of the other women had said anything about a connection between the two. Sarana looked at her hands again. *I am Yinock's daughter,* she thought. *Maybe I've seen the truth of his sign.*

After a moment's thought, she turned to the women sitting beside her; they were still chattering as before, though different women came and went.

"Maybe Yinock's city is about to return," Sarana said, a little softly.

"What's that, child?" An older woman.

"He might be a prophet—the man at the river. What if the Wayfarer's fall is a sign of Yinock's return—the return of the Great City of Old?"

"How can that be?" a woman asked, querulous. "If it means anything, it means the things of Yinock's time are dying. The bits and pieces of the old world are beginning to wear out and break."

Sarana had heard the same, but she persisted. "But when the city was taken up into heaven, these stones fell to earth, just like the Wayfarer." She rubbed her palm on the stone to emphasize her thought. "Maybe the Wayfarer's fall means the city is coming back."

The old woman shook her head. "It's a pretty thought, child, but Yinock abandoned us long ago. I do not think he will return."

"But the Lines say he—" Sarana began, but she was cut off.

"The Lines say Esana will come. And he will be preceded by a prophet of great power." The old woman waved her hand vaguely to the west. "Do you think this man at the river is the forerunner?"

Sarana shook her head. "He could be. I—I don't know."

"And you never will, child. Unless Esana comes and reveals all things." The woman did not speak unkindly. "We are just water women. You have your jars there. Do you think you know better than people who have seen and listened to him? They cannot say who or what he is. You ought to get back to the things that matter."

Sarana was reminded again of Abasha, who, at that moment, would have ended this soft rebuke by saying, *In submission is exaltation.* "None of us has seen him either," the middle-aged woman said. She gestured with her chin toward Sarana and said, "But like you said, it is a pretty thought. I would be glad to see the city return." The woman's eyes drifted upward.

"Perhaps you're right," Sarana said reflexively, answering the older woman's rebuke and turning her eyes back to the ground. But something smoldered in her heart. The absoluteness of the old woman's declaration, the finality of her edict, provoked a silent flame of contradiction.

I will be more than a water woman, she thought. And she clenched her hands in her lap. *I am of age. I do not have to remain a servant.*

But the prospect of renouncing her favored status as a temple servant and leaving the House of Jianin roused latent terrors. If she renounced her servitude before her jubilee, she would have nothing. No home, no money, no work. She would be one of the *nebini.*

"There is no shame in it, child." The old woman put a hand on Sarana's arm and squeezed gently, drawing her back to her place. "To be what we are is a great gift, too."

Sarana nodded slightly, but she did not look up. She looked at her jars and felt a baleful impulse to break them. Her jars, her clay children. The fragile offspring of clay and fire could not withstand her terrible, indestructible hands.

But the impulse withered quickly, subdued by a reflexive, bedrock aversion to broken jars. Her temple mother had repeated the apothegm daily: *A broken jar carries no water.* Sarana knew it was true, but her anger was not entirely slaked.

A path alongside a river appeared in her mind, and she imagined a little child folded within the curves of her jar—a child nursed by her unceasing efforts at the Well of Geb. And in that moment, she saw the endless string of clay children she would bear, day after day, year after year. *To be what we are is a great gift, too.*

Sarana prodded one of her jars with her toes. Hollow bulbs of clay, fired to withstand the force of water. Mere receptacles. That was something she learned from Abasha, too, and it came to her now with renewed force. *Servitude is merely a receptacle—like this jar. What matters is what you put inside of it. But remember, child, humility is harder to trap than water.*

The familiar memory of her temple mother's wrinkled face crossed her consciousness, filling her with mixed feelings. In her moments of vanity, Sarana secretly hoped her own face would never bear such signs of degeneration. But when she remembered the quiet, peaceful days they had spent in the ordered courtyards of the temple complex, and when she recalled her temple mother's kindly face, Sarana knew the old woman's deliberate, gnarled hands had captured something greater than vain dreams.

The women around her continued their endless talking.

Sarana looked down at her empty jars, snared by her anger, held in place by what she knew to be true. She told herself she should get back to work, but the silent admonition held no force. The old woman's words stung. *Do you think you know better than people who have seen and listened to him?* No. The old woman was right. A woman of the well knew nothing of the broader world. Not really. Cast-off tales, dim echoes of the truth, crumbs from an elusive table far above the world of servitude.

Sarana felt the tears before she understood them. And then, as she blinked them back, she realized just how empty she felt. And her anger grew. She looked down at her jars again. In her master's house, she knew, the other servants waited for her, waited for the water she would bring to them. Her jars, and whatever she could trap within them, would never forsake her. *In submission is exaltation.*

But something had changed. She did not want to return home.

CHAPTER TWO.
SON OF HRUSK.

In the Hruskan Quarter, Neturu Dam walked quickly among the small, crowded homes of his impoverished countrymen. He wore colorful Hruskan attire, ear jewels, and a thin gold chain of rank around his neck. He glanced instinctively at doorways and alleys, alert. Though he did not expect an attack—at least not yet—the patterns of his training, the habits of his youth, were not easily discarded or forgotten.

He turned onto the *churk*, and the lavish brawl of the Hruskan market enveloped him. Wealth replaced poverty. Rows of tables and racks lined the place, and colorfully dressed Hruskans milled noisily from one table to the next. They laughed easily and talked loudly. Vibrant clothing, tapestries, and carpets draped the tables.

But Neturu ignored the beckoning merchants, immune. He was the son and heir of the on-Dam, the emissary of Hrusk; he had grown up in Noot at the heart of Hrusk's wealth and power. He could not be persuaded with the wealth of the world.

At the far end of the *churk*, he skirted a little group of old women who routinely gathered to share stories, woes, and unsolicited observations. Their good-natured jibes and salutations—tossed out almost at random to passersby—drew him out of his gloomier thoughts.

"Such a *nice* young man," one of them called. He nodded and gave them a good-natured wink, and their kindly, dark faces wrinkled pleasantly and broke into smiles. He heard them cackle in his wake as he entered a narrow alley.

The walls drew inward, but the little street was familiar to him. Overhead, thin ropes traversed the narrow gap between the second-story windows of the buildings, and assorted clothing hung like varicolored flags, filling the alley with a filtered, softened glow of sunlight.

Momentarily awed by such a simple glory, he slowed. Absurdly sentimental tears formed in his eyes, and he shook his head, recalling the close, narrow streets of Noot, where people hung their clothing in just the same way. The streets of his childhood. He had grown soft, nostalgic for home, and the weight of his thoughts only heightened his emotions. He wondered if he would ever see his home in Noot again.

He resumed his quick pace, checking cross streets and avoiding vagrants who slept—or feigned sleep—in dusky doorways and corners. Asleep or not, their daytime slumbers did not speak well of them. He sometimes felt the urge to kick them from his path. But such thoughts were unworthy of his new commitments.

A moment later, he emerged from the alleyway and stepped onto the *ulaka*. A familiar pride tinged his thoughts as his eyes played over the design of the broad, cobblestone street. Its mosaic stones lay in precise, flowing patterns, accented with sinuous, intertwining lines of lighter and darker stones. There was no street like it in all of the great city. A work of art. His father had commissioned it to showcase the superiority of Hruskan artistry and workmanship.

My father, he thought sorrowfully.

He arrived at his destination. The consular house sat like a miniature temple in its imported Hruskan jungle. Relatively few Hruskan plants could withstand the colder climate of the Great City, but his father had insisted on finding and cultivating those that could. *A garden of our own intransigence*, his father had said.

Broad-leafed plants lined the short avenue leading to the house, and here and there, blooms and flowers adorned the trees and bushes.

Columns of rosy stone bracketed the front door, and above the entryway a small porch overlooked the grounds. His father had insisted on making the house a reflection of their homeland. Each stone had been hauled from the *skala* quarries of hari-Hrusk at great expense.

The guards at the doors bowed as he entered, each removing his hand from the hilt of his curving sword. But their unceasing loyalty did not comfort him. Rumors of war were filtering into the Great City, and the bin-Yinocki were slowly awakening to the threat of a long-harbored hatred. The pieces of the broken southern lands had slowly rebuilt a semblance of the past, and some families believed it was time to renew the bloodlines of Hrusk.

But do the Yinoi have reason to fear? He did not know.

The bin-Yinocki had slaughtered and subjugated the southern lands with legendary ease. Unstoppable with their Daniti warriors—armed with their ancient weapons of marvelous power—the bin-Yinocki had claimed dominion in Hrusk and hari-Hrusk, all the way down to the northern fringe of the *pustinya*. And for more than a hundred years, the people of Hrusk had lain silently in the dust, always believing any attempt to throw off their oppressors would bring greater humiliation.

But rumors suggested the power of the Daniti was waning. Their ancient weapons were failing, and the bin-Yinocki were incapable of repairing them.

And if they are failing, perhaps we can conquer. Perhaps.

Either way, there would be blood.

Inside, Neturu slowed his hurried steps, dreading what he was about to do. But there was no turning back. Not in his mind. He went straight to his father's council room, where he found a group of men discussing the recent outbreaks of violence in Hrusk. Some of them, Neturu knew from previous meetings, were convinced the time was ripe to pluck victory from the hands of the *Yinoi*—as if war were nothing more than sending men into an orchard to harvest the *kivich*. Ignoring them, Neturu went straight to his father.

"Neturu, my son," his father said, breaking abruptly, perhaps hopefully, from the conversation.

"Father."

The other men quieted. For a moment, there was a tenseness in their eyes and around their mouths. A few glanced at one another, as if they already knew what Neturu would say. The others watched the on-Dam. The recent rift between the on-Dam and his son was not a secret. Neturu's baptism by the *Yinoi* heretic had ignited controversy and speculation. And it had prompted the on-Dam to lay down an ultimatum: renounce or be ostracized.

The on-Dam did not flinch. "You have had three days. Have you seen the folly of your decision?"

Neturu glanced at the other men and shook his head. "No, father."

"You have made up your mind, then?"

Neturu nodded and reached inside his shirt. He withdrew the small bronze medallion he wore around his neck—a little star with eight points, the symbol of his new faith. Some of the gathered men tried to get a better look at it, but Neturu tucked it back inside his clothing.

"I believe he is a man of God," Neturu said. He looked at his father's hard, brown face, the stern nobility carved there by nearly a century of hard training and tradition. He expected to see anger, but the on-Dam's dark eyes held sorrow.

"Will you not remember the faces of your Fathers? Of even your own father?"

For a moment, Neturu's anger flared, and he wanted to explain his decision again. His new faith did not require him to forsake the Hruskan Fathers. His father knew that; Neturu had explained it carefully, more than once. *How many times do I have to say it?* But he knew his father's anger and sorrow could not be reconciled with the unknown god of a renegade *Yinoi* prophet.

"We've been through those gates before," Neturu said.

"Then you know what I must do," the on-Dam said.

Neturu blinked, suddenly uncertain, and he felt weakness trembling at the sides of his mouth. But then he pressed his lips together and nodded.

"I know, father."

He still secretly hoped his father would reconsider, but he knew it would not happen. He understood the demands of his father's position. The politics of Hrusk were unforgiving, and the timing of his conversion to an alien religion could not have been worse. Even before he confessed, he knew the probable consequences of his conversion. And he knew what he had to do. He never seriously considered deception. Silence alone would have been a lie. He owed a greater duty to his father. The father deserves to know the heart of the son, even if it divides them.

The silence stretched, and for a moment Neturu's hope lived. Perhaps his father had repented of his oath.

"You are not my son," the on-Dam said finally, his voice flat.

Neturu nodded, knowing his voice would fail him if he tried to respond too quickly. After a momentary silence, one of the on-Dam's assistants started to say something, but the on-Dam silenced him with a curt left-handed gesture. Silence descended upon the room, and Neturu knew the silence would remain until he responded to the on-Dam's declaration. If he were to act with honor, nothing could displace the words tradition required. He would not add shame to his father's sorrow.

Neturu removed the golden chain of rank from around his neck. "You are not my father," he said. He held out the sign of his rank and dropped it into his father's hand. *But in my heart you will always be my father, and I think I will always be your son. I know it.*

The on-Dam took one long look into his former son's eyes. Then he nodded and turned away, hands clasped behind his back. Neturu waited for his once-father to name his successor, but the on-Dam stood silent.

The on-Dam finally looked toward the door and gestured to one of the guards. "Remove this trespasser."

The guard nodded and turned his gaze upon Neturu. The gathered men clamored for the name of the on-Dam's intended heir, and Neturu followed the guard from the room, never to see his father again. But as Neturu left, he heard the on-Dam's voice. It was clear above the other voices and full of sorrow.

He said, "Such a son as I once had cannot be replaced so easily."

CHAPTER THREE.
LOST CHILD.

Sarana blinked away the watery heat in her eyes and glanced around the place of the well. The other women—including the one who had rebuked her—continued their chatter. New women joined the conversation, and some left. The women shifted, the stories did not. To the women of the well, the prophet was merely a happening, a thing to talk about, an eidolon of gossip.

But he was out there at the river.

People saw him every day.

Sarana wiped one of her eyes and blinked several times, her anger hot in her throat, her heart smoldering. That old woman did not know everything. The prophet at the river and the Wayfarer's fall were linked; she felt it. Unlike the other women of the well, she had found a connection.

I am Yinock's daughter.

Again she glanced around at the gathered women. They perched like a flock of desert-hued birds on the white ruins of Yinock's ancient city, rising and settling, waiting to be enskied. They stood in lines among the stones, jars resting on hips and heads. They had no answers; they could not unravel the truth from the knotted tales and rumors. She chewed her lower lip, deliberating, tasting her anger.

She did not have to stay; she could go see the prophet for herself. She stood.

A woman beside her looked up, a seeming question in her eyes, and Sarana felt a shift of attention in her direction. Long habit, and a little guilt, urged her to return to her labors, to fulfil expectations. When a water woman stood, she took her jars; she went to draw water, or she returned home. *In submission is exaltation.* At her feet, her jars waited beside the stone relic from Yinock's city.

"I'm going to see him," she said quietly. And before anyone could respond, she turned and threaded her way through the mingling servants of the well, leaving her jars beside the stone. A woman behind her said something—a question, an admonition—but Sarana ignored her. She worried someone would try to stop her. No one did.

A broad road led away from the temple district, straight to the western gates. Sarana walked with her eyes down, looking up from time to time, a little worried she might encounter someone from her master's house. She had never been all the way to the western gates—she had no need to go there—but she knew how to get there. Her temple mother had prepared her, taught her how to make her way around the city. Though she knew little about the Hruskan Quarter or the wealthy quarter where many of the elders resided, she knew every street and byway leading to the Well of Geb; she knew the little markets and the great market *bokovala.* She knew where the gates lay.

Once, she and her temple mother had walked as far as the Almoners Square, where dusty pilgrims and other supplicants made offerings after entering the city. That day had been special. Abasha had gestured further down the street and told her about the Pilgrim's Gate and the road that crossed the Geblon Valley to Gazelem. Sarana smiled at the memory. Her temple mother had given her a tenth-*tok* to drop into one of the coffers where a priest had watched with vigilant eyes. Her little coin had seemed so small. But the priest had smiled at her, and her heart had felt full.

This time she passed by the Almoners Square without stopping. Pilgrims still gathered at the coffers, but she had no coins to give, even if she had wanted to.

Doubts about her errand persisted. But when she thought about going back to the well, her heart cringed and hardened. The old woman's rebuke—and the words Sarana imagined the old woman would utter if she returned without seeing the prophet—prodded her on. She would not go back. The other water women were probably talking about her now, marveling at her departure. The thought lit a fierce smile, but she quickly suppressed it.

She kept looking ahead, expecting to see the city gates at a distance, looming. But all at once, they were before her—great, grey slabs of northern *hrestak* wood—seemingly pinned back against the city walls by the press of travelers. Guards of the watch stood on either side, but they glanced only occasionally, indifferently, at the competing traffic. Wagons, cattle, and people clogged the entry— some coming, some going. One of the guards stood beside a gesticulating man, laughing, and Sarana wondered why the guards were even there. Then, before she could give it any further thought, she was through.

But the city did not end. A sprawling warren of narrow streets and makeshift markets cluttered the hillside. Merchants and peddlers lined the road, calling their wares. Food vendors offered meat pastries, cinnamon bread, and fruit. The smell of the hot bread and savory meats reminded Sarana of the fresh bread and cucumbers being served for the midday meal at home. She was hungry.

Farther away from the city, little clusters of houses, stables, and small work yards replaced the relentless markets. And here and there, women sat in groups or worked alone. Some wove simple rugs or sewed clothing. Some nursed infant children. Others ground flour and scooped it into little bins, their calloused hands massaging the grinding stones with practiced ease. They smiled at one another. Some scowled. They talked easily and laughed; they argued.

Sarana envied them.

It was all so different from the ordered life she knew—so vibrant. Even the loquacious women at the well seemed dull and faded in comparison. The place of water was more contained, quieter—an ordered confluence of women.

Beyond the scree of the city, the road stretched out onto a grassy plain.

Traffic thinned. Breezy air, fitful, but fresh from the north, tugged at the edges of her shawl, caressing her face. A measureless host of purple wildflowers bobbed and fluttered across the gentle slope, and speckles of white, red, and yellow blooms spiced the land. Swaying grasses shone green and gold in the late morning light, and in the cradle of the valley, the Geblon flowed in lazy curves, fringed with tall, tufted grasses and willowy trees. Sarana's lips parted, and she slowed, astonished by the beauty of it.

Abruptly, the reality of what she had done crashed through her, and a feral joy burned away the remnant of her doubts. She was outside the city; she was on her way to see the prophet. And she was almost there. Already she could see the crossroads and the gathered people in the valley below. That creature of rumor, the prophet, was almost within sight. She hastened onward.

Blossoming *plesa* trees lined the river and meandering *desarati* flew languidly from branch to branch, lighting here and there among the little oval leaves and silvery blossoms, gathering and dispersing the lifeblood of the flowers. Sarana moved slowly through the loosely-gathered throng, tilting her head back and forth as she made her way forward, straining to get a glimpse of the man she had come to see.

And then she saw him standing in the river. The prophet.

He was just a man.

Dark hair and simple clothing. He could have been any one of the myriad common men she had seen on her way out of the city. And, yet, people had gathered at the river's edge to listen to him.

Could he be the forerunner? She was still a little distance from him— too far to hear what he was saying, so she moved closer. His voice rose over the soft babble of the crowd, becoming clearer as she drew nearer.

And then she heard him: ". . . they will not. For they believe they are still the keepers of the great key of redemption."

Sarana looked at some of the people standing nearby, wondering what he might be talking about. But the camaraderie of the well had not followed her to this place; she was alone. So she just listened.

"But they will be abased, and servants will rule over them." The prophet reached out toward the riverbank, his palm upturned, and said, "You have this chance to ready yourselves for the coming day of restoration. You all have this chance, this day."

He paused, continued. "But not for many days more. The world has become an ash heap, burned over by the false fires of hypocrisy." The prophet pointed to the east, toward the Great City. "That city on the hill, the so-called Great City of the bin-Yinocki, is but a shadow of Yinock's ancient handiwork. The true flame has burned out."

A mutter rippled through the crowd, and Sarana looked around again. A few angry faces and accusations of blasphemy, some bland expressions of a restrained outrage, but mostly the people continued as before—some talking, some disinterested, some laughing. A few exhorted their neighbors to listen.

Sarana stepped a little closer to the river, skirting a group of richly-dressed young men. They looked like idle pleasure seekers. She kept her eyes down.

The prophet continued. "But the day comes . . ." He paused and held up his hand. "The day comes when God will kneel beside the dwindling fires of the world and rekindle the flames with a gust of his everlasting breath—like a smith with his bellows." He held out his arms. "And the living coals will ignite the fire of the world again."

The prophet scanned the bank, and Sarana looked down, not wanting to be seen by him—a childish impulse. She heard someone call out, jeering, asking when God was going to clean out the hearth.

"But who will be the living coals?" The prophet's voice carried across the water, undeterred. "Who will burn brightly on that day? Who will restore the ancient glory of the world?"

Sarana looked up, half expecting he would be looking at her. He was not. He let his questions hang over the gathered people. A moment passed.

And then he said, "Come. Come and be baptized. Make yourselves ready for the day of restoration."

A man stepped out into the river. And all at once, the spectacle changed.

Sarana stared. The man walked slowly, uncertainly, slipping on slick stones. He stumbled, and water sloshed up the side of his body before he could catch himself. The prophet held a hand out in his direction, taking him by the wrist when he came within reach. The prophet spoke then, softly, his head inclined toward the suppliant. Sarana could not hear the words, but the man nodded.

Louder, the prophet said, "Having authority from Almighty God, I baptize you in preparation for his kingdom. *Es-prida*." The prophet pushed the man gently back, down under the water.

Little details sank into Sarana's eyes—the prophet's ragged clothing, the knotted muscles of his arms, the swirling water where the baptized man disappeared beneath the flowing surface of the river. The world seemed quieter for a moment. People could not help but watch in silent expectation. And then the man emerged, dripping with water. The prophet pulled him up, steadied him. The man wiped his face with his hands and blew out a pent up breath, smiling.

The surrounding babble of the assembled watchers reasserted itself, and the prophet released his new adherent. There were others lined up on the shore, waiting for baptism; the next person stepped out into the river.

Sarana glanced around, wondering what other people thought of it all. Her own thoughts moiled, a bit befuddled, tinged with wonder, streaked with anger. A strange melange of emotions. *Who will be the living coals?* The prophet's question stirred her mind. The Children of Yinock were God's chosen. But the thought of joining those people, walking out into the river—it was a compelling image. She moved closer to the riverbank, stepping up beside the group of people waiting to be baptized.

A memory of her own baptism surfaced, starkly different. A line of temple children—all who had reached the age of accountability— had descended into the secluded, sacred basements of the temple, dressed in white robes.

The temple baptistry featured a round font set flush into the floor. A low stone border lined the lip of the little pool, but at four points around the perimeter, water flowed out through narrow channels cut into the floor, symbolic of the four rivers of paradise. The streams flowed outward toward the walls of the baptistry and disappeared in the gloom. The farthest reaches of the room were dim, unlit, but the baptismal font glowed with an otherworldly light, illuminated from above by recessed lights of ancient manufacture—a consecrated oasis of light and water in the dim wilderness of the world.

She remembered the luxurious warmth of the baptismal sea. A kindly old priest standing waist-deep within had helped her down the submerged steps. His bright eyes had shone with reflected light, and his wispy head had wobbled a little as he spoke the words of her baptism, his voice raspy with age.

Afterward, her temple mother had helped her change out of her wet clothing, and she had said, *It is a special privilege to be baptized here in the temple—in the House of Esana. Do not forget the gift God has given you.*

Sarana clenched her jaw. She had not forgotten. The memory was graven upon her mind.

At the water's edge, some of the newly baptized gathered. Many of them smiled; a few stood looking out over the river. Sarana looked back at the prophet. Her thoughts grew unsettled, vaguely hostile, a little befuddled. *Did I really think this man was connected to the Wayfarer's fall?* The idea seemed foolish.

But she had been so sure.

And now he did look at her. The river was practically at her feet; the prophet's hand was stretched out toward her. The noise of the crowd was pointed at her back.

She took a small step back, her thoughts reeling back to her conversation at the well. Tales of a fallen star, evocative rumors, idle suppositions. The fiery seed of the fallen Wayfarer had landed in fecund soil. And her pride had watered it with vanity and anger. She could not recall what she had hoped to gain by abandoning her servitude. Renouncing her servitude would be utter folly. Her master was a good man; the house she served was an honorable house, a safe haven. She looked down at her hands.

In submission is exaltation. The memory of Abasha's words jolted her.

She looked around, half expecting her old temple mother to be standing beside her. But she was alone in a crowd of strangers, and

Abasha was probably dead. Ten years had passed since she had seen the old woman—ten years on the long path to exaltation.

Except she had strayed again, discarded her duties.

By now her absence had surely been noticed, and she was a long way from her master's house. *What will I tell Telasa?* The headwoman of the house would be looking for her, wanting an explanation for her tardiness. Perhaps if she hurried, she could blame the crowds at the well, or say she had decided to stop by the prayer wall. That was somewhat true. She had passed by the prayer wall.

Only a moment had passed. His hand was stretched out still.

But the hope of returning to her duties unscathed impelled her to instinctive action; she immediately turned and made her way back to the road. Someone jeered at her, mocking her apparent fear and flight from the prophet. But her mind was fixed on getting back; she hurried on without pause or concern for the crowd.

A part of her derided the idea that she could go back and reclaim her jars. She was already lost. A little part of her hoped her jars were still there, waiting for her to return. Or that one of the women had taken charge of them in her absence. But mostly—too late to do her any good—she berated her foolishness for leaving in the first place. Her temple mother had warned her against disobedience. Abasha had told her the day would come when she would have to cast away all vanity and gather up humility.

Humility is harder to trap than water.

Back at the place of the well, she returned to the stone she had vacated earlier. Her jars were gone. And so were the women she had been sitting with. They had been replaced by other women, and none of them had seen her jars. Sarana scanned the assembled women, straining for help. There was none. She checked the neighboring stones, thinking she might have misremembered where she had been. But her jars were gone. Her master was sure to punish her for losing them, and she was helpless before him.

The Lines spoke clearly to her circumstances, fearful words. She was in her master's hand, and once rebellious, the servant need not be trusted again. Only mercy could save her.

Too late she realized she could have saved herself by taking the simple precaution of carrying her jars with her. No one would have discovered her folly then.

But she had been too intent on her own desires. Too driven by pride.

"I'm being punished," she whispered, and her tears dropped like fallen angels into the dust at her feet, balling up into moist globes of dirt. "God has seen my folly, and he is punishing me."

CHAPTER FOUR.

DEBTOR.

"The Lines give me leave to release you from your servitude."

Her master, Gibson bin Jianin, spoke without looking at her. He had been writing something at his table when she arrived, but he had arisen. He stood facing a window, leaning against the table, one hand resting on the dark, polished wood. Dwindling afternoon sunlight brushed his face. Several piles of paper, an inkwell, a day book for recording receipts and expenditures, and a small pitcher of water sat on the table near at hand. On the far side of the room, through an arched doorway and half concealed by a partially drawn curtain, was her master's bedroom. It lay in shadow.

"Is that what you desire?" he asked.

Sarana shook her head without looking up, oozing penitence, straining to hear any words of forgiveness that might escape his lips. The stones of the floor were cool against her forehead—soothing compared to her master's countenance.

A return to the temple for reassignment would be better. She would have to start her servitude anew, but it would be better than a release. If he released her, she would be without house, bereft, and the other houses would shun her as a slothful servant. She would have no place to stay, nothing to eat.

The depth of her folly, the stark reality of her existence, lay limp upon her shoulders like a tattered robe, revealing and scant. Half the harlots in the Great City were former water women. Or so said the rumormongers.

When she did not speak, Gibson looked at her and said, "Tell me why you abandoned your jars."

She answered softly, carefully. "To go down to the river."

"And why?"

His voice was mild, but she feared what he might say with his next breath. She shook her head again and put her forehead on the stones, waiting for his words, waiting for his inevitable wrath.

The silence stretched out painfully. She dared not look upon him, but she could feel his gaze upon her. Or at least she thought she could. In all the days of her servitude, she had never been so afraid and sorrowful. Her years of obedience and adherence to the lines— ten years of faithful servitude—had come to an ignominious end. It was all lost, and she felt the enormous weight of her guilt like an unalterable decree of heaven.

Gibson rapped his knuckles on the table, startling her. He walked to the window and sat on the bench there, resting his arm on the windowsill. Through that same window, Sarana had sometimes surveyed the plains and the lazy curves of the distant river, stealing glimpses and daydreaming. Her shame grew. Even in the presence of her master, in her master's house, she had not been faithful. And now the plains were a far-off land—once visited, never to be seen again. Her regret was bitter, unwanted, necessary.

"Forgive me," she said softly. She looked up for the barest moment, glancing at him through dark locks of hair that had fallen from under her shawl.

Silence.

"God has punished me for my folly." Her lurking bitterness eclipsed her grief, and she turned her gaze back toward the floor, afraid he would see her true feelings. She clenched her teeth, forestalling further tears, and looked up again.

Gibson did not respond, but she felt a change. He turned toward the window again and gazed into the distance, toward Gazelem. It was something he did often, and Sarana imagined he was thinking of his wife, who had returned to Gazelem to live with her parents. He rarely mentioned her, but Sarana knew he still hoped for her return. The servants of the house were quiet about it, but they saw and heard enough to know their master's heart.

She watched the play of light and shadow on his face and neck, and she recalled happier occasions—occasions when she was simply serving and pouring water for his dusty feet. More than once she had imagined herself in a different role in her master's house. To be married, to be a wife in the House of Jianin, would set her free.

Impossible. Especially now.

Finally, Gibson spoke, but he did not turn from the window. "Perhaps God *has* punished you," he said.

Sarana rose up slightly from the floor.

"But who am I to undo God's punishment?" he asked softly. He seemed almost on the verge of laughter. Light and shadow, shifting. Then he turned and said, "You will not be able to serve as you once did."

Sarana sat up on her knees. "Please," she said. "I will never go to the river again. Please don't send me away."

Gibson shook his head and chuckled involuntarily. Then he sobered and said, "I'm not going to send you away. That's not what I meant. I just mean things cannot go back to what they were." He stepped toward her and held out his hand.

She looked at his hand and swallowed, uncertain. "I'm sorry, Lord Jianin. I won't go out there again. I'm sorry."

"I'm not angry about that. Not anymore."

For a moment, she imagined cruel punishments inflicted on other unprofitable servants. Not by Gibson, but by other masters. Some had been lashed and cast out of their homes; some had been sold to slavers who beat them and abused them. Or so it was said. She did not know such women, but she had heard such tales at the well. And her temple mother had warned her sternly not to forsake her duties.

"Come," Gibson said. His hand was still outstretched.

Sarana took his hand and stood, reluctant but with growing relief. Her master's face had softened.

"I want to tell you something." He directed her to the other end of the bench and let go of her hand.

"My Lord?" She felt too close, too small. She had never touched his hand in quite the same way, and the touch of his fingers lingered on her skin—and in her mind.

"I've been master of this house for many years now, and I've had many people serve me. Some, like Kaina, even served my father. And every one of them has earned my wrath at one time or another. Can you guess how many servants I have sent away?"

Sarana knew of none during the ten years she had served. "No, my Lord."

"I've never sent anyone away. But not because they've all served me faithfully without fail. Some have failed me. And now you." Gibson studied her for a moment and allowed the silence to stretch out between them. Then he looked out the window again and softly bounced his palm on the window sill.

"Do you know—" Gibson halted. "Have you ever been told about the revelation ceremony in the temple?"

"I have heard of it, my Lord."

"But do you know what it is? What is said and done in it?"

"No, my Lord."

Gibson nodded. "Only those who've been through it know everything, but there are aspects that can be shared."

Sarana waited.

"There is a room in the temple, the Room of Revelation, and those who participate in the ceremony must make certain covenants. I can't talk about those, but I can tell you about one aspect of the revelation itself." Gibson paused, looked in Sarana's eyes. "It concerns the Line of *Es*. It is the first line in the revelatory ceremony. 'When he drinks, he will ever thirst.' Did you know that?"

She shook her head. "No, my Lord."

"It refers to our first father's dilemma. Being immortal, he could not die; he had no need to drink. And yet, he knew drinking from the river in the intransigent garden would be pleasurable. The water was cool and would provide respite from the heat of the day. And God had also told him it would quicken his seed, so he and our first mother could bring children into the world. But as you know, God also told him that if he drank, he would always thirst, and he would eventually die."

Gibson smiled. "Some priests will tell you the story is just symbolic—that it is merely representative of real events and we don't know what really happened." Gibson shrugged. "That may be, or it may be an accurate history. But we use the Line of *Es* to define our existence. It *is* real, one way or another. And what you did today was merely a continuation of the choice our first father and mother made so many years ago—you *are* our first parents' daughter."

Sarana tried to understand, but she could not resolve her questions. *Is he saying it was right? Does he mean I was right to do it?* Her training had not prepared her to treat with her master in this manner.

Gibson continued. "During the revelation, we sit in darkness. And then a curtain is pulled open behind us and light from a window in an adjoining room falls on the wall in front of us. We see shadows moving on the wall, but we are not permitted to turn and see the people who are standing in the light. Instead, we only hear their voices and see the shadows of their movements—shadows of things to come."

He paused. "Like the Line of *Es*, the shadow plays are symbolic. We receive instruction through them, but there are many things that have not yet been revealed—though they will be. We are promised one day, we, too, will be allowed beyond the veil, so we can walk in the light. And in that world of light, we will drink straight from the source of all wisdom and knowledge, and the allure of sin will have no power over us—no ability to convince us that through sin we might find some degree of happiness."

Gibson looked away from her and fell silent. Sarana had been so taken by his words she had forgotten, for a moment, her earlier peril.

"I'm not angry with you, Sarana. I was, but not now. We know from God's dealings with his children that the sin is often less important than our actions afterward." One side of Gibson's mouth quirked upward. "What I'm trying to say is, I forgive you for leaving your jars to be stolen. But you must learn from this choice. And I may have additional duties for you to perform in the coming days."

"Yes, my Lord. Thank you, my Lord."

Gibson stood and walked back to his table; he sat in one of the chairs and picked up a sheet of paper from one of the piles. "So, now that you have been to see this man at the river, what can you tell me about him?"

Sarana stared, snared by his unexpected question. Fear of punishment had shunted the prophet to the back of her mind.

Gibson put the paper down and looked at her. "I know you have seen him," he said. "It is no great mystery what is going on down there. But I did not have to guess. One of my men came from Gazelem today, and he stopped to listen to the man. He saw you near the water's edge, watching the baptisms. He thought he recognized you, but he wasn't sure until he saw your mark." Gibson held up his arm and pointed at his wrist.

Sarana let her gaze fall to the floor. "Forgive me, my Lord. I should have told you I went to see him."

"I just want to know why. What is it about the man?"

"Because I thought—" She stopped. "I only went to watch him, my Lord." *To be free of you*, she thought, and she inhaled sharply. She had nearly spoken the words aloud. And they were not the truth. Not really. But neither was what she had said. The truth lay somewhere in between. And mixed into it were her foolish imaginings about the Great City of Old and its flight into the heavens.

"And yet you abandoned your jars." Gibson shook his head. "Why would you risk so much to see him?"

"That was wrong, my Lord." *And it was stupid*. She felt the tenseness of her face as she stifled her internal recriminations.

"It was wrong," Gibson said. "But we are past that. So tell me what you know about this man at the river."

"I know nothing." Sarana bit her lower lip.

"Some say he is a prophet."

She did not answer. Her earlier speculations about the fallen Wayfarer and the return of the City of Old seemed meaningless and childish. She could not bring herself to mention them.

"Some say he is Esana."

Still she did not answer. Gibson considered her silence.

"I'm not angry you went to see him," he said.

Sarana looked at the floor, desperate to avoid his questions. Gibson had always been a good and courteous master. He never mistreated his servants. But she had never disobeyed him, either, and she had never forsaken her duties. She had never abandoned her jars—though she had once broken one.

"You refuse to tell me?"

She shook her head. "I—I don't know what to think of him. I have heard the stories about him, but I have only seen him once. I—" she paused. "I am afraid, my Lord." She forced herself to look into his eyes.

Gibson looked at her for a moment. And then he nodded. "I understand. But I expect more from you now."

As his eyes probed hers, Sarana slowly realized he truly was not angry. Not any longer. It was as he said. And though she knew not what, her master's brooding eyes held something other than anger. They were dark, but they were mild. Something Abasha often said came to mind. *There is naught to fear but God's wrath. But fear not even that, if you are willing to repent. He is slow to anger.*

A knock at the chamber door crashed through her memories, and she turned.

Ganon was there, holding a large log book. He nodded at her and stepped inside as Gibson motioned for him to enter.

"We can continue later," Gibson said. "You can go back to work. But after today, things cannot be as they were."

CHAPTER FIVE.

BROKEN BONES.

The once-son of the on-Dam slipped into an open doorway and looked back the way he had come. An uncharacteristic silence seemed to fill the street.

And then they rounded the corner. Four of them.

They had come upon him near the *churk*—four men dressed in the bright colors of the Hruskan citizenry. They had tried to blend in with the crowds, but he had seen them coming, faces hard and pitiless. He had been looking for them, and he knew what they intended. He had escaped their initial attack by running through the market, but they had given chase. He did not recognize any of them, but he did not need to.

News of his ostracization had burned through the Hruskan Quarter like a wind of fire on the grassy plains of hari-Hrusk. It was an opportunity his father's enemies could not overlook. They dared not act while he was yet the son of the on-Dam, but once the tie was broken, they could strike without justifying open retribution. This was the ancient way, and Neturu had expected it.

As Neturu watched, the men spread out and advanced down the narrow street. They moved with fluid grace, absolute certainty. From the look of them, Neturu would have wagered his father's wealth they were *hinavu*—selected from among the secret bodyguards of some notable Hruskan. Neturu coldly calculated his chances and concluded they would beat him, even if they were not *hinavu*. Their numbers and evident training gave them an insurmountable advantage. He would have to run, but it was unlikely he could evade them for long. And if he continued to run, he would simply be fatigued when they finally ran him down. *Better to face them fresh if I have to*, he concluded. *And I think I must.*

Neturu stepped out of the doorway. The oncoming men walked toward him without faltering. Neturu watched them carefully, plotting to incapacitate at least one of them as quickly as possible. When they were several steps away, Neturu turned and ran down the street, hoping they would think he had lost his nerve. He turned right at the end of the street and fled just ahead of his pursuers.

He sprinted past an alley. Another. At the third opportunity he threw himself between the buildings. He bounced off the wall and raced down the alley. Overhead, lines of hanging clothes drooped between the buildings, stagnant and drab. One of his pursuers was swifter than the others. Neturu heard him drawing closer. It was time.

Ahead, the alley emerged onto a narrow street. Neturu slowed abruptly and went to the left. He was counting on unbridled pursuit. After rounding the corner, he immediately halted and spun to his right, swinging his right arm outward as he turned. The abrupt stop left him off-balance and diminished his attack, but as he spun he aimed his fist at the approximate level of his pursuer's throat.

For a moment, he feared his pursuer was not close enough—he feared his clenched fist would simply pass through the air. But even as the thought formed, the man emerged from the alley, and Neturu's fist connected with his mouth and nose. Pain erupted in his hand, but Neturu's triumph bellowed out of him.

The impact threw the man's head backward, and Neturu felt the man's teeth and nose crack. Blood erupted. The man's body continued forward, and then he tumbled onto his back, clutching his face.

The others emerged from the alley. They slowed, but they were coming too fast. The first stumbled over the fallen one and tumbled to the ground. Neturu delivered a quick kick to his ribs, but the man was already rolling to his right, and the kick did little harm. In a fluid motion, the man was back on his feet and circling to Neturu's left. The last two men emerged from the alley. One approached Neturu head on; the other moved to Neturu's right. Neturu still had open street behind him, but his breathing had quickened. If he ran again, he would tire. His attackers advanced, wary.

Neturu lunged at the last man to emerge from the alley. But before he could reach him, pain erupted in his lower back. His attackers were fast—faster than he anticipated. The kick sent him sprawling toward his intended target, off balance. A fragment of time seemed to abruptly expand, and in that moment, Neturu felt not fear but peace. *It will be all right.* And then: *This is the path I have chosen.* A rush of movement as time collapsed and vanished; Neturu put his hands up to shield himself. A fist caught his jaw and whipped his head around. He kept his feet but staggered crazily, arms flailing for any type of purchase.

And then they were on him.

For a few seconds, Neturu fought. He landed a few blows on two of his attackers, blocked some of their attacks, but he could not bring any of them down. They circled him and struck simultaneously from different sides, moving in tandem, reading each other's moves, cooperating seamlessly. If one of them needed to disengage, he did, and the others closed in. They had no individual honor or pride; they were a single weapon. One after another, they battered him with their fists and feet.

Neturu began to question his choices. *Maybe I should have kept running. Maybe I never should have told my father.* And then a hard blow to the side of his head silenced internal doubts.

One of the men threw him to the ground, and Neturu covered his face with his arms and curled up as tightly as he could. Hard blows came from all sides; pain cocooned him, transformed him. And then sharp pain cracked through his side as one of his ribs broke beneath a well-placed kick. He felt his body spasm and uncoil. A foot smashed down on his left shin, breaking his bones. But his assailants did not kill him. And, dimly, Neturu realized they were not trying to kill him.

At least not yet. And then the beating stopped, and for a long moment, Neturu lay in expectant agony.

Someone was speaking. The words were calm.

"Open your eyes, once-son of the on-Dam—once-son of Hrusk." The voice was level. "Open them."

Neturu slowly let his arms fall down, and he opened his eyes. His attackers stood in a circle around him. The man whose face he had smashed stood right in front of him, looking down upon him. He spoke, and Neturu saw one of his front teeth had cracked off at an angle, leaving a triangular gap. His nose was swollen, and blood—hastily swiped away—streaked his lips and chin. Neturu could not help but feel a small degree of satisfaction.

"Once-son of Hrusk, you are found wanting by the Fathers of Hrusk. You have forgotten the face of your father."

The spokesman knelt on one knee in front of Neturu and unfastened the silver clasp holding Neturu's cloak around his neck. The man wiped the cloak roughly across Neturu's face; it came away bloody. He handed the cloak over his shoulder to one of the others, and then he spat on Neturu's cheek.

"The Fathers do not want your blood on their hands, once-son of Hrusk. But you will not show yourself among your once-brethren again." The man leaned closer and cupped one of Neturu's cheeks in his hand, directing Neturu's gaze into his own. "Do you understand?"

Neturu opened his mouth to speak, and pain jabbed him in the side. "Yes," he said.

The spokesman's gaze roamed Neturu's face. "You have forgotten the face of your father," he said softly, earnestly. "But I will not forget yours."

"I fear . . ." Neturu blew out a shaky breath. "In this—" He winced with pain as he inhaled. "We have all . . . forgotten . . . our fathers' faces."

"Each man must hold what memories he can." The man gave Neturu a curt nod and rose. He turned and gestured to the other men.

Neturu lay in the street and watched them go, shuddering with pain. When they turned a corner, he rolled over and crawled to the side of the street, dragging his left leg painfully across the ground. Ramshackle buildings lined the sides of the street, and he sat with his back against an uneven, crumbling wall of stones. He pressed lightly on his ribs, assessing the damage. Pain etched through his innards, but he had suffered cracked ribs before, and this felt no worse than some of the injuries he received in training. He shifted his left leg and tried to rotate his foot. Pain lanced upward, and he sucked in a breath. That was not a training injury. The rest of his body was battered, but the pain was fading, dulling—persistent but manageable.

It could have been worse, he thought. He ran his hands over his face and winced as his fingers found tender places and cuts. His hands came away bloody. But it could have been much worse.

He got to his knees, using the wall to pull himself up. He tried to keep his weight on his right leg. Still, the accustomed movements of his left leg were hard to suppress, and he grunted and faltered briefly when he tried to use his left foot for leverage. When he gained his feet, he leaned against the wall and rested, his left leg hanging. A few people emerged from the surrounding buildings, returning to their lives. But they did not look at him, and Neturu did not seek their attention. They were Hruskans, and he could not show his face to them. He would not.

This is what I chose.

Neturu looked once more in the direction his attackers had gone— back toward the heart of the Hruskan Quarter. He dared not travel through the Quarter. His father's enemies would surely be watching for him, and a second meeting would not turn out so favorably.

He turned and took a shuffling hop-step in the other direction, steadying himself against the wall with his hands. He would have to exit the city on the north and make his way through the sprawling outer city.

He tried to believe he could make it.

But two hours later, as the shadow-laden streets grew darker, he faltered and fell to the ground, uncertain of his progress. It was not the first time he had fallen, and the palms of his hands were scraped, bloodied. He was not familiar with this part of the city. Vaguely, but without much force, he wondered why no one had come to his aid. He tried to get up, but his strength had dwindled to the perishing point. Around him, the streets were silent, sepulchral. The dust in his nostrils was acrid and smoky. In agony, he rolled over and let his head fall back on the ground. Above him, an indigo sky watched over him, on the cusp of revealing its glittering stars.

After a moment, he rolled his head to the side. A dark hovel hunched there in the shadows. An empty window and an open doorway looked out into the street. No hint of light, no noise, came from within. He gathered his strength and rolled over. More dust. He gathered his strength again and pushed up onto his hands and knees. Trembling, he crawled over to the doorway. No sound emerged, and nothing moved in the darkness.

As he dragged himself inside, wisps of putrescence infiltrated the air. He searched the floor with his hands but found nothing except a few pebbles in the dust. He reached the back of the room and found another doorway. He pulled himself forward and peered into the resident gloom. Nothing stirred, but just inside the second room, his fingers brushed against the folds of coarse fabric. He tugged and the rotten fabric ripped. Corruption and decay blossomed in the darkness, and a wave of putrescence repulsed him. He pushed himself back— too quickly—and cried out involuntarily as his left leg dragged across the floor.

A corpse. He had come farther east than he intended. He had reached the northeastern edge of the city—the ash-laden streets of the forsaken quarter, where the poor laid their dead to rest, leaving the bodies to be collected and burned by the scorchers, the city's garbage collectors. He retreated.

Near the front door, he found a corner and curled up, wanting to sleep, wanting to slip away into oblivion. Instead, he wept silently, exhausted.

I am no longer a son of Hrusk. He reached into his shirt and clutched the small, bronze star he wore around his neck. *But I have made promises to God.* The metal felt warm, and his promises to God were fiery jewels in the box of his heart.

CHAPTER SIX.

NEW JARS.

Sarana fled down the stairs, grateful for Ganon's timely arrival. In the hearth room she found Kaina shelling a bowl of *rebboth* seeds. The old woman looked up and raised her eyebrows.

"Still with us, I see."

Sarana walked over to the baskets beside the wall and scooped out a bowlful of the rough, brown seeds. She stood for a moment, staring down at the stacks of small baskets, the coffer of seeds, the jars, and the folded blankets. The long pattern of her servitude was broken, and she felt like an intruder.

"I was worried about you." Kaina's voice was raspy, good natured. "Earlier, I mean. When I heard you ran off." The older woman smiled and patted the floor.

Sarana tied on an apron. But she hesitated.

Kaina's hands moved unerringly as they split the rough husks of the *rebboth*, liberating the scarlet fruit within. Other workers had gathered the seeds throughout the day, and now the women of the house would spend the next few hours harvesting the tiny, precious fruits within. The familiar pattern continued.

Sarana put a folded blanket on the floor beside her old friend and sat.

"It's stronger than you think," Kaina said.

"What?"

"I just thought you could use a reminder."

"What is?"

"The product of your labors, child."

Sarana just shook her head.

But Kaina pressed on. "Each day, each task is a carefully laid stone. And over time, they make a path. A road. How long depends on your faith." Kaina paused for a moment, her hands resting in the bowl on her lap, her fingers buried in the brown seeds. "What you did today won't tear up all those stones."

Sarana nodded. Then: "Does everyone know?"

"I know. A few of the men. The others will find out. Telasa doesn't know what you did, but she knows something happened." Kaina shook her head. "And she knows your jars are gone—stolen." Kaina shrugged and went back to her work. "But in time, it won't interest them any longer."

Sarana picked up a seed and snapped the husk between her fingertips, careful not to crush the minuscule fruit within. If Telasa knew, she was bound to make things harder for Sarana. And that meant additional assignments.

"We are blessed with a good master," Kaina said softly. "I had no doubt he would treat you kindly. I am glad to see I was right."

"He was . . . kind," Sarana said, not wanting to contradict the older woman. "But he had some questions."

"What did you tell him?"

Sarana shrugged. "He knew I went out to see the prophet."

"And did you find what you were looking for?"

Obviously not. Sarana did not answer.

Kaina smiled, apparently unperturbed by the younger woman's silence. In a way Sarana did not understand, Kaina always seemed peaceful.

The two women worked, and Sarana mulled the old woman's question. Except for her thoughts about the City of Old, she could not exactly recall what she had thought right before abandoning her jars. Whatever had prodded her to act so rashly had vanished. Her fleeting notions of freedom—the joy she thought she felt in her brief wanderings—seemed reckless, childish. She was ashamed of her foolish pride. And though the weight of her disobedience was diminishing, her heart still ached. Abasha had warned her, prepared her.

And she had still given in.

Eventually, she spoke. "He wanted to know what I thought of him."

"Mmm."

"I wasn't sure what to tell him."

"Only the truth matters."

"I don't even remember why I thought it was so important. I just—I wanted to see him. And I thought I could—I don't know. Be free or something."

"It was a foolish thing to do," Kaina said.

Sarana glanced over, but Kaina was looking down. There was no scorn in the old woman, just gentle reproof. Sarana's gaze strayed to Kaina's gnarled hands. Darkened, lined with wrinkles, fingers curling slightly. So different from her own. And, yet, they shelled the *rebboth* with practiced ease, splitting the rough seeds methodically and expertly, rarely spilling any of the scarlet juice of the fruit within.

After so many years, those old hands had found a sort of perfection in servitude. *In submission is exaltation.* But even so, the old woman's fingertips were stained a pale red. It seemed no amount of skill could avoid those inevitable, indelible marks from the rough husks and the spilled juice of broken seeds.

My fingers are still white.

"Careful, child." Kaina's gentle admonition jarred her from her thoughts.

Sarana looked down and saw she had broken the fruit of the seed in her hands. Scarlet smears marred the tips of her fingers, and she silently cursed her inattention. The seeds represented substantial wealth, and she had been told, often, as a child—and occasionally by the head serving woman of the house—how valuable they were. The juice was used for inks and dyes, and they were prized in the far south, in Shal-Gashun, where the *rebboth* would not grow. They had to be harvested by hand to preserve the fragile fruit within.

Her temple mother said women sometimes used the diluted juice on their lips, to enhance their beauty. And secretly, in a rare moment of foolishness, the old woman had shown her how to dab her lips with juice from broken fruits. *It would have gone to waste, child, and we would not want that.* Sarana smiled at the memory, and at the stern admonition against actually practicing the habit. It was the one time she could remember Abasha ever straying from the Lines.

She wiped her fingers on her apron and examined them. Her hands, as yet, were unmarked. But even if she were a pure descendant of Yinock, eventually the minuscule spines of the rough husks would abrade her regenerative flesh into submission and mark a path for the scarlet juice of the *rebboth*, embroidering the stain of her servitude onto her fingertips. She would be marked.

Like Kaina.

She became aware of the faint but acrid smell of the freshly-split seeds—bitter, reminiscent of countless days, comforting. She wondered how it felt to be so old and slow and quiet.

For a moment Sarana recalled the women of the outer city—how they knelt outside their miserable homes, laughing and chattering, adding to the chaos of the outer city, mending baskets, preparing food, grinding grain to flour. If she had not been born to servitude, she might have been among those women, talking and laughing in the tumbled streets of the outer city.

"Did you go to the market today?" Sarana asked quietly.

Kaina looked up, and her practiced hands hesitated momentarily over her bowl of seeds. "Telasa no longer sends me to the market," she said.

Sarana continued her work, waiting for Kaina to go on.

Kaina wiped her fingers on her apron, leaving small dabs of scarlet. A rare break. "Just this month she stopped. She sends Ana in my stead." A pause. "I don't mind. Not really. It gives me a chance to sit with the other women and talk, or to pray at the temple. Or I just work in the vineyard. I don't miss the market."

Sarana merely nodded. Telasa was probably right to send someone younger.

"There's something you need to think about," Kaina said.

"What?"

"That this is your home. And it always will be."

"I—"

"Whatever it was, whatever you were looking for out there is not real. You cannot find happiness by running away from your place in life—from the place God has ordained for you. He knew you child—and you him—before you were born. And he knew the choices you would make when you came to this life. Now you must find out whether he was glad when he foresaw what you would become."

Sarana took this in without thought; she said, "Today, when I was at the well, talking with the other women, I thought I realized something."

"What was that?"

"It was about the Wayfarer."

"Ah yes, I heard about that. No one could stop talking about it earlier."

"I was talking about it with some of the women at the well."

"And what did you think?"

Sarana shook her head, trying to pass off her thoughts as unimportant. But she worried the old woman would know her heart. She faltered. "Do you really believe the ancient stories?" she asked.

"Of course, child."

"You really believe the City of Old will return?" She recalled again the tale of the city's departure, seeing in her mind how the great stones broke away and tumbled through the air, crashing onto the lorn plains below. Perhaps they, too, like the fallen Wayfarer, had spewed fire and burned as they fell. But that was not in any of the stories.

Kaina looked up at Sarana. "Don't you, child?"

"I—of course I do."

The old woman smiled, cushioning her eyes in webs of wrinkles. "It doesn't help to question God, child. I know what you're thinking, and I think I know why you went to see that so-called prophet at the

river. You were thinking that this life—" The old woman gestured
vaguely with her hand at their surroundings. "You were thinking it is
unjust. And freedom would be better. But God watches after his
children, and the day of his mercy hangs over us like a cloud." Kaina's
hands had returned to their work. The tiny husks cracked with a
steady rhythm. "When the storm comes, He will shelter those who
have looked unto Him in times of trial. You need not worry."

Sarana looked down at her bowl. *God is not the one I question*, she
thought. *God is not the one I question.* She was about to ask if Kaina had
ever left the city, but before she could speak, Kaina brushed off her
hands and picked up her empty bowl. Sarana worked until Kaina
returned with a fresh bowl of seeds.

"Have you ever been outside the city?"

"I was born outside the city," Kaina said as she resumed her work.
"I was brought here as a small child—after the war that subdued my
people. That was many years ago, long before you were born, after my
people were swept up in a war they did not cause and did not want.
Except for memories of my mother and grandmother, and the stories
they told me, I know nothing of my people's homeland."

Sarana nodded, but she felt no real emotion. The savage Kainites
had been subdued and taken captive by the bin-Yinocki more than a
hundred years earlier. The Kainite nation was only a memory, a story.

"But I do not mourn them," Kaina said. "Not any more. I was a
child of the temple after they took me from my family. I was brought
up in the House of Esana; I learned the stories of the bin-Yinocki.
And I've come to know my place. I am home here."

Sarana nodded; Kaina had a way of rambling.

"But the last time I left the city was when Father Jianin died. He
was buried in Talat, so we could not see him. But Gibson held a feast
for all of us in Gazelem."

Sarana looked up, a little surprised. "You have not left the city
since then?" Gibson's father had been dead for many years.

The old woman shrugged. "I have not had to. Our duties keep us
close to home."

"Have you—did you ever think about renouncing—when you

were younger?"

For several moments, Kaina did not answer; Sarana waited.

"Children of captivity do not have the same privileges as dedicated children," Kaina said. "We cannot renounce our servitude and live by the mercy of Esana. We must wait for our jubilee."

Sarana nodded; she should have thought of that. She asked, "How long until your jubilee?"

The old woman laughed softly. "I am a hundred and twenty-seven years old, child. My second jubilee has come and gone."

Sarana's hands stilled and she looked up, her eyes wide. "But the Lines don't allow a third servitude. How—" She cut off her question. "Does Lord Jianin know?" But she knew the question was absurd even as she spoke it. He knew.

Kaina smiled. "He knows; it has all been recorded. I was brought to the House of Jianin in my eighth year. I served my first master, Father Jianin, for forty years, until my jubilee. It was recorded in the temple, and Father Jianin offered me my freedom. But I decided to stay. After he died, I served his son—our master—for another term. And then my second jubilee was recorded. That was nearly thirty years ago. If the Lines allowed it, I would be approaching my third jubilee."

"But you're still a servant. Lord Jianin should have freed you."

"Oh, well, he did. He did. I'm a free woman. He came to me on the day of my second jubilee and told me the Lines no longer gave him any hold over me. He even had the money for my remission in hand. A double portion for my second jubilee. I still remember the day clearly—the money was in a beautiful *rebboth*-colored bag of very fine material. I still have it." Kaina chuckled. "If he hadn't told me, I wouldn't have known the day myself. I hadn't thought about it for . . . I don't know how long."

"But why didn't you go free?"

Kaina laughed. "I am free. But the Lines don't preserve old women from thieves and robbers. The Lines do not give me a bed to sleep in. Where would I go? I asked to stay, and he said I could."

"But you had the money," Sarana said. "And it's the law."

Kaina laughed again. "The money would have kept me alive for some time—you're right about that. But not forever. Besides, I couldn't leave my home. And I had no desire to leave our master." Kaina shrugged. "There was nothing better for me, child. After so many years of servitude, I was ready to rest. And you will be, too. This is your home."

Sarana said nothing, but for a moment she remembered her abandoned jars. And she considered the possibility that Kaina was right. If her blood was weak, she would begin to show the first signs of age within thirty or forty years. Maybe fifty.

"None of us looks forward to it," Kaina said softly. "Not even you. After today, you should know that. The world out there is not our place."

"Part of me—I think . . ." Sarana blinked rapidly. "Part of me wishes I had stayed out there. For a moment, when I was standing on the riverbank, I thought about walking out to him to be baptized. A part of me wishes I'd had the courage to do it."

Kaina offered a small smile.

"I can't decide what is right," Sarana said.

Kaina looked at Sarana with soft eyes. "You are correct, of course. You must simply *do* what is right." The old woman smiled.

And after a moment, Sarana shook her head, amused by the old aphorism despite her melancholy thoughts.

When her bowl was empty, Sarana tossed the empty husks into the fire. They crackled and flared, somehow joyful. The wealth she had harvested this evening was sufficient to feed the entire house for a month. A month's worth of harvesting the tiny fruits amounted to a quantity of riches Sarana could barely fathom. And then there was Kaina's work beside her own, and the work of some of the other women when time allowed. Daily fortunes.

As she washed her hands, she remembered how, as a small girl, she had secretly lamented how easily the water sluiced the *rebboth* juice from her fingers. In the temple, beneath Abasha's constant care, she had once looked forward to the seemingly distant day when her own fingers would bear the stains of her servitude. She had wanted so much to be like her kindly mother in every way. She did not know exactly when that had changed.

She dried her hands and was about to retrieve her jars from their customary place beside the hearth when she remembered they were gone. She turned. There were many empty jars along the wall, but they were only house jars, smaller than her jars for carrying water to and from the well, and she felt the loss of her own jars deeply.

Kaina came up beside her. "There's something for you back there." A slight smile accompanied the old woman's words. She gestured back toward the women's quarters and gave her a nudge in the back, prodding her to go look.

On her bed sat two new jars.

She picked one up. The familiar balance of well-made water jars passed through her hands. Comforting. She had gone most of the day without her jars, and their absence was made stark by this renewal. Her palm caressed the bulging belly of the clay. Her master's mercy was complete. Or nearly so. The jar was nicely made, well balanced, but plain. Neither jar was adorned with the flower-like pattern that had circled the neck of one of her old jars. But he probably did not know what her other jars looked like. He could not be blamed.

Outside, twilight lay upon the city. Shadows draped the courtyard with their soft gloom, and the great, gnarled *hresta* tree in the center of the yard stood black against the night sky. The pungent smell of burning leaves drifted through the air, and through the arched, stone doorway to the orchard, she saw Telasa and Ana burning piles of old leaves and sticks—the cast-off detritus of winter. The warm firelight groped outward among the apple and plum trees, and bright sparks flowed heavenward when the wood popped and snapped.

Something the prophet said returned to mind: *Who will be the living coals?* She gazed upward for a few moments, watching until the eastern sky was indigo and speckled with light. *The Wayfarer is no more*, she thought. *But I am back home.*

Jars in hand, she crossed the yard and went to the basin to fill them.

CHAPTER SEVEN.

MERCHANT.

Twilight deepened into night, and throughout the city, soft firelight bloomed in windows and spilled through doorways. From his window, Gibson could see signs of the slow and scattered progress of lamp lighters. Their progression through the streets, and the trail of tiny flame lights in their wake, made him think of caterpillars. This was a familiar thought, inspired by the spring festival of the Gashuni, and he smiled unconsciously.

His gaze twitched to the west toward Gazelem, where the lights of the jewel city lay upon the distant hills.

But he did not let his thoughts linger there.

A little to the north, in the heart of the city, the ever-burning lights of the temple cast a diffuse dome of white light into the sky. And when he found himself scanning the heavens, his thoughts turned to the fallen Wayfarer. But he had no answers for the questions plaguing the city. He could not discern the meaning of the Wayfarer's fall. And he doubted he ever would. He frowned.

How can anyone know?

He had gotten word of the Wayfarer's spectacular demise two days earlier, and he had been waiting to see what effect it would work upon the people. The response of his young water woman was but one among many. From various quarters there were worse reports: violence, whispers of rebellion, suicides.

But there were other reactions, too. Where some saw darkness, others saw opportunity or hope. Enterprising mystagogues were already sowing hints of marvelous new secrets to be had. Simpler folk cherished thoughts of Yinock returning in a burning chariot.

Whatever came of it, Gibson's trade would undoubtedly be affected. Trade always followed the mood of the people. And one way or another, Hrusk would have to be placated.

He turned from the window, and after locking his door, he retrieved a wooden box from the chest at the foot of his bed. A long, metal cylinder lay within. Flawlessly smooth and unblemished, the cylinder had no apparent opening.

He took hold of one end and twisted gently. The invisible seal of the canister broke with a soft *tsss*, and he shook out two rolled maps and laid them on his table.

They were thinner than ordinary travel maps—more like the thin sheets of metal the Hruskans used for their sacred texts—and they were made of a white, seemingly indestructible material. The map features stood out in vivid color. And, with the exception of a circumscribed triangle impressed into the right-hand corner of each map, they were completely smooth.

But only one of the maps was useful.

Gibson traced his finger over the landscape and marveled, as he always did, at the flawless reproduction of the world in miniature. *Initial Survey, Primary Continent (K336:2), 3265:7:29.* The map bore no other title or place names, but certain features of the western half of the continent were easy to pick out.

The Geblon meandered down out of the land northward, terminating in the sea far to the south, where Noot lay in the heart of the Hruskan domain. The coastal lands of hari-Hrusk, the *pustinya*, and Shal-Gashun were also familiar to his traveler's eyes. And though he had not traveled to the lands east of Shal-Gashun, the sea folk and shippers of the southern kingdom confirmed that a string of islands stretched away from the southeast corner of the continent, just as the map showed.

The other map was a mystery. *Initial Survey, Island Continent*

(K336:2), 3265:7:29. Aside from small costal islands, and the islands east of Shal-Gashun, Gibson knew nothing about any islands. The few sea folk he had queried knew nothing. Or at least they would not say if they did.

And, yet, Gibson knew the island continent was real. His family had used the primary map to great advantage for generations.

The old road to Shal-Gashun had followed the hari-Hruskan seashore, traversing sparsely inhabited lands before venturing across a thin finger of the *pustinya*—an arid wasteland separating the lands of Shal-Gashun from the rest of the world. Caravans to Shal-Gashun had traveled the old road at their peril, heavily guarded against thieves and robbers—often behind schedule, and sometimes at great loss. *And worst of all,* his father had been fond of saying, *with knife-thin profit margins.*

But that was before the House of Jianin had ventured to cross the interior regions of the *pustinya.*

It had been a reckless gambit. Or so it had seemed to outsiders.

Gibson smiled, predatory. Except for a few members of the House of Jianin, no one knew the secret that made the venture possible.

His eyes drifted over the primary map to a small green dot deep within the *pustinya*, a speck of verdant life in the midst of the desert.

Believing in the precise handiwork of the ancient cartographers, Gibson's grandfather had set out for that point on the map, surmising it marked an oasis in the wilderness. And it had—a small, lush valley amid the interminable dunes and stony palisades of the *pustinya*. The Oasis of Rume. So called by his grandfather because of the flowering *rumesa* trees he found there upon his arrival.

Gibson shook his head, smiling slightly. His grandfather's gambit had risked both wealth and lives. Disaster and death would have been his reward if the ancient map had been wrong. One man had died, bitten by a poisonous, spiny serpent that dwelt in the deep desert. But something like that could have occurred anywhere; there were always risks to trading with Shal-Gashun.

Returning his gaze to the Geblon, he followed the course of the winding river with his fingertip. The road south followed the river all the way to Noot, where the mouth of the river disgorged its waters into the ocean. His eyes strayed to the southern tip of the continent, where Shal-Gashun rested in warmer climes. The unmistakable Bay of Bal-Ala was there, rendered in tiny, perfect detail.

If I could, I'd go to Shal-Gashun.

For a moment the thin, ornate spires of the Gashuni temples appeared in the light of his imagination. He saw the faces of people he had known there, the hospitable courtyards of the caravansaries, and the jungle-shrouded, holy mountain overlooking the jewel-blue Bay of Bal-Ala.

Why not go?

He laid his hand on the map and closed his eyes. He could not see a path to security for his house. He needed what his grandfather had found: some new source of wealth or success, something that would make him even more powerful.

The lands to the north held little promise. There were no cities there, no people; and several years earlier, an excursion led by the Daniti—to rediscover the foundations of the Great City of Old—had returned with nothing but tales of icy desolation. Over the mountains to the west lay the cold sea and a desolate, rocky coast. Few people. And to the east was only the impoverished shadow of the Kainite nation. But there could be other people, other nations across the vast plains of the interior.

Briefly he looked at the map of the island continent. There were, perhaps, treasures to be found there.

He rolled up the maps and slid them back into the cylinder. The metal skin sealed itself, and Gibson shook his head, marveling at the technology of his ancestors. Then he put the case away and unlocked his door.

He had hoped the relics would inspire some plan. But he felt no certainty.

Rumors of war in Hrusk had grown ominous, and the rise of the prophet had coincided with the growing unrest. *And now the Wayfarer has fallen.* Gibson stood in his bedroom window overlooking the yard, brooding.

And then he saw Sarana hurrying across the courtyard with her jars. Her new jars. He smiled, nostalgic for different days. Sarana had trouble with jars; she had broken her first set within a month of coming to the house. He recalled the day. Still a child, she had wept unendingly. Or would have, if Gibson had not told her all young girls were given inexpensive training jars that broke too easily.

He half laughed. She had been young enough to almost believe him—if only because it was better to believe—and she had lacked the desire to convince herself otherwise. And, after receiving new jars, she had returned to her labors still a child—a water girl with cropped, uncovered hair and dark, questioning eyes, slipping noiselessly from room to room. But then, seemingly not long after, she had changed. One evening she had knelt to pour his water, and when she had stood, her placid face—the smooth, unworried face of a young woman—had peered at him from beneath the folds of her shawl.

The ephemeral passage of time.

But she had not just grown older. There were times when he looked at her and imagined—if only for a glimpsed moment—he was looking at a daughter of one of the Great Houses. But no child of the ancient bloodline would have been given to the House of Jianin—to the house of a mere merchant. Such children were identified and assigned to the Great Houses of antiquity—to be married to privileged sons, to bear children who carried the attenuated thread of Yinock's immortality.

Still, the blood of Yinock was stronger in her than in many others. He had seen the regenerative power of her blood at work more than once.

A knock broke his revery, and he went back to his work.

"Come," he said.

Sarana entered noiselessly and knelt beside his foot basin to pour water. She laid a folded towel beside the basin, stood, and retreated a step.

He sat down, removed his sandals, and washed his feet, soaking them in the hot water. Year by year, he took greater pleasure in such small things. Finally, he looked up at her and smiled slightly. "Before you came, I was remembering the day you broke your first jars."

Sarana looked down. "I remember that day, Lord Jianin."

He was about to tell her it was a fond memory, but he forbore, turning instead to business. "You know . . . you are not alone in your curiosity." As he spoke, he dried his feet and put on house shoes. "Many people go to see him every day. Hundreds of them. So you are not alone. He intrigues *me*. He teaches strange things, and yet, people are drawn to him. Many join him in baptism."

Sarana nodded; she said, "I've heard the stories about him. The women at the well talk about him."

"I'm sure they do." Gibson stared at his water woman. "Were you tempted?"

"My Lord?"

"Were you tempted to join yourself to him?"

"I . . . was, my Lord."

Gibson picked up the half empty jar of water at his feet, and turned it slowly in his hands, as if admiring it. "Mercy," he said quietly, almost to himself. "The workmanship of man molded into mercy."

Sarana looked carefully at him. "My Lord?"

"I was just thinking." He paused. "This has been a strange day. With everyone talking about the Wayfarer, and this prophet." Gibson held out the jar and Sarana took it. "Perhaps today it is easier to forgive acts of harmless disobedience. But it is good you did not join yourself to him. I cannot have the servants of my household turning after strange gods."

"I did not mean—"

"In that, there can be no compromise."

She nodded. "Yes, my Lord."

Gibson picked up the foot basin and emptied it out the window. The water splashed away in the darkness, running into one of the gutters and down to the orchard. Sarana reached out, belatedly, but he had done her job before she could intervene.

Gibson smiled. "Don't be troubled. When I was a boy, my father made me work among the servants of the house for a full year. You might recall I made Maran do the same. I learned every job, and I even spent many nights with the watchmen." Gibson put the basin back in its place. "I learned that work is good. And that there is no indignity in performing the labors of this House. It is an honor."

Sarana looked down at the jar in her hands.

"It is time, I think, for you to learn something about my work." Gibson walked to his table and picked up a small bag. He reached in and drew out a handful of coins. He laid the coins on the table. "I am a man of business." Gibson counted out several coins and put the remainder back into the sack. "What you see here—this is what I spent today to replace your jars. This is your debt to me." Gibson walked around to the other side of the table and sat down across from Sarana. "How will you repay this debt?"

"I . . ." Sarana bit her lower lip. "I will never forsake my duties again, my Lord."

Gibson shook his head. "You owe me that already."

A silence followed, and Gibson watched as she worked through the problem his words posed. Everything she had belonged to the House of Jianin. She was merely a steward of a few of his possessions. Her brow furrowed slightly, and her dark eyes quickened with thought. He waited for her to respond.

Finally, she spoke. "I don't know, my Lord. I have nothing."

Gibson smiled, pleased. "You find yourself in a common predicament. But fear not. I want to employ you in a new task." Gibson put a hand on the table and tapped his finger. "You see those coins. Each one represents a day's wage."

Sarana looked at the coins. Two new jars. A week's labor. Gibson waited for her to respond.

"I don't understand," she said.

"You know I employ some of my servants?"

"Yes. But I am a servant of the temple. Abasha said—my temple mother—she said I cannot take payment."

"She spoke only of your sacred duty to serve. Your covenant applies only to your labors for this House—your assigned servitude. But I am talking about my personal business. In that, I am free to pay you, I can hire you like any other person."

Sarana continued to look at the coins, her brow furrowed. She said, "But I spend every day serving here."

Gibson nodded. "True. But as your master, I can also grant you leave to rest from your duties. Which I am willing to do—partly—to allow you to repay this debt."

"I don't understand. Why would you grant me leave from my duties, and then pay me money to perform them?"

"I won't. In fact, you will still have your duties to complete. But at times, perhaps a few hours each day, I will release you from your duties so you can earn the money to repay your debt."

"But what other work can I do?" Sarana's face flushed, and she looked back down at the floor.

Gibson heard the slight emphasis, and he silently considered his young water woman, her softly boiling frustration. And then he smiled slightly. "I want you to tell me more about this man at the river—this prophet."

Sarana looked up, surprise in her eyes. "But I know nothing. I only know what people have said . . . and what I saw today."

Gibson nodded. "But you can find out more. And in return for your efforts, I'll pay you a fair price."

"But how can I—"

Gibson stopped her with an upheld hand, tasting impatience. "You know more than you think, Sarana. And you are capable of discovering more. You showed that today. And though I cannot condone your disobedience, I *can* take advantage of it. That is the challenge after any transgression—to become better because of it." He rubbed his chin with a finger. "So let's begin there. You have a debt that needs to be repaid. I will not force you to repay it, but I'm offering you a chance to do so. Do you think you want to try?"

"I—" Sarana stuttered, stopped. Her lips parted and she blinked a few times. "I want to try," she said.

"Good."

"But what should I do?"

"That is the question." Gibson stood and walked around the table.

He swept the coins into his left hand and shook them softly, meditating on the problem. The coins clinked softly, pleasingly. "Maybe I should send you out to the river again," he said. "I have a man who keeps me informed about this prophet, but he might not see what you see. You could also bring me the stories told at the well." Gibson tightened his fist around the coins, and he turned and looked at Sarana.

Sarana opened her mouth slightly, as if to speak, but she said nothing. Gibson nodded as if she had asked him a question.

He continued. "It could be profitable. I'd like to hear more about how people take his words."

"I think I could do it, my Lord." Her eyes were down.

"Well, we do not have to settle it now. Think on it, and let me know tomorrow what your thoughts are. I will think on it too."

After his young water woman departed, Gibson stood at the window and let his thoughts wander out to Gazelem—and to inevitable thoughts about his wife. His wife would not have counseled leniency with Sarana. And certainly not another trip to the river. She would have warned him it was foolish to encourage greater independence among his servants. And she would have predicted some dire consequence.

Gibson closed his eyes and scratched his eyebrow. His wife was usually right, of course. But in this case, a mix of mercy and mercenary instinct seemed right.

CHAPTER EIGHT.

WATCHMAN.

An hour after sunset, Gibson looked up from his work, alerted by the sound of someone coming toward his room. Tobin appeared in the doorway, and Gibson gestured for him to enter.

"A message arrived for you, my Lord." Tobin held out an envelope and then put it on the desk.

"A message? From?"

"We could not tell. The man who delivered it would not identify himself or say who sent him. He wore a heavy cowl; we could not see his face."

Gibson felt a touch of anticipation. "Nothing else?"

"No, my Lord."

After Tobin left, Gibson picked up the envelope and turned it over in his hands, examining it slowly. No markings. The paper felt heavy, expensive. He cut open the envelope and removed a folded sheet from within. Expensive product, thick but smooth, and made with soft fibers. It had probably come from Hrusk. He rubbed it between his thumb and forefinger, and then he opened it up. The message was short, written by a careful hand in scarlet ink: *Your house is not in order.*

For a moment, Gibson's mind balked. He read the words again, accepting their reality only slowly. He knew what it meant. But he never imagined he would face such an accusation. *Your house is not in order.* The shame of it built slowly. And then some anger, too. *What does anyone have against me that would lead to this?* Nothing.

Gibson tossed the note down on his table. A pile of his own papers and a costly bottle of *rebboth* ink sat beside a brightly burning candle. The stark words of the note glared at him, illuminated in the soft glow of the candle. *Your house is not in order.*

Outside, darkness blanketed the empty yard. Small glimmers of light outlined the gatehouse door where it was not flush within its frame. Gibson rapped on the door and walked inside. Ganon stood up from his chair beside the outer window.

"My Lord."

"The messenger," Gibson said. He paused. "Tobin said he didn't identify himself. Did you see anything else? Can you describe him?"

"No, my Lord, nothing useful. He wore a heavy robe and had a hood over his face. He only said a few words. Then he turned and walked away."

"What did he say?"

" 'For your master.' And then he gave me the envelope. I tried to call him back, to question him, but he just walked away."

Gibson shook his head, trying to think of anything else to ask. But there was nothing more to discover. The messenger could have been anyone, a hired courier. And he knew what the message portended in any event. The Council—or someone on the Council—was seeking to have him removed. The hard-won seat of the House of Jianin was being challenged. He imagined he would learn soon enough what his anonymous accuser had against him.

"Thank you, Ganon."

Gibson closed the gatehouse door and went back toward the house. An old, but formidable, *hresta* tree grew in the middle of the courtyard, and he stood for a moment beneath its dark canopy. He needed to get back to work—he had work to finish before morning, when his next caravan headed south to Noot—but he wanted a moment alone, somewhere he could sort out his thoughts.

The leafy darkness of the vineyard engulfed him, and, after stumbling into a stack of baskets, he walked quietly among the rows, cautiously avoiding the unruly, thorny branches.

In the southwest corner of the vineyard, at the farthest point from the house, a little-used watchtower stood black against the sky. In times past, in his grandfather's days, thieves and foraging animals had been more common. But as the city grew, the wildness of the hills had been driven back.

Or perhaps we've just grown more complacent.

Atop the little tower, Gibson looked to the west and south, his eyes sliding away from Gazelem. Night had erased the road, but campfires and travelers' lanterns marked its course across the land. Gibson smiled. Men sat around those fires, eating savory dishes, singing, and recounting tales. He knew their easy camaraderie; he had lived the life of the road with his own father, traveling and trading and sharing the travails of the road.

He closed his eyes.

Many nights he had lain beneath the endless expanse of the desert sky—a sky so broad, so bespeckled with glory, it defied comprehension. Nothing seemed so vast as the desert sky on a clear night. Nothing. Southeast of Noot, after the mountains receded beneath the horizon, the heavens stretched from one edge of the world to the other, glittering and infinite. On those nights, he knew God was watching over him with his invisible, glass eyes.

Gibson looked up, remembering the vastness of the starry firmament. But in the Great City, there was too much light, too much pollution from below. The bejeweled weave of heaven's folds was but a scant blanket. To the northeast lay Pekel and its ever-burning wasteland of garbage pits and ashy fields, the reddish glow of its orange-black fires a fell dawn. Closer, though, and far brighter, stood the blocky bulk of the temple. Its ancient lamps bathed its walls with an otherworldly radiance and cast a pearly luminescence high into the night sky.

He looked south again and blew out a breath. Musing about the night sky would not solve the problem he was facing.

Your house is not in order.

He wondered if rumors of war in Hrusk, or the Wayfarer's fall, had emboldened a rival or enemy to act. It was no secret he favored amiable relations with Hrusk. He had repeatedly proposed changes to trade rules, hoping to equalize relations. His manifest sympathy for Hrusk could easily be characterized as something more nefarious. It seemed unlikely, though, as there were many in the Council who agreed—if only silently—that some change was necessary.

There were other possibilities.

His wealth and influence had grown among the merchant houses —a source of envy and, perhaps, anger. But his success had not come to the great detriment of any particular house. At least not recently. His grandfather's exploits in crossing the *pustinya* had destroyed trade alliances and boosted the House of Jianin's wealth and power considerably, but many years had passed since then.

Which means little. He chided himself. The note delivered to his door could have been the first step of a plan intended to bear fruit sixty years hence, or it could have been the penultimate step of a sixty-year-old plan on the cusp of fruition.

He stood in the dark a bit longer, savoring the stillness of the watchtower.

Someone thought there was something amiss in his house. He would have to find it. And remedy it.

When he returned to his room, the small candle on his desk still burned. The flame floated above a placid pool of wax poised like water in an overfull cup. He pushed aside the anonymous message and finished a letter to his steward in Noot. It felt futile in the face of impending destruction to write about the mundane needs of his business. But rumors of war were only rumors, and anonymous threats of expulsion from the Council were only threats.

Gibson looked over the letter. As he did so, a sharp rap sounded on his door, startling him. But the intrusion was expected. His business manager, Nef. Gibson motioned him in.

"An eventful day," Nef said. His deep-set eyes met Gibson's.

"You might say so." Gibson laughed and put aside his letter. "You did the right thing sending me word about Sarana. Telasa would have reported the missing jars, no doubt, but knowing the whole story was useful."

"I knew you would want to know."

"So, what else have you brought me?"

"Many stories abroad, today. One, in particular. The Quarter was in turmoil. As he threatened, the on-Dam ostracized his son—the boy would not renounce the prophet—and it had immediate repercussions. Several men chased the boy down and attacked him. He was severely beaten. There are dire rumors about his fate, but no one claims to know what actually happened to him. None of my men could ascertain his whereabouts this evening. He could be dead."

Gibson nodded, well aware of the politics in the Quarter. "You may be right. I hope not, for the boy's sake. But perhaps not ours." He smiled ruefully. "We don't need another Hruskan son rising up against his father. The Quarter is bad enough."

"It's not likely. According to all accounts, the boy and his father were genuinely close. And—" Nef held up a finger. "The on-Dam has not yet named an heir."

Gibson weighed that information for several seconds. "I wonder . . . does the boy have any other relatives in the city?"

Nef shrugged. "Undoubtedly there are cousins, if not others. But there are no close ties that I know of. His mother still resides in Hrusk, in Noot."

"Find out. If the Quarter divides into factions over this, we'll need to know how it affects our trade alliances. Not that we can be certain about any of it." Gibson paused, and then he asked, "What of the prophet?"

"There were around four hundred people at the river today, with many coming and going. As you know, Sarana was among them."

"I dealt with her earlier," Gibson said, waving his hand.

"There were seventy-eight baptisms."

"Seventy-eight," Gibson said. "Are things slowing down at all?"

Nef frowned. "I think not. There have been around two thousand baptisms, I'd say. And there are probably more. We don't watch him constantly, and there were many before we started counting."

Gibson tapped his fingers on the desk. "Two thousand. I knew the number was growing rapidly, but . . . you think that many?"

"Some days he baptizes well over a hundred. Once he baptized around two hundred. Of course, there's no way of knowing how many of them are still actual supporters." He shrugged. "Some of them could have renounced their belief, or never had much to begin with. A lot of them might not even understand what they have joined. Maybe some have been counted twice."

Gibson grunted softly. "Doesn't really matter. Either way, there are members of the Council who will use this prophet to play for power. He's become too powerful to ignore." *Especially to people like the Daniti.*

"He's been reckless," Nef said.

Gibson huffed air out through his nose. "Beyond reckless—if half the stories told about him are true. His arrogance has provoked the Council too much. And not at a good time." Gibson sobered, silently considering the prophet's probable future. The Daniti were clamoring for his arrest, which meant they wanted him dead or in prison, and no other House had spoken much in opposition. There were not many who wanted to stand against the Daniti. Not for something so trivial as a street preacher—and not with war lurking in Hrusk.

And I have other problems. Gibson picked up the note. "I need you to do one more thing for me." Gibson handed the note to Nef. "This came tonight."

Nef read the note. He flipped the paper over, looking for anything more.

"I need to know who sent it," Gibson said. "And I need to know what they think they have against me."

"How did it arrive?"

"Earlier this evening. A messenger dropped it off and left."

"That's not much to work with." Nef looked toward the window overlooking the courtyard. "Ganon should have followed him. It will be difficult to find much, I think." But his eyes had narrowed, his mind already at work.

"I also need to know where the other merchant houses stand."

Nef started to say something but then he stopped. One side of his mouth twitched briefly, and then he frowned.

"What?" Gibson said.

"It occurred to me that Lady Jianin could have useful insights."

"No," Gibson said. He met Nef's gaze and said nothing more.

Nef nodded and let his gaze drop. He rubbed his chin with two fingers. "I will find out what I can."

Gibson picked up a little stack of letters and handed them to Nef. "These must be delivered tonight, the van leaves in the morning."

Alone, Gibson went to his window and looked toward Gazelem. Nef was right, of course. The Lady Jianin—his absent wife—would probably know exactly what he ought to do. *Or at least she'd tell me exactly what I ought to do.*

Her insights into the slow machinations of the bin-Yinocki were usually correct, and her family's connections to people of power seemed endless. Even if he had not loved her, the marriage would have been a profitable partnership, if only for the trade information she sometimes gleaned from her ubiquitous contacts.

But not profitable enough for her. He clenched his jaw, angry and mournful. *By the Wayfarer,* he thought. *I miss her.*

CHAPTER NINE.

LOVE. WISDOM.

Sarana lay awake in the predawn gloom of the women's quarters. Twice during the night she had awakened, anxious, impelled out of sleep by her plan to get an early start. Each time, the constant chirping of the *noka-teets* had told her morning was too far off. But now the little night birds were quieting, and liminal light, grey and cool, blushed in the doorway, outlining the heavy curtain hanging there.

She eased out of bed, conscious of her sleeping sisters. Kaina lay in the bed next to hers, breathing deeply.

For a moment, Sarana looked down on her. *She is a woman of sorrows.*

The turn of her thoughts surprised her, and Sarana stood looking at the old woman for several seconds. But then she straightened the blankets of her bed and quietly fluffed her pillow. She had work to do. It was too early to go into the city, to the well, but she could fill the house jars and build up the fire for hot water. And when Ganon opened the gate, she would be ready to go. She removed her heavy shift, and the lingering coolness of the night stippled her bare skin. She shivered as she donned a thinner shift to wear beneath her robe.

After filling the house jars with water from the cistern, she put half a dozen of the smaller hearth jars in the oven. That done, she looked around and decided she had done everything she could before going to the well. She picked up her new jars and went outside to wait for the gates to open.

Only a few bright stars remained in the indigo expanse of heaven, and Sarana looked up at them through the branches of the *hresta* tree. Soon the other servants of the house would wake, and the ordinary operations of the house would commence. And when the gates opened, she would hurry to the well. *And then to the river.* The plan had formed the night before as she lay in her bed, thinking about her master's words.

A sound caught her attention and she looked toward the vineyard. She saw no one. But then, through the open archway, she saw several baskets scattered on the ground. *Probably knocked over during the night by the wind . . . or a small animal.* But animals rarely came inside the walls, except for birds. *Maybe they weren't stacked well last night.*

Leaving her jars beneath the *hresta*, she went into the vineyard and gathered up the baskets. The ground bore no marks of rummaging beasts. Just the normal passage of servants. And then she heard another sound, a soft scuffling. She rose up and peered over the tops of the rows of plants. In the leafy gloom, at the back side of the vineyard, a man was climbing down off the rear wall. He was dressed in dark clothing, and he moved wearily.

And then she recognized him. Maran bin Jianin.

She ducked down instinctively. *What is he doing?* There was no reason for him to be climbing over the wall and wandering around the vineyard. Or perhaps there was. Maran did not answer to her; he was the son of her master—he was the man she was destined to serve some day. And she served him even now.

If he went out secretly, there must have been a reason. Slowly her thoughts calmed. Maran was often entrusted with his father's business.

But does Gibson know?

Sarana backed out of the vineyard and hurried back to her place beneath the tree. She sat next to her jars and looked toward the gate, feigning no interest in the vineyard. A moment later, she heard him enter the yard behind her.

A tense moment of expectancy.

"Ah, Sarana, you're out early."

She turned, flinching at the sound of his voice even though she knew he was there. "Bin Jianin," she said.

"Getting an early start, I see."

"Yes, I . . . I wanted to get an early start after yesterday." She looked down, ashamed because it was truer than she thought it would be.

"Before you go out, could you please bring some hot water up to my room?"

"Yes, bin Jianin. Of course."

He thanked her and went inside. She wondered if he knew she had seen him sneaking in over the wall.

What was he doing? But even as she wondered, she went back inside; she had duties no matter what he had been doing. *You will not always know your master's heart. Your duty is to serve, not question.*

With iron tongs, she removed a hearth jar from the oven and mixed the hot water with some cold water in a partially-full house jar. Steam rose from the jar, and Sarana dipped her finger in to test it. *Perfect.* Just as Maran preferred. Scalding him would not satisfy her curiosity. He was her master, or master's son, and, thus, one and the same. She hurried up the stairs, discarding her questions.

His room was separated from Gibson's chambers by two empty rooms. One of the empty rooms had belonged to Gibson's wife; the other would have gone to a second wife. Or to Maran's betrothed.

She slowed, drawn into thoughtfulness by her common, if somewhat inchoate, dream of becoming a wife. It was not unheard of for a servant to be taken in marriage. Temple children were sometimes married to the sons of lesser elders. But not often. Not ever, as far as she knew personally. But there were stories among the women at the well. Rumors. And children of the blood were always taken by the Great Houses, to preserve the bloodline and raise up children.

She stopped in front of Maran's closed door, feeling foolish. If he had desires toward marriage, he would not look to her, the lowliest water woman of the house. She knocked.

"Come," he said.

She stepped into the room; he was standing beside his open window, looking out.

The west-facing window looked out upon the still shadowy valley. Gazelem sat in the distance, indistinct. But closer, in the sprawl of the lower city, the world had begun to stir. Hazy twists of smoke rose slowly from many houses, and distant, dreamy sounds floated on the still air.

At the foot of Maran's bed, Sarana knelt and poured the steaming water into his foot basin. For a moment, Maran did nothing, seeming about to speak, but then he sat on the end of his bed and put his feet into the water. She was careful not to meet his eyes as she took his right foot into her hands. Slowly, she rubbed away the thin, slick sheen of dust-become-mud that coated his toes.

So he walked some distance. Again she wondered where he had been —why he had slipped over the wall like a thief.

Her hands moved methodically to his other foot, rubbing the brown dirt from his skin, feeling the knobs of his bones, the tense lines of tendons. The familiar contours of feet were indelibly impressed upon her fingertips. As a child, as with all things, she had learned the ritual of washing feet from her temple mother. Abasha and the other children had regularly washed Sarana's feet, and Sarana had washed theirs, in remembrance of their servitude, and in training for their future labors.

A glance upward revealed his keen brown eyes looking down upon her. She wiped his feet with the soft cloth tied at her waist, dried her hands, and leaned back, waiting for his word—for his will. Unconsciously, she reached up and straightened her shawl, pushing back a stray lock of hair.

"Thank you," Maran said. "That will be all."

Sarana emptied the basin and gathered up the house jar. She hesitated. And for a moment, she almost dared to ask him where he had been that morning. Maran's gaze grew less sharp, became questioning.

Why don't we speak?

He looked at her a moment longer, and then he waved a hand in her direction, dismissing her.

Gibson awoke from a dream of the deep desert. He lay unmoving, eyes trained on the ceiling, hungry for the nostalgic happiness his dream had engendered. He was tempted to close his eyes and remain submerged beneath his blankets—to try to piece together the nubilous pieces of his subconscious yearning.

But pre-dawn light had already crept into his room, and the unmistakable sound of morning birdsong roused him to action. He swung his feet out of bed and walked across the cool stones to the foot of his bed, where he knelt. Softly he recited the Ten Lines.

As he dressed, he recalled his dream. The deep desert. A moonless night. The smell of the caravan thick in his nostrils—camels, sweat, leather, dust. And above him, the glittering expanse of heaven.

So vast, so strangely bright. Gibson rubbed his eyes, remembering dry eyes filmed with the dust of the road. There had been many nights like that, when sleepless, or just hungry for the eternal signs and wonders of heaven, he had lain awake and stared at the endless reaches of the star-strewn firmament.

No doubt the dream had been prompted by his musings the night before.

If only this day could be like those days. He splashed his face with cool water from his wash basin and ran his wet fingers back through his short, cropped hair. But even if he could return to his travels, the night sky would never be the same. *The Wayfarer is gone.*

After a meal of honeyed bread, apples, and lightly spiced sausages, Gibson sat back and looked out the window of his dining room into his vineyard. He was alone at the table, and he let his thoughts wander. His house was active with the familiar sounds of a new day, but the vineyard was still quiet, the leaves of the *rebboth* plants bobbing gently in a soft breeze. He felt the blessing of Esana in his mind.

Except for a few of the truly wealthy houses, none could match the vineyard of the House of Jianin. And among them all, none were more productive—a legacy of Gibson's grandmother, who had excelled in grafting one plant into another to produce stronger, more robust plants. She had, in her own quiet way, added immeasurably to the fortunes of the House of Jianin.

He summoned Telasa and asked her to send in Sarana. When Sarana did not come right away, Gibson wondered if she had already gone to the well. Finally, Telasa came back.

"Sarana is not in the house, Lord Jianin."

Gibson turned from the window and smiled. Telasa looked expectant, and he thought he knew what she was thinking. *What punishment will I mete out?* He chuckled softly. "It is a lucky thing you are here, then. Actually, when you see her, you will please remind her I am expecting . . . ah, increased efforts from her. Do you know where has she gone?"

"I don't know, my Lord. I looked, but I couldn't find her anywhere. She didn't leave word, but Ganon saw her leave with her jars. Kaina thinks she has gone early to the well. To draw water."

How carefully you choose your words, Gibson thought. *Suspicious woman.* "But she left without your noticing?" he asked.

A slight pause. "Yes, Lord."

"It is well. Undoubtedly she is making up for yesterday. Thank you."

Telasa dipped her chin and left the room. Gibson watched her go, smiling. She was a good, hard-working woman, but she seemed to have little kindness in her heart for Sarana. It must have galled her to hear Sarana had gone out to the river and seen the prophet.

Outside, in the courtyard, his stable master, Daran, had his black mare saddled and ready. Her coat shone in the morning light; her feet stepped lightly—a tad impatiently; she was ready for a jaunt. Gibson thanked Daran and rode out into the city, intending to take an indirect route to the council hall.

It's time to cast off my gloomy thoughts.

He left the upper city through the Merchant's Gate, moving at a leisurely pace along the New Road. From the upper city, the road led down to the valley, where it forked—the left fork curving south and eventually joining with the road to Noot, and the right fork turning north and skirting the rocky curve of the hill beneath the Upper City.

Gibson veered north and urged his horse to a canter. The stony ramparts of the hill rose up in jagged splendor, speckled with tenacious wild flowers and resolute patches of wispy grass. Brown ground-nesting wrens fluttered from their homes among the rocks and bounced from one small promontory to another, peeping viciously, taking flight briefly when Gibson passed beneath their portion of the world.

When he reached the Pilgrim's Road, he turned right again and went back up the hill toward the city. The tumble-down buildings of the outer city sprawled along the road like rockfall on the side of a mountain. Gibson eyed the gabbling denizens, the human miscellany, disquietly. If war reached the city, the people of the outer city would have no protection. And where the outer city abutted the city walls, the city would be harder to defend.

We have grown complacent and disorderly. Gibson frowned, and his jaw clenched. *Your house is not in order.*

He rode on into the city, trying not to fall back into gloomy ruminations. When he reached the Almoners Square, where priests stood sentinel, he slowed, got down from his mount, and dropped an offering into one of the alms boxes. Pilgrims and other travelers were doing the same, and enterprising urchins milled among them, hands out. Gibson guessed they did quite well.

When he arrived at the council hall, he turned his horse over to a young boy—a temple child in training. Gibson recognized him.

"Take good care of her, Tam."

"Yes, Lord Jianin."

Broad steps led up to the entrance of the blocky building. Over the open doorway, cut deep into the smooth face of the ancient stone lintel, were two words:

LOVE • WISDOM

Gibson smiled up at the words and entered, thinking, as he often did, that the Elders had long since learned to ignore the simple but vexing charge of the ancient artisan. There was even a longstanding argument over the meaning of the phrase. Love – Wisdom. Was it intended to command a love of wisdom? Or did it set forth two guiding principles for the leaders of the city? Was the first a prerequisite to the second? Were they complementary? Or were they somehow opposing precepts that had to be balanced?

The priests debated such things.

An unadorned, windowless hall led to the council chamber—a conduit filled with brisk movement and serious faces. Gibson felt his innards quiver as his thoughts turned to the terse message delivered the night before. But he did not think he would have to answer yet. The note was not a formal charge.

Several people greeted him as he descended the steps of the auditorium and took his customary seat among the newer, less powerful members of the Council. All around him, the great room thrummed with conversation. Women and men stood or sat, heads together, glancing from time to time around the room, nodding when their eyes met the gaze of a compatriot or rival.

Gibson's gaze turned to the High Elder's seat. Ableth bin Somith was already in his place, talking to Haran, one of the temple's ubiquitous priests. A moment later, the High Elder tapped the *gaz-lahi* on his arm rest. Its distinctive, glassy rap rang out through the room and demanded silence.

"Brothers and sisters—Elders of the Council." Ableth stood and held out his arms, giving the established greeting. "Though I come to you as the first, I will be the last. I will make judgment for our people."

"*Es-prida,*" Gibson said, responding with the others.

The room quieted and Ableth continued. "Many reports—you all have heard this, I am sure—have confirmed the fall of the Wayfarer and its immolation as it fell." Ableth raised his hands again, quieting the murmuring that rippled across the chamber.

"We cannot say what it signifies, but the priests assure me they are searching the Lines to discover its meaning. They will report to the Council what they find. Until then, we have more pressing concerns. There are, as many of you know, reports of increased fighting in Hrusk. There are rumors of impending war. We should not confuse rumors, of course, with, ah . . . actual facts."

"You accuse us of distorting the truth?"

Gibson turned—though he did not have to look to know who had spoken. Kim bith Dan's mellifluous voice was unmistakable. And she had a habit of speaking without being recognized by the presiding elder. Gibson's eyes lingered. Her lustrous, dark hair, stark against her fair skin, was drawn back and braided on the sides of her head.

"Not at all, Elder Dan." Ableth's hands rose in front of his body, his palms turned outward. "I simply suggest we need not be hasty."

Wisdom, Gibson thought, somewhat wryly. Careful inaction was the pinnacle of Ableth's wisdom.

"Such rumors arise from time to time," Ableth said, deliberate. "We need not reach for any unlikely conclusions."

"We do not think war is unlikely," Kim said.

"As you've made plain," Ableth said. "But the Council is not convinced, and the on-Dam has assured us he wants peace." Ableth's eyebrows raised slightly. "We know they fear the superior might of the Daniti. And they know they cannot succeed against us. The Daniti are too powerful."

Gibson watched Kim carefully. Ableth was pandering to her, but she believed his words. Or at least she would not suggest otherwise to the Council. The Daniti were her greatest vanity; she wore the strength of her warriors like a harlot wore perfume.

"But," Ableth said, pausing and turning slightly away from Kim. "How these rumors have affected the city cannot be ignored. Our peace is threatened in other ways. This man who styles himself a prophet is leading away the hearts of the people, plying them with these rumors of war. He has challenged our authority and accused the priests of leading the people astray." Ableth paused. "I have been in counsel with Elder Amin and believe we cannot stand idly by." He looked to his right.

"If you will permit me."

Gibson turned his gaze toward the familiar, resonant voice. Tendar bin Amin stood with his arms at his sides, a scarlet cloak draped from his shoulders. His serene, marble face surveyed the room. A man of ancient blood. And near him sat the eugenic scions of his house

—young immortals, or near immortals, of the House of Amin.

"I agree with Elder Somith," Tendar said. "The situation in Hrusk is only a minor concern—a situation we have dealt with time and again over the years. Hrusk can mount no serious attack upon our city." He paused, deliberate. "Assuming, of course, the accountings made to me are correct and the rumors about the Daniti are, in fact, merely rumor." Tendar looked at Kim, his gaze deceptively lazy.

"There is no truth to such tales," she said calmly.

Muttering spread across the room.

"As I suspected," Tendar said, overpowering the low murmur. "So, the immediate issue we must address is this man who mocks the holy prophets. And, of course, the rising discontent among the resident Hruskans—or those who might use the present disorder to effect change."

Gibson watched reactions around the room as Tendar described the prophet's recent deeds. A few seemed shocked when he reported that thousands had been baptized. Others appeared disinterested, bored.

Your house is not in order. The words delivered to his door the night before recurred in his mind.

Perhaps it was an indictment of them all.

"I am Treasurer of the Covenant," Tendar said finally. "And the storehouse of Esana must be preserved—every whit." He paused. "This so-called prophet must be arrested and brought before the Council. If he will not renounce and publicly renounce his lies—so that the people may see him for what he is—then he must be punished."

Ableth bin Somith held up his hands, as if forestalling interruption. "The solution to this problem will be discussed in the designated manner. I will cast the lots." The clatter of the lots filled the chamber. "It falls on Hannon bin Laban."

A long pause ensued while Hannon bin Laban, the oldest member of the Council, rose from his seat on shaky legs. Wisps of his white hair, which sprouted thick from his scalp, protruded wildly in all directions. "I see no reason to fight against this man who would call himself prophet. We have weathered such storms before, always coming through them with the help of God. This man will not overcome the people of God, nor will he threaten the peace of our people. Those who follow him are the dross. They pass judgment on themselves."

Gibson listened impassively as many of the older members of the Council voiced similar opinions. Only a few—mostly those with traditional ties to the Daniti—favored any strong action.

Finally, the lot fell upon Kim bith Dan. She stood. "My brothers and sisters. There is only one path open to us: we must move against this so-called prophet and destroy him. He must be killed for his blasphemous teachings, and those who have foolishly followed after him must renounce or suffer the consequences of their disobedience —as the Lines decree. I do not agree with those who see no threat in this man, and I do not agree that the reports from Hrusk are only the familiar stories we hear from year to year. There will be war, and we must be prepared. Ridding ourselves of this prophet is the first step of our purification. After that, we must diminish the risk of internal insecurity by taking action against the increasing numbers of Hruskans finding succor within our gates."

Gibson listened as Kim regaled the Council with carefully selected examples of righteous wars recorded in the Lines of the Law. *By the Wayfarer, she is beautiful*, he thought. And he smiled, a bit sadly, as he contemplated the now-useless oath. The Wayfarer was no more, it had fallen. He felt then how the loss of the Wayfarer, its destruction, had wounded the world.

When Kim finished, the orderly debate continued, one speaker at a time, chosen by random selection of the lots. *The God of the Sticks*, his father had been fond of saying. A small blasphemy. Gibson composed his thoughts, ordering what he would say, but the lot did not fall on him.

None of what he might say would surprise anyone.

His thoughts aligned with the older members of the Council who saw little danger in permitting the prophet to continue without interference—though he would want to keep a watchful eye.

Forbearance, deliberation, inaction. *Safety*, he thought; and the silent derision of his mental uttering surprised him.

But he did part ways with most of them when it came to trade. He wanted better trade with Hrusk; he was willing to make concessions that the old pride of the ancient houses would not—or could not—condone. That was not a safe stance; his outspokenness on that topic might have contributed to the warning he had received the night before.

Perhaps it is better if the lot does not find me. He looked around the room; he sensed unseen lines of power, taut with secret schemes. *Your house is not in order.*

He remembered then something new from his dream the night before. He had been deep in the desert, encamped in a familiar place. A gargantuan *drevesa* tree had loomed in the darkness beside him, its giant trunk pocked with hand-hewn niches. And in each small cavity, a tiny candle flame had burned. Little pockets of light circled upward, bright at eye level and dwindling as they rose higher toward the distant canopy.

So strange.

And there had been something else. A guard sitting motionlessly on a rock near the twinkling, glowing tree. A Hruskan. His dark skin had blended seamlessly with the night-drenched wasteland, and candlelight glinted on the thin golden chains crisscrossing his face and dangling from the rings in his ears and nose. He had smiled flashingly and put a finger to his lips, and his eyes had glowed like magical flakes of ivory.

It reminded Gibson of the first night he had stood watch. His father had assigned a more experienced man, a Hruskan mercenary, to sit with him, to train him.

"Got to thit here real thilent," the man had said, lisping to avoid hissing.

And Gibson had seen the man's teeth flash momentarily in the darkness, an ephemeral wedge of the moon captured. The man's uncanny eyes had turned back toward the black desert, and his right hand had tightened around the hilt of his long, curved sword. The blade had shone dully in the dark.

"Now ith the time when it'th motht dangerouth. Got to be careful out here on the edge. If you don't know what'th out there, you don't know how to prepare for it. And then you got trouble." A wink, and one glowing eye was snuffed momentarily, and then relit, in the darkness.

The tapping of the judgment stone drew him back to the Council chamber, dispelling his oneiric thoughts.

"My brothers and sisters." Elder Somith spread his hands again. "We will take the words of this Council into our hearts, seeking wisdom. And now, Kim bith Dan has a proposal to bring before the Council."

Along with the rest of the Elders, Gibson conceded the floor to Kim. But as he did, he recalled the ghostly face of the watchman from his dream. *Now is the time when it's most dangerous.* He smiled grimly, only half listening to Kim, who was prefacing her proposal with dire warnings from the Lines.

His dream had pushed his thoughts in another direction. The prophet was like a vast darkness beyond his camp. This man who had swayed the people of the city was as unknown to him as his wife in recent months. Everything he knew about the man had been observed by other eyes. He had been too lax—had relied too much on others to watch his gates.

It was time to venture out into the darkness himself.

I was foolish to wait so long. The lowliest of his water women had gone to see the prophet before he had thought to go himself. Amusing. But troubling, too.

He settled back into his seat and listened as the Council continued its slow machinations. Kim bith Dan was still intoning her unsubtle indictment against the prophet and other rebellious elements taking root in the city.

But then Kim paused, glanced slowly back at Ableth, and held up a document.

"This is my proposal," she said. "It is time to take a stronger hand with the Hruskan Quarter. If they are going to live here, they must respect our ancient traditions."

Kim began to read from the document in her hand.

CHAPTER TEN.

SCORCHERS.

A foot prodded Neturu's side, stoking the little fire smoldering in his broken rib. He awoke with a gasp.

"This one's not dead!" The voice shrilled slightly.

"Well this one back here is long past dead." The second voice was deep, sedate, but tinged with nascent laughter. "Looks like someone missed his rounds again."

The shrill-voiced man, now calmer, looked ready to spit. "We should make him come and get it."

Neturu squeezed his eyes shut and then he pushed himself up into a sitting position. He grunted through the pain. "Ah!" He coughed, his throat dry, sour. The man who had kicked him stepped back.

"Can you help me?" Neturu said, his voice croaking.

The man with the deep voice stepped out of the back room and looked down at Neturu. Black clothing adorned his imposing frame, and a tightly-wrapped, soot-darkened scarf that had once been blue, covered his head.

He smiled, playfully rueful. "We could do naught but help, I think, given your sorry state. I think anything we did would be an improvement. Still, I don't suppose you were asking for sarcasm or ill-timed *shalas*." The man winked.

Neturu smiled involuntarily at the man's use of the Hruskan word for jokes.

"I'm Doman," the big man said. "And this here is Saban." The man gestured to his companion. "And if I'm not mistaken, you are . . . Neturu." The dramatic pause was accompanied by an upraised finger.

"How—"

The man smiled. "It's no great mystery. You have fine clothes—fine enough to mark you as a son of privilege. You are Hruskan. And, more importantly, you have those fine new injuries." Doman crouched down beside him and, tenderly, turned Neturu's head to get a look at his left temple. Doman was a huge man, his arms corded with muscle.

The giant continued. "The rumors went wild yesterday about a certain son of Hrusk. You met a dozen different ends, I'd say. Though not one of them put you here. Can you walk? Saban, bring him some water."

"A little. My leg is broken."

"Ah."

Neturu drank deeply from the proffered bottle. He coughed, and water dribbled over his chin. Pain pierced his side. "Actually, I don't think I'll be able to walk."

"It's all right," Doman said. "We can load you into our cart. Come on, let's get him in. Looks like Mason will have to come back for the dead one after all. We cannot put them both in, I would say." Doman chuckled and Saban grinned along with him as they helped Neturu up. "You've saved us some unpleasant business, my friend."

But pain hammered Neturu into wincing, gasping wordlessness.

Finally, he lay in the back of the cart, breathing heavily.

"I don't suppose we can take you into the Hruskan Quarter, eh?" Doman looked north, considering. His hulking form blocked the early morning sun, and Neturu lay in his shadow. "We'll take you to our healer. What do you think, Saban? Lihana would be very sore if we didn't bring him to her."

Neturu closed his eyes. "Thank you," he said.

The cart rolled slowly behind the two scorchers, bumping painfully over the uneven streets of the forsaken quarter. At times, a foul mixture of stenches—decay, refuse, sewage—laced the air. Distant sounds of life—a man shouting, a child crying—drifted through the alleys and streets.

Neturu tried to control his breathing as a means of focusing his mind, but the jarring progress of the cart mercilessly drew him out. He reached into his shirt and clasped the tiny bronze star lying chained against his breast. It fit in the cave of his fist easily, small as a *zvesa* leaf. Its sharp points bit into the fleshy creases of his palm. He brought it out, and it flashed in the new sunlight.

Home, he thought. *At the center of all, is the great Governing One, the center—the place where Esana awaits the arrival of his taken. Home.* Though alien to his Hruskan upbringing, the prophet's words brought him some measure of relief.

And then he recalled his father's face. And he recalled the last words he had heard his father speak. *Such a son as I once had, cannot be replaced so easily.*

Silently, while the scorchers pulled and pushed the cart, Neturu allowed himself to weep. Tears cut runnels through the ash and dust on his face. And, eventually, still clutching the bronze token of his faith, he sank into half-conscious fatigue, waking and drifting through pain and moments of strange clarity.

At the northeast edge of the city, Doman pulled the cart off the side of the road and stopped beside the stone marker at the boundary of Pekel. He stood in front of the stone and whispered the Line of the Wayfarer: "Though I pass from one world to the next, I endure."

"Come on," Saban called.

"Fallen or not, it's still true," Doman said, his deep voice reverent. "Maybe more so now." Doman laughed as he turned away from the marker, and he turned his face upward. "And be with my unbelieving partner, too." This he said a little too loudly to be a prayer.

From the boundary, the land sloped down to the smoky fields of Pekel. Heaps of trash covered the valley, and ash blackened the earth. Here and there, scorchers moved slowly among the heaps, scavenging what they could from the refuse of the Great City and consigning the rest to the flames of the smoldering pits. The stench of garbage and fire mixed uneasily. Smoke boiled up from the ground and drifted east.

The cart slowed again, and Neturu tried to push himself up with one arm. But Doman put a hand on his shoulder and gently urged him to be still. "We have some distance to go, my friend. This is just a way station. Our homes are on the other side. But we have to make sure that body is retrieved. Saban is relaying a message for our idle-hands brother, Mason. Hold on now, I'll be right back."

A few moments later, Doman returned. "Here, I have something for you, for the pain." Doman held out cup. "It will make you sleepy, especially at first, but at least you won't feel the pain for a while."

Neturu drank the proffered relief and closed his eyes. It tasted like honey. Soon the cart rolled on, but Neturu lost track of where they were going. It seemed unimportant. And within a few minutes more, he slept.

Soft, throaty humming filled his ears when he awoke. Morning sunlight lit the small room, and beside a small stove, a woman fussed over a pot, stirring occasionally. Though her face was turned away, he heard the soft sounds of her quiet, aimless music. It was a tune he did not recognize.

"Hello," he said.

The woman turned. "Awake so soon," she said. "Good. That's good." She looked at him with dark eyes; she had a pleasant face— lined and slightly wrinkled around her eyes. Her hair was laced with grey.

"Where am I?"

"No need to worry. Wait, lie still there. You can't stand on that leg, anyway."

She helped him sit up against the wall. A coarse, tattered blanket adorned the cot, but the mattress beneath was soft. The pain in his leg had dulled considerably; it had been bandaged and set with a splint.

"My name is Lihana," she said.

"Is this Pekel?" he asked.

"Yes. You're—" The woman laughed quietly, without scorn. "I was about to say you're lucky Doman found you. Lucky. But here you are. Lying half dead in Pekel. Not so lucky, I guess." She made a gesture with her hand, circling her face. "Doman says you must have really pounded someone's fists." She smiled. "And from what I can guess, you've got a broken rib in there, too."

Neturu probed his side, gently prodding, trying to remember how it had felt the day before, but the pain felt distant. "Here, I think."

"Well, as I said." She looked around her small abode. "It may not be luck that brought you here, and you might be accustomed to more, but I will do what I can for you."

"No," Neturu said, negating her deprecations. "Truly, I thank you."

"Think not of it." The woman turned to the wall and produced a cup. She filled it with water. "Here, take a drink." She watched him carefully as he lifted the cup to his lips. The water was tepid but refreshing. "Can you eat a little? I have bread, butter, and a little milk."

"Yes, thank you."

As she laid bread and butter before him on a plate, Neturu looked around the room. Tattered rugs covered the floor. Shelves masked one wall, filled with assorted bits of junk and kitchen wares—chipped bowls and cups, a few large spoons, and some rags. The rags were folded neatly in a stack. Bundles of dry herbs hung above the bowls. Next to a wooden door, a small niche occupied the far wall. A home-made broom, a shawl, dilapidated boots, and a misshapen *klobunta* hat lay within. There was only the one room.

"Eat a little and rest."

"Thank you."

"At least you've nice manners. Doman said you're from Noot?"

"Yes."

"Ah." She turned back to the stove and stirred briefly. Then she took the pot from the heat and placed it on a makeshift hearth of five or six flat stones. The throaty hum returned.

"I don't know about your leg, to be honest," she said after a moment.

Neturu looked at the splint. It looked fine. "Did you dress it?"

"Me? Yes. Had help, though. Doman held you down when I

pulled the leg straight and set it. Even though you were only half-conscious, the pain made you thrash. But it needed to be set. It's a bad break." She poked out her lips and glanced again at the splint.

"Is it going to be all right?" he asked.

Again her lips poked out. "It could rot," she said finally. "Your color is pretty good, though. Pretty good."

Neturu tasted bitterness. *I need to get out of here. What can these scorchers know about healing?* But he knew he had nowhere else to go. The Hruskan Quarter was closed to him, and he would find little succor among the *Yinoi*. Not with events unfolding as they were. He looked at the middle-aged scorcher woman and, with eyes unaccustomed to humility, remembered that she owed him nothing. He was lucky to find himself in her care. He looked again at the bandage wrapped around his shin. "Thank you for setting it."

"Think not of it," she said. "We deal with harm here often enough."

Neturu finished his bread and handed the plate to the woman.

"Get some rest," she said. "You only slept about an hour."

"My . . . my name is Neturu," he said.

"Neturu." For a moment she seemed to consider his name. "I'm sorry about your father. Doman told me what happened to you up there."

"I . . ." But Neturu didn't know what to say.

Lihana went on. "I don't travel into the city, so I know little about it, myself. I suppose I should pay more attention. But some of us think it doesn't matter much what happens with Hrusk. Everyone needs garbage collectors." She shrugged and put her hand on the door. "I'll be back to check on you soon."

"Can I ask you a question? You've already done so much for me."

"What is it?"

"Do you know of the prophet? At the river?"

Lihana smiled. "I know of him," she said.

"I need to see him."

"He comes among the scorchers from time to time."

"Yes, I know."

Lihana dropped her hand from the door. "What do you need of him?"

"I—I don't really know. I've no where else to turn." In truth he had a vague hope the prophet would somehow get him out of Pekel. The prophet had many followers. Certainly someone could help.

"Hmm."

"Are you a follower of the prophet?" Neturu asked.

"I follow Esana," Lihana said. "As should you."

Neturu frowned and said, "I, too, follow Esana. The prophet teaches that Esana will return—"

"I know what the prophet teaches."

"Forgive me." Rudeness was not often on Neturu's lips.

"He will come to Pekel today or tomorrow. It is his way."

Neturu took the small bronze star from beneath his shirt. "Will you take this to him? Tell him that Neturu, once-son of the on-Dam of Hrusk, seeks him."

"I can tell him that without taking your charm."

It's not a charm, he thought. But he was shamed even by silent rudeness. "Thank you," he said softly.

"Rest now. If he comes tonight, I will see if I can speak to him. Maybe he will come."

CHAPTER ELEVEN.
STORYTELLER.

Sarana made several trips to the well without stopping to talk with the other women. A few women looked at her speculatively; a few whispered and cast narrow glances at her. She supposed they must have seen her abandon her jars, or heard gossip about it.

But she paid them little heed. The thought of going back to the river was filled with inevitable promise, and she knew Gibson would approve of what she had decided to do. She looked upon the other women with pity, scorning their gossip, knowing she was favored among them.

But slowly, her thoughts softened.

Even as she avoided lingering among the women-shrouded stones, her servitude renewed her, reminding her of her duties. Except for her master's grace, she might have been less than these women; and, as he said, their labors at the well were an honor. And she was no paragon. She knew how often her mind had succumbed to sloth and rebellion when she should have been working—how often she had sat on one of the stones at the place of water and dreamed of other lives.

Running off to the river was merely the first forbidden life she had chosen to live beyond the confines of her mind. Or, perhaps, the second. But she did not want to think about the day she had stepped, however briefly, into that house of levity, curious and greedy for the promised coins.

But now I can go to the river with my master's blessing.

The thought kindled a serene pride, and vanity, and she strove against it, grappling with the dissonance between the new privilege and her station. *Humility is harder to trap than water.*

When she finished her morning duties at the well, she put her jars beside her bed, hoping Telasa was less likely to see them there. She did not want the older woman to find them and wonder; she did not want to tell Telasa about Gibson's offer of working to pay her debt. *She only dreams of going where I can go, now.*

Smiling slightly, she went back to the hearth room to eat some dried fruits for a late breakfast. As she ate, she was already on the open plains, passing beneath the cloud-cluttered vastness of the wide blue sky, breathing the fresh breezes.

But Telasa grabbed her arm, startling her out of her thoughts. "Where have you been?"

"To . . . the well." Sarana stammered.

"Gibson called for you earlier. I had to go in your place and make excuses for you. Why did you leave the house so early?"

Sarana had no answer for Telasa's anger, and her thoughts fought for the reins of her tongue, stuttering and going no where.

"Well?"

"I'm sorry, Telasa. I went early to the well. I've made several trips already."

"And now?" Telasa held up a hand with her palm up. "Where are your jars?"

"They're beside my—"

"Were you leaving the house without them?"

Sarana looked at the older woman, her eyes widened by fear.

"Were you going back to the river?" Telasa interpreted Sarana's guilty silence in a worse light. "Were you going back to the Stair Market, to that house—"

"No! I wouldn't." Sarana flared anger. And then shame. The wheedling seducer of the Stair Market had snared her with his promises, and she seemed unable to cleanse herself.

But she had not lingered there.

Telasa whispered, with a touch of restrained fury, "We both know, Sarana. We both know your tendency to trouble. And though I've never told our master what you told me that day—because I was willing to believe your story—I *will* tell him if I ever think you've gone back there since."

"I wasn't going back. I won't." More than once, Sarana had regretted telling anyone about her little folly.

Telasa eyed her for a moment before continuing. "So where were you going?"

"I wasn't going anywhere. I went to the well early to carry out his will." The omission came easier than Sarana might have imagined.

"I see." Telasa's face softened slightly. "Our master talked to me this morning; he had a message for you."

"He did?" Sarana felt her heart quicken.

"Yes, he expects more of you today."

Sarana bowed her head. "I know. And I've already drawn the morning water."

"I know. I checked the basins when I couldn't find you."

"I promised him I'd carry out all of my duties."

Telasa frowned with exaggerated resignation. "Come on, then. I have work for you to do. You can begin by pitching in with the *rebboth*."

"Our master might have other work for me."

But Telasa hardly paused. "Well there's surely no need for you to draw more water right now. He told me this morning what he wanted you to do, and I intend to make sure of it. Today, you'll do as I say."

Sarana hesitated on the edge of obedience to Telasa. *Did Gibson give her special instructions for me? Is she lying?* There was little chance of that; Telasa might have been resentful, even bitter, but she was not prone to lies. The truth was harsh enough.

Telasa grabbed Sarana's arm. "Are you listening to me?"

"Yes."

"There's a lot to do today, and you can't laze about. The older women need help in the vineyard, and I expect you to work with them and the hired women until the midday meal."

Sarana nodded, her thoughts unraveling. Her plan to go to the river, to take the initiative in paying her debt, eroded and fell away. She watched silently as Telasa turned and walked out of the room. And then she followed in her wake. The older woman's questions—her accusations—still sounded in her mind.

When Sarana caught up with her and entered the hearth room, Telasa handed her a stack of empty baskets. "Fill these today. Get going."

Sarana walked across the courtyard, tempted to drop the baskets and run for the gates. Instead, she passed under the *hresta* and went into the vineyard. Other women were already scattered among the rows, seeking out the ready seeds. *Like crows in the rich merchant's field.* It was an old story that came to mind. *Some they will take; some they will forsake.*

She started to pluck the small, rough *rebboth* seeds from the vines.

Telasa had been right about one thing: there was work aplenty and some call for urgency. The baccate branches of the thorny plants were sagging, heavy with seeds. Many of the fruits would go to waste if they weren't picked within a few days; the over-ripe seeds would split and wither, leaving shriveled, worthless husks to litter the ground—probably sometime before Sabat.

As she worked, she relinquished her anger. But slowly. The *rebboth* needed to be harvested, and Gibson undoubtedly felt such matters were more important than her plan to listen to the prophet again. And he had not actually told her to go; she had formulated that plan during the night.

She pushed her hopes of temporary freedom from her mind and worked. *In submission is exaltation.*

The rough seeds and thorny branches of the *rebboth* abraded the skin of her fingertips and the backs of her hands. And, slowly, her flesh began to tingle and grow warm, seeming to pulse with the beat of her heart.

For several long minutes, she continued her labors, fingers questing among the thorny vines. But then she gave in to temptation and gazed upon her hands. She watched as a shallow red scratch on the back of her right hand lightened and smoothed away into nothingness, leaving only the unblemished perfection of her fair skin.

My blood is strong.

But then she upbraided herself, remembering a cold winter day when her temple mother had caught her playing the blood game with a group of children.

Do not put your faith in the hand of the flesh, child. No matter how strong it might be, it will fail you. The soft lash of Abasha's tongue had put a stop to her arrogant demonstration that day, but it had not laid to rest her vanity.

This day it was Kaina who reminded her of her place.

"They are beautiful—I will give you that." The old woman had come up alongside her in another row. She held up her wrinkled hands and cackled. "You see what has become of mine. Remember this is what awaits you."

"So you've said." Sarana smiled.

"It's no less true today."

Sarana watched as Kaina went back to work. The old woman's hands moved surely from one plant to the next, plucking the ready seeds, expert in their motions and discretion. It seemed both a shame and a blessing to become an old woman. So worn and tired, so expert and unnoticed.

"I'm surprised to see you here," Kaina said. "Usually you are still drawing water this time of morning."

"I—Telasa bid me work in the vineyard this morning—at Gibson's request."

"Are you sure of that? I thought maybe he had another duty for you today."

"Maybe he changed his mind."

The old woman nodded. "That happens, I guess."

But Sarana could see the old woman doubted the explanation. "Do you think Telasa was lying?"

"No, not that. But I'm not sure she knows the mind of our master. At least not as well as she might think." The old woman paused, and then she borrowed a saying from the Lines and applied it to Telasa.

"And, being misled by her own view of his will, she strays."

"Our first father knew not the mind of God," Sarana said, recalling the teachings of her temple mother.

"How true that was," Kaina said. "And still is." The old woman focused back on her work of picking the ripe seeds. She said, "You know the Lines well, child. I wish everyone paid them as much heed as you."

"I love the Lines," Sarana said. "I love the old stories."

"I can tell. You listen. Even to my stories."

"Abasha—my temple mother—said when all else passes away, the Lines will still remain. Strong, like an iron rod."

Kaina shook her head, but she said, "I suppose that's true."

The old woman's hands continued to work, and her head craned back and forth as she examined the fruits of the vine. "But in the end, only God remains unchanged. Only he deserves our unwavering faith."

"But the Lines *are* God's expressed will." Sarana said, earnest. "The Lines have endured since the days of our first parents."

Kaina continued to hunt and pluck the little fruits as she spoke. "That's true. But even the Lines change. The Lines aren't perfect."

Sarana looked up over the *rebboth* plants at the older woman. "That's not true."

The old woman looked up. "I'm not saying they aren't true. But they do change, they have—in small ways."

"But the Lines are God's word."

"They are a record of God's word. They are not God's word."

"I don't—that's the same thing."

Kaina smiled and said, "If only storytelling were so simple." She paused and then said, "You remember the story of our first parents."

Sarana nodded, pulling the story from memory, remembering the sound of Abasha's gravelly voice as the children sat at her feet. She had always enjoyed the Line of Creation. She had been fascinated by the mysterious words.

And God spoke his next Word: Uzum-Aman-doziv-telan, meaning, bring the man, or the lesser god, from the fertile earth, or plant the mind in a fertile spot.

Kaina said again, "Do you remember it? Do you remember how it ends?"

"I think so. 'After creating the world and seeing the destiny of all people, God placed Ish, who was later called Aram, and Ishana in paradise.' " Sarana spoke a little faster, gaining confidence. " 'And Aram lived there in happiness for many days, without being told what God truly wanted from him, and he knew not the mind of God.' "

"That's right." Kaina nodded and resumed her work among the vines. "And that's how you learned it. But when I was a child, the Line was different. A little. It—"

"What did it say?"

"It said, 'And Aram lived there after the manner of happiness for many days.' You see the difference."

Sarana shrugged. "The wording is a little different, but it still means the same thing."

"No," Kaina said. "It is quite different."

Sarana thought about the words. *And Aram lived there in happiness for many days.* It did not seem very different from Kaina's version. *And Aram lived there after the manner of happiness for many days.*

"It seems the same, to me."

Kaina nodded and spoke without stopping her work. "There is a great difference between 'happiness' and 'the manner of happiness.' We say Aram was happy in the intransigent garden, and that is what the Line says. But when I was a child, it said he lived after the manner of happiness." Kaina smiled slightly. "I think that means—the way it was taught when I was a child—he had no true happiness in the garden."

"But Aram *was* happy," Sarana said.

"That's what the Lines say now, yes, and that's what you were taught. That's what *I* was taught, too—that's what I was told the line meant. But I am not sure that's what it meant in the beginning. It doesn't really make sense; does it? To say he was happy. How could he have felt real happiness, if he had never felt sadness? In the intransigent garden, there was no death, no pain—nothing to cause him to sense any loss. He was a child, innocent—he hadn't yet learned to feel happiness. Not until he drank from the river."

"I was happy as a child."

"Yes, but the world had already fallen. You suffered deprivations —small as they were—and you felt sadness. And no doubt you felt happiness, too. But even so, what you felt was only the shadow of what you would come to know. With Aram, things were different. He was protected from harm of all sorts. He felt no fear, no grief, no pain —everything was provided for him. And I think, as a consequence, he never truly felt happiness—at least while he remained in the garden."

"He—" But Sarana was unsure of what she wanted to say. If Kaina was right, the Line of Creation had been changed, corrupted. She did not believe that. "I believe the Lines are true," she said.

"I do, too." Kaina paused. "I just don't believe the stories are the same as they used to be."

"But if the stories change, then they can't be true."

Kaina shook her head. "They still tell the story of our past, and the past is a true thing. The past is a true thing that remains the same."

The two women worked silently for a few moments, and Sarana struggled with her thoughts, knowing Kaina was wrong. The idle conversation of two of the hired women drifted across the vineyard.

Kaina continued. "My grandmother said if I did not remember the stories of my people—and tell them to my children—we would become a lost and forgotten people." Kaina smiled, but it was the resigned smile of a sorrow long savored and accepted. "We had our own stories—Kainish stories—but I do not remember them all, sadly. My grandmother was a storyteller of my people, and she made me promise to remember them."

"Your people had heathen beliefs."

"I have come to think so as well," Kaina said thoughtfully. "Though I'm not sure it matters. Perhaps all beliefs have become heathen in some way."

"They didn't even believe Esana would come," Sarana said.

The old woman shrugged slightly. "The idea had never occurred to them. And I thank God he has brought me to that knowledge." Kaina turned a palm toward heaven, her gnarled fingers extended as far as possible, ready to catch a stray drop of rain, as the saying went.

"But if you believe in Esana, how can you believe the Lines have changed?"

Kaina thought for a moment before she spoke. "Because my faith does not rest on the words of priests."

"You think the priests have changed the Lines?"

"I do."

"But why?"

"Because the men and women of God are losing their hold on the past. The stories are losing their power over people."

"That's not true."

"It is true, child. You can tell by the way people talk. And it's why they started to change the Lines in the first place, I think. When people start to doubt—when they cannot understand references to things lost, or when the Lines provide no ready answer—there is a natural desire to make things more understandable. I think the Lines have been changed in an attempt to renew their power."

Sarana considered Kaina's words. But she was still incredulous. *Who could change God's words?* Such a thing could not occur. God would not let it occur. "You must have remembered it wrong," she said.

For a moment, the old woman remained silent. "You might be right. The changes become the story after so many years, and the world is a forgetful place. I might be the last storyteller of my people, and my memory is not what it used to be."

"Storyteller?"

"Well, not like the Kainish storytellers of old. But when my people were conquered, I was charged by my grandmother to remember the stories of my people and pass them on to my own children." Kaina shrugged. "She did not know what would happen to the captive children of my people."

Sarana blinked, remembering the days and nights when Kaina had told them stories as they worked. "That's why you tell us stories."

"The storytellers of my people remembered by repeating the tales. That's how we recorded our history."

"You didn't have the Lines," Sarana said, smug.

"The storytellers were our Lines, child."

Sarana considered that.

"I'm not sure my people wrote down anything. And now we are disappearing, and our past is disappearing, too. When I am dead, many stories will cease to exist." The old woman smiled again, that smile.

"Someone should write them down."

Kaina shook her head. "Perhaps some storyteller has. But I doubt it."

"You've told us some of them."

"Only a few, child. Fragments of the longer story." Kaina smiled, a soft, sweet smile. "But now you can remember them and pass them on." The old woman gestured around the vineyard with her hand. "There will be other children who come here, and the stories of my people will live on in them in some small part." The old woman let her gaze linger on the young water woman for a moment, and then she went back to work.

Sarana remained silent, noncommittal. But the old woman's words stirred her thoughts.

CHAPTER TWELVE.
LAST DAYS.

The afternoon dwindled.

For nearly two hours—after fulfilling her afternoon duties at the well—Sarana had toiled at the western edge of the vineyard, reaping the thorny *rebboth*. Her flesh burned and throbbed, kneaded by the unceasing, reparative cycles of her blood. But she did not look at her hands—not directly—and she worked without giving in to temptation.

From the arched doorway at the top of the yard, Kaina called the hired women out of the vineyard to collect their pay. Distance diminished the old woman's voice, but even as Kaina's words floated across the yard, Sarana stood up, relieved. She arched backward and groaned lavishly as the bow of her back released. After a moment, she blinked and looked back down the row.

Just five or six more vines until the end of the row. Some of them drooped in the dusky shadows.

By the time she finished, her last basket hung heavy in her hand, heaped to the point of overflowing. A few of the vines at the end of the row had been heavy with seed, branches sagging, rich and ripe for harvest. She looked up toward the house and smiled contentedly: the broken path, the upturned stones of her servitude had been laid back in their place. Or at least she had begun anew.

For a moment, she stood motionless. And as her thoughts grew still, the softer sounds of the yard emerged from the gloaming: the susurrus of the breeze among the vines, the infinitesimal fluttering of a *rebboth* beetle's chitinous wings. Above her, the indigo sky promised stars.

But the Wayfarer is no more.

She leaned back against the wall, eyes heavenward.

I wish I had seen it fall, she thought. And she tried to imagine what the burning, falling star would have looked like. The images suggested by the women at the well blazed through the darkness of her imagination, flaming and casting off great burning trails of sparks and fire. And for a moment, she envisioned the falling stones of the Great City of Old.

I wish I had seen it.

When she emerged from the vineyard, Telasa was just finishing her inspection of the hired women's baskets. The last woman watched sharply as Telasa marked the ledger and counted out a pile of small coins.

Sarana walked closer, and Telasa looked up. For a moment, Telasa paused, and Sarana had the odd sense she had caught the older woman in some sort of impropriety. But Telasa was merely counting out pay; and, after looking at Sarana with half-lidded eyes, she turned back to her counting. She placed two more coins into the hired woman's hand, paused with an upraised finger, and then closed the money pouch.

"You can take the damaged for the remainder," Telasa said.

"I'd rather have the coin." The hired woman had not yet closed her hand. She held it open hopefully.

But Telasa shook her head. "You'll get more for the damaged seeds—especially if you take them to the Quarter." Telasa's eyes flitted toward Sarana and back to the hired woman. "Bring back the basket. Or it'll be deducted from your wages next time."

The hired woman relented—bound by the law—and Telasa turned back to the ledger.

Sarana was still wondering about the odd feeling of impropriety when Kaina touched her arm. "Come, child."

"Hmm?" Sarana turned.

"Come on." Kaina took her by the hand. "You've done enough work today. Come inside and I'll rinse and brush out your hair."

Sarana followed the older woman into the women's quarters, loosening her shawl and pulling it off as she crossed the threshold of their room. Ana was already there, sitting on her small bed, pulling her fingers through the wet tangles of her hair. A brush sat by her side.

"I heard you got in some trouble this morning." Ana's lips turned up archly, and her dark eyes widened. The girl was a natural rogue, a little older than Sarana and given to playful taunts. "Telasa's been keeping you busy today."

"You should know better than to repeat idle gossip," Kaina said.

"Telasa thought you might have run off again this morning." Ana let out a chuckle. "Surely you didn't lose *another* set of jars."

Kaina shook her head and smiled.

Sarana sat with her back to Kaina and tilted her head back, leaning back on her hands over a small basin. The old woman poured handfuls of water over her hair.

Throughout the day, Sarana's mind had strayed back to her confrontation with Telasa and her failed attempt to return to the river. She had resolved to try again in the morning, if she could slip away before Telasa found extra chores for her.

"So," Ana whispered, leaning toward Sarana. "What really happened when you lost your jars yesterday? Pelem said he heard you tried to run away. And your jars were stolen by someone on the road. He said you got as far as the river before you got scared and decided to come home."

"Pelem should stick to cleaning out the stalls," Kaina said. Her methodical fingers worked slowly through bunches of Sarana's wet hair.

Sarana looked over at Ana. "Where did he hear that?"

Ana shrugged carelessly. "Probably just talking with the other men—Ganon and Tobin, I would guess."

"My jars weren't stolen—not on the road. I left them at the well. And someone took them."

"You don't need to talk about it." Kaina cast a glance toward Ana. "Our master has forgiven you and given you new jars."

But Sarana wanted to talk about it. She did not want Pelem telling tales. And aside from second-hand bits of gossip gleaned from the crowds of women at the well, she had never had any story of her own to share.

Why shouldn't I tell Ana? She opened her mouth to speak, but Kaina spoke first.

"You should be content, child."

Ana giggled. "Old woman." But she did not speak unkindly. "If we ever want to have any fun, we'll have to wait until you're sleeping—which is often enough these days." Ana smiled broadly, and Sarana felt a familiar envy. When Ana smiled like that, her lips parted to form the most pleasing curves, framing her straight white teeth. She did not think her own smile—reflected and examined in the dimness of the cistern—had nearly the same beauty. On the other hand, Ana's blood was not strong.

"Maybe," Kaina said. "But then your transgressions will be your own." Kaina picked up the brush and pulled it through Sarana's hair several times. The little tangles relented.

"I *was* scared," Sarana said. "At the river, I got scared."

"Did you—" Ana paused and looked at Kaina; she wavered on the edge of speech.

"Don't worry about me," Kaina said. "I'm just an old woman. I hardly hear anything at all anymore."

Sarana rolled her eyes. But Ana still hesitated.

"What?" Sarana asked.

"So did you see him?"

Sarana nodded, and she was about to say more. But a wondrous thought took flame in her mind, and she paused. *She wants to see him, too.*

"What was he like?" Ana asked.

"You've heard the same stories I've heard," Sarana said. But even as she spoke, she knew the secondhand stories and gossip had become irrelevant. *What are stories compared to the man himself?*

"But you've actually *seen* him," Ana said. Her voice had returned to playful, but the roguish tone only highlighted the earnestness of her previous question. "So now you have to tell us what he's *really* like. The gossips in the markets cannot decide if he is baseborn and ugly or merely ragged around his lovely edges." Ana's eyebrows raised, and she caught the tip of her tongue between her front teeth.

Kaina laughed. "You wicked child."

Ana smiled her envy-inducing smile. "I cannot help how they talk about him."

Sarana looked to Kaina. The old woman smiled slightly. "It's not up to me, child. If you want to be his messenger, then speak."

Alone in his room, Gibson prayed.

He asked God to engrave the Lines upon his heart. But he felt little peace. Not after the day's events.

Through his window, a remnant of the sun shimmered red and orange over the tops of the hills, and strips of cloud hung high in the western sky, burning with yellow-white fire. He felt a familiar awe, dwarfed by an infinite design, but he could not douse his fears of an impending, bloody destruction.

Nef's arrival prodded him out of his brooding revery.

"What news?" Gibson asked.

"There are rumors the Council intends to seize control of the Quarter," Nef said.

Gibson looked back out over the city. "The decree is strict, but it doesn't go that far." He walked over to his table and sat down.

"What are the terms? I assume it will be posted."

"Yes, tomorrow. No practices of the Fathers within the city. If any Hruskan violates it, it will result in expulsion from the city. A second violation by any member of the same clan will result in expulsion of the entire clan." Gibson slid a piece of parchment across the table toward Nef—the full decree. "Convenient how they had these printed and ready for us. It is a reckless provocation, but at least that is all it is."

"But it could lead to more. Especially if they strictly enforce it."

Gibson nodded. "It could. But I hope it won't."

"Forgive me, my Lord, but hope is an unreliable protection."

"I will do what I can to see that it goes no further." But even as he said the words, he felt their frailty. Kim had not had to work very hard to persuade the Council to issue its decree. She had railed against the barbarous laws of the Hruskan Fathers and pointed to the recent ostracization of the on-Dam's son—and to the merciless retribution meted out upon him by the on-Dam's enemies.

This cannot be permitted, she had said. *We cannot have children killed in the streets, and we cannot have competing systems of laws.*

Gibson had not foreseen such capitalization of the young Hruskan's demise.

Nef put a hand on the table. "If the Council seeks to extend its power in the Quarter, there will be bloodshed."

"I'm sure you're right."

"More than that," Nef said. "That's what my Hruskan contacts are telling me."

Gibson put his thumb and forefinger into his eyes and rubbed gently. *And this is just the beginning. It's how we maintain our purity.* Gibson let out a breath. Time after time, outsiders, rebels, or heathens had been expelled, enslaved, killed. Once there had been magic in the world—or so his father had said—but those ancient sparks, held by dwindling bloodlines, had faded to cheap trickery and sleight of hand. Little true magic existed in the hands of God's children now.

"Their schools and prayer yards are still closed to the bin-Yinocki," Gibson said. "The decree changes none of that. It's my hope—" Gibson dropped his fingers from his eyes and looked at Nef. "It is my hope that any judgments rendered by the Fathers will take place there, in their places of learning and worship. And that will be communicated to the Fathers this evening."

"Will that be enough?"

"I think we still allow people to worship as they will," Gibson said, sardonic. "And it would be a hard task to police the prayer yards and the schools."

Nef nodded, thinking through the problem. But then he frowned.

"There are rumors circulating that you voted in favor of it."

Gibson looked up sharply. But his initial surprise dulled immediately. It was to be expected. *Your house is not in order.* "Just rumors," Gibson said. "Tell your contacts I did not vote for it. And let my business partners know, when you see them—especially Umeru and his coalition. I tried to speak against it, but it was quickly apparent that a group led by Kim had agreed beforehand to make it happen." Gibson's upper lip twitched on one side, a suppressed sneer. "You do not have to tell them that part."

"I'll talk to Umeru," Nef said.

"It sounds like you've encountered trouble over it."

"Some." Nef smiled. "Most are withholding judgment. But Umeru told me to tell you that he'd snap your scrawny *Yinoi* neck if the rumors held any truth."

The two men laughed. Gibson said, "He probably means it."

"I'll set things straight with him."

Gibson waved him on. Nef would do what he could, but the rumor's pestilential life cycle would have to be endured. "So what else do you have for me."

"The on-Dam's once son is still unaccounted for," Nef said.

"He's probably dead."

"Probably. But if so, there will be trouble. The Council blames the Fathers. But it's not likely anyone will take responsibility for his death. And there are already rumors in the Quarter that he was actually killed by agents of the Council."

Gibson mulled this information. *Was it possible?* It had been easy enough to assume agents of one of the Hruskan clans had taken the opportunity to strike at the on-Dam. But anyone could hire mercenaries and dress them up. And there had been time to do it. News of the young Hruskan's conversion, and the decision the on-Dam had placed before him, had circulated for days before the attack. *Time enough.*

"We need to know more," Gibson said, knowing that Nef would take steps.

"I'll take steps," Nef said.

Gibson chuckled without opening his mouth. "What of the prophet?"

"He baptized one hundred and three people today."

"One hundred and three." Gibson tapped a finger on his table. "There was some debate about him today. The Council will be forced to act soon. He has some powerful enemies."

"The House of Dan?"

"Not just Kim—though she was the loudest. There are others, too, who would see him silenced. Bin Amin, for one." Gibson frowned, recalling how Tendar had downplayed any concerns about war with Hrusk and turned the Council's attention to the prophet.

"They fear him," Nef said. "His influence is growing."

"Maybe," Gibson said. But his thoughts did not confirm the conclusion. The prophet's popularity seemed too minor a provocation to warrant such attention. There had been such men before—heretics, outcasts, philosophers of doom. They had largely been ignored. Still, none had moved the people like this man. None had drawn such ire from the priests, though all had been condemned by them.

All the more reason to see him for myself.

Nef waited, but Gibson didn't continue.

"I have nothing else to report," Nef said after a moment.

"Find out what you can about the men who attacked the on-Dam's son. And I have something for Urudu. Please have it delivered tonight." Gibson held up an envelope addressed to his steward in Gazelem.

After Nef left, Gibson extinguished the lamps and sat in the dusky darkness. For a long time he sat there, thinking. After a while, he recited the Ten Lines, lingering thoughtfully over each word.

And then, in the darkness of his room, he whispered the unspoken commandment God had intended his children to remember without being told: "And all these things shall be engraved upon your hearts."

CHAPTER THIRTEEN.
CROSSROADS.

When Neturu woke, the small room stood empty. A fire burned lowly in the hearth, and a round, covered pot sat on the hearthstones. The smell of fresh wheat cakes filled his nostrils, coaxing his belly to grumble. The night had passed.

And the prophet had not come.

Gently, he tested his leg, expecting more pain than he felt. He pushed himself up and leaned back against the wall. He had slept well. Once during the night he had awoken. The fire had been very low— mostly glowing coals, an occasional pulse of flame. But he had not lain awake long. He had dreamed of Hrusk, and of the hilly wilderness north of his family's estate in Noot.

My once family, he thought.

Lihana entered, carrying a fresh jar of water.

"Ah, you're already up. Good morning. I have water and some wheat cakes. Cooking beans for later. Are you hungry?"

"Yes."

"Sorry I've no milk. Some days I do, but most not." The scorcher woman shrugged, unashamed of her poverty.

He realized he was imposing on her greatly. "I think I still have a little money." He reached for his pocket, but then he regretted his thoughtlessness. "Forgive me, I don't mean any offense." Neturu looked down at the floor, thinking he had probably offended her.

"I have enough for my needs," she said without rancor. Then she handed him two wheat cakes on a cracked plate. "And for some of yours."

"I'm sorry for the trouble I've caused you."

"Think not of it," she said. She patted his hand. "I've had patients here before. But if you have any money, you are welcome to share it. We scorchers—none of us has great wealth—but we have enough. We share our burdens and our blessings."

Neturu ate the grainy cakes and sipped the cool water. He relished the strength of the cakes. They were still warm, and they were good.

"I spoke with some of the others last night," she said. "I told them how you're doing. Doman sends greetings."

"Ah," Neturu said. "I need to thank him properly. I am in his debt."

"So you are," Lihana said. "But it will keep until you are better. Or maybe he will find time to visit us."

"How long until my leg is healed?"

Lihana's countenance shifted—her eyes moving to his leg—and her lips pressed together briefly. "Your leg is maybe a little worse, I'm afraid."

Neturu felt for any pain from his leg. "I don't—but it feels much better."

Lihana shook her head. "The numbing paste takes away the pain, but when I looked this morning, the flesh around the wound was discolored. I put new wraps on it, but the wound may fester."

"You think it's worse?"

"It might be. I'm sorry." Lihana looked at him gravely, but gently.

He did not want to believe her. He wanted to weep. After a quiet moment, he said: "What can I do?"

"Nothing more than I've done already, unless we call the surgeon. A proper healer might be able to do more, but . . ." She trailed off for a moment. "Sometimes one of us is badly injured. If the wound festers, we can try to cleanse it. Sometimes that will work, but not always." She shrugged.

Neturu thought he knew what happened then. The limb was

removed. And even then there were no guarantees.

Lihana continued. "I washed the wound carefully, dressed it, and rubbed it with honey paste. So now we wait."

"How long?"

"Not more than a day."

A day. Neturu shook his head slightly. That did not seem hopeful. "You do not think it will get better."

"We can apply fire—if you ask it—but I fear we will have to burn you deeply to cleanse it." Lihana shook her head. "When they brought you to me, I had hoped it would get better on its own, but after cleaning you up—. Well, if it doesn't start to look a little better soon, you will have to decide what you want to do. I am sorry, Neturu. It was a bad break. The bone pierced the skin."

Neturu looked at the shoddy bandages, silent. *What will be, will be.* He could do nothing to bend the will of God. He could only bend himself. He looked into Lihana's kind eyes. "I want you to apply the fire."

Gibson raised his eyes above the converging traffic of the crossroads and glanced upriver. People were gathered along the river's eastern side, waiting. A few sat beneath the *plesa* trees. He saw no sign the prophet might be among them. It was too early for the man to have begun his rituals. Still, it looked like it would not be long.

On the other side of the Geblon, a steady flow of people made its way up the gently sloping hillside. Some of the merchant carts were accompanied by lightly-armed, hired men. But there was little to fear on the road to Gazelem. An occasional small theft. Rarely any violence.

At the outskirts of the town, traffic congealed. Vendors and beggars wandered among the accumulated people, precatory, calling their wares, asking for small gifts of charity. A group of ragged street *harimi* darted through the people, holding out their hands and pulling the tails of uncharitable travelers' animals. Gibson watched, amused, as ungenerous cart drivers cursed and flicked whips at the children's mischievous hands. The small, quick hands usually escaped unscathed.

But an occasional shriek betokened victory for the drivers.

At the city gates, Gibson raised a hand to the busy guards and nodded. He knew most of them. His wife's family had built part of its fortune providing protection for the Jewel City, and over the years Gibson had recommended many men for service. Some men just grew tired of the road.

But I never did. I miss it.

He was still thinking about the sprawling caravansary north of Shal-Gashun when he arrived at the lavish little house his wife had said they must have to increase their standing among the merchant houses and lesser branches of the Great Houses. He dismounted and led his mare around to the side entrance, where an arched doorway gave ingress for animals and deliveries. He pushed open the wooden door and walked inside.

Walkways of white pebbles curled among well-tended beds of bright yellow blooms and young apple trees. The scent of honey blossoms filled the air. As Gibson approached the stables, his personal steward, Urudu, emerged through the open doors.

Urudu took the proffered reins with one hand and gently laid a palm on the horse's forehead, rubbing affectionately.

"I am glad to see you, my Lord."

"She's glad to see you, too," Gibson said. "You spoil her."

Urudu smiled. "I give her only what she deserves. Come along." His words were directed to the horse.

Gibson chuckled and turned where he stood, taking in the beauty of his little garden; Urudu guided his charge through a pair of thick wooden doors into well-groomed stables. A minute later, he rejoined Gibson and they walked over to Urudu's quarters.

"We are ready?" Gibson asked.

"Yes. The clothes are right in here." Urudu gestured toward his room. A bed sat in one corner, a table in the other. A law box sat open on the table, the pages of the Lines stacked neatly inside. Gibson touched the side of the box, pleased. He had given it to Urudu a few years before. It was a fine box, if spare. Its unadorned quality matched his steward perfectly.

He changed into the plain clothes his steward had laid out on the bed. They fit well enough, and the hood was large. He would look like some sort of shiftless mystic. But he would not look like himself. And that was what he wanted.

Urudu was dressed to accompany him, but without the hood. Instead he wore a hari-Hruskan head scarf. He had exchanged his usual white robes for a brown tunic and dark-brown pants. But he had kept his fat-bladed knives strapped conspicuously around his waist.

"I didn't get a very good price for the clothes," Urudu said.

Gibson pulled the rope belt a bit tighter.

Urudu looked him over. "If you keep your face lowered, your identity will be safe. Are we going to the river?"

"Yes, to see him."

"I thought as much." Urudu rested his hands on the handles of his blades, and his dark eyes bored into the distance.

Gibson waited, certain his steward was about to say something more.

But Urudu's eyes snapped back a moment later, and he gestured toward the door. "I will walk a little behind you on our way out of town. We might as well minimize the number of people who see me walking with you."

Gibson nodded. Sensible enough. But he wondered what his steward had been on the cusp of saying.

They made their way through the weave of Gazelem's streets. Hand-carved wooden gates—insubstantial things made for beauty—gave glimpses of ornamental gardens behind walls of stone. And beyond, in the open windows of many of the houses, colorful curtains fluttered and undulated. The jewel city had succumbed to the opulence and decadence of the southern realms.

And then he saw one of Kim bith Dan's little enclaves. Two men stood outside the iron-enforced wooden gates. Gibson did not doubt their readiness, and he felt admiration for Kim's indomitable refusal to give way to anything—even if she might be part of the simmering plot against his house. *She is not merely a hammer swinging in the dark*, his father had said once. No. She saw the distant turns of time and planned for them. Her mind and her immortal beauty had beguiled the Council for generations.

Admiration twined slowly through Gibson's tangled thoughts.

But now she faces an unforeseen problem. Recent, persistent rumors said the ancient weapons of the Daniti were starting to fail. And the loss of those weapons would undoubtedly tangle the skeins of Kim's weaving designs. *And if there is war*—. But that fragment of thought died, useless. He had thought it hundreds of times already.

Gibson glanced back at Urudu. *A man of war.* His steward walked casually, but his hands were planted firmly on the handles of his knives, ready. In a blink, the knives could emerge, flashingly quick and deadly.

Once, in the empty, beautiful wastes of the deep desert, in the last stretch of the *pustinya* before reaching Shal-Gashun, Urudu had saved his life with those very knives. Gibson still remembered that barren, starkly beautiful stretch of wilderness. The robbers had risen up from the stones magically, appearing between one breath and the next. But their endeavor had failed; the fight had been short but brutal, and Urudu had forever earned his favored place among the servants of the House of Jianin.

Beyond Gazelem's gates, as they emerged from the crowds, Gibson again surveyed the wandering path of the river. Knots of travelers had formed at the crossroads, and even from a distance he could see people gathering purposefully beneath the lithely beautiful *plesa* trees, lingering at the water's edge to listen to the prophet.

Soon we meet, Gibson thought. He waited for Urudu to come up alongside him, and then he urged him onward with a nod.

CHAPTER FOURTEEN.

PROPHET.

Gibson walked slowly among the people gathered beneath the *plesa* trees. The prophet had not yet begun his sermons, but he was sitting among a ragged group of people a little distance upriver. He sat with his arms draped over his knees like a Shal-Gashuni idol. Gibson cast a glance over his shoulder and confirmed Urudu's staid presence; the Hruskan nodded slightly.

Gibson moved closer. The prophet wore coarse, brown clothing, and his ragged hair made him appear a wild man. But only at first glance, for his eyes were mild, not crazed, and his movements were slow and measured.

Then Gibson saw what his expectations had overclouded.

The man who called himself prophet was conversing casually with a small group of soot-besmirched scorchers. And while they talked, they ate, the prophet eating unhesitatingly from a communal loaf of bread—bread shared and touched by the unclean hands of filthy scorchers.

Gibson stepped closer and sat within hearing distance—but not too closely. He understood why the lingering crowds had not yet formed themselves into the usual mob: none of the bin-Yinocki would mingle with scorchers. None would ever think to share bread with them. He strained forward to hear the man's words.

"The priests and elders will not be warned," the prophet said softly. "They think they have no need for a man like me. But that is unimportant. I must remain here for a time, and those who come will come. Some will hear, but most will turn away. I have no need to raise the cry of warning where there are even more deaf ears."

"They will not hear us, either," one scorcher said.

"True," an old scorcher said. "We have petitioned many times for relief from the ban that keeps us from the temple. The Lines do not prohibit any from the courts of mercy."

Gibson watched from beneath his cowl. He was familiar with the scorchers' self-described plight, but their sacrifices were brought to the temple by proxies; they had no true complaint.

The prophet chewed his bread slowly, but then he gestured toward the city and said, "Perhaps you have not spoken loudly enough."

"Without us the city would drown in its garbage," the first scorcher said.

"That is not the answer," the old scorcher said.

For a moment, no one said anything. Gibson contemplated the implications of the prophet's soft-spoken invitation to rebellion. *If that's what it was.* The scorchers hauled refuse day and night and burned it in the smoking pits of Pekel. They maintained the midden piles. And they gathered the dead of the poor, the outcast. There would be horrible consequences if the scorchers ceased their labors.

"I agree," the prophet said. "But perhaps they have forgotten your sacrifices and need to be reminded."

"But how can we do anything?" the young scorcher said.

"I am but one man," the prophet said. "But I, too, have come to remind the children of Yinock of their duty—to tell them that they had gone astray. It's a time for remembrance, my young brother. And perhaps also change."

"Well, we cannot stop our work," the old scorcher said. "We've been paid to do our labors, and too many people would suffer needlessly. It is not our brothers and sisters that need correcting, it is the law." The old scorcher looked around the group. "Much as we'd like to punish the Council, we cannot stop our work. It's the work that will eventually cleanse us." The old scorcher looked around again.

"We cannot stop."

The other scorchers nodded and agreed, mostly, but the young scorcher who had spoken first was silent, thoughtful.

The prophet dusted off his hands and said, "That may be. But in the meantime, I have a message I must give to the people. But I will tell you first. Last night I had a dream. And I think it was a true dream. In my dream I saw a cloud overshadowing the city. A wind rose up, and for a while, the cloud threatened. And then it rained. And I cannot say how long it rained. A howl rose up from the city, but as the rain continued to fall, streams and rivers filled the streets, and all manner of dirt and filth washed out of the alleyways and markets. And soon, black rivers poured from the gates of the city. And after that, I saw many things—the rise and fall of great and spacious buildings, the coming and going of many multitudes. I—"

The prophet paused, and he looked upward. Then he returned his gaze to his listeners. "At the end, the overshadowing cloud transformed into fire and descended on the city. And when the cloud rose up into heaven, the Great City was gone."

The prophet stopped. He looked to his right, and then he looked to his left. "Blessed be the hearers of these words."

Gibson smirked. It took little effort to imagine the rivers of filth bearing away the priests and elders. It was not an unwelcome image, in some respects.

The old scorcher held up a hand to silence his companions. He asked: "Do you mean to say that the great day of Esana is near at hand?"

"Is it not promised in the Lines?" said the prophet. "He comes quickly."

Gibson shook his head. But even as he silently doubted, he reflected, as he often had, upon the promise of the Lines. *The day of his coming is near.*

"But when will Esana come?" the old scorcher asked. "When will he come to govern his people?"

"That I cannot say. But do not be misled by the teachings of a lost and fallen generation. Esana will not live among us in the Great City."

"But the Lines say that he will walk among his people. That he will heal the sick and afflicted." The old scorcher's hard eyes held the prophet's gaze.

The prophet held up a placating hand. "He *will* live among His people, my brother, as the Lines say. But He will not live here among the bin-Yinocki. We are not the only people under heaven. We are not the only lost children of God, and we are strangers here."

The prophet let his eyes move across the gathered scorchers. "God watches over many worlds, and he has planted his seed where he will. And he will send the gatherer where he will. Since the days of Yinock, the prophets have spoken of this."

Gibson stared. *How dare he rob the people of their promised Esana?* He stole a glance at Urudu who was looking grave.

The prophet continued. "In the lines, Yinock taught his sons and daughters that the children of Esana are as countless as the stars in the heavens. In the very beginning, Aram was promised that the generations of his children would be as countless as the stars. Is it any wonder that Esana might *live* among the stars as well? Did not Yinock's city flee into the heavens?"

The prophet looked from one face to another. He continued: "All of God's children dwell in the heavens, on their appointed worlds. And we—we came to this world by the hand of Yinock, from Yinock's homeland. But when our ancient fathers and mothers rebelled against the Order of Heaven, the Great City of Old abandoned its place and left us here, wayfarers." The prophet's brow crinkled. "And that is why the Lines seem to say that Esana will be born among us. They recite a prophesy that was first uttered on another world."

"A prophecy from another world?" Gibson loosed the question without thought.

The prophet raised his gaze over the heads of his nearest listeners. "Just so, my brother, another world. Our ancient fathers and mothers carried those prophecies with them to this place. This new world in the heavens."

"But the Lines say that God dwells in heaven," Gibson said.

"Heaven," the prophet said, "is like the great sea to the south. You, my brother, should understand this. There are many shores, but there is only one world sea. It encompasses all. Thus, to some, we live in the heavens. But when you look into the night sky, you see the stars and the dwelling place of many worlds. So ask yourself what our Father sees from the avenues of his holy city. Does he not see the stars when he peers into the depths of heaven? That is the answer to your question. God created the worlds, and we are but travelers on a shore far from home." The prophet looked into the darkness beneath the hood of Gibson's robe, finding Gibson's eyes.

"You cannot rewrite the Lines," Gibson said.

The prophet paused. "You think you know the Lines?"

"I know them well enough. My father was a poor man, but he taught me what he knew." The half lie did not burn his conscience too much. His father's father had once been poor.

"Ah, your father," the prophet said. He paused and nodded his head slightly, as if remembering Gibson's father. "Our fathers might have taught us the same words when we were children." A brief pause. "But time has changed our understanding. And now we walk divergent paths. Where will your path lead you?"

Gibson forced himself to meet the prophet's gaze. "If you were taught from the Lines, then why do you say Esana will not be born of a daughter of Yinock? Why do you concoct these tales to take away the people's hope?"

"I said nothing of his mother. And you need not lose hope. To those that listen, I say only that He will be born on the world of God's choosing. It matters not what world that may be." The prophet pointed in Gibson's direction. "But do not misunderstand: He will be born of a daughter of Yinock. As the Lines say."

Gibson said nothing.

"We are but a few lost shells cast up upon the shore." The prophet turned his attention to the group at large. "But rejoice, my brothers and sisters. Because we know that He shall come, and we can prepare for the day of His coming. This is His command: repent and be cleansed. Take the name of Esana and be saved—be baptized in the name of the promised one, and then you will be purified."

"But if he will not come to us, how can we be saved?" the old scorcher asked.

The prophet looked out over the crowd. "How can you be saved? The priests should have taught you this already. But they have forgotten the way to the homeland of our fathers. They walk on twisted paths—forbidden roads that lead to destruction." The prophet's gaze grew fierce. "They have lost the great key of the inimitable power of redemption."

Gibson glanced around, growing angry. But no one challenged the prophet. No one answered for the priests of God.

The prophet continued: "The priests have taught you according to their own wisdom and knowledge. And many of them teach the truth as far as they know it. But they have forgotten much. They have lost much. They have turned the Lines to their own purposes and lost the knowledge of redemption."

"I think you go too far," the old scorcher said.

"No, brother. I have not gone far enough. Not yet. But soon."

Gibson became aware of the crowd growing at his back. He could hear people telling their neighbors to listen. Others mocked. He heard voices proclaiming the prophet to be a man of God. He heard laughter. And then he heard a woman's voice near at hand, speaking softly, as to a confidante; she said, "He was instructed by the Spirit of Esana in the wilderness."

Gibson closed his eyes and shut out the world. It was time to leave. He felt it instinctively. *Every bargain exists within limits.* So his father had always said. He opened his eyes and saw the scorchers starting to disperse. He stood. But as he was about to turn away, the prophet's words broke through his thoughts.

"I do not choose my listeners; they choose me." The prophet's gaze swept across the gathered people. "You all chose me this day."

Gibson looked around at the gathered people. He thought someone must have asked a question or issued a challenge of some sort, but he could see no obvious target for the prophet's retort. When he looked back, he found the prophet staring at him. The prophet's dark, mild eyes had hardened; his gaze had found Gibson's hooded eyes unerringly. Gibson almost turned away. But he did not want to appear timid.

"Who told you to come here?" the prophet asked. "Who warned you that destruction comes to the Great City?"

Gibson steeled his gaze and maintained a careful silence.

After a moment, the prophet's lips curved up on one side. "Come, friend," he said, his voice softening. "Heed this warning and save yourself."

His voice was mild, and yet piercing, and the quiet power of his exhortation gouged a furrow in Gibson's mind. Gibson's former anger at the prophet's words fell away like autumnal leaves, brittle and spent. The prophet seemed about to say more, but then he turned away and began to speak loudly to the group slowly gathering in the wake of the departed scorchers. For a moment the quiet, compelling words repeated themselves in Gibson's mind.

Come friend. Heed this warning. Save yourself. There was strength in those words.

And did he know me? Did he see my face and recognize me?

Gibson saw then that the scorchers had all gone. And he felt exposed. He felt as if the prophet had torn away the hood and bared his head to the eyes of the multitude. It had not been wise to hesitate. *Every bargain exists within limits.* And what was his shoddy disguise before the burning eyes of the prophet?

He turned; he saw Urudu's unwavering presence, ever watchful, and he made his way toward the road. He kept his head down then and walked slowly. Urudu maintained a steady pace behind him.

CHAPTER FIFTEEN.

THIEF.

At the top of the old, stone stairway, Sarana paused and looked down at the busy Stair Market below. A cool morning breeze played fitfully, pleasantly, with the edges of her shawl, but it could not eliminate the fringe of guilt from her thoughts.

She had not overtly deceived Telasa. But her actions had been designed to give one impression while concealing her plan to slip away and go to the river.

After finishing at the well, she had taken up a basket and gone straight to work in the vineyard—without waiting for Telasa to direct her. And then, after Telasa had gone to market without giving her any other assignments, she had left. Her apparent diligence had disguised her rebellion, and she had known—or at least hoped—that it would.

I am about my master's business.

She started down the steps, and the voice of her temple mother sounded in her memory. *You cannot hide from the glass eyes of God, child.*

But not even Abasha's gentle words could divert her.

As she approached the city gates, she was forced to halt. A herd of sheep, recently sheared, crowded in through the gates, jostling quietly, bleating occasionally, as their shepherds guided them toward the temple and their deaths. With the Feast of Travelers approaching, the city's markets and streets murmured with pre-sacrificial life. These would be among the first to give their lives for the weary and the lost;

she looked on the sheep with a bleak compassion.

As a child, she had seen the periodic slaughter in the courts of mercy. The cacophony of ritual butchery, the supplications, the prayers. She had seen the blood-filled, stone gutters emptying into the underground drainage system. The priestly bowls of antiquity could not hold it all, and it flowed into cisterns, where blood-water vendors mixed it with water and sold it to farmers.

Sacrifice is the gift of Esana, she thought, consoling herself. But the dark eyes of the beasts seemed pitiable all the same.

Beyond the gates, the outer city drove away her morbid thoughts. The lively accretions of the outer city encroached on either side, and a profusion of narrow paths and alleys crossed and meandered from building to building. Her eyes drank in the tumble-down houses, the heaps of clothing and rags, the domestic detritus. And though she had only been there once before, the scenes of work and play—the thick-armed woman and darting children, the loafing men and heckling peddlers—seemed familiar and welcome.

But she quickly moved beyond the city, and as the chaotic shambles diminished, the road blended into the world, cutting across the hillside and drifting down into the grassy valley, where the sinuous line of the Geblon meandered among green banks and *plesa* trees. And as before, she felt awe blossom in her mind, huge and formless. She drifted to a stop on the side of the dusty road and inhaled the dry earth and warm air.

"Chay on peya ikola bo on zheya," she whispered silently. *When he drinks, he will ever thirst.* She descended into the valley, the Line of *Es* burning in her mind.

At the crossroads, she heard the prophet's voice rise over the crowd.

"The people of this city claim to be God's chosen people. They call themselves the bin-Yinocki, the Children of Yinock. The priests and elders sit in their libraries and trace their genealogies, and they claim the blessings of Esana by virtue of their birth." The prophet's dark eyes shot from one face to the next, fierce. "But any who claim blessings by blood will be disappointed, for God's chosen people are those who choose God."

A contradictory murmur rippled through the crowd.

"There are those who say otherwise, claiming a special birthright for the old bloodlines of Yinock." The prophet paused. "But God will raise up children from the byways and secret places of the wilderness if he desires. And when Esana comes, he will gather his children wherever they can be found and lay them up in the storehouse of his mercy."

Sarana slipped forward between two men and halted, unable to move closer without pressing her way through the crowd. She leaned to her right and could see the prophet standing near the riverbank, framed by the hanging branches of the *plesa* trees.

"They think their long lives are a sign of God's pleasure. But long lives of iniquity will not save them, and the pure bloodline of Yinock is only a quiet echo of a lost immortality. A thread of eternal life lingers in their veins but not in their hearts. They should rather live a brief life, while doing good."

The prophet pointed over the heads of the gathered people. "What you see there, that little city on the hill, is only a poor remnant. But do not think God has forsaken his children. Or that he will not call us to our ancient home. God does watch over his children, and he is calling to you now. All of you can heed his call and join your bloodlines to the heavenly lineage of God."

The prophet raised his voice over the growing clamor.

"*That* is the divine lineage," the prophet said. "But is there a priest or teacher among the bin-Yinocki who retains the knowledge of redemption? Does this tattered remnant of Yinock's offspring retain a remembrance of the great laws of heaven? Will you serve such shabby servants?" A murmur passed through the crowd. "You look forward to Esana, but you will not know him when you see him."

Shouted questions darted out of the murmuring crowd. But one loud voice near the front of the crowd drew the prophet's attention.

"Enough of your riddles. Speak plainly."

"I speak no riddles, brother."

"Ah . . . but you do not claim to speak plainly." The man stepped up next to the prophet and turned to face the crowd. "His words today wander like a drunkard. This morning, he said Esana will not live among this people. Now he says we will not recognize him when we see him."

The prophet shook his head and smiled. "You and I have traded words often enough, brother. I will no longer squander the time God has given me arguing with lawyers." The prophet put a hand on the man's shoulder, conciliatory. "There is little enough time in the world. Will you be ready when He comes?"

Another man stepped forward then, and his hand trembled beneath the weight of old age as he reached out and took hold of the prophet's arm. For a moment, the three men stood thus. And then the old man spoke. His soft voice quavered, and he spoke but a few words. "I have come to you from Noot, and I fear I will not live long enough to return home."

The prophet turned his gaze upon the old man. "Be not concerned. And do not place your hopes—or your fears—on the arm of the flesh." The prophet paused then and leaned down. "What is it you would like to ask?" The crowd had grown quieter.

"When will He be born?"

The lawyer spoke. "Don't expect an answer, father. We've asked that question before. What he cannot answer, he answers with riddles."

A man standing in front of Sarana shook his head, turned, and pushed his way back through the crowd, muttering. Sarana eased forward.

"Hear this," the prophet said, casting his voice high over the crowd. "Esana is like the rain that falls in a far off land. The rain gives life to the fruits of the earth, and the merchants who travel from place to place bring the fruit to your doorstep."

The lawyer rolled his eyes. "And you are a merchant. We know."

The prophet looked down and let his gaze linger on the face of his wizened inquisitor. "And hear this," he said, his face mild, his voice soft. "He was born before your mother weaned you. He was conceived before the stones of the temple were laid one upon another." The prophet put his hands on the old man's shoulders. "The sign of his birth is yet to come, but he has already drunk the bitter cup and passed through the vale of mortality."

The prophet looked off toward the city, his eyes bright. He said, "You will not find him here in the Great City, or in any of the cities from here to Shal-Gashun. For as I have said, he will not live among us. But he will yet come to this people in his own time, and they will see him with their own eyes."

The old man closed his eyes and nodded.

The road into the Great City steepened slightly near the crest of the hill, and Sarana paused, a little weary. And hungry. She had neglected any thought of food for a midday meal before leaving the house, and she felt her forgetfulness now.

And, yet, she did not want to return home straightaway. *What could he have meant? He was born before your mother weaned you.* It was not a saying she had ever heard among the women at the well; she wondered if it would be new to Gibson, too.

Among the tumbledown buildings of the outer city she watched a small boy and girl who ran from one person to another, hands outstretched, faces smudged with sweat and dust. Their golden-brown skin and colorful clothing marked them: *harimi.* Their dirty legs flashed as they ran from one person to another, seemingly in a race with one another. They came to her in turn and tugged on her robe, small and pitiful. And yet, they had hope. Sarana held out her empty hands and pointed to the mark of servitude on her wrist. The children ducked their heads, gracious in their penury, and moved quickly to the next person. Sarana watched their small bodies disappear into the traffic; she wondered where they lived.

Reluctantly, her thoughts turned toward home. The thought of retrieving her jars and returning to work weighed down her thoughts, onerous. Only a few hours had passed since she had gone to the well, but she felt restless. Her course had seemed to alter. Her temple mother had always said the course of life was like water among stones. *Water among stones, child. Sometimes altered by the impenetrable, but unstoppable no matter the difficulty of the way.* She smiled in remembrance of Abasha's words.

As she passed beyond the milling people inside the city gates, a large man stepped in front of her. Instinctively, she started to sidestep, her face down, but the man took hold of her arm. She looked up, alarmed.

"Servant of the House of Jianin," he said. He let go. He was a steward or a household guard of a wealthy householder. He wore light-colored pants and a dark blue shirt with long sleeves. A dark grey cape hung from his shoulders, and on his arms he wore thick gold bands.

He spoke again. "You are a servant of the House of Jianin."

"I am." Her hands felt conspicuously empty.

"Our master has asked us to bring you to him. He wishes to speak with you." A second man stood a little behind him.

"I . . ." She looked around. A nervous flutter infected her hands, and she clasped them together. Rote words came to mind. "I am about my master's business."

"As are we." The man's blue eyes narrowed. "And you are a servant of the temple. If a council member has need of your services, you must fulfil any reasonable requests."

Sarana nodded; she knew her duty. But she could not see how her training could assist any council member at that moment. Her jars were at home. Surely he had his own servants. She hesitated.

"Come. We will take you to him." The man gestured off to his side. A heavily curtained palanquin sat on the ground a few feet away. Several carriers knelt beside it, their hands in their laps.

And then she understood. The bearers were resting, and their master wanted her to fetch water for them. Relief filled her, and she smiled at her foolishness. She had performed such service before on several occasions. She had no jars with her, but he likely had one or two of his own for such circumstances.

"Do the bearers need water?" she asked.

The man pulled open the curtain and gestured toward the interior. It was empty. "Please get in. We will take you to our master."

Sarana stopped; she looked around again, nervous. The second man had stepped up close behind her. All around them, people went about their business. For a moment, she thought about running, but she did not think she would get away. And her fears felt foolish. These men would not harm her. She knew that. None of the leaders of the great houses would harm a servant of the temple. Gibson surely would not.

But what could their master want from me?

"Will it—" she stuttered. "Will it take long? I have other duties."

"It will take whatever time our master desires. But fear not. Our master does not wish to delay you unduly."

The words did little to quell her nervousness. "It . . ." she trailed off briefly. But then she looked up into his face. "It does not seem like a reasonable request. What you are asking."

A flicker in his eyes, and around his eyes, betrayed a momentary surprise, but the man merely said, "It is not your place to question our master."

"I just don't understand what he could want from me. My jars are at home."

The man let his gaze rest on her for a moment. "It is not for you to question," he said, brusque. "I know only that he sent me out to find you. If your master believes you have been used unreasonably, he may settle his grievance by petitioning the temple. Come." He gestured toward the open palanquin, peremptory.

They were not going to let her go. Sarana looked at each of the two men, hesitated a moment longer, and then ducked inside. The man followed after her and sat across from her. When the heavy curtain closed behind him, the darkness inside was nearly complete.

"It is not far," he said. Even as he spoke, the conveyance rose up and jumped forward. Sarana rocked backward a little but she caught herself. After a short time, she felt the palanquin change direction. One thought after another tumbled through her mind, chaotic. Unable to see outside, her feeling of peril grew. Like tendrils of water from a broken jar, her thoughts spilled in every direction, wasted and useless.

They changed direction again. One of the heavy curtains swayed outward, and a stab of light shot inward between the curtains. She caught a glimpse of the richly colored fabrics and pillows. Then it was dark again. A minute passed. They changed direction again. Outside, the sounds of the city became more distant. The steady beat of the bearers' feet became predominant.

A few minutes later, they stopped. The curtain opened to reveal a small, well-tended garden. A high wall encircled it, and near its center, an aged *plesa* tree spread its drooping branches over a small white bench of carved marble. Stepping-stone paths meandered among raised beds of flowers and shrubberies. She did not recognize any of the plants. There were no *rebboth*, no fruit trees—no useful plants she recognized. The men directed her across the garden to a door on the other side, and the man who had ridden with her drew a key from one of his pockets. The lintel bore an ornate inscription.

They walked down a short corridor and stepped into a long, rectangular chamber. Cushioned couches surrounded a low table at the far end of the room. A tall table of white stone stood in the center of the room, along with two tall chairs. Shelves lined the walls, and Sarana stared at the great number of books. The only time she had ever seen so many books was as a child, in the temple library.

The man told her to wait. His dark gaze settled on her, and then he and the other man left through an arched doorway on the opposite wall.

Sarana stood unmoving for several seconds, unsure of what to do. She dared not sit; she could not escape. Her escorts had locked the door leading back to the garden—she was a prisoner—and she knew not what lay through the other door. A glance through the arched doorway revealed a short corridor with another arched doorway at the other end. A white curtain blocked the other doorway, and she saw that a similar curtain could be drawn across the door where she stood. She almost took a step into the corridor, but then she backed away, clasping her hands.

Her hip brushed against the corner of the tall table, and, surprised, she turned to look at it. Its surface was smooth, glassy, almost lucent in the dim light of the room. She touched the top of it and felt a familiar quiver of energy. Like the ancient stones at the well, the table silently hummed against her fingertips. She walked slowly around the table, letting her fingers slide across the polished stone.

She found a delicately wrought handle set into the side of the table top. A drawer. She looked over her shoulder toward the door. She was still alone.

A long, narrow drawer slid out noiselessly. A jumble of golden jewelry lay inside. For a moment her surprise immobilized her. But then an impulsive thought shot through her mind. *Take one.* She looked toward the door again. No one. She reached into the drawer and pulled out a bracelet.

But it was not a bracelet. It was too small, and it was not an empty circle. She turned it slowly. A golden circle, and within, a delicately wrought triangle. The precise curves and angles seemed adamantine and silken at the same time. She ran a fingertip along the outside arc of the gold. There were several more in the drawer. She wondered if anyone would notice one was missing.

For a moment she stood with the ornament in hand, wondering if she would be caught. Then she shook herself and put it back in the drawer. She could not steal. No child of the temple would ever think to steal. Abasha had warned her against all forms of evil, and the Lines made plain that a thief was abominable in God's eyes.

What was I thinking? She started to close the drawer.

Take one.

This time the thought astonied her, and she stood quite still, her hand on the delicate handle of the drawer. The golden treasures lay piled inside, lorn, unimportant. Almost as if they had been forgotten.

Would it be so wrong to take one?

It would. She knew it would.

But they forced me to come here. They left me here. They locked me in here. They kidnapped me. Her thoughts evolved rapidly into recriminations against the master of the house, the man responsible for tearing her away from her duties.

And then she heard someone coming, and impulse prevailed. She grabbed one of the rings and tucked it inside her robe. The gold lay cold and accusatory upon the skin of her breast. Her blood pulsed, and she stepped back from the table guiltily.

When she looked up, the man who had told her to wait was standing in the doorway. He stared at her for a moment.

Did he see? Sarana felt her heart thump.

Then he beckoned her into the hallway. "This way," he said.

Through the arched doorway and into another room at the end of the little hall, they entered a sunlit room. A large window looked out over the city, the temple visible in the distance. A man stood facing the window; a scarlet cloak hung from his shoulders. He did not turn when she entered.

Her escort spoke. "You will kneel before our master."

Sarana obeyed, instinctively. *In submission is exaltation.*

The man at the window spoke. "You are Gibson's servant, of the House of Jianin."

Sarana looked up. The man still faced the window, his back turned to her.

"Are you not?" His tone increased.

"Yes, my Lord."

"I expect your master will be grateful to me when he learns what I have learned." The man did not turn, but he turned his head slightly to the side.

Sarana put her forehead to the floor. *What is he talking about?*

"You need not fear me, child. It is between you and your master. But it is my duty to tell him you have been leaving the city." He paused. "And that you have been listening to that heretic who preaches at the river. One of my men saw you on the road—saw the mark you bear on your wrist."

Sarana looked up, relieved. Now she understood. "But he already knows."

"Does he? Your master, Lord Gibson?"

"Yes, my Lord."

"Gibson bin Jianin knows you have gone to the river to listen to that heretic?"

"He does."

"Do you speak truly, child?" The man stood unmoving.

"I do, my Lord. I had his permission to go."

"I see." The man stood with his back to her for a long minute. Then he gestured with his left hand. "Well, then. You are free to go." Sarana felt a hand on her shoulder, and her escort started to direct her back the way she had come.

But as she turned, the man spoke again, his voice sharp: "Wait."

He had turned away from the window; he was staring at her. He took a step toward her, and Sarana turned her eyes down, reluctant to meet his examination.

He stopped a few steps away from her and reached out, his palm up, his fingers slightly curled, as if he were about to raise up her chin. But he stopped without touching her and then drew back his hand. Sarana raised her eyes a little. His hands were sculpted and pale, immaculate. Like her own.

"You are a temple child," he said. "A bonded servant?"

"Yes, my Lord."

"Did you know your parents?"

Sarana shook her head. "I never knew them. I was dedicated as a baby. My temple mother said I was given by my mother to be raised in the House of Esana."

"I see." A pause. "How long have you been in service to your master?"

"Ten years."

Another pause. Sarana could feel his lingering gaze. She grew uncomfortable.

"Ten years," he said again. "I think I have seen you before, child. You would have been in the temple at the same time as several children who came to serve in my house. Who was your temple mother?"

"Abasha bith Svetlan."

"And you have served in the House of Jianin from the beginning —since you reached the age of accountability? The house of your master, Gibson bin Jianin?"

"Yes, my Lord."

Abruptly he turned and walked back to the window, the hem of his scarlet cloak flaring outward slightly as he turned. Sarana thought she heard a whispered word, and she dared a glance. His left hand was clenched at his side.

He said, "You have served your master well, child. You may go."

Her escort directed her back through the hallway to the room where she had waited earlier. Sarana glanced at the little table. The cold circle of gold had disappeared against the warmth of her flesh. But she knew it was there. In the terrible moments of her brief confrontation with the master of the house, she had forgotten her theft, her guilt. But she knew it lay beneath the folds of her robe, shrouded. She thought about trying to put it back in the drawer, but she dared not be caught. Then her escort was directing her out, back toward the garden where the palanquin waited.

In darkness they moved through the city streets. Sarana thought about hiding the little golden circle beneath the pillows, but she forbore, fearing that when it was found, it would be traced back to her. She thought about dropping it through the curtains, but that seemed worse than stealing it. Conscious of her guilt, she suffered in silence.

When they came to a stop, the man pulled open the curtain and nodded toward the opening. "The temple is just down there. That way. I trust you can find your way home from here."

Standing alone in the street, Sarana watched as the palanquin moved away and disappeared around a corner. The whole encounter seemed unreal. *What will the others think? Can I even tell them? Should I?* She would tell Kaina. And she would tell Gibson. But as for the rest—she floundered, uncertain.

A quick glance at her surroundings, and she turned toward the temple, falling in with a stream of pilgrims. They flowed into a large courtyard and washed up onto the broad steps of the prayer wall. Some of the supplicants went straight up the steps, but others spread out among the vendors in the yard. Prayer vendors and hymnists stood beside their tables and kiosks, selling words to offer to God.

Some were scrawled on small squares of paper. Some were written in scrolls, carefully rolled and sealed, expensive. The cheapest were scratched into shards of clay and old potsherds. But no written prayer was required; the poorest simply climbed the steps and offered the prayers of their hearts.

Nearly a year had passed since Sarana had joined the unending multitude of boiling supplicants at the top of the steps. She started up the broad steps, empty handed. *Maybe that was God's hidden purpose behind them taking me today—to bring me to this place. Maybe I need to be here now, this minute.* And then she remembered the stolen gold lying against her breast, and she faltered. *Can a thief offer prayers at the wall?*

Near the top of the steps, she moved slowly into the straining mass of the faithful, a little fearful, troubled by her new guilt. But once among the men and woman who had come to make their pleas, she calmed and simply strove forward. The wall was a repository of power, and all of its lore unfolded in her mind, gargantuan and awesome. A place of worship, of importuning; a place of promise. The place where Esana would one day stand and call forth the children of His City.

The thought of Esana calling his chosen immediately filled her. It was an event she had once dreamed, and she had always held it as a sort of token in her mind: a robed figure standing atop the wall—a man bathed in heaven, wreathed by a red and empyreal sky. And beyond him, towering into the heavens, a landscape of clouds—a misty, *kolobian* landscape of cloudy bluffs and terraces effused with the rosy light of an expiring world.

There were few things she felt certain of. But her faith in that future moment had never wavered. He would come.

The blank-faced stones confronted her. The smooth, fair flesh of her hands complemented the intransigent whiteness of the wall, and she imagined—as she often did—the connection between her blood and the ancient stones. Some said the stones had once been inscribed with the Ten Great Lines, but the unrelenting hands of sinners had worn away the words. Some said only the ghostly shadow of some of the letters could be seen at certain times, at certain angles. Others said the wall had always been unmarked, but people saw visions of inscriptions, and the inscriptions changed to suit the needs of those who sought God's guidance.

But Sarana had never seen anything.

She frowned and closed her eyes.

It was time to offer her prayer, but her mind grew dim, alien. The crush of bodies grew inexorable, and she moved to her right, pushed toward one of the arched doorways giving ingress to the inner courtyard. Behind her, people continued to press forward, pushing the center toward the edges. She had heard excitedly-uttered stories, morbid stories, about people who had died trying to offer up prayers, crushed by the heedless faithful. But she did not really believe them.

A few feet from the doorway, she closed her eyes, slowed. She disliked the mix of despair and hope on the people's faces. She tried to hold her breath against the smell of so many bodies.

Her outstretched hands rested on the smooth stones. Just a few feet away, temple guards stood by the doorway, ushering people inside, away from the wall. She would have to finish quickly.

But what do I say?

The warm stones slid beneath her hands as the inexorable sea of bodies crashed slowly against the immovable place of prayers. After generations of worship, the currents at the base of the wall were almost instinctual. She tried to think of true words.

This is the first great commandment of the world: Thou shalt not steal from God. Seek not my treasures among dumb stones or in the workmanship of your hands.

A rough shove pushed her half a step sideways and she stumbled. She opened her eyes. No visions. Then she remembered the prophet standing in the river.

Who will be the living coals?

Her mind turned the question over, finding no answer.

Then the crowd surged and a man beside her stepped on her foot. Her feet became entangled, and she fell sideways, reaching out with a hand to break her fall. She clutched at a man beside her, but he shook her off, intent upon his own silent needs. She came down on her hands and knees. A heedless supplicant stepped on her splayed hand, grinding her palm into the earth. She cried out and clawed upward.

And then relief surged through her. Many hands reached down and pulled her to her feet. Words of concern came from all sides. "Are you hurt?"—"Are you all right?" Ashamed by her fear, she said nothing and pushed her way to the side. Behind her, the press of the people's prayers reasserted itself.

The waiting guards directed her through the doorway.

Once through, she stepped to her right and clung to the wall of the inner courtyard. The pain in her hand faded, and she looked at her abraded flesh. A small patch of redness marked her pain, but almost no sign remained of her injury. And even as she watched, the color drained away, leaving smooth white flesh. Unblemished. The reparative power of her blood had kindled quickly and burned away the wound.

But shame still tinged her thoughts, and she felt tears brimming in the cups of her eyes. She blinked, looked around. No one in the bustling crowd returned her gaze; she was quite alone.

CHAPTER SIXTEEN.

NEW COVENANT.

Near the gates of Gazelem, Gibson glanced at Urudu and said, "Let's take the long way around."

Urudu nodded and they turned onto the *hodari-misa*, leaving behind the dust and the noise, the need for silence. Yet they walked in silence. When they had passed the first bend, Gibson drew back his hood and walked with his head bare in the breeze.

The path of the *hodari* circled south around Gazelem. It dipped and curved across the hillside, meandering among trees and skirting rocky outcroppings. An occasional traveler sat on one of the rocky shelves of the hillside, resting, meditating in one of the *hodari*'s shady refuges. Gibson nodded to them as he passed.

They soon came to a familiar place—a rocky stretch of path overhung by large trees growing above the trail. Gibson stopped and stood on an outcropping of flat stone; he looked south over the plains. The road to Noot drew his gaze, but his thoughts did not follow. He bit the inside of his upper lip and shook his head. One thought kept rising up: *Foolish.*

He was still a little dumbfounded, and a little angry, the prophet had drawn him out so easily. He had not intended to say or do anything; he had only wanted to see the man for himself. But the man had snared him with unexpected rhetoric. He had expected to hear words his men had already reported to him; he had expected to find a charismatic man who had sparked interest with a few new ideas.

"It was foolish for me to speak out like that."

Urudu shrugged. "That was . . . maybe not so good. But I don't think anyone recognized you. I saw none I know. I expect few employed by the great houses venture so close while the scorchers are there."

Gibson reflected silently. He might not have either, if he had realized sooner who the prophet's companions were. "That was surprising—that he ate with scorchers."

"He is not conventional."

Gibson laughed. "So I noticed." Then he equivocated, starting to rationalize what he had heard. "But, in truth, most of what he said was plain enough, if sometimes evasive." Gibson looked over his shoulder and looked at his steward. "What do you think of him?"

"When I listen to him, I find I almost believe him." Urudu quirked a wry eyebrow and shook his head. "He can be compelling. And they say he easily confounds the priests who challenge him. But this new Esana he teaches—it's too strange to think Esana will live on another world. I cannot accept it."

Gibson nodded and turned his eyes back to the road. "And yet we believe Yinock came from another world. The Lines say as much." He paused. "Still, it's what draws people to him. This idea—this otherworldly Esana. It's strange. It gives people something to talk about. Something they can use to say they're different. Or better than ordinary folks. It's a truth no one can refute. But one day it will be refuted."

Gibson sat on a shelf of stone protruding from the hillside and rolled the stem of an old, brown *hresta* leaf between his fingers. The branches overhead wore the bright new leaves of spring, still stunted by youth.

"There have been others, though. Self-proclaimed prophets and miracle workers. A few of the Godless. Some were popular."

Urudu frowned. "If—"

But Gibson talked over him. "But none has ever taught a new Esana. They've always taught either that the people have forgotten the teachings of Esana, gone astray . . . or that there is no Esana."

"This man has never denied Esana."

"Mmm," Gibson said. "Little good it will do him, though. The Council will not tolerate him for long. What he teaches *is* a denial of the one true Esana. At least that's how most of them see it."

Urudu nodded, worry creasing his face. "I know," he said. "And it surprises me so many still gather to him." The Hruskan looked into the distance, pausing, impregnating his words. "People I would not have expected. Or suspected."

Gibson looked at his steward. "Who?"

Urudu returned Gibson's gaze unflinchingly. "My brother."

"Your brother?" Gibson said, surprised. "Reb has joined with them?"

"He believes this prophet is a man of God." Urudu's face hardened. "He has been urging me to be baptized. He says he can introduce me to the man, if I want to meet him."

Gibson looked at his steward thoughtfully. *How long has he hidden this from me? Did he think to keep it secret for his brother's sake?* No. Urudu had saved his life and risked his own to protect the fortunes of House Jianin too many times. Gibson let his gaze drift toward the south. *Such a formidable fighter, and a trustworthy man, and yet . . . what compromises might blood wring from a man?*

But Reb was not a brother by blood. He was a street child, a lonely hari-Hruskan Urudu had befriended many years before—a child uplifted through Urudu's kindness and loyalty. The stern Hruskan had shared his lunches with him, taught him, trained him in the art of work, and, finally, recommended him for employment in Gibson's stables in Gazelem. Gibson still remembered something his steward had said that day: *A man of blood has no right to a son. But God has blessed me with a brother.*

"Thank you for telling me, my friend. I know what it cost you."

"You pay me well for my services," Urudu said, trying to be light.

Gibson chuckled, but he felt sadness. *Is that it then? Money?* But he immediately repented; he knew it was not so. Urudu was worthy of more confidence. Still, the man's joking words reached down to a

deeper truth. Friend or not, his steward was a servant of the House of
Jianin, bestowed by the temple and bound by a lesser tie than love.

"It did not cost me much, my Lord," Urudu said quietly. "Reb
knew I would tell you. He said I was right to do it."

Gibson nodded, thinking, *You raised him well.* But he said nothing.
Then: "When did you find out?"

"Three days ago."

"Ah." The master of the House of Jianin tasted bitterness, some
anger.

Your house is not in order. The impeccably-penned words rose up,
crimson, the image of them scribed indelibly on his mind. And behind
them, only a shadowy accuser. Perhaps Reb's affiliation with the
prophet was part of that. He wondered then how the prophet had
gathered such power, and how his house had come to be in such
jeopardy. He stood to lose much. And people would suffer if his
house fell from power—his son, servants, employees, business
associates. Money could only accomplish so much. And what money
he had would vanish beside the vast wealth of the House of Dan. Or
Amin. No merchant's wealth could withstand the treasuries of the
great, ancient houses.

But it can buy new jars. The thought came unbidden, and Gibson's
thoughts turned to his errant water woman. Another proof of the
prophet's power.

But proof of my own as well. Even a small sum of money turned to the
purpose had awed and liberated his water woman. But it had not been
the money. The money had been important—necessary even, to
purchase the new jars—but no amount of money could have restored
Sarana to grace. Gibson's thoughts stepped from one stone to
another, moving along a path he had previously only dimly seen in
isolated moments of contemplation.

Urudu waited quietly, expecting his master to say something more.
But when Gibson remained silent, he pressed on. "I probably should
have told you sooner. I fear I have failed you in this thing."

"No," Gibson said. "I was thinking about something my father
once told me. He said every bargain exists within limits."

Urudu nodded, familiar with the saying.

"But one night he said something I'd never heard before. He said, Grace is infinite because it can remedy the irremediable." He paused. "We were at Rume. You remember what Rume was like—at night."

"I remember."

"I had second watch that night, on the south side. About an hour in, my father came out of his tent and sat beside me. You know how he was at night. Restless. It was one of those clear, moonless nights, when the stars are just—" Gibson shrugged.

Urudu nodded, silent, knowing without further words what Gibson meant, and the dark empyrean, luminous with innumerable stars, shone in the collective memory of their minds. Unimaginably beautiful.

"We looked at the stars for a while, and he made me find the constellations—testing me. The Leaf, the Virgin, the Great Wheel of the South. He said God placed the stars to guide his children. He called them landmarks in the wilderness of heaven. And he said if I ever doubted God's grace I should go into the wilderness and wait for a clear moonless night. Light no fires. The darker the better. And then look up. The darkest nights most fully reveal heaven's glories. So he said."

Gibson smiled. Beneath the sky of memory, with his father beside him, the prophet's words did not seem so strange. *Grace is infinite, son. Grace is infinite because it can remedy the irremediable.* He blinked, cleared his vision. His father had been killed by a band of thieves on a routine trip to Noot. He would never know what his father would have made of the prophet's teachings. *Probably not much. But would he have scoffed at an otherworldly Esana?* Maybe. But maybe not.

"He warned me the House of Jianin—its power—existed within limits. He said a day might come when I could no longer rely on it to sustain me. Or my family. He quoted the Lines; he said, Do not put your trust in the arm of the flesh. " Gibson looked at his steward. "I didn't really believe him. But I do now."

"Has there been a threat?"

"A warning."

"Who—"

"I don't know. One of the great houses, I assume. I received notice that my house is not in order." Gibson shook his head. "It is not a charge I can withstand, I think. Not with things as they are. And not with my well-known sympathies for Hrusk. It's not the sort of charge that requires much proof. And if there is war in Hrusk . . ." He laughed, but joylessly.

"What must be done?"

"That is the question, my friend. That is the question."

The two men sat silently. After a moment, Urudu put his hand over Gibson's and said, "I am with you."

Gibson looked down at the dark, heavy hand covering his own. The silver mark of Urudu's servitude hung from the small chain around his wrist.

"Listen, my friend." Gibson looked hard into his steward's eyes, and his resolve hardened. "I'm going to change the affairs of my house. I've begun to make some preparations . . . for whatever may come. And I don't think my house will be a safe haven any longer."

"You think there will be war."

"Likely, likely. But the more pressing matter is the warning I received the other night. If they aim to destroy my house, I will leave little for them." Gibson looked south, feeling the draw of the road. "I miss the road."

"I miss it, too, my Lord. I would gladly go back to it." A pause. "Are you thinking of going south?"

Gibson shook his head. "Only if I could reach Shal-Gashun. But war would make that difficult. At least if I hope to save any with me."

"I meant what I said, my Lord. Whether there is war or not."

"I know." Gibson looked into his servant's eyes again. "I know. But it's time to change the affairs of my house. There may not be room for servants and temple children any longer."

"Do you mean to give up my temple bond?"

"Not like that, my friend—not to the temple." He smiled. "Could I ever get by without your services?" Gibson laughed, encouraging his servant to levity.

Urudu grinned, and a hand strayed unconsciously to one of the knives at his waist. "Of course not."

"So the question is, do you want to be free?"

CHAPTER SEVENTEEN.
SECRET COMBINATIONS.

Sarana waited for her master to speak.

"It was a trap," Gibson said. And a small smile bent one side of his mouth.

She felt a prick of fear. *A trap.* She tried to understand. But she saw nothing in the encounter to suggest a trap.

Gibson had questioned her at length, and she had told him everything she could remember. Except for the theft. She had described the walled garden and the rooms of the house. She had described the palanquin, the men who had taken her, the things she had seen inside the house, and anything she could recall about the surreptitious lord of the house.

"Was there nothing else?" Gibson asked.

Sarana slowly shook her head. "No, my Lord."

"Tell me," Gibson said. "The door with writing on the lintel. Do you think you could recognize any of the words?"

Sarana kneaded half of her lower lip with her teeth and shook her head. "I don't think—I don't know."

"Here, sit."

Gibson placed a sheet of paper on the table in front of her and wrote several words. She stared at the bewildering curves and lines, knowing she would fail this task. She shook her head.

"I'm sorry, my Lord."

"Let's try this." He wrote several letters. "Do you recognize any of these letters?"

She stared at the letters for several seconds. Hot shame filled her mouth. "No, my Lord." Her words felt thick.

Gibson walked around the table and stood facing the bookshelves. His finger tapped restlessly against his leg. He said, "It's a pity you don't know how to read. I taught Urudu many years ago, and all of my agents are well versed." He looked at her and drew in and let out a breath through his nostrils. "If I had taught you, I might be better off now." He turned and looked out the window.

After a short silence, Sarana spoke. "My Lord?"

"Hmm?" Gibson's thoughts had wandered momentarily, discovering paths he had never seen before.

"How was it a trap?"

The Lord of the House of Jianin looked at his water woman. Even a few days before, she would not have dared to inquire—not merely to satisfy her curiosity. He decided to tell her. "Whoever it was—it might have been Elder Amin, I think it was—wanted to gather evidence against me. There has been a threat against me—against the House of Jianin— and someone is gathering evidence to use against me in the Council."

"Did I give him—"

Gibson broke off her sentence. "Yes. But you could not have known. When you told him I gave you permission, you gave him evidence he can use against me. There are members of the Council who will say I must sympathize with this prophet and his followers. They will say I have allowed the members of my house to go whoring after a false god and a renegade prophet. An unknowable Esana."

Sarana's mouth filled with anger. "But I didn't know."

"You cannot help being a child," he said. "It is what you are. It is what you were trained to be. And to remain."

He felt a pang; he regretted the words. Sarana seemed not to have heard him.

"But how did they know what I would tell them?"

"They could only guess." Gibson paused momentarily, thinking.

"But they would have used anything you said against me. If you had gone without my knowledge, they could have used that. A servant straying from her duties—a master unable to control his house— would have confirmed the charge against me."

"I thought I had to answer him."

"You did. By the Lines, a servant must answer to the priests and elders. But not all servants are as faithful as you."

Sarana felt an objection rise up. The broken path of her servitude was barely mended, the stones still rumpled and uneven in her mind. She was not faithful.

"I should have seen the danger, myself," Gibson said. "I should have realized you could become a target." He walked over to his bookshelf and took down a slate and a piece of chalk. "I told you before that things could not remain the same between us—after you broke your servitude."

"Yes, my Lord."

"So, I have something for you to do." He put the slate on the table in front of her and wrote a series of letters. She thought for a moment he wanted her to look again, to see if she recognized any of the letters. She started to shake her head.

"You can do this," he said, holding up a staying hand. "You can. I am going to teach you to read them."

A moment of fear paralyzed her. She stared at her master.

He said, "I think, perhaps, I need to change many things." He looked down at the slate and continued. "There are seventy-five letters in all—twenty-five simple letters and fifty variations of the five root letters." He tapped the slate with his finger. "These five are the root letters. The first is *ah*. Say it."

Sarana looked at the slate. Her master's finger pointed to the first letter. She said, "*Ah*." Then she looked back up at her master's face.

"*Ah* is written like this. Watch." His hand slowly drew a duplicate of the first letter as she watched. "Now you try." He pointed to the empty space below his letters. "Learning to write them will help you remember them."

Sarana took the thin, sharp chalk from her master's hand. Her mind blazed. She drew slowly, and a trembling, wavering imitation of her master's sure strokes stuttered from her fingertips. But she could feel no disappointment.

"Good," he said. "Good. Practice will make you more sure." He pointed to the second letter. "This is the second root letter—*ehah*." He showed her how to draw the letter, and they repeated his instruction for each of the letters. And when the slate was full of her attempts, Gibson wiped it clean and started the exercise again.

They continued for several minutes.

Finally, Gibson said, "That's enough for now. You will have to keep practicing, but you need to give your hand a rest."

Sarana looked at the slate. The imperfect lines of her efforts could not match the grace of her master's hand. But her attempts had improved.

"Once you have mastered the root letters, I will teach you the other simple letters. And, finally, you will learn the complex or combination letters. Some call them the variations."

"What is the difference?"

"The difference?"

"Between the basic letters and the others—the variations." She liked the name. She liked the sound of it. *Variations.*

Gibson smiled, prodded by the question into a recollection of his father. He savored his memory for a moment and then said, after a huff of laughter, "My father said the difference was beauty." He shook his head, remembering his father's irritation with a faction of merchants who had urged him to join their efforts to convince the Council that a simplified alphabet should become the standard.

"The variations—the complex or combination letters—are essentially the combination of a root letter with one of the other basic letters. But they form something new." Gibson took the slate. "The first variation of *ah* is *ahf*. See, it's written like this." He demonstrated. "But in simplified letters, instead of one complex letter, you would just write the two basic letters *ah* and *fay*, like this." Gibson put the slate back down in front of her.

She recognized the letter *ah* but the other letters were still foreign to her.

"The advantage of the simplified alphabet is that a person need only learn the twenty-five basic letters, instead of seventy-five. There is no need for the combination letters. It's easier to learn, so some say it is better."

"If it's better, why not use it?"

"That's where people disagree. The simplified alphabet is easier to learn, but it represents a loss. My father called it a degradation. It meant losing some of the beauty of our language. Our heritage. Our history. The legacy of Yinock." He shrugged, suggesting an indifference he did not feel. "And consider: a person who cannot read the complex letters would not be able to read the Lines of the Law. Or any of the ancient writings of our people. In fact—" But Gibson stopped.

His water woman could read nothing. *And she certainly won't understand this.* He looked at her, feeling a bit ridiculous. But her serene face merely looked up at him, waiting. He decided to continue.

"I was going to say, some people believe we have already lost much. Scholars have found combination letters in ancient copies of the Lines that we do not use. They can be deciphered by context, but no one really knows whether those combinations are examples of lost combinations, errors, or attempts at innovation by some long-dead scribe. One group of scholars believes the alphabet has undergone at least one simplification to reduce the number of letters to seventy-five—the twenty-five basic letters plus the most common variations."

Sarana was silent; she did not understand what it all meant. But then Kaina's words came back to her. "Do you mean that the Lines have changed?"

He did not answer her question; instead, he said, "If the alphabet were simplified— reduced to the basic letters—the Lines would have to be rewritten to make them understandable to people who know only the basic letters. An unacceptable loss. A limited set of characters, a less educated literate populace, a loss of beautiful combinations that have been used in poetry and artwork for generations." Gibson shook his head and smiled ruefully, but happily.

He had not thought about his father's views on the question of alphabet simplification for years. The push to change the alphabet had died, but his father's views still inhabited his mind like ghosts.

"Some said simplification would be used to create ignorance—to create a low-literate class of people who could not read the ancient texts, which are full of combinations. But there is widespread illiteracy regardless of the alphabet." Gibson glanced at Sarana, silently cognizant of the accepted illiteracy of servants.

"Those who argued for simplification said an easier alphabet—the elimination of all the combinations—would improve literacy. They thought any literacy was better than none. They said more people would be able to learn. And they said the Lines could be rewritten with simplified letters." Gibson shook his head before continuing. "Still, there have long been rumors that the priests have access to ancient books—books handed down from the days of Yinock— books full of secret combinations that the priests will not reveal to anyone outside the priesthood."

"What's the truth?" Sarana asked.

"Ah, well, nothing so easy as that." He smiled. And for a moment he said nothing more, content with his silent belief that *truth* about matters of scholarly debate can rarely be distilled so easily, or acceptably. But when he saw his water woman was waiting for his answer, he groped forward. "I guess I agree with my father, that we should keep the old letters. Some of them are beautiful, and they make our language more . . . pure."

"Pure?"

"Perfect is the better word, perhaps. The beauty and complexity of the variations is not their only virtue. They are more concise. Let me show you."

Gibson took the slate again and wiped it clean. Then he took the chalk and said, "Watch." He started to write a series of letters.

"In simplified letters, your name is written like this—*sah, ah, rah, ah, nahl, ah.*" He wrote each letter as he spoke, pausing after each one. "Six letters. But using the variations, it is written with four: *sah, ahr, ahn, ah.* See? Just four letters." He pointed to the second letter. "*Ah* and *rah* combine and become *ahr.* And then *ah* and *nahl* combine to make the third letter, *ahn*. If a whole book were written in simplified letters, the book might be half again as long as a book written with the variations."

Sarana stared at the letters for a few moments. Then she said, "So if there were more variations, a book might be even shorter."

"That's right." Gibson looked at his water woman, thinking he might praise her rapid insight. But her eyes were rapt upon the little slate as she examined the letters; he said nothing for several moments.

Sarana touched the letters of her name, lightly tracing the lines. Her hand was close to her master's hand, smooth and white against the slate, like living chalk. She imagined the lines flowing from her gliding fingertip. And then, as her finger moved from the second to third letter of her name, she saw how the two forms could be combined to create the variation *ahr*. She glanced up at Gibson, astonished. But she quickly looked back down, away from his gaze, and continued to stare at the letters.

There was a logic to the combination of the letters. A clear pattern. And she saw how ancient minds must have created the variation. Her eyes leaped to the next variation in her name—*ahn*—and she again saw the logic of the combination. And then she wondered whether similar logic could be used to combine more letters. But the slate offered no more variations. She looked at the simple letters of her name. *Could the letter* ah *be combined with* sah? The root letter *ah* had a sinuous line that remained when the letter was combined with other letters.

She looked up at Gibson. "Can *ah* be combined with *sah*?"

"Yes. *Ahs* is the ninth variation of *ah*. It's written like this."

Sarana stared at the new variation. Deep wonder filled her mind. The sinuous line remained as she had expected, and the remainder of the variation followed the logic she had foreseen. "It's just what I thought!" she said, excited. "They're not hard at all. I think I could learn all of the variations at once."

Gibson laughed, contented and amused. His young water woman's serene, fair face had kindled with silent joy. "Slowly, Sarana. You will need to keep practicing. And when you have these mastered, I will teach you the next set."

CHAPTER EIGHTEEN.

THE TALE OF NAINA-NAH-NAULUMA.

Somehow, nothing changed. The events of the day receded; the words of the prophet became distant; and the waylaying—the draped palanquin, the walled garden, the secretive elder—seemed unreal, like a story. Within moments of leaving her master's study, her life in the House of Jianin reclaimed her.

She went back to her labors at the well. And when she had finished there, Telasa sent her to work with the hired women in the vineyard. The endless monotony of plucking the *rebboth* quelled her simmering thoughts. Only the quiet, decayed remnants of an unexpected joy— the product of learning a few letters—remained.

And then the day drew to a close. And she found herself beside the hearth, mashing beans for the evening meal, recounting her day to Kaina. They were alone amid the ordinary bustle of the house. The old woman's methodical hands paused from time to time and sprinkled powdered spices into their bowls. The scent of redolent pepper, freshly ground, hung in the air.

"I wish I could have told him more," Sarana said. "I felt so foolish."

"You could not be expected to know an elder you had never seen. Surely our master was not angry about that."

"No. But I wanted—" Sarana shrugged and closed her eyes as she shook her head. "I felt so useless. I wanted to find the answer for him—to do something to help him."

"You wanted to be more than you are," Kaina said.

"I just wanted—"

"You wanted to be bigger than you are, more important." Kaina smiled. "Your pride roused in your heart. As it does for all of us from time to time."

Humility is harder to trap than water. Sarana looked into her bowl of beans.

Kaina leaned over and looked at her bowl. "I can finish the rest. You should probably see to some of those." She gestured toward the hearth where the empty house jars outnumbered the full by a goodly number.

Outside, a drape of wispy clouds had caught the last illumination of the fleeing sun, the light rosy. Sarana descended into the water house, and her skin prickled pleasantly, aroused by the subterranean chill. Someone had been there recently—probably Pelem watering the horses—and the dusk-black water undulated lazily and slapped quietly in the corners of the cistern.

All at once, the words of the prophet came back to her.

He was born before your mother weaned you. He was conceived before the stones of the temple were laid one upon another. The momentous words of the prophet—temporarily driven from her mind by the subsequent events of the day—seemed to fill the little chamber. And she realized she had not told Gibson what she had heard. She had not told him about the confrontation between the prophet and the crowd, or about the old man from Noot who had taken hold of the prophet's arm and obtained an answer for his question.

He was born before your mother weaned you.

The words were plain enough but utterly alien. *He was conceived before the stones of the temple were laid one upon another.* She could not accept them. They contradicted everything she knew about Esana. They were impossible.

And yet, when she imagined Esana had been born—that he had lived and breathed and walked among his people—she felt a glimmer of gladness in her heart.

She wanted it to be true; she wanted the prophet to be right.

In the garden of her mind, she felt a slithering uncertainty, but the seed watered by the prophet's words slowly produced a shoot. She thought she should tell Gibson. He had said he wanted to hear what she heard.

But he had other people who reported to him. And she had work to do. She could tell him when she next took him water.

For a while, she worked without conscious thought, walking back and forth across the yard with the little house jars. Overhead, the dimming heavens evolved through permutations of gold and pink and violet.

When she returned to her place in the hearth room, Kaina had finished with the beans and she was shelling the *rebboth*. Ana knelt beside the hearth, kneading dough for the next day's bread; the smell of nascent loaves lay heavy in the air. Ana looked up and smiled. Sarana put on an apron and joined the old woman. The cracking husks and the faint, acrid smell of the *rebboth* enveloped her.

Ana spoke first. "I heard the prophet was accused of blasphemy today."

"What?" Sarana looked up.

Ana shook her head, pouting, her eyes wide with concern. "That's not good news for you, Sara. You're probably bound for *zahyel*."

"Quiet child," Kaina said. "Don't joke about the gated land."

Ana smiled and looked down, returning to her kneading. "It's Sarana should be worried. I'm not. The gated land has not opened its maw to devour me." Ana glanced up at Sarana and smiled archly.

Kaina cast an irritated glance at Ana's playful impudence.

"What did you hear?" Sarana said, amused.

"Oh. Well." Ana shrugged, replacing her wickedness with nonchalance. "He said Esana already came, that he was born a long time ago—years and years ago—and is dead. People say he has broken faith, that he is teaching a false Esana."

"He was already doing that," Kaina said.

"A priest even went down to the river and warned him to be silent. But the prophet wouldn't. That's what I heard, anyway."

Sarana realized she had stopped working; she was staring at Ana stupidly.

"What?" Ana said.

Sarana looked down and set her hands to work again. "I heard what he said. I was there." She shook her head, her eyes down.

"You were there?" Ana's eyes had gone wide again. And then she glanced at the door, checking instinctively for the watchful presence of Telasa.

"She had permission," Kaina said.

"What happened?"

"It was the strangest thing. He—" Sarana broke off. "A man was arguing with him. And then there was this old man from Noot who went up and asked him when Esana would be born. No one thought he would answer. And I was thinking, No one knows—like the Lines say." Sarana looked up. "But I wanted to know. And then the prophet looked at the old man, and he had this look in his eyes. It was so gentle. He said Esana was born before the old man's mother weaned him."

Kaina snorted softly.

"That's impossible," Ana said.

"You see," Kaina said. "He teaches a false Esana."

"I thought so, too," Sarana said, responding to Ana. "He couldn't have been born so long ago—not according to the Lines." She paused. "But you should have seen him. Part of me wanted it to be true. I was thinking later . . . it would be wonderful if he was already alive."

"But it is not true," Kaina said.

"I know," Sarana said. "But what if Esana *did* live a long time ago."

The old woman thought for several moments. "It raises an interesting question, I will say that. Would it be more difficult to place our faith in him now?" The old woman paused. "Is it more difficult to have faith in an Esana who lived long ago or an Esana who will be born in the future?"

"But he says Esana lived on another world," Ana said, impatient.

"True," the old woman said. "His teachings cannot be right. But what if this prophet had said Esana was living in Noot? You've never been to Noot—you cannot go there. Would the distance between this place and Noot destroy your faith?"

Sarana considered the old woman's words. "The Line of *Nahoy-Es* says he will be born to a daughter of Yinock."

"True," Kaina said. "But Yinock has children in Noot. He has them among the remnants of my own people."

"Not pure descendants," Sarana said.

Kaina ignored the comment with a wave of her hand. "The question is, would the lengths between the Great City and Noot destroy your faith in Esana? Would any distance rob Esana of his power to save his people?"

"The prophet wasn't talking about Noot," Ana said.

"Does any distance, or any number of years, matter to Esana?" Kaina asked. "If Esana had lived on another world in a past age, would our faith in him be in vain?"

"I think we have another heretic here," Ana said, turning to Sarana. Her eyes twinkled with anticipation.

"No, child," Kaina said. "There is only one true faith. These tales merely caused me to wonder aloud."

"But . . ." Sarana trailed off quickly. She was not sure what she wanted to say.

Kaina was quiet for a long moment. "I've only heard a little of what he teaches. And mostly from old women and rumormongers." She cast a glance at Ana. "I cannot believe in another Esana born on a distant world. I do not understand why people would *want* to believe in someone they or their children will never see. The ancient prophets said Esana would live and walk among his people. They said He would succor his people and free them from bondage."

"Maybe they are tired of waiting for him," Ana said, her voice softer than usual.

"People do get tired," Kaina said. Her gnarled hands came to rest in her bowl, having split the last seed. But instead of stopping to refill her bowl, she continued, "And it can make them restless, ready to believe anything that gives them hope. There's one old woman in the

Stair Market who is convinced the Taking has already begun—that missing children must have been taken up to live with God."

"I've never heard that," Sarana said.

"But you've heard stranger news, now," Kaina said. "That Esana was born before an old man was weaned from his mother's breast. What is that compared to an old woman's hope that children are being taken up to God rather than stolen?"

Kaina picked up her bowl of *rebboth* husks and emptied it into the fire. When she had refilled the bowl, she said, "I'm going to tell you one of the ancient tales of my people—a story about the importance of keeping faith. You talked about *zahyel* opening its maw to swallow up the unfaithful, but in times past, the earth did open its mouth and swallow up the treasures of my people. Because of evildoers."

"Ah," Ana said, finding her usual voice. "A kainish tale of superstitious dread. We were warned about such tales by our temple mothers."

Kaina responded slowly, deliberately, without ire. "You Yinocki do not understood our stories," she said. "When you hear about the deep wonders of the world you see only darkness and magic. But you do not hear the story. This tale teaches the importance of holding on to goodness. It was told among the women of my people, and it was always remembered and passed on—mother to daughter, grandmother to daughter. Down through generations of women. You are not kainish women, but now I'm going to pass it on to you."

"And make us heathens, like you," Ana said, her voice playful.

"I'd like to hear it," Sarana said.

"So." Kaina looked at each of the young women before starting. "There was a woman in the ancient days, named Naina-Nah-Nauluma, which means infinite and eternal in the heavenly language. She entered the world when the world began, and it was prophesied she would live for ten thousand years."

"I guess that didn't come true," Ana said.

Kaina ignored the interruption. "It was prophesied the people would be blessed if they followed Naina's counsel. They called her Naina, because her full name, Naina-Nah-Nauluma, was too sacred.

And too long." Kaina smiled.

"Naina Nala Lala Luna," Ana said, and she flashed her envy-inducing smile.

"It was a long name," Kaina said, glancing at Ana, unperturbed. "My grandmother always made that foolish little joke about her long name."

"Did the people listen to her?" Sarana asked.

"For many years, they did," Kaina said. "And the people did prosper, and they were greatly blessed. They became a great people." Kaina paused. "But in her heart, Naina knew the people would eventually turn away from her. She foresaw the people would lose faith in her—that she would be forgotten and lost in obscurity."

"Not even a true child of Yinock can live for ten thousand years," Sarana said.

"Naina was one of the ancients—those we call the Ancients of Days. They could do great and marvelous works."

"If they were so powerful, what happened to them?" Ana said.

"I asked my grandmother that same question once. She told me to think about another question. She said, If God is so powerful, why does he hide? She said when I could see the goodness in God's absence, I would see the true beauty of the world."

Ana shook her head, her face troubled. "God does not hide," she said.

Kaina smiled. "You think on it. Now listen, and I will tell you what happened to Naina. She was a peculiar woman. She had to be carried from place to place, and in the beginning, a certain man was appointed to be her guardian. His name was Shensa-Nahman, which means messenger of God in the heavenly language."

"Shensa-Nahman," Sarana said, testing the feel of it.

"He was one of the ancient immortals. But of all the immortals, he had been given the power to travel the heavenly realm and return to the world to guide his children. But then, one day, God told Shensa-Nahman it was his time to leave the world and dwell forever in the distant heavens. So Shensa-Nahman called his children together and told them they would have to care for Naina. He selected one of his sons to be the next guardian, and he blessed him specially for that purpose. He told his children she would guide them like a loving mother, so long as they cared for her and preserved her from harm. He warned them, however, that because the world had become wicked, she must never touch the ground." Kaina stopped and smiled again. "My grandmother always said, if we had preserved Naina, we never would have fallen captive to your people."

"What happened?" Sarana asked.

"Forty generations of guardians cared for Naina, and the guardians became rich and powerful. And then came the last guardian—a man named Shev. Shev was a wicked and slothful man, and he would not listen to Naina's counsel. He refused to carry her from place to place. And, yet, he feared the warning of Shensa-Nahman, and he did not let her touch the ground. Shev made slaves hold her, and he kept her locked in a room. Shev told the people she had to be protected.

"Year after year, Naina remained confined, and the slaves and the children of those slaves, served her in captivity. Naina sent messages to Shev, warning him she would soon perish if he did not let her see the sun, but he would not listen. And when she did not die, Shev's heart grew even harder, and he said Naina had become a liar.

"But it was Shev who lied. Naina was one of the ancients, so she did not die immediately. She became weaker and weaker. After another year, she ceased to speak, and her face no longer glowed with the light of the ancient heavens. The righteous few who remained in the land began to fear for her life. Finally, a poor but righteous man went to Shev and pleaded on Naina's behalf. For three days he begged, pleading with Shev and promising his eternal servitude if Shev would bring Naina out into the sunlight.

"Shev grew angry and said, 'If you want to serve, then you will serve Naina for the remainder of your days.' Shev cast out the other slaves and made the man serve Naina alone. But on the third day, when they took food in to him, he was alone. He said Naina had spoken to him and told him to put her on the ground. He said Naina told him her time had come to return to her Mother Earth. But she said one day she would rise again and feel the sun on her face. The man said that when he put her on the ground, the earth opened up and swallowed her." Kaina stopped and looked at the two younger women. "And that is the story of Naina-Nah-Nauluma, the story of how the last of the Ancients of Days was lost to us."

Sarana considered the end of the story, not knowing what to say.

"It seems like a strange story to tell little girls," Ana said.

"Undoubtedly strange to your Yinocki ears," Kaina said. Then the old woman smiled and said, "And full of heathen notions and superstitious dread."

Ana smiled and said, "Beware little ones. Naina is down there. Waiting. And she just might grab you and pull you down into the earth."

"Her story is not a fearful story," Kaina said. "It is a hopeful story, if sorrowful." The old woman stood up slowly and emptied her bowl of *rebboth* husks into the fire. They crackled and spit sparks.

"But do you think it is true?" Sarana said.

Kaina spoke slowly. "Is it true? I think so. Maybe not in some of its particulars, I suppose. But that doesn't matter much. Not really. The words are not truth. The truth lies somewhere behind—or beyond—the words. The words are a guide to the truth."

"But if the words are not true . . ." Sarana said, puzzling.

"It is the past that matters, child. The past of which the story speaks is true. A few words can never capture the complexity of the countless lives of Naina's time. A story conceals far more than it reveals. All those people, all those choices, all those events. But the words remind us that the past is there."

Kaina pressed her fingertips against her breast and said, "And your own heart—with all of its beauty and meanness, with all of its hopes and fears—can provide the hidden texts the story cannot recount. Shev really did live, and he was a wicked man. And because of his sloth, the last of the ancients was lost to my people. We can still learn from the story, and we are free to search out the unspoken truths that lie beyond the story itself."

Telasa walked into the room, and the women stopped talking. For a moment, Telasa looked from one woman to the next, expectant, but when no one spoke, she examined the house jars, nodded, and turned to Sarana. "Come with me, Sarana. We need to bring in the wash."

Outside, the wash lines stretched darkly in the orchard. Just enough twilight hung over the world to finish the work. A cloudy sky foreshadowed a dark night.

Across the courtyard, the gates had closed out the rest of the world, and for a moment Sarana's thoughts turned dark, rebellious. She eyed Telasa. The older woman moved briskly, decisively along a line of clothes. Sarana started on one of the other lines, and as she pulled down the clothes, she thought about the raucous women of the outer city. The teeming alleys contrasted starkly with the dark orchard of her merchant master, and it seemed impossible the orderly darkness could satisfy her.

And then she recalled the quiet wonders of the temple complex where she had spent her childhood. There, among the ancient buildings, small lamps had illuminated the footpaths and doorways with soft white light. Starlike, the minuscule lights were too small to produce much light, but they glowed serenely through the nights— small white fruits with glittering cores—making paths of light through the dark courtyards. Such beauty. It seemed impossible that anything less ordered could seduce her.

But if the prophet were to be believed, the temple had been corrupted by priestcraft and deceit. Its ancient wonders had fallen into the hands of evil stewards who had lost the knowledge of redemption. And, as if to mark the prophet's words, the Wayfarer had fallen from heaven. The old wonders of the world were dying. *Like Naina.*

Dear Abasha, she thought. *What am I to do?* Her silent plea was immediately answered, as it always was when she called on her old temple mother. *Your duty, child. In submission is exaltation.*

Sarana finished the line and laid the last carefully folded robe into her basket. She tasted her feelings delicately. *I am a vessel. In submission is exaltation.* She let out a breath and followed Telasa back into the house.

CHAPTER NINETEEN.

NEWBORN.

Dawn was still some hours away, but Neturu could see no stars from where he sat in the slow-moving cart.

The smell of old fire burdened the humid darkness, and in the black heavens, towering thunder clouds lurked, illuminated betimes with flashes of fulgurant fire. Beside him, Doman strode silently, his eyes closed, his hand on the side of the cart to guide his steps. Neturu thought he might be praying. The big, soft-spoken man had promised to do so on Neturu's behalf when he had come by Lihana's home the night before. *All men need strength to withstand the fire*, he had said. Neturu had not felt much comforted.

Saban pulled the cart slowly to avoid jolts and jounces, and Pekel unfolded before Neturu's eyes in the darkness. The scorchers' stone homes stood close together in rows, sometimes sharing walls. Beyond the clustered homes, the cart passed into a realm Neturu had never fully conceived. Heaps of trash lined the path, and the path branched and wove among them, serpentine, twisting among the heaps and weaving toward the burning pits.

"Not far now," Doman said.

His companion had opened his eyes, and Neturu asked, "What is this place?"

"This is Pekel, my friend." The obtuse response seemed to give Doman some sort of perverse pleasure; the big man smiled, a little slyly.

"But what are all these piles. Why haven't you burned this?"

"Ah. These are the recycling heaps. All the trash is brought here first and sorted. We salvage everything we can. We repair and reuse many things the careless folk of the city toss away." Doman smiled and shrugged. "What we cannot use, we sell, if we can. And the rest is burned."

"You sell trash?"

Doman laughed. "We don't sell it to people like you."

Neturu quieted, feeling rebuked.

Doman sobered. "You might be surprised what people throw away," he said. "Especially among the great houses. And many of us are skilled in useful crafts. There is a seamstress here—Hana—who can make incredible clothing. She sorts through the piles of old clothes, blankets, rags—whatever types of fabric are salvaged—and she creates new things. Sometimes she simply repairs old clothing, but when she can't, she uses what she can to make new items. Most of what we have—our clothes and everything else—was salvaged from the trash heaps of the city."

"I had no idea," Neturu said. He looked at the heaps stretching out in all directions, and the scope of the work dwarfed him. A separate economy unfolded in his mind, and he imagined an army of scorchers picking over the heaps of trash like coordinated insects. He marveled. And then he shook his head. "But how do you sell to the Yinoi? Surely they won't take goods from you. Anything you scorchers touch is unclean."

"Yes," Doman said. "But there are ways to handle that." He paused. "You have no reservations dealing with us."

"I am not a Yinoi. I'm not bound by their false superstitions."

Doman nodded, smiling slightly. "We use middle buyers."

"Middle buyers?"

"People who aren't bound by their *superstitions*—and who want to make some money." Doman laughed. "Sometimes we sell to Hruskan traders. The middle buyers buy our goods—at a good price—and resell them. Many of them are traveling merchants who sell their wares along the road to Noot. Once our goods pass through a middle buyer, they are clean. I can only assume—and hope—the middle buyers do what they must to be purified themselves."

"You think their dealings with you make them unclean?"

"By the Lines, we are unclean. And any who deal with us are unclean." Doman looked over at him. "You are unclean."

Neturu looked out over the heaps. He refrained from expressing his disdain for the backward beliefs of the *Yinoi*. "How do you manage it all?"

Doman looked out over the heaps for a moment. "We have an administrator who oversees the work. And we all work together. We all share what we have."

Again the image of swarming insects arose in Neturu's mind. "How many scorchers are there?"

"I don't know with certainty. Probably around seven hundred. Maybe a few more than that. The administrator would know. He keeps count when people pass away. When new people come. Or children are born. We told him when you arrived." Doman smiled and shrugged. "Wasn't sure if you'd stay, but I guessed you'd be here for a little while at least."

"Children." Neturu said it quietly. The thought of children being born and living in Pekel had never occurred to him. He had just not thought of it. But now generations unfolded in his mind, rolling back in time, and forward, a great scroll. "Do people often come here?" he asked.

"No." Doman shook his head. "A few find refuge here. Not many come by choice. Few are ever condemned to Pekel."

Neturu looked out over the heaps of trash. The thought of living in Pekel—of joining ranks with a people who spent their days sorting through trash—was unimaginably alien. But when Doman had asked him the night before where he intended to go, Neturu had not had an answer. He would find no help in the Quarter—none he could trust. He had no way to get to Hrusk. And the prophet had not come as he had hoped.

The cart slowed, stopped. Doman helped Neturu get out, and

Neturu stood with his weight on his good leg, and a hand on
Doman's shoulder. A stone table stood beside one of the great
burning pits, silhouetted against the glow of fire. Neturu felt himself
quail. Saban came around from the front of the cart.

"Come," Doman said.

As Neturu sat on the edge of the table, a man emerged from the
burning pit. He carried a large water jar, holding it with metal tongs.
He put the jar beside the table; a wisp of steam emerged from its open
mouth. Two more scorchers were laboring to place a large brazier
near the foot of the table.

"The surgeon," Doman said to Neturu.

The man turned toward them. "All is ready here. Where is
Lihana?"

Doman gestured with his chin over his shoulder. "She and the
others are coming on behind. They'll be along in a moment. I brought
Neturu here first to meet you, since he is new among us."

The surgeon turned to Neturu. "I'm Taelon."

"Neturu."

"I know who you are—once son of the on-Dam. The news of you
reached me quickly, after Lihana took a look at your leg." Taelon
looked up into the sky, forehead creased. "I'm hoping it doesn't rain.
We don't need that." He looked back at Neturu. "Doman tells me you
were in bad shape when he found you. You have Lihana to thank for
the improvement. She has true healer's hands."

"I am grateful to her."

"I don't know if you'll be grateful to me. Let's have a look."

Neturu sat back on the table. Taelon took off the bandage and
peered at the injury in the firelight. He pressed lightly on the inflamed
skin with his fingertips. "Hmm. Lihana was right about the infection."
The surgeon looked into Neturu's eyes. "Doman says you have
courage. Are you ready?"

"Tell me what will happen."

Taelon nodded. "I'll cut in first and drain the wound. I'll clean it
out as much as I can. But I'll have to work fast; there will be bleeding.
Then I'll cut away the infected flesh—as much as I can—and burn the

wound to purify it and close it. The burning implements are in the fire, here." He gestured toward the brazier. "They are ready. " He paused. "The pain . . . will be very great. You can bite down on something if you like, but do not be ashamed to cry out." Taelon put a hand on Neturu's shoulder. "No one can withstand the fire—it is natural to voice your pain. We'll get started soon."

Neturu looked doubtfully at the dark sky. It was still too early, too dark. "It's too dark for you to work," he said.

Taelon shook his head and smiled. "You would be correct—except you don't know our ways. In Pekel, all such work is done by night." He picked up a small bag sitting at the end of the table; hard objects clacked softly inside. "Today you will see one of our ancient glories." He loosened the top of the bag. Soft, white light flowed upward out of the bag, and Taelon reached down into it, his hand occluding and then being suffused by white light. He drew out a small, bright object. A translucent, shining stone.

Neturu's lips parted, but he said nothing. Taelon held out the stone, and the light flowed outward, bathing the table in a soft white radiance. Neturu stretched out a hand but then drew back. He had heard rumors of the miraculous relics of the *Yinoi*. And not just rumors. He had seen the dome of light over the temple when night fell; he had seen the ancient well house of Geb and its inexhaustible pumps.

But the translucent stone exceeded any hidden wonders of the temple. It lay exposed in Taelon's palm, an undimmed bit of glory, a source of awe. Neturu's eyes strayed to the bag in Taelon's other hand. Then he looked at Taelon.

"We call it a Nohak stone."

"How—where did you—where did it come from?" Neturu asked.

"They belong to us." Taelon's voice had a grim edge. But then his countenance lightened, and he spoke softly. "Nohak constructed them in the days of Yinock, in our homeland. And we have preserved them since the city fled."

Neturu stared again at the shining stone, enthralled by the simplicity and impossibility of it. A radiant core of living light, encased in translucent stone. *How could a man construct something like that?* He was about to ask if he could hold it, but he stopped himself and said, "It is truly marvelous."

Taelon put the stone away, and the dimness of Pekel collapsed back around them. "As you can see, you needn't worry about the darkness."

Neturu nodded absently, his thoughts jumbled. The miracle of the Nohak stone unfolded slowly in his mind, and he suddenly comprehended the unbreakable faith of some of the *Yinoi*. The wonders of Yinock's days—seen close at hand—provided a tangible token of things otherwise unseen.

"Do you have any other questions about the surgery?" Taelon glanced to his left, out toward the recycling heaps. "I think the others are all here and ready."

"No. No. I'm ready." Neturu felt his heart quicken.

"I will get the others."

Neturu lay back on the table. The handles of the burning implements protruded from the mouth of the brazier, and within, bright coals blazed. He closed his eyes and focused his thoughts. He put his hand over his chest and felt the tiny, bronze star beneath his clothing. Fear fluttered in his breast, and he pushed it down. He thought instead about Hrusk, his old friends, his once home, his mother. And he thought about how he had turned—if only slightly— from the faces of his fathers.

Just then he felt a hand on his shoulder. Lihana stood over him. She cradled a small, round crock against her body with one hand. She looked at him for a moment, and then she caressed his forehead gently. "You sure know how to put yourself into trouble, boy. I am sorry it has come to this."

Neturu smiled up at the scorcher woman. "I was thinking of my mother a moment ago, and my old home in Hrusk. I was wondering how she will take the news that I am no longer her son. That is—I know how she will react publicly. She would not betray my father— my once father—that way. But I wonder what she will hold in her heart."

Lihana put her hand over his and said, "Be still. You will always be her son."

"By my fathers, I hope you are right." Neturu stopped talking, and he looked toward the burning pit. He did not want to weep, but his fear was making him weak, mawkish, and he felt his resolve wavering. Lihana patted his hand once more, and then she joined Taelon and Doman, where they stood talking beside the pit. Neturu closed his eyes and waited for them to finish their preparations.

A few moments later, light bloomed around him and Neturu felt several hands take hold of him. Taelon had fastened the Nohak stone into a headband above his eyes, and the soft light radiated outward, illuminating the space between them. He had a knife in his hand, and he dipped the knife and his hands deep into the jar of steaming water. He held them there for several moments, and when he pulled them out, steam rose up from his flesh. "Let's begin," he said.

Neturu clenched the sides of the table with both hands. Doman stood above him, his strong hands on Neturu's shoulders, pushing him down. Two other men stood on either side of the stone table, holding Neturu's legs. Lihana stood by, her hands clasped around her little crock of honey paste. She stood ready to salve the wound. They all wore Nohak stones on their foreheads.

Taelon did not delay. Neturu felt the knife part his skin. The anticipated pain followed, but it was bearable. He reminded himself to breath regularly, and he held fast to the sides of the table, bearing up under Taelon's determined hands. Taelon pressed and probed, his fingers sure and strong. The pain grew, and Neturu thought he felt the knife at work. He closed his eyes and forced his thoughts away. He thought again of distant Hrusk.

Doman said something about washing, but Neturu did not hear the words. Then hot raw pain erupted in his leg and Neturu's eyes flicked open involuntarily. He cried out briefly, abruptly, catching himself too late. He stammered but could not speak; he grunted through his clenched jaw and breathed desperately through his nostrils. He found Doman's eyes.

And then Taelon spoke. "It's bleeding clean. I'm going to flush it again." He paused and his eyes flashed up toward Neturu's face. "Be ready."

Neturu watched as Taelon poured a clear liquid over the wound. Another jolt of raw pain shot into his leg, and Doman's hands pressed down a bit harder. Neturu's breathing became loud, interspersed with repressed grunts. Taelon put aside the flask and quickly donned a brown leather glove. He retrieved one of the heated implements from the brazier. The tip emerged from the coals glowing. A burning half circle of white-hot metal pressed its image onto Neturu's eyes. *Like a mid-month moon hanging over the sea*, he thought, his mind straying.

"Secure his legs," Taelon said.

A coiling fear abruptly unwound in Neturu's breast—commanding, impelling him to flight—but no time remained to avoid the impending calamity. And Doman's hands were strong and sure. Taelon laid the hot metal in the wound, and Neturu cried out and strained upward. A flaming flower took root in his flesh—bright and magnificent. Doman's hands pressed down implacably, and Neturu clenched his eyes against the focused agony of the fire. A moment later, the searing metal etched his leg again. Taelon had drawn another implement from the brazier beside the table. This time Neturu stifled his cry.

And then Taelon said, "That's it."

After long moments, Doman's hands lifted. Neturu looked up at the dark sky as people moved around the table—illuminated beings in the darkness, marked by the burning stars on their foreheads. The threatened thunderstorm had not come. He heard Taelon's voice giving soft commands to his assistants. Exhaustion dulled his thoughts, and he wanted to close his eyes and push away the pain. He looked down when gentle hands began administering to his wound. Lihana was there. The scorcher woman scooped honey paste from her little crock and gently pressed it onto his wounded flesh. The anesthetic in the concoction started its slow work. Then she loosely wrapped his leg, humming one of her soft tunes.

Neturu became conscious of tears on his cheeks, and he reached up and brushed them away, unsure of himself. His hands felt cramped from clutching the sides of the table. He thought then he must have slipped into unconsciousness for a moment. It was dark again. Doman no longer stood over him, and the pain in his leg had dulled, become distant. Lihana had finished her work. He blinked away the tears of his ordeal and looked up into the sky.

To the north, the clouds had thinned, and a few bright rearward stars of the departing night stood out in the darkness. Neturu recalled something the prophet had said to his followers just a few days before. *If we could comprehend God's fires—the everlasting burnings that await the faithful in the heavenly abode—we would begin to comprehend the unending wonder of our unrevealed natures. You are gods!* Neturu's hand strayed to the small bronze star upon his breast. He felt a warmth in his bosom; he imagined a small flame burning there.

He sat up then, careful not to move his leg. The others stood a short way off, conversing. They no longer wore the Nohak stones. Lihana saw him sit up, and she pulled Doman over to the table.

"Your leg will heal, I think." Lihana looked at him with one of her small smiles.

Doman nodded. "You managed well."

Neturu looked down at the wrapping. "I thank you." He touched the soft cloth bandage lightly. *A recycled piece of trash.* He smiled, amused. Everything Lihana had provided for him—blankets, cups, plates, utensils—was probably trash. Scavenged remains of other lives. He looked back toward the heaps of recycled trash; he saw the place with new eyes. He saw now a wholesomeness in what had been only corruption and filth. All of the past and future labors of simple people piled up and waiting.

God is merciful, he thought. "I think I'd like to stay here," he said.

Doman and Lihana both smiled.

CHAPTER TWENTY.

EARTHEN VESSELS.

Traffic roiled in the streets, and Sarana and Kaina wended their way toward the Well of Geb. Procrastinators and backsliders crowded around them, driven to urgency by the impending Sabat, and Sarana recalled the teachings of her temple mother. *Sabat will not delay, so you cannot delay. What can be done today, must be done today.*

Sarana smiled at the memory, unconcerned. She had worked hard to reclaim her servitude, and the week's labors were nearly complete. There was still the matter of her debt to Gibson. But for that, she needed to find time to go out to the river.

Kaina caught her eye and gestured toward the side of the street. A line of old women sat there, selling pickled vegetables, sour cabbage, and dried fruits. A few had small tables, but most of them simply sold their wares from baskets and small barrels. Sarana smelled the sharp tang of pickled cucumbers, and she looked longingly at the containers beside one of the women. Dark, shiny pickles lay half submerged in tangy juices. The House of Jianin did not produce pickles, and Sarana never could be satisfied with the small portions she received.

"Wait a moment while I say hello to one of my sisters," Kaina said.

Sarana nodded and followed along.

Kaina exchanged greetings with a woman who was selling bundles of herbs. The woman's aged, pudgy face was kindly, and she answered in the soft-syllabled tongue of the Kainites. Sarana listened carefully, but she understood none of it. Kaina gestured toward the street and the face of the pudgy woman grew thoughtful, her eyes narrowing. Sarana wondered what they were talking about, but she soon turned and watched as a line of carts rolled by. Dark-skinned Hruskans drove the carts, their faces stern, their eyes intent, watchful. Their animals were dusty and weary, and she wondered if they had come all the way from Noot. Images of that far-off city rose up in her mind, a mirage. Her eyes met the eyes of one of the men, and she flinched. An uncharacteristic anger smoldered in his countenance.

Kaina touched her arm. "Come, child. I'm finished here."

At the Well of Geb, they found an open place on one of the stones. Sarana closed her eyes and lifted her face to the sun. For a moment, she imagined the heat and light of the sun were flowing through her, mingling with the thrumming energy of the stone. She smiled as her thoughts flowed outward, evolving strangely.

"What are you smiling about?" Kaina asked.

Sarana looked at the old woman, her eyes still dazzled by the sun through her eyelids. "I was—" She faltered. "I just had a strange thought." She paused, trying to fit her thoughts into words. "When I felt the sunlight on my face, I thought—I imagined how the light might have . . ." She shook her head, still trying to find words. "How it might have filled up the stone. And how the stone might have become light instead of stone. Or how the light and the stone might have been made of the same thing. And I suddenly felt like . . . if I looked up into the sun long enough, I might be filled up with light and become light."

Kaina stared. "You have strange thoughts, child."

Sarana laughed. "And you have a strange tongue. What were you talking to that Kainite woman about?"

"You."

"Me?"

"I wanted to know if she had heard anything about a young woman being picked up by two men and a fancy palanquin. I thought she might be able to help us discover who took you the other day. Word of such things sometimes gets around. If anyone saw it."

"Did she hear anything?"

"No. I would have told you. But she will keep her ears and eyes open."

"You think she will hear something?"

"She might. I also told her what you told me—about the men, the house, the palanquin. She could not tell me anything, but she will ask her friends."

Sarana felt hope kindle in her bosom. She keenly felt the shame of disappointing her master, and she worried about what she had said to the man who questioned her. He had trapped her easily, and she had not even known it until Gibson told her later. If Kaina could find out anything—if they could identify the man—perhaps she could undo her folly a little. And find favor in Gibson's eyes.

"Do not hope for too much," Kaina said, reading her expression. "But my kainish sisters will do what they can."

Sarana looked down at her jars, turning her attention to something mundane, trying to cover her eagerness. "I did not know you had sisters among the Kainites."

"There are not many of us. But those that remain . . ." Kaina shrugged. "We still rely on one another."

"Do you always speak Kainish?"

"We do." Kaina shook her head; she chuckled. "It's how we carry on the fight."

"What do you mean?"

"It's an old saying with us. A meaningless jest, now. We could not withstand the armies of the bin-Yinocki. But after our nation fell, we held on to little things. Our language, our crafts." Kaina waved a hand. "My mother changed my name to Kaina. And we never called ourselves Kainites. Though that has changed."

"But you *are* Kainites."

"The Yinoi called us Kainites. But we had another name for ourselves, a kainish name. *Kainan-shahb-ahmanshah.* The people of the everlasting promise."

Sarana laughed. "It's so long."

"We shortened it to Kainan usually—the people. Which is why the bin-Yinocki took to calling us Kainites."

"So your name—Kaina—means 'the people'?"

Kaina shook her head. "Kaina means just one. And because it ends with *ah*, it means a woman of the people." She smiled.

"That's . . . strange," Sarana said. "But nice, too," she added.

"My kainish name was Kala-shansa," the old woman said softly. "Kala-shansa. It makes me think of my mother. She called me Kala. And my grandmother, too."

Sarana repeated the name in her mind. *Kala-shansa.* She liked the sound of it. "Kala-shansa," she said. "Is that right?"

Kaina nodded.

"I like it."

"Thank you, child. I always liked it, too."

"Why don't you use it now?"

"My mother gave me a new name when I was taken to the temple. She did not want me to forget my people. I feel like I would lose something if I gave up my new name, now."

"Kala-shansa," Sarana said slowly. "I never knew my mother. But she must have been a child of Yinock." She looked at her hands, their perfect whiteness. "Abasha said I was a daughter of Yinock, and that I should always remember that."

"She was right, child."

"Will you tell me some words in Kainish?" Sarana asked.

The old woman blinked, surprised. Then she smiled. "Of course," she said.

Sarana waited.

"But where should I begin?" Kaina looked around. And then she held up her jar. "Here," she said. "This is *zhiv.*"

"Z-zheev? That's a jar?"

"Yes, *zhiv.*"

"What does it mean?"

Kaina laughed. "It means jar."

Sarana was momentarily surprised. "I mean why do you call it zheev?"

"Why do you call it a jar?" Kaina said.

Sarana shrugged. "That's just what it is."

"No, child, it is *zhiv*. And my people should know because jars were given to us by the creator long ago. My grandmother told me the story of jars when I was a child."

"Jars were given to you by God?"

The old woman nodded gravely. "Yes, long ago. My people were the first to have jars." Kaina spoke with a trace of pride. And playfulness.

"How do—no they weren't," Sarana said.

"Have I never told you the story of Samo's jars?"

Sarana laughed. "You have a story for everything."

The old woman smiled and looked around the place of water. Then she said, "This is still one of my favorite places. I used to imagine, sometimes, when I came here, when I was younger, that I was free—that I was just a woman drawing water for my own household."

Sarana looked down; she ran a finger around the rim of one of her jars. She knew such thoughts. But she did not want to talk about them.

Kaina continued, "It was foolish, I suppose, to wish for that."

Sarana looked up. "Will you tell me the story about jars?"

The old woman smiled and looked over at her. She said, "Very well. It began like this. In the beginning, the world was empty, and there was only one man. And his name was Samo, because he was all alone. But soon, other things came into the world. Animals and trees and plants. So Samo took care of the animals, and he watched over all the trees and plants; and for a long time, he was happy in his solitude. But then one day he realized he was alone. He saw that many animals had companions, and he wondered why he did not. He became lonely. So he decided that he would look for a companion. And he thought it would be good to have the most beautiful thing on the earth as his companion, so he began searching for the most beautiful thing on earth."

"Did he find a woman?" Sarana asked.

"Be patient, child." Kaina smiled, adjusted her shawl, and

continued. "He searched for many days. And on the first day, he found a beautiful flower, but he had already seen many beautiful flowers, so he decided to keep looking. On the second day, he found a beautiful tree, but he had also seen many beautiful trees."

Kaina paused. "And what do you think he found on the third day?"

"I . . . don't know," Sarana said.

"Just try."

Sarana thought for a moment. "A river?"

"That's right! How did you know that?"

"I just guessed." Sarana smiled.

"He did. He found a beautiful river flowing through a valley, and its waters were cool and refreshing. But he had seen many beautiful rivers, so he decided to keep looking. And what do you think he found on the fourth day?"

Sarana shook her head. "I don't know. Maybe some sort of bird?"

"That's right again," Kaina said, smiling.

And Sarana felt a thrill of wonder. She had guessed correctly again.

"He found a bird of paradisiacal beauty. Its feathers were indigo blue, and its eyes were sky-blue. And when it soared through the air—" Kaina gestured with her hand. "It made the heart yearn for heaven. But Samo had seen many beautiful birds, so he decided to keep looking. And what do you think he found on the fifth day?"

This time Sarana closed her eyes and tried to imagine something beautiful. She immediately recalled the windblown grasses of the valley; the *plesa* trees beside the River Geblon; the humming *desarati* among the blossoms and flowers. And then she remembered something else from several days earlier. But she knew it would not be what Samo had found.

"Go ahead, child, tell me what you think."

Sarana looked up toward the sky. "Mist," she said. "In the early morning sunlight." She looked back at Kaina.

The old storyteller looked impressed. "That's right."

This time the young water woman balked. "That can't be—I just thought of it because I saw it in the orchard last week. And I thought the trees looked so beautiful, half hidden in the mist."

"But it is right." The old woman spoke solemnly. "He awoke on the morning of the fifth day, and he saw a fine mist in the early morning light. It hung in the air like a veil of thin, white silk, and it shone in the sunlight. And the world was made mysterious and beautiful." Kaina paused. "But Samo had seen many morning mists, so he decided to keep searching. Now . . . I won't ask you what he found on the next day because he searched and searched for many days, and this story would become much too long if I tried to tell you everything."

Sarana let out an impatient snort, exasperated but amused. She realized her guesses had been made a part of the story. Abasha had played similar tricks with the temple children in her charge.

"But here is an important thing to remember, child. Every day he searched, Samo found something more beautiful than the day before. For that is the nature of the world. And that is how we know that there is no end to beauty."

"And then what happened?"

"After many days of searching, Samo came to the edge of the desert, and he was too afraid to cross it. Soon it began to get dark, and he was feeling tired. So he sat down under a tree and fell asleep. And for six days he did this, trying to decide if he should cross the desert. And every day, he was too afraid to go on. But then, on the seventh day, he decided he would either cross the desert or die trying.

"And so he started across the desert. But he soon grew weary, and he fell down in the sand. He could walk no further. And he grew thirsty. But then he saw something he had never seen before. It was a woman, and she was carrying something on her head. Samo tried to speak to her, but his mouth was too dry."

"She was carrying a jar, wasn't she?"

"Yes, child. And she gave Samo water from her jar, and when he was able to speak, Samo said, 'Of all things in the world, you are surely the most beautiful. I hope you will stay with me for the rest of my days.' And the woman said, 'I won't stay with you, but I will give you this.' Then she handed the jar to Samo. And Samo said, 'what do you call this thing?' And the woman said 'I do not know what you will call it.' And Samo said, 'I will find a name for it.' So Samo finished crossing the desert, and the woman revealed to Samo the secret homeland of our people—my people."

"Did the woman and Samo get married?" Sarana asked.

"No. After she had shown Samo to his new home, she said, 'My work is finished here,' and she grew old and died. And Samo was soon very lonely again, but the land was desolate of other creatures. So one day he mixed dust and water in his jar, and it formed clay. He took the clay from the jar and fashioned a woman's body, in the image of the woman who had found him in the desert. Then he laid the clay woman in the sun to dry.

"The next morning, when he awoke, the woman made from clay was bathing in the river by his house. And Samo said, 'Now I am a maker, and I will call this vessel *zhiv*. And from that day forth, he created children—sons and daughters from clay.

"And for each of his daughters, he made a little jar. He fashioned each jar out of the same earth they were made of. And in that way, his sons and daughters were able to cross the desert and settle the fruitful land where Samo had begun his search." Kaina paused. "And that, child, is where my people come from. So you see, my people were the first to bring jars into the world. So it is not so strange to call a jar *zhiv*."

"That can't be true," Sarana said, smiling. But she liked the story.

CHAPTER TWENTY-ONE.

CONSPIRATORS.

Your house is not in order.

The words had gained clarity in Gibson's mind, and he looked across the table at Nef, who stood stone faced and grim, waiting for Gibson's response to his report.

Tomith bin Somith, the youngest son of the Great House Somith, had confessed to his father: the prophet and his followers intended to overthrow the Council. And Tomith had implicated Maran in the conspiracy.

"How certain is this information?"

Nef hesitated. "The words are certain enough. Elder Somith is putting out the word through his most trusted men."

"But it could mean many things," Gibson said. He did not want to think Maran would be so reckless—so foolish. He preferred to believe he had been falsely implicated. "Tell me exactly what was said about my son."

Nef shook his head. "Very little, in fact. Tomith named him as a follower of the prophet, along with a few others of political importance—Jasmin bith Oren, Sebrana bith Lucas. A few children of the lesser houses—Toran bin Naftalik, Ganon bin Naftalik, Anara bith Corum. And the Hruskan boy, Neturu."

"Neturu," Gibson said. "Do you have word of him?"

"No. He has vanished."

Gibson could tell it irked Nef. "There is the possibility that Tomith's story is misinformation. It could be a lure. For me or for one of the others. To draw us out—to convince us to openly condemn the prophet and quash the accusations made against our houses."

Nef silently deferred to Gibson's reasoning.

"It does little good to speculate," Gibson said finally, picking up the broken thread of his thoughts. "We cannot know Tomith's motives, or whether he's an agent of his father or others. It could all be a ruse, or it could be true." Gibson tapped his upper lip with his fist. "Of course, it doesn't have to be true to be effective. The question is whether the Council will act on this. A charge of conspiracy may be enough. Kim has been arguing for the prophet's arrest for some time. Those who do not agree with her after this may find themselves isolated."

Nef said, "Why stand with the prophet at all?"

"I don't," Gibson said. "But I cannot join with the Daniti in taking him down. Their efforts are a prelude to war."

Nef nodded. "There are factions on both sides that would like to see war. The Daniti are not solely to blame."

"True enough," Gibson said. "Though I doubt the Hruskan Fathers would be foolish enough to attack the Great City."

"What of Maran?" Nef asked.

"When he returns from Gazelem, I will confront him." Gibson glanced toward his window and turned away, troubled by any reminder of his wife's self-imposed exile in Gazelem. "But I cannot ignore any possibility. For now, I must assume Tomith's accusation is true." Gibson paused. "I hope it is not, but I want you to watch Maran carefully. If he's been visiting the prophet or his followers in secret, your men can surely follow him."

"Surely, my Lord."

"Do whatever is necessary."

Nef nodded slowly.

"One more thing," Gibson said. "After today, Urudu will be free of his servitude, but he will remain in my employ. He has purchased his freedom. Or he will within the hour. I am meeting with him shortly."

Nef's face became contemplative; his lower lip pushing outward. He said, "Will it be public knowledge? Need it be?"

"Not immediately. But it must be recorded at the temple to be valid."

Nef nodded.

"And I have to give the eleemosynary tenth to the priests. I can't retain that."

"No, of course," Nef said. "I ask only because Hruskans are already feeling the effects of the Council's edict. If there is war in Hrusk, it will be difficult for any Hruskan to remain in the city. Maybe impossible. But as your bonded servant—." Nef shrugged; he did not finish the sentence.

Gibson considered Nef's words. "You may be right. He will have to make that choice. But I will warn him. Thank you."

Nef left.

Alone, Gibson walked to his window and looked out toward Gazelem. He stood there for several minutes, and his mind turned from one thing to another, passing from each without conclusion. Kim bith Dan. The fallen Wayfarer. The threat against his house. The prophet. His wife. His son. The strands of his indeterminate thoughts overlapped and turned upon themselves. He did not know how to quell the forces threatening to break apart his house. After several moments he chided himself. *I still have work to do*, he thought.

Urudu and his brother stood when Gibson entered the room. Telasa had laid out cups, a tall pitcher of water, a bowl of fruit. Neither man had eaten the offered food, but Reb was eyeing the *kivich*.

"I'm glad to see you, my friend."

"Lord Jianin."

"You and your brother are welcome here."

"I thank you, my Lord."

Gibson gestured toward their seats, urging them to sit back down.

"Please," he said, turning a hand toward the bowl. "The *kivich* are at their best." He picked up the pitcher and poured water into the cups.

Reb picked up his cup and took a sip.

Urudu held his cup but did not drink. "I have the price you requested of me," he said. "As you know, I cannot pay the full amount." Urudu took a bag from inside his robes and placed it on the table. "It falls well short of the bond." Urudu looked up at his master. "I am in your hands."

"It is enough," Gibson said. "As I said before." He opened the bag and poured the coins out. They jingled onto the tabletop. For a servant, they represented an enormous sum. *The price of a man's freedom*, Gibson thought. *And not enough by the Lines*. He picked up a single-*tok* coin and thought back to his meeting with Sarana. Her trip to the river, her lost jars, her debt. She would never have the means to buy her freedom; she would have to wait for her jubilee.

"You have saved all of this?" Gibson asked.

"Every *tok*. It is all I have."

Gibson considered the pile of coins. Compared to his own fortune, Urudu's savings were insignificant. And yet, the coins on the table seemed far more significant than any amount of money Gibson had ever seen. He tossed the coin back. He glanced at Reb. The keeper of his stables in Gazelem merely watched. There were words to say; the Lines of the Law required a revocation of the bond.

"Before I accept this, you should think about the possible consequences," Gibson said.

"My Lord?"

"If there is war." Gibson paused. "If there is war, it may not be safe for you in the Great City. Not for any free Hruskan."

"I have considered that. Reb and I talked about it last night." Urudu glanced at his brother. "But I think even servants like me will not be safe if there is war. And if there is not, so much the better. Either way, you will have my services."

Gibson felt the warmth of Urudu's loyalty. Familiar, expected, humbling. He nodded. "Then there is no reason to delay. By the Lines, the bond is revoked." He raked through the pile of coins and drew out ten coins. One hundred *toki*. He put the coins into a small pouch and held it out to Urudu. The little bag seemed pitifully small. "By the Lines, a tenth part is returned to the faithful servant. And by the Lines, a tenth part will also be returned to God for the nurturing of the hungry and naked. I will deliver the *talah* to the temple, where it will be recorded."

"Thank you, my Lord." Urudu took the small pouch and tucked it inside his robe. In Urudu's hands, Gibson thought the bag looked even smaller. But the joy in his former servant's face was evident.

"I cannot help but think the Lines have dealt unjustly with you," Gibson said.

Urudu did not respond immediately. Then he said, "The Lines are as they are, my Lord. We follow them as we may." Urudu's eyes dropped briefly, but then he looked up. "But my faithfulness was not bought with coin or tradition."

Gibson nodded, finding that he could not answer.

"We thank you," Reb said into the silence.

Gibson looked at Urudu's brother. Though edged with Hruskan sharpness, the shape of Reb's face was rounder, softer. The lineage of Yinock was clearly visible in his features and in his light brown skin. He was smaller than his brother, and his dark eyes were mellower.

"You puzzle me, Reb." Gibson took a miniature orange from the bowl and began to peel it. "Urudu told me you've joined the so-called prophet down at the river. I'd like to ask you some questions." Gibson divided the orange into slices.

"I thought you might. Urudu told me he was going to tell you of my baptism."

"You don't fear the loss of your employment?"

Reb shrugged. "That is a risk I accepted from the beginning."

"But you hoped I would not discover it."

"At first. But after I told Urudu . . . I knew he would tell you."

Gibson laughed, a little amused by Reb's fearlessness and gratified by Reb's foreknowledge of Urudu's loyalty. "Your candor surprises me," he said.

"I guess we are on the same feet," Reb said. "I had thought that the elders of the city had forgotten the ways of redemption—so it is taught by our prophet. But you . . . you are a savior upon the shores of promise, you are *esana* to my brother, and you have formed him out of new clay."

Gibson held up a warding hand, shocked. "What do you mean by that?"

Reb blinked and took a breath. "Forgive me, Elder Jianin. I know it sounds strange to you, but I don't mean any disrespect to God. I only mean that you are merciful. I meant that you have extended the hand of mercy to my brother and become, in a small way, more like Esana. When we do his work, we are like smaller versions of Him. When my brother told me of your promise to free him, I could not help thinking you are a great man. But I wavered. I could not believe it was true. But now I have seen the operation of redemption with my own eyes."

"I see." Gibson felt a frown upon his lips. The taste of heresy lingered. *It's no wonder the Daniti abhor you.*

"We need more leaders like you," Reb said.

Gibson shook his head. "I'm only a merchant."

"You're an Elder of the Council," Reb said.

Gibson raised his voice slightly. "Do you think I can stand against the will of the Council? Do you think I would?"

Reb's face quickly stilled. But Gibson had sensed an affirmation on his lips.

"There is a dearth of good men and women in the Council," Reb said. "But you have not lost the knowledge of redemption."

"Your prophet says otherwise," Gibson said. "I do not think he has exempted any of us from his condemnation."

"He speaks generally," Reb said. "But he makes allowances for repentance. And he invites all to repent."

Gibson shook his head, amused. But his amusement died quickly. "Your dedication is admirable, Reb, but the prophet has drawn the ire of the Council. I fear for him. And his followers."

"God's messengers always draw the ire of the world," Reb said.

The glib answer was irritating. "You have yet to see what war will bring. When war breaks out in Hrusk, there will be no forbearance for heretics." Gibson paused and allowed his thoughts to still. "If there is war, you will all be forced to recant, or you will be put to death. It won't matter that the war is distant, or easily won. It will give the priests and elders a reason to cleanse the city. Surely you know this from the Lines."

Reb spoke slowly. "This has been . . . discussed among us. But surely the Council would not take such action these days."

Gibson looked at Urudu. He looked back at Reb. "You need to realize how wrong you are. I can tell you how the Daniti will act if they get the support they need in the Council. If there is war, they will not allow any division in the city. They will demand unity. They will destroy your so-called prophet and they will put an end to his followers."

"The prophet has warned us that troubled times approach."

Another glib answer. Gibson rubbed his eyes with his thumb and forefinger, impatient and irritated; he said, "It's more than troubled times, Reb. Heretics who do not renounce will be killed. You need to tell the others what awaits them if they persist in following the prophet."

"I will," Reb said. "Coming from you, the warning will not be taken lightly."

For a moment none of them said anything.

"Is there a conspiracy to overthrow the Council?" Gibson asked.

Reb flinched, startled. "Of course not. We seek nothing more than to worship God and follow Esana."

"Nothing of greater consequence?"

"There is nothing of greater consequence," Reb said.

Gibson laughed once, a quick exhalation. This time the glib answer really was amusing. "Of course. You are quite right."

Telasa stepped into the room. "Lord Jianin," she said. "Maran has returned from Gazelem."

The whole house seemed to have grown quiet. Gibson looked at his son and felt his anger dull. He was a little surprised.

But Maran's frank admissions had removed the keen edge of his wrath. Maran had been baptized because he believed Esana had sent the prophet to renew the faith of the bin-Yinocki. He and the on-Dam's son had been baptized on the same day. There was no conspiracy to overthrow the Council; he did not seek power. He simply believed the prophet was God's messenger. Or so he said.

"You should have told me you were baptized, son."

"I knew I would have to. But I didn't have Neturu's courage."

"Or the same loyalty to your father." Gibson spoke with only a little heat, and he relented quickly. "Though it did him little good in the end."

Maran looked down. "We've been hoping Neturu might have escaped—that he's hiding somewhere."

Gibson shook his head. "My men have been looking for word of him, but they haven't heard anything. The boy's blood-smeared cloak was delivered to the on-Dam—the same day he was ostracized. A clear message."

"But it doesn't mean he's dead. Even if it was his blood. We heard that, too."

"True. But it does not bode well for him either."

Maran looked up. "So what do we do now?"

"You've put me in a difficult situation, son. No one in the Council will speak for your prophet. No one will stand against the Daniti. I will not abandon you, but I don't know how to protect you. I stand alone in the Council, or nearly alone. There are a few who believe the prophet should not be persecuted, but no one will speak for him now—not with war looming."

"But it sounds like you would support him."

"No. Do not misunderstand. I am only convinced this persecution will end in bloodshed, and I wish to avoid that. But siding with the prophet has become too dangerous. Kim wants to extend her influence over the city, and she will use the prophet if she can. With troubles increasing in the South, she knows she can push for stronger control in the city. It has already begun. The inner vessel must be clean."

Maran nodded; he understood.

"I went to see your prophet," Gibson said. "I've been watching him for some time, and I thought I needed to see him for myself."

"Did you listen to him?" Maran's eyes showed hope.

"Yes, and now I know why the Daniti are able to use him. He seemed ready to incite any sort of rebellion. He has no respect for the priests and the elders. He mocks them openly and condemns them. And he teaches an unknown Esana."

"He doesn't teach an unknown Esana," Maran said.

"I won't argue that with you." Gibson held up a hand. "Regardless of what you believe—what you say he teaches—it is a matter of perception."

"Didn't you feel the truth of his teachings?"

"No." Gibson shook his head. "I—son, I have heard such men before. They come at different times and seasons, but they are all the same in the end. I'll admit, this prophet speaks strange things, new things—even some compelling things. But he is like any number of self-proclaimed prophets who have come before him. He draws the people away from the faith and traditions of Yinock."

"He teaches the words of Yinock. He is not—"

"I will not argue it, Maran. I have heard him teach, and I understand what you are trying to tell me. I can even understand why people want to follow him. He shows courage. He inspires people, and he offers them something new. But new is not necessarily true." Gibson paused. "And you have to understand: charges will be brought against him now that Tomith has revealed the conspiracy."

"There is no conspiracy."

"Perception, son. It doesn't have to be true," Gibson said. "Sometimes the conspiracy is in the eye of the beholder. And if someone wants to see evil, he will. The very fact that so many of you joined—that you hoped to convince members of the Council to accept his teachings—could be viewed as a conspiracy. Your prophet will be convicted on the strength of such evidence. And with war threatening in Hrusk—and there will be war, I fear—the Daniti will succeed in having him executed." Gibson rubbed his face; he felt weary. "And then his followers will have to make a choice. Anyone who won't renounce his teachings will probably suffer the same punishment."

"That's just further proof," Maran said. "The Council has lost its bearings. You only have to look at what's happening right now to see that it has lost its way. The prophet is right in that. You must see that."

"I would not go so far. But I agree that it needs to alter its course."

"Then we need to alter its course."

"So it's come to that," Gibson said, smiling slightly. "Now you want me to join your conspiracy."

Maran let that jest flutter to the ground.

"You'd better start by telling me everything you know about the prophet." Gibson laughed resignedly. "At least then I might learn what charges the Council will bring against you. Tell me what you know."

Later that night, Gibson made his way through the dark vineyard and climbed the ladder of the old watchtower. The moon had not yet risen. His eyes found the lights of Gazelem in the distance, and for a moment, his thoughts turned to his wife. But then he looked up at the stars and let his thoughts wander. *Worlds without end.* Surely there were worlds without end. The Lines said as much. But Gibson had never considered what their purpose might be. He wondered why not.

Why did God fill the heavens with worlds?

His eyes found the Leaf, and he looked at the three bright stars of the stem. The center star was the brightest.

Many worlds. And Esana will be born on one of them. Or so said the prophet. Gibson let his eyes move across the sky. A few arcane Lines referred to the stars as governing bodies, and the prophet seemed to have seized upon them. *These are the governing ones. These are the governing bodies in heaven; and the name of the greatest among them is Kolob, because it is near unto me.*

A sound across the vineyard drew his attention. He saw a lamp moving through the darkness. Telasa walked in the glow of its small flame. Nef came behind her. When they reached the wall, Telasa stopped, and Nef came on alone. Gibson heard Nef enter the room below. He turned and put his hands on the window sill.

Nef climbed up the ladder and stepped into the watch room. "There is war in Hrusk," he said.

Chapter Twenty-two.
Sabat.

That night Gibson dreamed. But when he awoke in the morning, he could recall only incomplete images and sequences. Maran. Urudu. An old woman. Ruined buildings. He swung out of bed. The night-washed stones chilled his feet. Outside, birds had begun to sing.

Today is Sabat, he remembered. And abruptly the world changed. He knelt and recited the Ten Lines. He reflected upon the events of the past few days, but the problems of the Great City receded. Maran's embroilment in the affairs of the prophet grew distant, and he felt peace. It was a temporary reprieve, he knew, but the influence of Sabat was far reaching. The history of the bin-Yinocki flowed in six-day bursts.

He walked to his window and looked out over the city. The line between light and shadow dipped and staggered across the uneven tops of the buildings. His eyes were drawn to the temple complex, and he thought that today, at least, he would find peace within its walls. He turned his eyes toward Gazelem. The white buildings of the jewel city shone in the morning light. *Perhaps my wife looks toward the Great City.*

But she had been gone too long to believe that.

I was a fool to even hope she might return. And now—. Gibson cut off the pessimistic thought. Any designs she might have had for Maran, and by extension herself, could never be realized now. And so her return was even less likely. Her plan of forging an alliance between the merchant House of Jianin with the Great House of Somith could never be salvaged, even if Gibson wanted to bless a union between Maran and Tiana bith Somith. Gibson clenched his jaw. He could not deny that the union between their houses would have greatly increased the prominence of his house.

But now there is war in Hrusk, and Maran has been implicated in a conspiracy.

Gibson turned from the window and began to pace slowly. War in Hrusk. Nef's report had been certain. He brushed away thoughts of Maran's prospects. Maran's chance of a high place in the Council, meager though it might have been, was probably lost. He might even have maneuvered Maran to a position of strength and wealth, despite the declined marriage with Somith, but those days were past. *Your house is not in order.*

He stopped his pacing. The peace of Sabat had fled at the thought of war. But he thought he knew what he had to do. Maran had to leave the city before the Council moved against the prophet. Perhaps as far as Shal-Gashun. Too many events had come together at once. Too many for a single man to contain or turn aside.

Even if Maran escaped the reach of the Council, the House of Jianin would remain on the outskirts of power for a long, long time. Gibson could not precisely calculate the price of Maran's affiliation with the prophet, but generations of labor would be lost.

He found himself at the window again, staring at Gazelem. But as he looked over the empty, breezy plains, he was again calmed by the stillness of Sabat. No caravans moved on the road, and no people roved from place to place. No dust rose above the snaking length of the road south. Sabat had stilled the waters of commerce, and only God's creation moved. It was a hallowing experience to look upon the face of the world and see only the designs of God.

The house emptied as the servants left for worship. Gibson waited until they were all gone, and then he went downstairs.

In the common room, he noticed the neatly-stacked bowls and carefully stowed jars. He took a full jar from the hearth and poured the proper measure into the foot basin by the door. He carefully washed his feet. *On the day of Sabat, each will complete his own labors.* A small loaf of bread lay on the table, a knife and a small jar of honey beside it. Gibson cut three slices for himself. He dripped honey on it and ate slowly. It was fine wheat bread, ground, kneaded, formed, and baked in his own house. Made on the day before Sabat. He had not made it with his own hands, but it felt like cake in his mouth.

A few minutes passed. *Sabat.* Gibson let the word fill his mind.

A slash of sunlight cut through the gloom of the sanctuary, illuminating a swath of golden, floating motes. Sarana looked over her shoulder, and saw a man silhouetted against the glowing daylight. The door closed abruptly, but the imprint of the shaft of light lingered in her eyes, blinding her. Then the worshipers sat up, the prayer of reconciliation freshly fallen from their lips. Softly spoken words, shuffling, and the clearing of throats were the only sounds. Sarana turned back toward the altar, embarrassed by her inattention. Had she been praying, she might not have been distracted by the interrupting light.

A soft hymn broke the near silence, and Sarana joined her voice to the throng of worshipers. The tune was sorrowful and repetitive, the words like husky leaves on the wind. They sang of Yinock's departed city and the children who sought the farseer in vain. But there was the ever-present promise of Yinock's return, of the city built anew.

When the singing stopped, a man and a woman went forward to the law box at the altar. Together they lifted the lid and reached inside. The Lines of the Law lay within the box. Many worshipers had used the scroll, and its edges were worn. Its original beauty had dimmed.

Sarana watched as they turned the upper scroll bar. Ancient lines of print emerged from the dark curl of the scroll. The man and the woman placed the scroll on the altar and knelt.

The priest read: "And Jeru said: 'In those days of tribulation and discord, the multitudes of the chosen will be hungry and wasted like dry leaves. And some will say there is bread in a far country, but the wise will not listen. Then there will be empty cities on the earth, for God will not suffer his people to prosper in wickedness. And those who follow after fools will be cast down.' Es-prida." The priest stepped back from the altar, and said, "And so we see the folly of straying after fools who make empty promises of sustenance that we cannot see. God has given us what we need if we will but follow his laws. But we cannot prosper in wickedness." The priest continued on for several minutes, recounting the story of Jeru, describing the fate of the unrighteous.

The priest finally finished.

"Es-prida," Sarana said; the multitude spoke with her.

More prayers rose to heaven, and another hymn filled the church. The sound of joyful music was sweet, and Sarana listened to the melody thankfully, remembering the bright days of her childhood. The great doors opened and closed as the congregation sang the final hymn; formal worship had ended, and people came and went as they pleased, some leaving for home and others arriving for the next reading of the Lines. The servants of the House of Jianin always attended the earliest service.

When the hymn ended, Kaina stood up slowly and motioned toward the door. "Come, child. Let's walk a bit."

Sarana stood. The great doors stood open: light and people passed through the opening. *Like leaves in a stream of light*, she thought. The image pleased her.

Outside, the streets of the Great City were subdued. People walked slowly, and their quiet voices combined and filled the streets with a strangely comforting muttering. Beggars sat at busy intersections, but they pleaded for charity with brevity, softly spoken. Their efforts garnered a few coins, and the murmuring shroud of Sabat-hushed voices was occasionally broken by the tink of a tenth-*tok* in a beggar's cup.

"I wish I could read the great scroll," Sarana said.

"Did you learn another set of letters last night?"

"Yes. He says I'm doing well."

"In time, you'll be able to read anything you want."

"But not the great scroll."

"Ah. But our master has his own copy of the Lines. Perhaps he would let you read from that."

They walked quietly back to the house, talking softly. They did not hurry. When they arrived home, some of the other servants were gathering in the yard, preparing for the morning meal. Some sat beneath the *hresta* tree. Sarana saw Pelem among them. He smiled at her and waved. Sarana's spirits lifted a bit higher. She hurried inside to help the others bring out the food.

Gibson knelt on the cool marble floor, refusing himself the luxury of a prayer pillow. He touched his head to the floor and prayed for the safety of his people. Women and men of the great houses knelt in rows all around him. Sabat held them in sway. But slowly, one by one, they rose up from their prayers. Gibson delayed. He waited until only a few remained on their knees. Then he sat up.

Large windows stood open to the sunlight. Sheer white curtains shifted slightly in the breeze. The worshipers sat around the room in a wide semi-circle around the law box and the altar.

Gibson watched as two young acolytes slowly approached the altar. They ran their hands over the gilded edges of the law box and opened it reverently. They had been trained for this service, and they performed their work flawlessly. They lifted the Lines of the Law from the box. Each reading was transcribed onto its own sheet, with accompanying priestly commentary.

The priest spoke: "And Jeru said: 'In those days of tribulation and broken houses, the multitudes of the chosen will be hungry and wasted like dry leaves. And some will say there is bread in a far country, and the wise will know the truth, for they shall be taught of God. Then there will be empty cities on the earth, for God will not suffer his people to prosper in wickedness. And those who follow after fools will be cast down.' Es-prida."

"Es-prida," the worshipers said.

The priest continued. "At the time of Jeru, the great houses of the bin-Yinocki had become fragmented. No single ruler had presided over the children of Yinock for several years, and there was no governing council. And the nine-year famine was at its peak, with approximately four years remaining—though they did not know that then. Jeru's words were a pronouncement of contemporaneous woe and should not be viewed as prophecy. But we can, of course, learn from what he said. There are still 'fools' who would lead our people astray, promising them hidden treasures they cannot see, and we must guard against such things. There is no bread in a far-off land; there is no hidden bread to be 'taken' by those who will seek it. This city is the repository of his Revelation; God will not use the wicked instrumentalities of this world—unheralded messengers and vagabonds—to preserve the children of Yinock."

Gibson listened with practiced detachment. Jeru's words and a veiled tirade against the prophet were of little import. He could read the Lines on his own, and he already knew what the priests thought of the prophet. There were other things to hear and see at worship, and he had noticed a subtle, silent overlay of restraint—something more than the indifference that usually overlay the Council at times of worship. The events of the week simmered beneath the calm of Sabat.

Eventually, the priest finished his speaking, closing with the traditional words of supplication. Gibson and the rest of them responded in kind. The acolytes returned the Lines to the law box and left. Gibson remembered his days as a trainee in the priesthood. Like all children of the great houses, he had been versed in the initiatory mysteries of priestly conduct. He had attained acolyte status—the highest of the lower order—and upon his ordination to the higher order of the holy priesthood, his father had withdrawn him from further priestly education. After that he had gone to Shal-Gashun. He had spent five years there and in Noot, and on the roads that lay between them.

Maran was on the cusp of completing his acolyte training.

Another acolyte went forward and offered up the petition of the Council. Maran had stood in that spot in recent weeks, probably within days of joining himself to the prophet in baptism. The thought was disquieting.

The prayer ended, and Gibson felt the familiar guilt of having ignored the petition. The congregation began to sing, but Gibson's mind continued down other paths. He realized Maran could be stripped of his priesthood. Until that moment, Gibson had feared only the loss of place and prestige. But if the Council took action against the prophet and his followers, Maran could not hope to enter the higher order of the priesthood.

As the hymn concluded, members of the congregation stood and extended the hand of fellowship to one another. It was a tradition of the Council. Gibson felt a hand on his shoulder, and he heard his name; he turned.

Tendar bin Amin held out his hand.

"Tendar," Gibson said. They clasped hands.

"I have been meaning to speak with you, Gibson. There is a matter of some importance between us."

"Oh?"

"Sabat, my brother. May I come to your house during the week? Perhaps in the next day or two."

"Of course. My house is open to all."

"Yes, I have noticed." Tendar's face revealed nothing. "But you might want to reconsider the wisdom of that course."

Gibson tensed. "I would not close my door to you," he said.

"We shall meet later, then." Tendar smiled. "Sabat, my brother."

"Sabat," Gibson said.

Tendar walked away, extending his hand and greeting others. Gibson watched him go. Tendar consorted openly with the Daniti, but he remained quietly aloof from most, secure within his own sphere of power. Tendar's father had unsuccessfully courted Kim bith Dan at one time, and reportedly she had spurned him. But even so, among the many houses, Kim had chosen the House of Amin as her ally. *Curious*, Gibson thought, and not for the first time.

He glanced around the room. A few people were leaving, but most were content to linger a bit longer. Events in the Great City had precipitated a general inclination to linger where there might be information. Even on Sabat. Gibson approached a small group of three elders—Ableth bin Somith, Elana bith Somith, and Rebran bin Telan.

Elana extended the hand of fellowship. "Gibson," she said.

"Sabat, Elana."

"We were talking about this man who calls himself a prophet."

Gibson smiled slightly. "And what do you think?"

"His treatment of the priests and this Council is reprehensible. He will break down the confidence of the people."

"He might," Gibson said. "Or he might simply pass out of favor, in time. People can be fickle. He could dwindle to insignificance."

"I doubt that," Ableth said.

Gibson shrugged. "There have been others who did."

"He is performing baptisms," Ableth said. "He is building a rival church. He teaches a wild brand of the gospel, and hundreds—actually thousands—follow him. He represents himself as some kind of a deliverer." Ableth toyed with a gold ring on his left hand.

"I have heard he teaches Esana," Gibson said.

"An unknowable Esana," Ableth said.

"I have not heard that," Gibson said.

"Not in those terms," Rebran said. "He says Esana will not live among the bin-Yinocki. That Esana will live on a distant world."

"He says we have been misled by the Lines," Ableth said.

"A man's belief is his own," Gibson said.

A look passed between Ableth and Elana.

"We need not fear him," Gibson said.

"We don't fear him," Ableth said. "But he has broken the law, and it is our duty to stop him. We must act as we have been entrusted by the Lines. It is our sacred duty. He draws away the people, and it is our duty to bring them back to the teachings of Yinock."

"Has he done more than express his beliefs?" Gibson looked around the group.

"Much more, if some accounts are to be believed," Elana said. "The Daniti have caught him in some sort of mischief. They claim some kind of conspiracy is underway."

"I have heard the same," Rebran said.

"They call it a conspiracy," Gibson said. "But is there cause to go after him as the Daniti intend?" Even as he spoke, he felt the weakness of his stance. Maran had compromised his neutrality. And these people knew it.

"They attempted to convert my own son," Ableth said, grave. "And the man has compelled thousands more to his cause. As you know."

Gibson shook his head. "But how many of them actually believe? How many of them even know what they have done? They will not endure. People cannot believe in an unfulfillable myth for long." Gibson looked at each of their faces. "Will they have faith in a being who will live out his life on some distant world?"

"He teaches a disfigured form of Esana," Ableth said.

"So much so that it cannot endure," Gibson said. "He has taken the promise of Esana and made it even more remote. He will stretch their faith to the breaking point with his stories of an otherworldly Esana." Gibson paused. "And I think he will come to naught."

"Do you?" Tendar bin Amin had come up behind Gibson and joined the group. Gibson turned to face him.

"I do," Gibson said.

"Some are not so confident," Tendar said.

"What do you think the Council should do?" Ableth asked, looking at Gibson.

"Sabat," Rebran said.

Gibson faced the first elder, contemplating the undisguised political question; Ableth returned his gaze levelly.

"Sabat," Tendar said, when Gibson did not respond. "The prophet, as he is called, is perhaps too closely embroiled in the political affairs of the Council to discuss him, or his teachings, on the day of reconciliation."

"Yes," Ableth said. "But what stand is appropriate? In terms of our moral responsibilities."

"I think the Council should ignore him," Gibson said.

"I think you underestimate his power over the people," Ableth said. "He has drawn thousands away from the teachings of Esana."

"That is not technically correct," Tendar said. "He has drawn thousands away from what you say are the teachings of Esana." Tendar's tone was mild.

"Not what I say," Ableth said. "What the Lines say, what the priests say."

"Perhaps that is true," Gibson said. "I have watched him, too—from afar. And I've thought he might be trying to capitalize on the current turmoil in the city. But I don't think he represents any real danger to the church. He preaches the word as he understands it." Gibson paused, calculating; the others did not interrupt. "The Council has no need to fight this man. If he is not of God, then he will come to naught; but if he is of God, then we would do better not to fight against him."

Tendar bin Amin rubbed his chin softly, thoughtfully. Ableth and Elana shared another glance. Rebran looked embarrassed.

"Hmm," Tendar said finally. "I think you have stated an untenable position, brother. No, we cannot simply ignore him. We cannot—we dare not—take the teachings of Esana so lightly. And we cannot cast off the misguided souls of our people so nonchalantly. We have a sacred duty to follow the words of Esana, and we have a sacred duty to lead this people in the paths of righteousness. If we do not, then their sins are upon our heads."

"Yes," Ableth said.

Tendar continued: "To ignore this man is to ignore the duties put upon us by the Lines. To take the position you have advocated is to take no position at all. We should be compelled to take the position that is right."

Gibson had to agree; he nodded. "Perhaps you are right."

"The Council should consider its course of action soon," Ableth said.

"Sabat," Tendar said, then. "Let's not speak further about it. Not today."

"Sabat," Gibson said.

The others repeated the admonition, but Gibson felt weary. The day was broken, and any semblance of reconciliation had fled. *So much for Sabat.* He turned to leave, wary of further conversation. As he walked slowly toward the door, he extended the hand of fellowship to those he passed. A few spoke polite words; no one else mentioned the prophet. Gibson stopped at the doorway and looked back. Tendar was still talking to Elana and Ableth; Rebran had moved away to another group.

Gibson's gaze fell back onto Tendar. The usually silent man had rarely spoken to him, and nothing beyond brief pleasantries.

Perhaps he seeks business. But he knew it was not so.

In the vineyard, the newly-ripe *rebboth* had not been harvested. The plants drooped beneath the weight of the unharvested seeds. Sarana walked slowly down one of the rows, pensive. After the midday meal, her thoughts had turned inward as she contemplated her actions in the days leading up to Sabat. She could not recall a time when she had failed in so many ways.

And yet, she felt little remorse. Disobedience had born unexpected fruits.

She let her fingers drift over the tops of the vines. The leaves bobbed and fluttered beneath her touch.

As a girl, she had once picked a seed on Sabat.

That day, against the remembered admonitions of her temple mother, a perverse desire to defy God had taken root in her thoughts, and she had given in. Alone in the vineyard, unseen by anyone, she had defied the prohibition against work and picked a seed. But her little victory over God had been bitter in the end. Ashamed, she had run to the back of the vineyard and thrown the little fruit over the wall. Not only had she labored on Sabat, she had wasted a portion of her master's substance. Promises and vows—never to do it again—had accompanied her prayers for forgiveness.

But she had accumulated new sins since then, and worse.

From inside her robe she pulled out the golden trinket she had stolen. It hung from a string tied around her neck. She sat down between the rows and held it up. It twisted slowly on the string and shone in the sunlight. The precise edges and smooth curves of the metal bespoke a perfection born of ancient days.

A tremble passed through her as she contemplated the antiquity of the thing in her hand. A relic of the Great City. She imagined a woman of the ancient days holding it in her hands, laughing. A smile curved Sarana's lips, but then she frowned. It must have had some purpose, but she could divine no use for it—unless it was jewelry. It fit easily in the palm of her hand. There had been several more in the drawer, but she was not sure if they had all been the same.

I should show it to Gibson. A recurring thought.

He might know what it was, or where it came from. But she dared not reveal her crime to him. Confessing the loss of her jars had been humiliating and terrifying. It seemed even worse to tell him she had stolen something from an elder of the city.

But he kidnapped me, she thought. *And Gibson said he was trying to trap me.* The crimes of the reclusive elder had grown in her mind. *He tried to trap me.*

But she had not known that then, when she stole it. She had acted impulsively, her justifications only half formed. It had been wrong to take it. And dangerous. And she could have been caught. She recriminated herself again, berating herself with a question: *What if he had seen me?* But the servant had not said anything. He must not have seen.

Her conscience flinched, and she looked around suddenly, certain someone must have come into the vineyard behind her and seen her ill-gotten treasure. But she was still alone. The *rebboth* leaves nodded lazily, and the stillness of Sabat hung over the orderly rows. No one had seen her or the proof of her crime. She tucked the stolen artifact back inside her clothing.

A quiet certainty filled her mind. She would keep it, and she would keep it secret. No one would ever know. She would never tell anyone.

But God knows.

Abasha spoke softly in her memories.

No sin—no thought or deed—can be concealed from the glass eyes of God.

Gently, firmly, her temple mother's words returned to her. Abasha had taught her that simple truth: silence would never resolve sin. She had warned her about the gated land and the fate of unrepentant sinners.

But if you avoid sin in the beginning, you will never have anything to hide.

Sarana looked down at the ground. A little pool of anger swallowed up Abasha's words. *No one can be perfect*, she thought. But the silent retort sounded childish. Her temple mother had not demanded perfection. *The sin is often less important than our actions afterward.* That was what Gibson had said. Sarana ran the tip of her finger through the dirt and drew the letter *ah*. The other letters followed, and for a moment, she slowly drew the letters over and over, her thoughts disjointed. Then she stopped. She drew her knees up to her chest and rested her chin on top of them.

"In submission is exaltation," she said softly, finally.

But the whispered invocation did little to quell her thoughts. She lacked Abasha's quiet authority, and her words were lacking and weak. Her temple mother's deliberate voice, made raspy with age, had carried an irresistible power. When the old woman had spoken, the undeniable truth of her words was evident.

Beside her, just below the level of her eyes, a branch hung heavy with *rebboth* seeds. She raised up the drooping branch with her finger. Some of the seeds were on the edge of ruination, ready to spoil. She took hold of one of them. Ripe, it parted easily from its place with a quiet snap. No resistance. The branch swayed beneath the remaining seeds, and she was left holding the one seed between her fingertips.

Anguish tied a knot in her breast. She had broken Sabat. Just like she had as a child. Remorse blossomed then, and it was bitter.

I did not mean to do it.

And, yet, she had. She had known what might happen when she took hold of the seed. She had plucked innumerable seeds in the past; she knew how easily a ripe seed would part from its branch. She had no excuse. Tears formed in her eyes. She clenched her fist, and the prickly husk bit into her palm. A scarlet drop of juice escaped between her fingers and seeped across her knuckle.

When she emerged from the vineyard, she heard soft laughter

from beneath the *hresta*. For a moment she felt their laughter as if it had been directed at her. But it was just Ana laughing at something one of the others had said. She passed by them with her hand clenched.

ʹ The hearth room was empty, as she had hoped, and she dipped her hand into the washbasin. Most of the juice rinsed off, but a pale, scarlet stain remained. She scrubbed mercilessly with the pumice, excoriating her palm and fingers. Pain relieved her anguish, but it did not last. The reparative cycles of her blood quickly restored her damaged flesh. And for once, the perfect whiteness of her hands did not fill her spirit with secret pride. Those white hands hid perdition.

CHAPTER TWENTY-THREE.
STOLEN WATERS.

Sabat passed away, and like dry bones quickening with the hot breath of God, the Great City roused in the pale glimmering of the coming morning.

Sarana set off as soon as the house gates opened, anxious to finish her duties at the well. She hoped to reach the river early. But as she neared the place of water, congested streets slowed her progress. A little further, and a loitering mass of people filled the street. Some people still moved through the crowds in slow-moving rivulets, but a festive air hung over the streets as people stood talking and laughing in small groups.

And then she heard what some of the people were saying. The prophet had come to the Well of Geb.

Sarana hurried onward, but she soon found it difficult to continue. The street grew more crowded. At the outskirts of the place of water, the people had gathered to spectate and listen. Sarana looked doubtfully at her jars. She would not be able to draw water, and they made it difficult to move forward. For a moment she stood on her toes, trying to see over the multitude. Then she turned and retreated. Once free of the throng she rushed home as fast as she could.

"Kaina!" She found the old woman in the hearth room.

"The old woman looked up, smiling. "I hear you. What is it child? You haven't finished at the well, surely."

"The prophet. He's come to the well. He's there right now."

Kaina's eyebrows raised up. "He's there? He's at the well?"

"I didn't see him, but everyone was talking about it, and the streets were filled with people. I couldn't get through them. Not with my jars."

"Well, child, that . . . is interesting news."

"I'm going back. After I put my jars away."

Telasa walked into the room. Her mouth tightened. "What are you doing?"

Sarana hesitated. Then she said, "I am about our master's business."

"But you haven't drawn any water."

"I couldn't." The small triumph curled Sarana's lips.

But Telasa pressed on. "What do you mean? What's going on?" She turned to Kaina, but the older woman merely smiled.

"It's impossible right now," Sarana said. And the tale poured out of her.

Telasa listened, incredulous and angry. "He's gone too far," she said. "We need water. The house needs water."

Kaina held up a placating hand. "He won't be allowed to stay. Sarana can draw water later in the day. After he's gone."

"I'll finish in the evening," Sarana said.

Telasa folded her arms and looked at Sarana sternly. "The week has just begun, Sarana. The house still needs water—whether he is there or not."

Sarana tasted defiance, and she could not quell it. "I will find time," she said.

"So you will," Telasa said. Then she looked around the room, mentally checking the order of things. "I will inform our master." Telasa left.

"Well," Kaina said, thoughtful. "This has been an unexpected turn. But if you are going back, you should probably go now. She might try to find some way to keep you here."

Sarana hurried to follow the old woman's advice.

At the place of water, the great stones had been overrun, but

Sarana could see the prophet standing near the steps leading down to the place of water. At first she wondered how she could see him, but then she realized he was standing on a pile of stones. The ancient stones had been moved from their resting places, and a few of them had been stacked up for the prophet to stand on. The erstwhile benches had become a pedestal, and the prophet's arms were outstretched like the branches of a leafless tree.

An instinctive anger flared in Sarana's mind. *What has he done?*

But then the prophet's voice descended on the people. "I will tell you again. The day of warning has become a day of decision. There will be no more peaceful days in the city of Yinock. There will be no more days of indolent pride. There will be only strife, and the works you have wrought will be wrought upon you by an unforgiving taskmaster. And yet, even now, there is time to save yourselves. The waters of baptism are shallow, fleeing before the drought, but they are not yet dry."

Sarana pressed forward a bit more and finally met an unyielding wall of bodies. Even the steps leading down to the water were covered with people. The guards at the well house had either abandoned their posts or been forced out by the masses. The gates to the well stood open.

"This place is a dry, unfruitful place," the prophet called out. "You call it the place of water, but these waters will be dust in your bellies. You water women come to this place to draw water for your masters. You servants of the great houses come. You servants of the temple also come. You all come here to draw water, but as Sam said in the days of Morin, the Well of Geb will not always succor the lips of the Children of Yinock."

Murmurs passed through the crowd.

The prophet raised his voice. "I say now that the waters of Geb will dwindle to a dusty fountain. Throw down your jars and free yourself from this curse of dust! Drink not of the waters of Geb, for after today, the waters will turn to dust in your bellies." The prophet looked at the people surrounding his perch. Then he reached down and took a jar from a woman by his side. Her hands trailed after the jar and hung in the air briefly. "Throw down your jars and be free," the prophet said.

He turned and threw the jar. Sarana heard the rare but familiar sound of shattering clay as the jar crashed against the wall on the far side of the water. The broken shards dropped and fell into the waters of Geb.

And then she heard the crash of another jar. And another.

And then more jars broke against stone. Throughout the crowd, jars shattered. On every side, Sarana watched as people grabbed up jars and threw them down upon the stones of the streets. And then Sarana heard the cries of women. They called out, wailing. The sound of unwilling rebellion.

"No!" "No!" The stricken wails of women rose above the multitude. The sound of breaking jars diminished, but still they fell against the stones.

"It is enough," the prophet cried. His voice stilled the people, but a few final jars sundered in the silence. "The Lines of the Law are fulfilled. These bonds are broken, and the hopeful are released from their fetters." He raised his hands high over his head and turned his eyes toward heaven. The multitude watched him, wondering, and Sarana almost expected God's fiery wrath to strike him down.

"Esana will succor those who are taken. He will gather the far-flung leaves of the tree and reunite the lost Children of Yinock." The prophet looked back down upon the people. His strong arms lowered slowly, and he shook his head. "The day is drawing to a close, and there is little time for decisions. If you will be saved, be saved."

Sarana inched closer. The breaking of the jars had loosened the tightly packed people. She felt shards of broken pottery beneath her feet and she winced.

"If you will be baptized, there is water here," the prophet said, softer now. "I will take you into the kingdom until the waters are dry. Save yourselves while this day lingers, for soon night falls, and then I will await the will of Esana."

The prophet descended and made his way toward the well. A cry rose up from many throats, and the crowd surged toward the place of water. The small gaps among the people closed, and Sarana felt herself caught in the multitude's inexorable grasp. She moved forward with the people around her, but the crowd's movement quickly slowed and stilled. She stood at the top of the broad steps leading down to the well. Ahead of her, people were organizing at the gates of the well house. They stood in the stone duct, up to their knees in water, and the waters of Geb flowed around them. Several women cried out, urging the people to get out—to stop profaning the waters of Geb.

A few men were holding people back from the well house. They directed the people to form lines, and they created a space in front of the gates. Sarana watched as the first person stepped inside to the deeper waters within. She looked then at the faces of the people around her, wondering who they were and what they were thinking. Many of them spoke to their neighbors, rejoicing that the day of deliverance had come. A few prayed softly, and here and there, shouts of praise rose out of the multitude. *"Ashiana!" "Ashiana!"*

Sarana looked helplessly at the people standing in the water, her feelings mixed, her thoughts raging. The teachings of her youth rejected the actions of the mob, but her heart yearned to join them. The unbounded joy and excitement she had felt when she first abandoned her jars and fled the boundaries of the city had returned. But this time the prophet had come to her.

The sacred Line of *Es* rose to her lips: "When he drinks, he will ever thirst." But it seemed different—the inchoation of some new prayer, not the prayer her lips had muttered so many countless times before. She took a step toward the well, moving with the crowd. At her feet, broken pieces of fired clay mingled with the dust.

A tense silence hung over the assembled elders as the delegation from Hrusk filed out of the council chamber. A few of the Hruskans looked ready for a fight, their faces hard, their eyes implacable. Gibson eyed the on-Dam, impressed by the Hruskan leader's calm strength. From all reports, the on-Dam was a hard man, but he did not relish war. And he had said he desired peace. But he had also delivered demands—foremost that they be allowed to live according to their own customs, as guided by the Hruskan Fathers. Plainly they feared being driven from their homes. Gibson considered the hundreds of families living in the Hruskan Quarter, and he wondered fleetingly about the on-Dam's missing son.

A tap on his shoulder snapped him out of his thoughts. It was Nef; he spoke softly. "The prophet is baptizing at the well of Geb."

Gibson turned in his seat. "What?"

Nef told him what the prophet had done. As Nef spoke, Gibson saw others were receiving the same news from their own people. He heard a few loud voices, a tinge of outrage. A general muttering rose throughout the council chamber. Gibson looked at Tendar bin Amin; Tendar was looking out over the room, a finger on his chin. A man stood by his side, talking softly.

Messengers scurried about the council chamber, and after several moments, the glassy rap of the *gaz-lahi* restored order. Elder Somith stood and announced, "We will adjourn."

Gibson smiled, grimly amused. He imagined the members of the Council trying to save a caravan trapped in a dry wash. He saw the boiling clouds of a sudden, unexpected storm; he saw the elders in their pristine robes, running back and forth, and looking at the sky as the first fat drops of rain fell among them.

When he emerged from the Council Hall, Gibson turned toward the central sector and the Well of Geb. Nef walked beside him.

"He arrived early in the morning," Nef said. "There were only two guards there, and they were not prepared for his arrival. There were simply too many people for them to contend with."

"Any violence?"

"No. No fighting. He took them by surprise."

Gibson looked at Nef and said, "He took us all by surprise." Then he smiled, feeling an inordinate degree of pleasure. "I think even Kim was caught out. It's been a year of years since she was taken by surprise."

"There was something more." Nef remained focused. "There was an incident after he started preaching. Apparently he grabbed a woman's jar and threw it against a wall. It set off a reaction, and a number of people joined in. Many jars were broken, and not all of them willingly."

"What happened?"

Nef shook his head. "From what I can tell, not much. There wasn't much they could do. Many of them were probably just women who had gone to draw water, and they were just caught up or trapped in the crowd."

"Ah," Gibson said. And he pondered what symbolism the people of the city would find in such events. Then he looked up and said, "Let's go see what we can see."

Long before they reached the place of water, the streets grew hectic. All manner of people filled the streets, and opportunistic vendors walked their wares through the crowds. Gibson surveyed the masses and decided he had gone far enough.

Aside from the spectacle of it, he doubted he would learn anything. And after this, there would be no more tales about him— either at the well or the crossroads. The prophet had chosen his end by bringing his strange rebellion into the city and defiling the Well of Geb. He had taken an irrevocable step and inflicted irremediable harm. The Daniti would not have to wait for any deeper combination of power to set them in motion; they were free to act immediately. Some would fault them if they did not.

Gibson's thoughts collapsed into smaller and smaller certainties. Only one viable path remained for his wayward son. Escape.

Maran would have to leave the city immediately.

"We need to make some arrangements," Gibson said. Nef nodded.

When they reached the house, Gibson itched to pull out his family's maps, but he took out ink and paper instead. "I need a van ready to leave the city at my word." He began writing an inventory. "A medium-sized van should be sufficient. We may only have a few days to get him out of the city. Four or five days at most." Gibson paused and looked up, realizing that he had not told Nef what he planned to do. "I need to send Maran away. After the Daniti take down the prophet, they will round up his followers. With the fighting in Hrusk, tensions will be higher, and the Daniti will have an excuse. Things could become brutal."

Nef frowned. "It could be dangerous in Hrusk, as well."

"I'm less concerned about that. The Daniti will probably quell the uprising there quickly, and it will take some time for Maran to reach Noot. Between here and Noot, the road offers little danger."

"The Council can still reach him in Noot."

"He won't stay there. I will send him on to Shal-Gashun."

"Ah."

"He would have gone there soon anyway. I would have sent him to learn the route and establish himself with our contacts there. Though ideally I would have gone with him." Gibson looked toward the window. "He can remain there indefinitely while I work things out here. He will be safe there."

CHAPTER TWENTY-FOUR.

MELEK'S CHOICE.

Gibson was in the orchard looking at his trees, his mind churning, when Telasa found him and told him Elder Amin had come and requested to see him. He steeled himself, remembering their conversation on Sabat. *Your house is not in order.*

In the courtyard, Ana and Kaina were sitting beneath the *hresta* grinding grain with smooth white stones. He watched them for a moment before going inside. Their movements were both arduous and soothing; a murmur of quiet conversation overlay their labors. Gibson recalled the many hours he had devoted to the same work, and he clenched and unclenched his fingers.

In the guest hall, Tendar stood before one of the windows with his back to the door. He was looking at the women working in the vineyard. A *rebboth*-red cloak hung from his shoulders, an ostentatious display of wealth. Its deep scarlet hue stood in sharp contrast to the white drapes of the windows. When he turned, Gibson noticed the thin gold chains around his neck and the rings of gold on his fingers, ornaments he had not been wearing on Sabat. His angular face was smooth, practically unmarred by the long ages he had seen. The blood of Yinock ran deep.

"You are welcome in my house, Elder Amin." Gibson gestured for him to sit.

"Forgive me if I have come at an inopportune time," Tendar said.

"No doubt the prophet's recent actions have inconvenienced your house, as they have mine."

"I have been expecting you," Gibson said.

Telasa entered with a bowl of *kivich* and a round, glass pitcher. She placed the bowl before Tendar and poured glasses of water. Kneeling, she offered to wash Tendar's feet, but he placed a hand on her shoulder and said, "It is well. I have not come far."

Telasa inclined her head and departed.

"So, you have come to continue our conversation on Sabat," Gibson said.

"Ah, a man of business." Tendar took one of the small brown fruits and began to peel away the thin husk with his long nails, revealing the soft, green flesh within. "Formalities are not the hallmarks of your success. Though I must admit that I also sometimes prefer directness." Tendar held up the little fruit and appraised it with his eyes. "This fruit looks excellent," he said, and he popped the little morsel into his mouth.

Gibson gestured toward the bowl. "These were the first to reach the city. My van was the first from Shal-Gashun this year, as it usually is."

"The best I've tasted this season, I think. But as you undoubtedly know, I usually buy from Elder Somith's interests."

Gibson shrugged. "I have no trouble with my inventory. You are welcome to buy lesser goods."

Tendar chuckled. "Quite." He took another fruit from the bowl and turned it between his long, slender fingers. "I have come to offer you my advice."

"Am I in need of advice?"

Tendar was quiet for a moment; he let his gaze linger. "Your house is not in order, brother. I'm talking about Maran."

Gibson kept his face calm. "I've heard what people are saying."

"If there were any doubts about Maran's involvement with the so-called prophet, you resolved them on Sabat. Anyone who heard your self-serving remarks could have deciphered the truth. You do not want to fight him because he has already found a way into your home. But the day of decision is upon us now."

"Has the Council reached a decision I'm not aware of?"

Tendar shook his head and let his gaze drop. "No. But this so-called prophet has forced a choice upon us." He poked his nail through the skin of the second fruit and began to peel it carefully. "This heretic threatens the very foundation of our nation."

"An overstatement, I think."

"Not according to the Daniti." Tendar looked up. "We have a duty, brother. This 'prophet' has drawn a significant part of the city to his ranks, including several children of the great houses. The crossroads, and now the Well of Geb, have become symbols of dissension among the people. He teaches an Esana who is unknown to us, and he draws the hearts of the people away from God."

"A more pressing problem demands our attention," Gibson said. "There is fighting in Noot, and it threatens to get worse. Does the prophet threaten the lives of so many, that we can ignore the real threat of Hrusk?"

"The Daniti will settle the issue in Noot," Tendar said. "But don't forget what you plainly know. We cannot have division here if we are to stand against any concerted efforts by Hrusk. We cannot have heresy among our people. We cannot be divided."

"So you think I have gone after this prophet, too."

"No. I know you, brother. Everyone knows you hold fast to the teachings of Esana. Or at least that you always have." Tendar's green eyes were placid. "It is your son who has fallen."

Gibson waited.

"Tomith bin Ableth has confessed his involvement in the conspiracy, and he has revealed the extent of this so-called prophet's influence among the great houses."

"You truly think these children plan to overthrow the Council?"

Tendar returned Gibson's gaze. "Do you think we can ignore the risk? Or that we can allow our children to fall into apostasy?"

"Some inquiry is warranted," Gibson conceded. "I have spoken to my son, and I intend to correct his actions. But we are talking about youthful indiscretions committed by impetuous children—not a conspiracy."

"I agree. To call it a conspiracy of any real weight, at the moment, might be an exaggeration. But—" Tendar held up a finger. "You cannot deny that this heretic has urged rebellion, and many people have answered his invitation. And in light of his actions at the well today, the Council's response must be unequivocal."

Gibson took a sip of water. This was no less than what he had expected. "So what do you want from me?"

"It's not a matter of what *I* want," Tendar said, with subtle emphasis. "I'm sure you agree that the leadership of the city must remain in the hands of the righteous. As treasurer, this is my constant desire."

Gibson smiled, predatory. "You have me. How could I disagree?" *And how can I agree without saying you are righteous?* "But you still haven't told me what you want."

Tendar appeared to think for a moment. "Let me tell you what I expect will happen." A pause. "Because he was forthcoming and openly remorseful, Tomith will be granted a reprieve by the Council. And in due time, if he follows the counsel of his father, and if he proves himself faithful, he will take the place of his father. Though I think questions could arise over his fitness to preside."

Gibson waited.

Tendar continued. "But Tomith was the only one to come forward on his own. The others persist in their rebellion, or they have merely confessed their wrongdoing when compelled by outside circumstances."

"You want me to persuade Maran."

"No. That might change things somewhat, but based on reports I've heard . . . let me say, I don't believe Maran will turn from his new-found faith. And even if he did, it would not be enough for some. They would doubt his sincerity." Tendar looked steadily at Gibson. "He will not be pardoned."

Gibson tasted anger. Tendar's certainty, his bluntness, evinced a combination of power that exceeded his expectations. "So why come to me at all?" he asked.

"Because there is more at stake than Maran's future. In the coming days, many will question whether you should retain your seat."

"I will answer any charge I must answer," Gibson said.

"But with my backing, you will also defeat any charge."

Gibson spoke levelly. "And if I want your backing?"

Tendar's voice took on a quiet, grim solidity. "My terms are simple. When I ask for it—and I will not always do so—you will give me your support on matters brought before the Council. You will do this without ever revealing our agreement. And in return, you will keep your seat. You will have my backing against the charges that are surely coming against you."

Gibson considered Tendar's words.

Tendar continued, his voice firm. "You will retain your seat, and everything your family has built will continue. There is no need for unnecessary sacrifices."

"But there will be," Gibson said. "When the Daniti go after the prophet's followers, there will be blood. Many of them will not renounce him. My son could be among them."

Tendar's stony eyes did not waver. "You said you will correct his actions. But if he will not repent, it may be better for him to pay the price in blood. He was baptized by a heretic, and he has since officiated in the House of Esana. He has carried the law box; he has mocked God."

Gibson felt a hollowness in his breast. The indictment was too close to his own thoughts.

"You need not answer for your son," Tendar said. "You cannot. But you can save yourself and the remainder of your household. You are unpopular in certain circles of the Council—you have no friends among the Daniti—but I can promise you continued standing if you will agree to join your voice with mine."

"My first concern is my son."

Tendar said nothing for several seconds. "The Council might be persuaded to spare his life, but he will not take your seat."

"I did not build this house for myself," Gibson said.

Tendar shrugged. "But you did not build it for him alone, either. Unlike your father, you have abandoned the road. You have become a man of position, you know the allure of power. Are you willing to give that up? Are you willing to give up everything you have built?"

Gibson said nothing for a moment, mulling the words. There was some truth in them, and the thought of losing everything his family had built grieved him deeply. But there was no real question. "I'm not willing to sacrifice my son."

"You are above such savagery?" Tendar smiled.

Gibson did not answer. His thoughts turned to Shal-Gashun. The House of Jianin had assets there and strong contacts among the Gashuni. Maran would be safe there—for years, if necessary. The prophet would fade into obscurity, and these days would become unimportant, a relic of history.

Tendar pressed on. "The Lines require sacrifice, brother. Do they not say that the man who will lose his life shall find it?" He paused. "You recall the story of Melek."

"I know it," Gibson said.

"Now it is your son playing in the fields beyond the city wall, and you are the gatekeeper. The armies of Tanus are advancing on the gates, and you have to make a choice. Do you run out to save your son, only to lose the city? Or do you close the gates and save the city? It is impossible to save them both. The greater good demands your sacrifice."

Gibson knew the story. Melek had closed the gates. Instead of allowing the city to perish, he had sacrificed his son. The armies of Tanus had killed the boy, and Melek had mourned the loss of his little son with bitter tears.

But what he remembered most was his own father's declaration. Gibson had been a boy when he had first heard the story and asked his father about it. *Don't you believe it, my boy. The tale of Melek is a tale of coercion and ignorance. If such a choice is ever put before me, I'll come for you.* Gibson felt a strange triumph fill his mouth.

"You've picked the wrong story," he said.

"The—"

Gibson cut him off. "The person who made up that story did not know—did not understand—the great plan of redemption. Melek's son was an innocent child who died in ignorance of any sacrifice, and Melek could have made another choice, perhaps a better choice." Gibson smiled his predatory smile again. "It would have been right for Melek to let the citizens fight for themselves while he went to save his son. In some cases, it is necessary to leave the many to save the one."

Tendar raised his voice slightly. "You would cavil about such things? One day, a man will make Melek's choice. He will close the gates and sacrifice his son. And he will be great in the eyes of the people."

"I won't be coerced by political pressure to give up my son. Such games have no place in the councils of God's servants."

"You speak rashly," Tendar said quietly. "God is political."

"That's heresy."

Tendar's implacable voice continued. "Not at all. Do you think the ancient war of heaven was without sides? Do you think we were advocates of nothing? That our brothers and sisters who fell into perdition—and for whom we wept—were banished because of something other than their politics?"

Tendar shook his head and continued. "No, Gibson. The politics of men were learned in the temples of heaven. God is political, and he fights the war as we do. He fights for the souls of men."

"You think killing this prophet is God's will?"

Tendar spoke slowly. "It is better that one man should die than that the children of Yinock be led astray in unbelief. If he is not stopped, he could lead this people to utter destruction."

"You don't know that," Gibson said. "And it won't be just one man."

When Tendar did not immediately respond, Gibson leaned back in his seat; he said, "We do not have to kill him."

Tendar turned his gaze toward the window. He stood for several seconds without saying anything; then he said, "You are very like your father."

Gibson flinched; he had not expected that.

"I knew him, of course, before he was killed." Tendar glanced at Gibson, and then he looked back out the window. "I knew your grandfather, too, when he was but a lesser merchant. But for his astonishing feat of opening the wilderness road to Shal-Gashun—his discovery of the Oasis of Rume—the House of Jianin would be little more than a family of peddlers." Tendar stood. "I'm offering you a chance to continue the legacy of your family, Gibson. You and I could accomplish many things together."

"If I'll be your servant."

"If we work together," Tendar said. He frowned. "You doubt my sincerity. But my aim remains what it has always been. We must preserve what remains of Yinock's city. And we must restore our ancient greatness."

Gibson shook his head. "A hopeless dream. We don't have the ability, the knowledge." But a wistful yearning twined though his mind, and his thoughts turned to the ancient maps his family had followed across the deadly *pustinya*.

"What we once were, we can become again," Tendar said, growing earnest. "And with the Wayfarer fallen from heaven, we are closer than ever before."

"What do you mean?"

Tendar paused. He looked at Gibson for a moment, and then one eyebrow raised just slightly. "It is a sign. And perhaps more. Not all of the ancient relics of Yinock's time have lost their power." Tendar adjusted his cloak on his shoulders. "I will look for your support when the Council meets. I hope to get it."

After Tendar had gone, Gibson pondered what Tendar had said about the fallen Wayfarer. *A sign, and perhaps more.*

Gibson could not fathom what he meant. According to every report, the Wayfarer had burned violently and crashed down in the Southern Sea, far to the south. A spectacle, to be sure.

But what more might he see in it? The Council had, as yet, issued no formal proclamation about it, and the priests had offered little more than cryptic words about signs and wonders in the heavens—which meant they knew nothing.

"So what does he see in it?" Gibson said softly. He stood looking out his window for a long while, but he could not find an answer.

CHAPTER TWENTY-FIVE.

DAUGHTER OF YINOCK.

Cool water flowed around Sarana's legs.

A moment earlier, she had stood on the last long step leading down to the water, dreading what she was about to do. And then she had done the unthinkable—she had quietly recited the Line of *Es* and stepped down into the sacred waters of Geb.

And she was not alone in desecrating the waters. The gate to the well house stood open, and the clear-flowing waters of the basin were turbulent and muddied by the feet of hundreds. Ordinary men and women had taken the place of the temple guards, and they called out, directing the thronging people, scowling at times and speaking sharply. Beyond them, inside the well house, the prophet stood in the waist-deep waters, baptizing.

As Sarana drew closer, a woman moving down the line gestured with her hands and said, "Line up against the wall. People need to be able to get out." A couple of men were doing the same, working to hold back the crowd and provide an outlet for the people who had already been baptized.

At the threshold of the well house, Sarana saw more steps descending into the deeper waters within. The man in front of her stepped down onto the first step, silently waiting for his turn. He was older, his hair a mix of black and grey. His hands looked strong, his face gentle, and Sarana wondered, as she had several times while waiting behind him, what had drawn him to the prophet. But she did not ask him; she was not sure she could answer the question for herself.

She stepped up to the open door. Inside, the words of the prophet's baptism echoed off the stone walls of the enclosure. He dipped a woman beneath the waters and brought her back up. Sinuous lines of reflected light crawled over the walls and ceiling, mirroring the rippling waters.

Just inside the doorway, Sarana stared at the little blue rectangle set into the doorframe. Its soft light shone as it had in every day of her memory. She reached toward it, hesitated, and then touched it gently. Cool, somehow smoother than glass, its latent power hummed, almost imperceptible. She spread her hand out and pushed her palm up against it. Around the edge, glass and stone had been precisely melded; she felt no seam, no flaw. An image appeared in her mind—the first letter Gibson had taught her—and she drew it on the glass with her fingertip. Lines of evanescent light flowed from her finger, seemingly inside the glass. And then a symbol appeared at the top of the ancient panel—a triangle within a circle.

A little worried, she let her hand drop and she looked around. No one seemed to be paying any attention to her. And then the man in front of her moved half a step forward. It was almost time.

With a backward glance at the glowing panel, Sarana stepped down into the deeper waters of the pool. Her robe billowed slightly, and the cold waters rose up to her waist. She gasped slightly, a little surprised at how cold the water was. She took a breath and stepped forward. In front of her, the grey-haired man stepped toward the prophet, and the prophet took hold of one of his wrists and directed him where to stand.

"Are you ready?" the prophet asked.

"Yes. But it's cold," the man said.

The prophet smiled. "I'll be quick, then." He raised his gaze to heaven and offered the words of his baptism. He spoke loudly, and his voice filled the small chamber. Then he plunged the man beneath the waters.

When he came up, the man let out a little whoop, and Sarana felt an answering smile form on her lips. The prophet laughed and clapped him on the back. The man shook his head and wiped streams of water out of his eyes. Then he clasped the prophet's right hand with both hands and thanked him. The prophet nodded and then turned toward Sarana, his hand outstretched.

She stood unmoving in the water.

"Time is growing short," the prophet said. He looked over her shoulder toward the doorway. His eyes lingered there a moment before he looked back at her.

Sarana stepped forward, and he took hold of her wrist and turned her so she faced the doorway. Hundreds still waited outside, and the closest people in line were all looking at her, just as she had been looking at the people who were baptized before her. One of them might have been wondering about her as they stood waiting in line.

The prophet raised his hand. And then he stopped. He held up her wrist and looked at the little silver token of her servitude. His eyes turned to hers. "You wear the mark of the House of Jianin, child."

Sarana felt her body tense.

The prophet inclined his head; he spoke softly. "Does your master know what you do here?"

Sarana wanted to flee, but the prophet still held her wrist.

"Does he?"

"I—I am here with my master's permission," she said. It was not a direct lie; she had spoken truth. But it tasted like a lie. She turned her eyes down toward the rippling water. Her mind was filled with dread and uncertainty; her calm had fled.

The prophet stared at her, his eyes soft. "Forgive me, daughter of Yinock, for my questions. But I have been waiting for you. And I saw you in the doorway. Wait here." The prophet let go of her wrist and climbed the steps. Water dripped from his arms, and he stood in the open door, encased in sunlight. Sarana watched as he reached toward the glowing rectangle in the doorframe, but the people crowding around him blocked her view. She could not see what he did.

Then he turned and addressed the crowd, gesturing backward with his right hand. "You see before you a daughter of Yinock, and a servant of one of the great houses. It is as I said—even the lowly of the great houses will be greater than their masters. Today is this prophecy fulfilled. And in days to come, the lowly will rise to even greater fame." The prophet turned and stepped back down into the waters.

Sarana stared, open mouthed.

"Time is short," the prophet said when he returned to her side. "Will you place your hope in Esana?"

"I was baptized as a child in the House of Esana."

"As was I. But come. If you will put your hope in Esana, I will take the pride of your youth from you."

Sarana did not understand what he meant, but the words were spoken gently, without accusation, and they called to mind the idle moments of vanity she had often indulged in at the well, in the vineyard, or beneath the giant *hresta* in the yard. And then she recalled the broken *rebboth* seed she had plucked on Sabat. Her right hand rose to her chest, and she looked up at the prophet. A hope of being cleansed moved her.

"I will put my hope in Esana," she said.

The prophet nodded and took hold of her. He raised his eyes to heaven and spoke the words of his baptism. Sarana closed her eyes, a little worried, wondering if she should bend her knees. She started to lean back, and the prophet pushed her beneath the waters. Cold water poured into her clothing, shocking her, and then the world was gone, muted and excluded by the water. But it only lasted a moment, and she reemerged into the world.

As she came up, the shawl of her robe fell backward, like a cowl, full of water. Water dripped into her eyes, and she wiped it away, smiling. Blinking, she ran her hands back over the top of her head and looked up at the prophet. He returned her smile. Then he gestured toward the doorway and looked away; the next person was waiting.

Sarana trudged up the steps, her wet clothing clinging to her body. But in the doorway, she halted, her eyes drawn to the doorframe. The little glassy panel had changed. It glowed with a soft, amber light.

"What happened to it?" Sarana directed her question to a man standing in the doorway. He looked surprised, but his face was open. "What happened to it?" she repeated, urgent.

"To what?" The man answered slowly.

She pointed. "It's blue. It's supposed to be blue."

The man turned and glanced at the panel; he shrugged. "I don't know anything about it. But it's not blue." His unconcern frustrated her; he was not a man familiar with the well. None of nearby people seemed to understand what she was saying.

A woman took hold of Sarana's arm and gently pulled her toward the door. "Come along, make room."

Sarana looked back at the prophet, wondering what he had done, but she allowed herself to be ushered out of the well house.

The recently baptized congregated at the top of the steps leading up from the well. Some talked and laughed; some embraced; some sat alone. She passed by them and made her way through the crowd, preoccupied. In all her years of servitude, the well had never changed; the light had always been there, softly glowing in the doorway. *What did he do?*

Away from the place of water, away from the multitude, she walked through the streets in silence, her mind working. Whatever she had expected to feel, she felt only confusion. And a little anger.

The prophet had done something; he had changed something. The more she thought about it, the more she felt the enormity of his actions. The place of water had been transfigured. The stones had been moved from their places, the waters had been tainted by countless feet, the guards had been driven away, and the well house had been turned into a baptistry. And he had done more than that. Jars had been broken and trampled. Women and servants of the well had been forced out of their customary place. Her anger grew.

And after everything, she still needed to draw water.

A voice brought her to an abrupt stop. A man stepped in front of her. "Young lady! Young lady, pause a moment!"

She looked up; she had come to the Stair Market. The voice belonged to the man who worked there, calling and enticing people into his house of levity. He stood before her now, his arms held out to block her way. A broad smile filled his face, and the silken folds of his shirt sleeves shimmered in the sunlight. A glance revealed he still wore his shoes with curled up toes.

She tried to step around him, but he shuffled to his right. "Wait a moment, wait a moment. You look a bit bedraggled. Perhaps you need assistance?"

"Let me pass."

"Don't be angry. I only want to ask you a question. A question." His voice joked, but his eyes were determined.

"I will not answer you." Sarana tried to push past him, but he caught hold of her arm and stopped her. She looked into his face, astonished and afraid—shocked he would put his hands on her.

"Don't be afraid," he said. "Tell me where you're going."

She pulled back from him, a little bewildered; she could not understand why he had accosted her. "Let me go. I am a servant of the House of Jianin." She held up the silver mark on her wrist.

Immediately he released her. "Oh ho," he said, mockingly, holding up his hands. "I should not have guessed that. Forgive me. I meant no harm." He stepped back, his hands upheld, his broad smile flashing. His eyes shone with jollity; his voice became stentorian. "Be on your way then, servant of the House of Jianin." He laughed and continued in a more friendly voice, "But you might want to . . .." He trailed off, still smiling, and gestured vaguely at her, twirling his finger in her direction over her head.

Sarana hurried past him, confused. She did not understand. But she felt eyes turned upon her, and she felt her neck and face flush. When she reached the steps, she stopped to adjust her robes.

It was then she realized her head was uncovered.

Her long hair lay in loose coils on her shoulders, dark and lustrous in the sunlight, still wet from her baptism. For a moment she stared, stricken, not understanding what had happened. But then she recalled how her shawl had slipped off her head when she came up out of the water. She looked around.

People were staring. A woman scowled. Sarana quickly replaced her shawl, angry at her thoughtlessness. She had brought shame on her master's house, and she had nearly returned home wet and disheveled.

What would I have told Telasa?

She berated herself silently; she did not know what she planned to tell anyone. Not even Kaina.

Like a vagrant, she sat in a corner of the market and stared at the ground. The jocund invitations to the house of levity still sounded near the stairs. She closed her eyes and waited for her clothes to dry. It did not take long. And then she made her way up the stairs, still avoiding the eyes of anyone in the market. She needed to get back to work, back to her broken servitude.

But when she arrived home, the thought of confronting Telasa, or of answering Kaina's or Ana's questions, seemed too perilous. So she slipped into the women's quarters and took up her jars. She could not draw water from the defiled well—not while so many still trod in its waters—but she did not want to be at the house.

So she would wait. But not at the house.

At the place of water, the crowd around the steps had abated somewhat, and a few of the ancient stones had been reclaimed by water women. They sat with their jars at their feet, waiting for the people to leave—waiting for the inexorable compulsion of water to restore the world to its proper frame. *Chay on peya ikola bo on zheya*, she thought. *When he drinks, he will ever thirst.*

But even though some women had returned, the place of water had not returned to its former state. Some of the ancient stones were still stacked where the prophet and his followers had moved them. Some had been moved from their ancient resting places, revealing slight, perfectly smooth indentations in the ground. Her eyes kept going back to those marks; she wanted the stones back in their places. Those smooth places in the earth had cradled the ancient stones for generations.

An irreparable harm had been inflicted. Or so it seemed. They never should have been moved. The moments of time those stones had been out of their earthly cradles could never be retrieved, even if they were moved back.

Sarana looked up. A murmur passed slowly through the people. Something was happening nearer the water. Words filtered through the crowd. Then people at the water's edge began to shout, and the clamor spread outward. "The water's going down." "It's going down!"

The multitude contracted inward toward the well house. A few tried to hold back the rush of people, vainly trying to maintain order. Chaos unfolded and the orderly line leading into the well house collapsed into a compact mass. And then it ended. The roiling crowd became still and then slowly unknotted. The clamor changed: "It's gone." "The water's gone." "It's dry."

Sarana rose to her feet, and dread filled her breast. *It's dry?* She had heard the words, but her mind instinctively rebelled. *That's impossible.* It could not be true; the well of Geb had never failed.

As she watched, the prophet emerged from the throng. Men and women importuned him, took hold of his arms, but he merely shook his head and pulled away from their grasping hands. He ascended his stony perch and said, "I am finished. There is no more water at hand." He looked around. "Go to the river if you seek water. Night falls, and there is no more work to be done. My time here is finished."

Tromping feet drew Sarana's attention, and she turned to see a column of armed guards marching into the place of water. They spread out among the stones in pairs, directing people to stand back. Their commander drew close to the prophet; he held a small tablet in his hand. Two men stood at his back, hands clenched on the hilts of their swords. A small group of men stood their ground in front of the prophet. A silence slowly descended on the place of water; the sounds of the city seemed distant.

The commander spoke. "In the name of the Council, and by the dictate of the high priest, you are under arrest for desecrating properties held in sacred trust by the temple. You are suspected of heresy, inciting rebellion, and treason. Your specific crimes will be enumerated at a future date."

No one moved.

The commander raised his voice. "By further order of the high priest, all unauthorized people are forbidden to touch the waters of the Well of Geb or to remain in its environs. Water women, residents of the central sector, and bonded servants of the temple will be permitted to draw as deemed acceptable by the regular captain of the guard stationed here." A brief pause. "It is so ordered. *Es-prida!*"

˒ A few people responded to the show of authority, moving slowly, if somewhat reluctantly, away. Several people called out—some derisively, some plaintively—that there was no water. The captain ignored them, his eyes fixed on the prophet and his followers. The group of men in front of the prophet did not stir. A few stood with clenched fists, their faces stony. Others in the crowd moved to join them, mostly men but a few women, too. The temple guards began to coalesce around their leader. Sarana watched, eyes wide, as the conflict ripened.

But then the prophet spoke. "Stop. Wait. I will go with them." He gently pushed his way through the men who sought to protect him; he held out his hands toward the officer. The commander nodded and gestured for his men to come forward. They took hold of the prophet and walked him away from the well.

One of the prophet's followers stepped forward. "Where are you taking him?"

"You can address any grievance to the Council." The commander of the guard turned. "All of you people disperse. You women—if you seek to draw water, present yourself to the captain." He gestured toward one of the guards.

"Sir?" A woman holding a jar on her hip stepped forward. "The well is dry."

The plight of the women finally reached him, and he turned questioningly toward the well. He directed one of his men to go and look.

Sarana did not wait for the conclusion of his investigation. She picked up her jars and walked over to the steps leading down to the water's edge. Only remnants of the waters remained. Bits of broken jars lay scattered about, and the light in the doorway of the well house had gone dark. Either the source had failed, or the ancient pumps had finally ceased their work.

Sarana sat on the top step. An old woman sat beside her. The Line of *Es* flowed through her mind, repeating. But the water was gone. *Now what?*

Chapter Twenty-six.
Daniti.

As the sun sank toward the hills of Gazelem, a supple, segmented caterpillar of armored warriors stepped onto the patterned cobbles of the *ulaka*. A steady tromp accompanied their rapid march, and the streets of the Hruskan Quarter became desolate and empty before them. Here and there, a dark face watched them pass—some angry, some fearful—but no one emerged to stand against them.

Nine triads—three full squads—formed the column, and an officer flanked each squad. Not far distant, two more columns converged toward the same location: the house of the on-Dam, the heart of the Hruskan Quarter.

Shouting and the clash of weapons rose in the distance, and the column leader glanced toward it. It meant only one thing: one of the other columns had encountered resistance. But it was some distance away—too far away to worry about. *Like heaven*, the column leader thought. He smiled, grim, but exultant. The sound of death was sweet to him—redolent smoke from the thurible of war.

A second column streamed into view, and the two unopposed columns reached the on-Dam's house almost simultaneously. The massing soldiers separated into triads and formed two lines. Eighteen warriors armed with the ancient weapons of the Daniti formed the first rank. A second rank armed with swords stood close behind.

Serene in its imported jungle, the house of the on-Dam appeared empty. The guards normally outside its doors were gone, and the broad leaves of the exotic plants bobbed gently on a soft breeze. The late-afternoon light suffused the rosy stones of the pillars and walls, glancing off some of the glass windows.

A man stepped out onto a small upper-level porch. The on-Dam. He raised his voice over the nascent battleground. "You Daniti have no authority here. You must leave the Hruskan Quarter."

The commanding officer of the Daniti stepped forward. "You no longer hold the privileges of rank and power, man of Hrusk. Our nations are at war. You may elect to surrender, but you must do so immediately—without any delay or attempts at placation. You must tell me now. And let me be clear." He paused, waited. "Let me be clear. And for the third time, let me be clear. If you do not surrender immediately—if you do not surrender at this very moment—we will raze this compound to the ground. No stone will remain upon stone."

"I must consult—"

"You will not consult!" The officer stepped back to the second rank.

And the Daniti discharged their weapons.

Blazing streams of light—the bright, sundering blades of the Daniti's irresistible weapons—tore through the on-Dam's ornamental plants and trees. A roar poured out of the warriors, and they took a step forward, activating their weapons in short bursts and sweeping them in precise, destructive arcs. The ordered flower beds and walkways erupted, the plants snapping and sagging. Little stone benches and decorative columns fell to pieces, and the sandstone pavers of the walkways buckled and cracked.

The Daniti advanced, wading through the detritus of their destruction. Billowing dust and smoke enveloped them, and the beams of directed energy bloomed, the light expanding and scorching the swirling air.

A few steps further, and a volley of projectiles rained down on them from the upper windows—spears, arrows, stones, bits of broken furniture, and household items of every sort. A few of the Daniti staggered, and one dropped to one knee, stunned by a heavy blow to the head. But most of them pressed on, protected by their supple, impervious armor. Their reflective face plates turned aside the arrows and stones easily.

As they came within range of the house, the bright beams tore into it, cutting deep gouges in the rosy stones. The columns beneath the porch fell. For a moment the porch held, but then it collapsed, grinding downward inexorably and magnificently. Great chunks of stone tumbled to the ground.

And then the forces of the on-Dam poured out of the doors and windows of the crumpling ruin, swords and improvised implements of battle held high over their heads—a dark wave of yelling men and women. Most of them fell in the next instant, cut down by the radiant beams. The remainder crashed into the line, curved swords flashing down in wicked arcs, chopping again and again. Fury drove them, and the ancient cutting weapons of the Daniti momentarily lost their efficacy as the battle moved to close quarters, making it difficult to turn the beams without endangering their companions. One of the Daniti fell beneath the onslaught. Another.

But the shift in the battle was brief. The second rank of the Daniti had followed in the wake of the first, and they jumped forward with their swords to meet the furious onslaught. The first rank fell back with practiced restraint, and as opportunity arose, they cut down their attackers with short, precise shots.

The Hruskans tried to break through. But the line held. They were too few, the Daniti too powerful.

One by one the Hruskans fell. And, finally, the last of the on-Dam's little force was cut down. The screams, the clash of weapons, the blaze of the beams all ceased.

The commanding officer of the Daniti walked among the dead, his sword in hand. Dust and the stench of an otherworldly fire hung in the air. He gestured toward the house, flicking his sword. "Make sure the on-Dam is dead. Leave none alive. And then finish what we came to do. Not one stone left on another."

The once son of the on-Dam stood on his unbroken leg and

situated his new crutches under his arms. The little street in front of Lihana's house was empty, and Neturu looked down its length, determined to reach the garbage heaps where Lihana and several others were sorting and salvaging trash. He took the first step.

He was halfway there when he heard Doman calling to him from behind. He stopped and looked over his shoulder. Doman was jogging alongside his cart, and Saban was in his usual place, pulling. In their haste, the cart jounced and shuddered. Neturu smiled at the sight. The way they went out of their way to carry him around was gratifying.

As they drew nearer, Neturu's smile faded. Doman's face looked harsh.

"What is it?"

"There's been a fight," Doman said. He paused. "The Daniti attacked your father's house. And there are reports of war in Noot. People are saying an army of Hrusk is heading toward the city."

Neturu blinked, caught off guard. The words assailed his mind. An army of Hrusk. An attack on his father's house. "Is my father alive?" he asked.

"We don't know."

Neturu tried to stand still, but he felt himself tremble. "Here," he said, taking hold of both crutches with one hand. "Help me back to Lihana's house."

Saban took hold of one arm, and Doman the other. They eased him into the cart and placed the crutches next to him. And then Saban went around and took hold of the handles. The cart began to roll. Doman lent his strength from behind.

"We've been called out," Doman said. "But I wanted to tell you before we left."

"Called out?"

"We received orders to bring all available carts to the house of the on-Dam. To remove the spoils. And the dead."

"The Council sent a messenger," Saban said over his shoulder. "Right after we finished our last haul from the city."

Neturu turned his gaze away. The warmongering of recent weeks

filled his head, the folly of it now terrible and certain. His father and
his men could not have stood against the Daniti. The on-Dam's
personal forces were too small, and the Daniti too powerful. He
wondered how many of his father's advisors now lay among the
Hruskan dead. A vicious thought erupted. *I hope they're all dead.*

"He might not have been there when it happened," Doman said.
"We don't know who was killed."

Neturu shook his head gently. "No. I'm certain he was there."

"You can't be sure."

"The Daniti would not have attacked otherwise."

"He might have fled."

"You don't know my father."

They arrived at Lihana's door, and Saban walked around to the
back of the cart. They were about to help him down.

"Wait," Neturu said. "I want to come with you."

Doman looked at him, his dark eyes troubled. "You said you can't
go back to the Quarter. It won't be safe."

Neturu shook his head. "They won't be looking for me. Not now.
I am less than nothing now."

"That gap-toothed fellow you told me about might feel otherwise."

Neturu smiled involuntarily at Doman's words. But he sobered.
"He won't seek vengeance now—if he still lives. My father's political
enemies cannot hurt him any more with my blood."

From Lihana's house they traveled out of Pekel along the main
road, stopping briefly to join the other scorchers assembling for the
job. Neturu had never seen so many scorchers together at one time.
Twenty hand carts and a dozen or more large wagons lined the road.
Sixty or seventy scorchers attended them.

On the road out of Pekel, Doman paused at the boundary marker
and recited the Line of the Wayfarer. Neturu listened to the softly
uttered words. *Though I pass from one world to the next, I endure.* He knew
Doman repeated the line every time he crossed the boundary, and he
wondered at the hope and fatalism that seemed to find expression in
the words. For Doman, the fiery fall of the Wayfarer had simply been
the ultimate and long-awaited fulfilment of the words he had so often

uttered. The immolation of the Wayfarer was merely a translation of the wandering star into something new.

When they reached the Hruskan Quarter, Neturu kept his head down. He had spoken boldly in Pekel, but his confidence waned as they drew nearer his father's house. The streets were full of people, but the customary boisterousness of the South had been replaced with quiet determination. Many people were preparing to leave. Fear of the Daniti was driving them out.

A short distance from the on-Dam's house, the line of carts stopped. The lead carts had reached the destination. Neturu looked down the line, but his father's house was not yet in sight. He took up his crutches and eased down out of the cart.

"I'm going on ahead," he said.

Doman looked at Saban, and the smaller man nodded and said he would bring the cart up.

When the broken remains of the on-Dam's house came into sight, Neturu halted. "God of my fathers," he said. "What have they done?"

The old tales his father had told him about the Daniti had not prepared him for the utter devastation. The house of the on-Dam was no more. Where it had stood, great piles of sundered stones lay in jumbled heaps, broken and pulverized by the irresistible weapons of the Daniti. Dust hung in the air, a miasma of obliteration.

Neturu took a step forward, but his crutches made it difficult to walk down the gouged and broken path. He grimaced as he steadied himself. Just a few days before, he had strode down that path to meet with his father for the last time.

A few scorchers had already begun the work of retrieving the dead. They picked their way through the trampled plants and broken stones of the on-Dam's gardens.

"Come," Doman said. "We will look for your father."

It did not take long to find him. The on-Dam lay among the dead in the yard, his curved sword still in his hand. Another fighter lay on top of him. Neturu stared at the lifeless forms. He did not recognize the man on top.

"Shall I pick him up?" Doman asked.

"Take these others," Neturu said. "I will stay here with him."

Doman pulled the dead man off of the on-Dam and carried him away toward the wagons. Neturu settled onto the ground. A deep grief huddled in his throat, but he swallowed and made no sound. His father had died as many Hruskans would have wanted to die—standing against the *Yinoi* in battle. He picked up the curved sword from his father's hand. His father's sword. His father had owned it for as long as he could remember, and Neturu had once thought he would inherit it. To take it now would just be theft. Looting. But he did not put it down. He looked around.

Dozens of scorchers had entered the ruins, and they were sifting through the mangled remains of the house and gardens. They worked fast. Searching, sorting, stacking. Some carried away bodies to the waiting carts, and others made piles of salvageable items. Not far away, two scorchers were piling up weapons and armor. A momentary anger ignited in Neturu's mind; he nearly yelled at them to stop. But then he realized it all belonged to them now. Everything salvaged would belong to the scorcher community. A desolation filled his head.

He had thought he wanted to stay with the scorchers. But sitting in the midst of their insectile efficiency he felt isolated, detached. *I don't belong here.* He yearned to see Noot again. Not this lifeless city. He thought of his mother there, unaware she had lost her son and her husband among the *Yinoi* within a matter of days. A thin anger watered in his mouth, and he closed his eyes.

Doman returned for another of the dead. Neturu looked up.

"Your father's sword." The big man stood thinking for a moment. "I think if we ask, the director would allow you to keep it."

Neturu looked down at the sword. He wanted to keep it. But he said, "It would have gone to my father's heir. It's not mine to keep." He laid the sword down beside his father and used his crutches to stand up.

Doman stood looking at him for several moments. Then he said, "The ways of your people do not matter in Pekel."

Neturu turned his head sharply. "They are still my ways." His anger emerged from his grief, fully formed. Tears trembled in his eyes.

Doman nodded slightly. "I'm sorry, Neturu. By the Wayfarer, if I could change what happened here, I would."

Neturu let out a breath, faltering. He blinked and tears made tiny runnels down his cheeks. And then he looked around, abashed. As the once son of the on-Dam, he had no claim to anything there. If he wished to mourn, he could mourn in the secret rooms of his heart. "I should have stayed in Pekel."

Doman said. "That wouldn't have changed anything."

"I shouldn't have come."

But as Doman carried away another body, Neturu looked down at his father's face. The still features were no longer so stern—they were no longer the features he had known—but he recalled the last words he had heard his father speak.

Such a son as I once had, cannot be replaced so easily.

He lingered a moment longer. He did not want to forget the face of his father.

"I've never seen anything like it," Nef said.

Gibson waited for him to continue.

"The fighting was done by the time I arrived. But the Daniti weren't finished." Nef shook his head slightly as he sought words. "There were old Hruskan women, and some men, kneeling in the street with their hands in the air. They were pleading with the Daniti. Some of the old woman were mourning and wailing. But the Daniti—they didn't stop. They just kept going. They turned their weapons on the gardens, the on-Dam's house, the stables—everything. They destroyed everything."

Gibson tapped a finger on his table. He had never seen the Daniti fight, and Nef's evident awe inflamed his imagination. A curious part of him wished he had been there to see it. Old stories said a single Daniti warrior could cut down twenty men in as many seconds. It was said their weapons had been made by modifying ancient tools used in former times to cut stones from the mountains. There was a saying among the Daniti: *Our force can move mountains.*

"A part of me wishes I had seen it," Gibson said.

"It was—I've never seen anything like it," Nef said.

"They wanted to send a message. And they wanted their vengeance for what happened in Noot." Gibson tapped a report on the table in front of him. A Hruskan army had routed the small Yinocki forces there. Gibson continued, "Did they kill the on-Dam?"

"If he was there, he is dead. No one survived."

"How many were killed?"

"Dozens. There were several Daniti wounded. But I don't know if any of them were killed. I do not think so."

Gibson lightly rubbed his forehead with his fingertips. He let out a breath and said, "Kim has requested *avilah* for all of her warriors. She is ready to go to war."

"Has the Council agreed?"

"That decision belongs to the temple, but it will be granted. It probably already has. But with the Well of Geb defunct, it will be harder to purify so many. Water will have to be brought up from the river."

"The priests will be busy," Nef said.

"And the servants," Gibson said with a shake of his head. "The temple mothers will have to take their little ones down to the river if the well remains dry. For that matter, my own servants will have to go down too."

Nef's face looked troubled.

"What is it?" Gibson asked.

"It was wrong of him to use the well like that." Nef's eyes narrowed. "I will admit I'm glad he was arrested."

Gibson raised his eyebrows, a little surprised. He had not thought Nef cared much about such things. "I was angry, too."

"But how did he stop it?"

Gibson was surprised again. The inquiry evinced a puzzlement, a vulnerability he had never observed in Nef. But it was not difficult to understand. Against the expectations of ordinary people, the prophet had worked a wonder. He had evoked comparisons to ancient precedents. He had become a miracle worker.

"I don't know," Gibson said. Silently he considered the reports he had received. "But however it happened, the prophet has brought more trouble on himself than he can handle. Especially in light of this." He tapped the report again. "It won't be long before Kim moves against the prophet's followers. Time is running out."

For a moment, neither man spoke.

"The van will be ready at your word," Nef said.

Gibson nodded, but he did not speak immediately. Now that the time for a decision was upon him, he questioned every plan he had considered. And he feared Tendar was somehow impelling him down a path to ruin. But he could see only one path to follow. It was time for Maran to leave the city, but he could not send him to Noot.

Gibson said, "At a steady march, the Hruskan army could be here in eight days."

"We won't have that long."

"No. In a day or two, traffic around the city will be restricted. And closely watched." He shook his head. "And I can't let them stop the van. Maran's only hope is to get out of the city immediately."

"That shouldn't be a problem," Nef said. "I was concerned about drawing too much attention, so I organized the van into several smaller parts and moved them to the outer city. They are ready to go—as soon as you decide where to send them."

"Excellent." Gibson smiled. And for a moment he calculated, tracing lines across the map in his mind. The van could not travel the road south, but Maran's best chance lay in reaching Shal-Gashun. *So, how to get there.* It was a question he had been pondering.

Gibson took up a sheet of paper and quickly drew a rough map with a few lines. "Here," he said. He continued to write directions. "The hill country to the east is passable. There are only small settlements, and they can be avoided easily. If the wagons pass through this region—generally through here—the van can eventually gather in a small valley here." He pointed to a spot with his finger. "It's a good place, and there is fresh water there."

Nef's keen eyes examined the paper. "How will we know it?"

"Urudu knows the place; he has been there with me. He will have to go with the first group. And Maran, too. They can post a few men to bring the others in. The rest of the van should be able to get close enough with directions."

Nef traced his finger over the roughly drawn map, and for a moment he said nothing. Then, "To reach Shal-Gashun will be difficult. Reaching the *pustinya* will be hard enough. But if the *pustinya* reaches too far north in these eastern regions, it will be difficult to reach Rume."

Gibson nodded. But in his mind, he saw the far more detailed map of his family, and he knew Nef's concern was unfounded. The *pustinya* stretched far to the east, but its northern edge followed a nearly straight line. If they did not travel too far east, Rume would be within reach.

Though it will be across unfamiliar land.

He said, "It is a harder journey than I imagined for Maran on his first trip to Shal-Gashun. I would have preferred to send him through Noot, on the road."

Nef rubbed his chin. "So when will they leave?"

"We cannot wait any longer. The van leaves tonight."

CHAPTER TWENTY-SEVEN.

VISIONARY.

Sarana paused in the hallway outside her master's room. The usual warmth of the little lamps on his table had been extinguished. Gloom reigned within.

Gibson had departed for Gazelem late in the day, and he would not return for two or three days. *Two days at least.* His promise to teach her the next set of letters had fallen by the wayside. She would have to wait. But she would not be idle.

The hallway was empty behind her; she stepped inside the room. Though it was dim, she moved quickly, unerringly to the shelves along the wall opposite the window. Gibson kept the little slate and several sticks of chalk there. Her hands quested in the darkness. She found the little cup he had put there to hold the chalk. But she could not find the slate. She slid her hand along the shelf. Not there. For a moment she stood still, wondering where he might have put it.

When she turned back toward the table, she stopped. Telasa was in the doorway, watching her.

But it was not so. It was only a partially open door down the hallway—a patch of darkness in the lighter hallway. Her guilty conscience had transformed it into the shape of someone standing in the doorway. Her beating heart calmed, but only a little. With Gibson gone, there was no reason for her to be in her master's room, and she worried Telasa might catch her. She dared not delay any longer. She tucked a piece of chalk inside her robe; she would have to do without the slate.

Back beside the hearth, she knelt and arranged the warming jars beside the fire. It was just as well Gibson had gone to Gazelem. She was already worrying about how to obtain enough water, and fewer people in the house would make her job easier. Maran was gone, too—supposedly getting ready for his first trip to Noot. But Pelem said that was unlikely. Not with war in Hrusk. Especially after what the Daniti had done to the on-Dam and his household.

Sarana moved some of the jars of water from the back toward the front, nearer the fire, and she moved those at the front to the back. *The first shall be last, and the last shall be first,* she thought. Just as her temple mother had intoned all those nights ago. Sarana smiled.

Every night, Abasha had turned down the lights in the great room and stoked the hearth of the training house. The dark eyes of the girls had shone with reflected firelight in the darkness. *The first shall be last, and the last shall be first.* The old woman had always smiled so kindly upon them when she said the second part, and Sarana had known she was thinking of them.

The house grew quiet.

Sarana straightened the stacks of baskets and closed up the bins of freshly-picked *rebboth.* A few things still needed doing, but she did not hurry. It was her night to bank the fire, and it gave her an excuse to linger. When she finished the day's labors, she wanted to practice her letters. But she would wait until the other women were sleeping.

Neturu stared into the little fire Lihana had built up. The evening meal was past, and most of the household chores had been done. The scorcher woman had put a hand on his shoulder briefly, comforting him; but then she had retreated into silence, content to be there with him in her little home.

A soft tap on the door drew Lihana's gaze away from a small pile of odd bits of cloth she was sorting. "Come in," she said.

The door opened, and Doman stepped inside. He had a bundle in his arms, and he walked over to where Lihana was sitting. "I've

brought you some things," he said. "Look at this." He opened the
bundle and started to sort some items on the table.

Neturu glanced over, but he was not interested. There were
probably things in that pile from his father's house. *Maybe even some of
my things.* He turned back to the fire and watched the little flames. A
few minutes later, Doman stepped in front of him and Neturu looked
up. The giant scorcher was holding a folded blanket in his hands. But
there was something wrapped up inside. Neturu stared.

"I brought you this," Doman said. And he unwrapped the sword
of the on-Dam.

"Did you—" But Neturu stopped before finishing the question.

"I didn't ask the director," Doman said. He glanced over at
Lihana. "I decided it belonged to you. So I took it."

Neturu shook his head. "But it doesn't." He spoke without
conviction. The sight of the sword had sparked a tremulous joy within
his breast. He had keenly wanted to take the blade earlier. He had
regretted his choice. But he had also chastised himself for doubting
the rightness of his decision.

"It was your father's sword," Doman said. "It should be yours."
He sat and laid the sword across his knees. "I also took this. Your
father's ring." He placed the ring on the floor in front of him.

Lihana looked down at the curving blade and the golden ring.
"Oh, Doman," she said.

"I have been thinking," Doman said slowly.

"You know I trust your judgment," Lihana said. "But others must
have seen you take it. The director will hear of it."

"If it comes to that, I will make my case with the director. But I
don't think anyone knows I have them. Except you. There were a
great many swords in the weapons cart, and they won't be counted
and catalogued until tonight or tomorrow."

Lihana shook her head. "And you think I should remain silent."

Doman shrugged, his face calm. "Perhaps not, Liha. But consider
carefully what I'm about to say. This sword, and the ring, may be
lawfully his." He turned to Neturu. "I've been thinking about this all
day, my friend. About the future. Your future."

"I—"

But Doman did not let him speak. "With the destruction of your house, there may not be anyone left—anyone of consequence—who knows your status. Your father and all of his counselors were killed. Many believed you were killed on that first day by your father's enemies. But here you are. And from what I can learn, your father never named a new heir before his death."

Neturu's intended protest dwindled away. It was possible Doman was right.

"You could reclaim your place," Doman said.

The room grew quiet.

"It would be a lie," Neturu said finally.

"Would it?" Doman rested his hand on the hilt of the on-Dam's sword. "Do you know that? And who would gainsay you?"

Neturu thought for a moment. "The legalities are murky. Challenges could be made, but you could be right." Neturu wondered how many people still living knew the reason for his once-father's decision to ostracize him. He shook his head and said, "Well, it doesn't matter. Not now. There is nothing to reclaim."

"There is still your family in Hrusk," Doman said. "Your mother is there. And war is coming to the Great City. People are saying the Hruskan army routed the Yinocki forces in Noot."

"It means little," Neturu said. "They will not be able to stand against the Daniti."

"But if they do." Doman shrugged. "If they do, everything changes."

"And you think I should take my father's place."

Doman nodded. "You need to think about it. I know you are not happy here. Not now. And if the Hruskan army is successful . . . it would be better, for all of us, if you were the on-Dam."

Neturu considered the scorcher's words, and he wondered at the audacity of the proposal. The on-Dam's house had been reduced to dust and rubble, but in Doman's view it was still there to be reclaimed, an indestructible construct of mind, not breakable by the hands of men. *Is that what he sees? And why did I not?* Neturu tried to imagine a future where he stood as on-Dam over the people of the Great City. But the exigencies of the present crowded his mind. "And if the *Yinoi* destroy my people?"

Doman turned a hand over in his lap and said, "Then nothing need come of it, and you will be no worse off than you are now. If the bin-Yinocki prevail, then you can either remain here with us, or try to escape to Noot. You could return to your mother."

"My mother," Neturu said. "She will soon receive reports, or at least rumors, of my ostracization, if she has not already. And then she'll hear about my father." Neturu shook his head. "A lot of people know my father ostracized me. There won't be any way to conceal that."

"But you might not need to. He never named an heir."

"If there is any question, the Hruskan Fathers will have to sort out his succession."

"As far as you are concerned, there will be nothing to sort out if you do not make a claim," Doman said.

"True enough," Neturu said. "But it will be contested. You do not know the politics of Hrusk." Neturu remembered the words his gap-toothed assailant had whispered. *You have forgotten the face of your father. But I will not forget yours.*

Doman picked up the sword from his lap and held it out to Neturu. "Though I pass from one world to the next, I endure," he said.

Neturu looked at he sword. And then he picked up the little ring.

As he considered what to say, what to do, a knock sounded at the door and Saban leaned inside. His mouth sneered a bit, and he said, "You're not going to believe this. But we're being called out again. Nearly every wagon."

"It's the middle of the night," Doman said. "And the wagons are still loaded down from this afternoon." Doman glanced at Neturu.

"Not any more," Saban said. "They're being emptied right now. The director has called out everyone to empty them where they stand. There's another big job in the Upper City, and it'll all be sorted out later, I guess. It's a *prekleti* mad house."

No one said anything for a moment.

"And we'll still have to make our normal runs tomorrow," Doman said. But he was already getting to his feet and readying his mind to work. He wrapped the on-Dam's sword back inside the blanket and set it on Lihana's little table.

"I'll come, too," Neturu said. He had clutched his father's ring in his fist when Saban had entered. He slid it onto his finger and picked up his crutches.

Sarana looked over the little lines of letters she had drawn on the smooth stones of the hearth room floor. The low light from the fire tinged her work with gold. Each letter Gibson had taught her, each variation, had become familiar to her, and she drew them now with ease—more precisely, too, and smaller, though still not perfectly.

For a moment, she admired her work. Then, with a damp cloth, she wiped them away and started again, enjoying the sharpness of the letters against the water-darkened stone. The beauty and perfection of her master's hand still eluded her. But she was close, and she could see the forms in her mind.

A repeating matrix of letters flowed from her hand, but after several minutes, she left off writing her lessons and wrote the combinations of her name. *Sah, ahr, ahn, ah.* Twice more she wrote it, enamored. She had pieced together a few other simple words, and with the last two combinations of her name, she had discovered she could write a few other names. She wrote them out. And then she paused.

A new word had taken form in her mind. The sacred name of Esana. At least she thought she had got it right: the ninth variation of *ehah*, the sixth variation of *ah*, and the basic letter *ah*. The word appeared on the stone: *ehas, ahn, ah.*

"Esana," she whispered.

She stared at the little group of letters, full of awe. *Ehas, ahn, ah.* They added a new dimension to her devotion, and for a tingling moment she almost felt Esana was going to answer her call. Writing the letters and reading them aloud felt like a special invocation.

But no discernible answer came to her whispered call. The stones of the hearth room were as silent as the stones of the temple wall.

Except that they were not.

All around her, the stony tablets of the hearth room were filled with her carefully written letters. A new feeling filled her, and she looked at her hands, enthralled. But not with the secret pride that so often impelled her to admire their inimitable beauty.

Now they held a power she had never imagined or contemplated. They had become tools of curious workmanship, a conduit for thought. Like the ancient scribes of the Lines, she had captured a bit of truth with her handiwork. The lines of letters had passed from her mind, through her hand, and onto the surface of the stone. She had become a scribe of indecipherable messages; she had written her own revelation.

But it was not all indecipherable. She traced the name of Esana with her finger, captivated. Three letters. A word encapsulating the hope of an entire nation, an entire world.

A vision opened in her mind. And she thought she saw how the variations had once been part of a single whole. The letters of the sacred name blazed before her eyes, and on the stones all around her, the sinuous variations flowed and combined, made molten by the power of her thoughts. Each variation expressed a tiny part of the whole, each one unlocked a bit of truth.

But there was more. The variations were an outward expression—beautiful in their design—but a deep and secret word lay hidden beneath them all. And she thought if she were to put enough of the letters together—if she could but find the correct combinations—she might be able to discern the hidden word buried beneath them. It seemed the variations were all a part of a fragmented truth, a truth that had been broken into smaller and smaller parts, until, alone, each part resembled only itself.

It made her want to weep. And at the same time, she wanted to shout, to rejoice.

Compared to the secret word, the letters she had written on the stones of the floor were the indecipherable markings of an unlearned child. But the irreducible truth of them could not be repressed. Each one was a key. And beneath them, like the leaves of a book, layer upon layer of complex variations stretched down into the earth, striving toward the hidden seed from which they had sprung. The flat stones of the hearth room floor had become the lid of a secret law box. She imagined prying up the stone and finding pages of hidden Lines beneath.

You are a little coal, but I will make you a whirlwind of fire.

A quiet snap in the fireplace broke her revery. Her vision faded. In the dim light of the dwindling fire, the letters on the stones were barely visible. She looked up. A flowing mist of heat and light, the guttering orange flames of the hearth, licked and slid over the edges of the blackened remains of the wood. Jars lined the hearth, and in the warm darkness, bowls and baskets lurked, neatly stacked. It was time to bank the fire and go to bed. And it was time to clean off the stones.

But as she reached for the little cloth to wipe the floor, she heard raised voices and the sound of someone running across the courtyard. Pelem. Even before he entered, she knew the sound of his approach.

He ran into the room, stopping when he saw her on the floor. "Sarana. What are you doing?"

"I was just . . . I'm cleaning the floor." She gestured vaguely at the stones. "I was practicing the letters Lord Jianin taught me."

Pelem looked at the floor. But then he shook his head. "You need to get up. Get the others up."

"What's going on?"

"There are soldiers at the gate."

Chapter Twenty-eight.
House of Order.

Gibson watched the little lamps approach along the dark path of the *hodari*. A pair of travelers was coming slowly toward him, each carrying a small oil lamp, and he strained to see them better. One was his wife, or so he had been led to believe. They were too far away to tell.

The message had arrived late, just as he was getting ready for bed. *I will come in three hours to the place where you made your vow to me. —L.*

The note could have only one meaning, if it had come from his wife. To most, it would mean little, even if they knew who had written it. But Gibson knew. And even though Nef had warned him it could be a trap, Gibson had decided he would go to the appointed meeting place. It was the first time in months his wife had shown any willingness to see him. For that alone he might have gone, but it was possible she had other important information. Even Nef had acknowledged that.

The two travelers stopped when they reached the place where Nef stood waiting for them. Gibson watched, anxious. But then Nef bowed slightly, and one of the travelers continued on. Gibson turned away, his mind stripped down to a single thought: *She came.*

He felt the dread and hopeful anticipation of seeing his wife after several months of separation. He wondered again what could have impelled her to seek a meeting with him in the middle of the night.

No doubt she knew of Maran's entanglement with the prophet and his followers.

But why would she arrange a meeting out here, in the middle of the night? He had no sure answers. He could not guess what her motives might be.

And then she was there. He heard her walk up behind him, her steps deliberate in the darkness. He turned. The light from her little lamp had joined his own, and her pale Yinocki features looked up at him from beneath her shawl.

"Lisana," he said.

"You fool."

Sarana gathered with the other servants beneath the branches of the giant *hresta.* Torches lit the courtyard and created shadows in the doorways. A small cohort of soldiers had filled the yard. Their captain directed men here and there throughout the house and grounds.

Light glowed in the upper windows, and sounds of disruption filtered down into the yard. Sarana felt her anger wax. But it was impotent. She looked over at Ganon, who stood with his head bowed, eyes toward the ground. Blood dripped from his chin, running down from a cut on his cheek. He had tried to stop the soldiers from entering the yard, protesting their authority to enter without Lord Jianin's consent, but they had forced their way in. And when Ganon had tried to block their way, the captain had struck him across the face with the hilt of his sword.

Telasa still looked defiant, but even her sharp tongue had been dulled. They were just servants; there was nothing they could do.

"Servants of the House of Jianin." The captain stepped up in front of them. He passed his eyes over them. Then he read from the pronouncement in his hand. "All who walk the path of exaltation are entitled to a house of order. That your comings and goings may be in the name of Esana; that your greetings and farewells may be in the name of Esana; that you may serve with hands uplifted unto the Most High." He paused. "But the Lord of this House, the Lord Jianin, has not maintained a house of order." The captain paused and let the import of his words grow.

Ganon raised his eyes, and Sarana thought she saw his fists harden. "And so," the captain said. "You will be restored to a house of order. By order of the Council of Elders and of the House of the Most High this house is forfeit, and it will be reduced and stripped of all honors of office and rights of property. And you—"

He stopped; Kaina had stepped forward with her hands upheld. "What has our master done?"

Seeing her age, the captain's mien softened. "It is not my errand to discuss the workings of the Council. But you need not be concerned, sister. If you have done no wrong, you will be spared your master's fate." He raised his voice to include the rest of the group. "And you. Your bonds have been reclaimed by the temple, and you all will be given to new houses."

Sarana shrank within, and murmurs erupted from some of the others. But Kaina was not finished. "I am a free woman," she said.

The soldier looked down at her wrist. "You wear the mark of Jianin."

"Only by choice. The Lord Jianin redeemed my bond many years ago. But I have remained with him, and he has kept me in his household. He is a good master."

"It's true," Telasa said, stepping forward a pace. "She must be accorded all the rights of a free woman." A few others murmured agreement.

The captain looked back and forth between the two women. He blinked slowly, and his gaze settled on Kaina. "Do you have proof?"

"Inside," she said, gesturing toward the house. "The Lord Jianin gave me my tenth on the day he redeemed my bond. I have kept it ever since. And the *talah* was recorded in the temple, according to the Lines. But I'm an old woman. Your own eyes can tell you my jubilees have come and gone."

One of the soldiers approached and whispered something in the captain's ear. The captain nodded. He turned his attention back to Kaina. "Perhaps, but I have my orders. If you can show me proof you're not a servant, I will let you go." He gestured toward the soldier at his side. "Go with her. And help her carry her things out of the house. You can take only what belongs to you."

Kaina put a hand on the captain's shoulder. "Thank you, child. The Lord Jianin would thank you for treating an old woman of his house with respect."

Kaina and the soldier went inside and the remainder waited in silence. The captain turned and looked at the house, pensive. Sarana looked over her shoulder at Ana. They were each as helpless as the other. Sarana offered a small smile and let her gaze wander among the other servants of the house. And then she realized Pelem was not among them. She looked over the group again. He was not there. Her thoughts quickened. He had come inside to rouse the women. *But where did he go?* She had gone straight back to wake the others; she had not seen where he went. Sarana looked back at the house. *What's taking her so long?*

After a few long minutes, Kaina emerged from the house. The soldier walked behind her, carrying a small bundle of clothing, a blanket, and a small hearth jar.

"Show me the tenth," the captain said.

Kaina handed him her little sack of coins. The captain emptied the coins into his palm and appraised them. "This is a nice bag," he said, rubbing the soft fabric. And then he carefully tipped the coins back inside.

"It was his way to treat us well," Kaina said. "If you knew our master, you would not do what you are about to do. You would refuse."

The captain hardened. "I do not exercise my own will in this." He handed the little bag back. "You are free to go your own way. Or stay. It matters not to me."

He looked back down at the pronouncement in his hand and started reading again; he raised his voice. "By order of the Council of Elders and the House of the Most High, this house is forfeit. All honors of office are removed, all rights of property are extinguished. You servants—your bonds are reclaimed by the House of the Most High. All allegiance to your former master is dissolved. And if you have separated yourself from the true faith, you must recant and submit to the will of Esana."

The captain paused and let his gaze traverse the gathered members of the household; he asked, "Are there any among you who have followed after the heretic who defiled the well of Geb?"

Sarana's heart quickened. She felt the soldier's gaze had focused on her, and a diminutive voice in her bosom urged her to step forward. And for a brief moment, she imagined doing it. A galvanic idea. But fear had reduced her; her instinct was to hide. She looked around. *Who knows what I've done?* But she had told no one. Kaina might have guessed. Ana and Pelem knew she had been going to see him. Telasa was staring at her; Telasa certainly knew some of what she had been doing.

And then Telasa turned and spoke to the captain. "We are a house of faith," she said. "We hold the hope of Esana in our hearts."

"Then it will be well with you," the captain said.

Sarana's fear turned to watery relief.

The captain continued. "I speak the will of the Council and the will of the House of the Most High. It is my duty to carry it out. *Es-prida!*"

As he spoke, several soldiers closed in around the huddled servants.

"You are advised not to interfere." The captain turned toward the house.

A soldier emerged from the hearth room holding a large jar. For a moment, Sarana did not understand what was happening. But then he threw the jar down and shards exploded outward. Sarana flinched. A large curved shard spun outward and rocked back and forth on its convex side. Kaina touched her back, steadying her. The old woman said something, but Sarana did not hear it. Her eyes were fixed on the scattered pieces of clay.

And then the destruction continued. From one of the upper windows, a soldier hurled down a wooden chair. It hit the ground with a crack, and a leg splintered and broke off. The house disgorged several more items. Jars, plates, a box, a stack of baskets, a foot basin. They smashed and clattered on the ground. The servants of the house grew restive. But they could do nothing. And then a soldier with a sword in one hand and a handful of severed *rebboth* vines in the other emerged from the vineyard. He walked to the growing pile of broken and discarded items and tossed the fruit-laden vines onto the heap.

Sarana cried out—a gasp, an incoherent outcry. But Kaina held her arm, and Ganon turned and held out his arms, forestalling any attempt by any of them to interfere. Sarana struggled briefly against Kaina's grip, angry, broken; but she quickly gave up, knowing she could do nothing. The enormity of the act crushed down onto her, and she stared at the mutilated vines. Some of those plants had been growing in their master's vineyard for decades. Generations of vines had grown out of the careful husbandry of Gibson's grandmother, whose deliberate hands and farseeing mind had coaxed greatness out of a poor patch of earth.

The breakage subsided. Clothing and bedding still fell from the upper windows by the armload, but the rain of breakable items ceased. The soldier in the hearth room emerged with more jars, but these he lined up on the ground. Some of the others started piling things up into heaps. They might have been readying goods for transport. Except that the sound of chopping axes still came from the orchard, and the soldier in the vineyard emerged with another handful of ruined vines.

"Why are they saving some things?" Sarana asked. The moment of crisis had passed, and several of the servants had started talking quietly.

"I don't know," Kaina said.

"It is symbolic," Telasa said, moving over to stand beside them. "They have to destroy some things. To show that the house is forfeit. But the rest will be saved and given over to the scorchers. According to the Priestly Lines. Look." She gestured toward the gate with her head.

A line of carts had arrived from Pekel.

"Ah," Kaina said. "A nicely arranged plan."

"Everything will be unclean once they seize it," Telasa said.

Sarana said nothing, but she thought, *Once they take it, what does it matter if it's unclean? At least they didn't break my new jars.*

Telasa glanced at the captain, calculating. His attention had shifted to the work of his men. She turned her gaze upon Sarana. "What do you know about this? We all know you've been going to see him—and Gibson allowed it. Did you join the prophet?"

Sarana looked at Kaina, wordlessly beseeching her aid, but the old woman merely raised her eyebrows. Sarana looked back at the head water woman. She thought about lying, but she shrank instinctively from it. And then she realized her silence had already betrayed her. A moment of silence passed among them.

"I see," Telasa said softly. "And did our master know?"

Sarana shook her head and her resistance trickled away. "I . . . never told him. I was one of the people at the well today. I might have ended up telling him. But I didn't tell him when I got home. And then he left for Gazelem." She clung to that last thought, but it was a poor rationalization for her silence. She had thought to hide her baptism away.

Telasa stared at her. "You always promised to cause trouble in this house." But the usual fire in her eyes did not kindle.

"This is not a time to be thinking of old transgressions," Kaina said. "And none of it will matter in a day or two anyway."

"What do you mean?" Telasa asked.

The old woman shrugged. "Only that you will not be house sisters in a day or two. The temple has reclaimed your bonds. And when you are given to new houses, it will not be to the same house."

This silenced the women again. Then Telasa spoke. "You are right. Even if there were a house that could use us all, they won't keep us together."

"I won't go to a different house," Sarana said.

"You won't have a choice," Telasa said. "Your bond is already forfeit. Your servitude no longer belongs to the House of Jianin."

Sarana hardened her will. "Gibson won't let this happen."

Telasa shook her head. "It's already done, and he's not here."

"But he's only in Gazelem."

"Maybe. But he could have been arrested. Or maybe he was warned this was coming, and he left the city altogether."

"He wouldn't just leave us," Sarana said.

Telasa rubbed the lower half of her face; her eyes betrayed anguish.

"We can't worry about that," Kaina said. "And it's time to do something we can do. Look at them." The old woman gestured toward the heap of broken items and ruined vines. The scorchers had begun sorting through it. "They know it's valuable, but they'll ruin half the seeds before they're done. Probably not one of them has ever harvested it."

Sarana almost snarled. "You think we should help them?"

"The vines are already destroyed, child. It's worse to let it all go to waste. And perhaps we can do something for our master, in the end."

With their little lamps burning beside them, Gibson and Lisana sat within arm's reach of each other on the stony hillside of the *hodari*.

"You must tell me," Lisana said. "Has he already left the city?"

Gibson considered the question, but he did not speak immediately. Partly he just wanted to look at her. She had pulled back her shawl, and the dark furl of her hair hung down her back, held in place with silver combs. Ageless Yinocki beauty limned her features; he knew she would outlive him by many, many years. His eyes kept glancing at the little line at the right side of her mouth—a little line etched there by her slightly quirky smile. She used to smile often. And he had often traced that little line with his finger and then tipped her chin upward.

By the Wayfarer, she is beautiful, he thought.

Her sharp eyes caught him. "He's my son, too," she said, ignoring his silent adoration.

"He is safe. He is with Urudu." He did not want to answer her question. He was not sure he could trust her. Her family was too closely tied to the great houses. But if she spoke truly, she had come to warn him that Tendar intended to move against him very soon, within a day or two.

But the very fact she knew Tendar's plan was proof, possibly, that she was in his confidence.

"So he is gone," she said, guessing. But to Gibson it looked as if she were deeply relieved.

"You are glad," Gibson said.

"I didn't want him to go. I wanted to see him before he left." She looked to the south, as if trying to see him. "But I'm glad you acted quickly." Gibson thought maybe her eyes shone a little more in the lamp light.

"Perhaps I'm not such a fool as you thought." Her greeting had stung a little.

She laughed, but without much mirth; she did not turn to look at him. "Don't presume too much. You deserve credit for keeping him safe. But you let everything else be destroyed."

"You're exaggerating." Gibson spoke calmly. This landscape was familiar, the arguments comfortable.

Now she did turn. "You refuse to understand what's happening— what's already happened." She pressed the tip of her finger down on her knee. "There's been an agreement among the councilors. Tendar bin Amin already has the votes he needs to divest you of your house. To put it in order."

Gibson felt his certainty erode; a dismal sickness filled his bosom. "Any vote will have to come before the Council," he said.

This time her laugh was abrupt. "It will. But the vote that matters has already taken place. And he will act quickly. You never understood how these things work."

"I know well enough." Gibson sat back. "So they're going to hold me responsible for Maran's error."

"It's more than that. Though that would probably be enough with things as they are, with the Hruskan army a step before the door." Lisana looked out over the dark plains. "You won't be the only one."

"What else do they have against me?"

Lisana paused before answering. "Tendar says he has admissions from a servant of your house—confirmed by two witnesses—that you permitted her to go and listen to the heretic. Heresy in your bloodline, and fostering heresy in your household. More than enough to put your house in order."

Gibson nodded. "I thought as much. Sarana told me herself a man questioned her. His men snatched her right off the street. I thought it might be Tendar. And then he came to see me—and tried to buy me."

"So it's true."

"Are you here to confirm the allegations?" An unworthy retort. But a part of him still wondered what her motives were.

"Did she tell you as well that she was baptized?"

Gibson blinked, focused. "What?"

"That foolish girl has brought down your house. And you let it happen." Her voice was harsh.

"She wasn't baptized."

"You didn't give her permission to do that, too?"

"No."

Lisana shook her head. "Well it won't matter. There are witnesses who say they saw a servant of the House of Jianin baptized. At the Well of Geb, no less. And they heard her say she had your permission."

Gibson felt the same twisting sickness in his belly. *Why would she do that?* But it could be lies.

"You were always too kind, too understanding," Lisana said, softening. "Like your father. You never took a hard line with your household."

His wife's words were kindly meant—at least in her uncompromising way—but they sounded too much like one of their old arguments. "Everyone deserves kindness," he said, defensive.

"And now you see the return it brings."

Gibson grew quiet. "Why are you here, Lis?"

"I wanted to warn you. And to make sure our son is safe." Her lips parted, and she seemed on the verge of saying something more.

"Maran is safe," he said. "And if I can get him to Shal-Gashun, he can stay there until it is safe to return."

"It's a long road to Shal-Gashun," Lisana said softly.

Gibson smiled, a bit sadly. It was one of his father's old sayings—a saying his father had applied to any difficult task. "It is," he agreed. "But Urudu is with him, and most of my best men."

Lisana blinked rapidly. "You should think about going, too."

Her words surprised him, but he responded without pause. "It's better if I maintain a semblance of normalcy," he said.

"When they put your house in order, you will have nothing here. Your house will be forfeit, your property stripped from you. If they permit you any stewardship at all—if you even want one—you will be beholden to one of the Great Houses. It's what Tendar wants, I think. Part of what he wants, anyway."

"I also promised you I would never return to the road."

"Maran's no longer a child," Lisana said. "And neither am I."

Gibson recalled the evening he had made his vow to her. They had not been married long—just over a year—and the idea of never parting from one another was still little more than a few spoken words. It had changed that night, though, when she had told him their child was on the way.

They had gone to the *hodari* for a late-afternoon walk, and, as they often did, they had stopped where the path wound through sun-dappled pools of shade. He had been looking into her face, his fingers curled beneath her jaw, tipping her face upward, and she had said, *I can see the road in your eyes.* He had laughed, thinking her words were inspired by the tales of the road he had been telling her.

But then she said he needed to let the next van go to Shal-Gashun without him. He could not risk the road now. Now that their child was coming. For a moment he had only stared, and then he had slid his hand down over the front of her body and rested his palm on her stomach. And he had stared at the spot where his hand lay. A child in her womb, a tiny captive star, its own constellation in the dark interior of her flesh. He had promised her that day he would never leave her.

"I told you then I could see the road in your eyes," Lisana said, joining him in his memory. "I was the fool, I guess, to think that it would ever be different."

"I have kept my vow."

"I know. However unhappily." She smiled in his direction. "But you won't now. You cannot." Lisana looked south into the vast darkness of the night-drenched plains.

Gibson felt his mind move south. *Perhaps she's right.* He looked at the line of her profile, softened, but clear in the lamplight. An embodiment of the ordered aspects of his life. But absent lately. And he still longed for her.

"A house of order," he said softly.

She turned. "What?"

"Maybe Tendar is right." He shook his head, hesitated. "I received a warning the other night. It was just a note; it said, 'Your house is not in order.' I was angry when it came. I wondered how they dared to do it. But maybe it's true." Gibson looked into Lisana's eyes. And then he decided to reveal his heart. "I never should have let us be apart. I should have found a way for us to be together."

But she did not reciprocate. "It's too late for that."

"They can't take everything from me."

"Your house is lost. And you won't be happy here with what they leave you."

Gibson leaned forward. "We wouldn't have to stay here. I—we have holdings from here to Shal-Gashun. All throughout hari-Hrusk, in fact." He paused, calculating. "My holdings in Noot might be lost, but Shal-Gashun is beyond the reach of the Council. And you could finally see Rume."

Lisana shook her head. "I can't leave my family. The Great City is my home."

"We wouldn't have to stay there forever," Gibson said. But they had returned to a familiar landscape, and he knew such assurances meant nothing to Lisana. He floundered. Then he looked down the *hodari*. Nef was approaching, loping through the darkness quickly. Gibson stood and held up a hand to forestall any further argument; Lisana looked over her shoulder.

"Forgive me, my Lord. But I have an urgent message." Nef paused, looked toward Lisana.

"Go on," Gibson said.

"Speak," Lisana said at the same time.

"One of my men just brought word. Your house has been seized."

CHAPTER TWENTY-NINE.
THE OLDEST STORY.

Twice Sarana had quietly wept as she sorted through the *rebboth* vines. But mostly her anger held sway.

Kaina had convinced the captain he should allow the women of the house to aid the scorchers in harvesting the ruined remains of the vineyard. He could not stop Kaina; she was a free woman. But he agreed it made no sense to prolong the scorchers' labors when there were willing workers standing idly by. *And besides,* Kaina had said to the captain, *they don't know what they're doing.* And she was right. The work of plucking the seeds without breaking them or damaging the fruit within was more delicate than most people knew.

And so, in the small, dark hours of the night, surrounded by the locust efficiency of the scorchers, the serving women of the House of Jianin harvested the last of their master's fruits.

"I have one more story to tell you," Kaina said.

Sarana looked up.

"The story of Svetlaba-Hansha. My mother said it is the oldest story. It is the first story of my people." Kaina picked up one of the ruined vines and laid it across her lap. Her practiced hands went to work on the rough, brown seeds, plucking them and dropping them into the basket at her side.

"Kainish nonsense," Telasa muttered, but loudly enough to be heard.

Kaina pressed on. "Long ago, before you were born—before I was born—before your grandmother's grandmother's grandmother was born—there was a place where the youthful immortals dwelt. No one remembers the name of that place, so we just call it *Predan-shomo-telo.*" Kaina paused, smiled. "The place without days."

Her gravel voice continued, deliberate. "In Predan-shomo-telo no one ever died or became ill. There were plenty of fruit trees, and the *desarati*—we Kainites called them *shebulsa*—produced honey all the time. The flowers never withered, and there was an endless diversity of beauty. People never harmed one another because there was no need to harm anyone. There was enough food for everyone, and everyone had his own home."

"Like paradise," Ana said.

"Yes, a place like paradise. There were flowing rivers and towering trees, high mountains, and glorious lands. All manner of beautiful things lived there, and there was no enmity. There was no fear, for the immortals could not be harmed. And for an age of ages, they lived there after the manner of happiness."

Kaina paused to look at the other women. "But some of them were not content in the place without days. And rumors began to spread that there was a better place—a place where they could find true happiness. Then some of the immortals began to feel sad, and they began to weep."

"And that," Telasa said. "Is where rain comes from."

Ana giggled.

Kaina smiled, amused. She was used to Telasa's disdain for anything not found in the Lines. "Even an unlikely truth is sometimes true," Kaina said. "But you are wrong, of course. Every child knows the rain comes from the wool of the great lamb in the sky. Even the street *harimi* will tell you that."

Sarana smiled along with Kaina, and Ana giggled again. Telasa merely shook her head and continued to work.

"What happened next?" Sarana said.

"Many of the immortals were sad. But not all. One of the wisest and kindest of the immortals was Svetlaba-Hansha, and he went from place to place, telling the others there was a better place. And he said they would find true happiness only if they left the place without days. He said there was an unseen world where they would gain wisdom and power."

Kaina examined the vine in her lap and laid it aside. She picked up another and kept working as she spoke. "Most of the other immortals refused to believe him. They said there could be no greater happiness than the happiness of Predan-shomo-telo. But eventually, he began to convince some of them he was right, for he was filled with wisdom, and many said he must have gained his wisdom in the unseen world. And they started trying to convince others. And soon the whole of Predan-shomo-telo was divided between those who believed in the unseen world, and those who did not."

Kaina paused and looked toward the house. The soldiers seemed to have finished inside, and they were standing around in small groups, keeping out of the way of the scorchers. She returned to her work. "At last the unbelievers told the others they should leave the place without days. They said, 'If you are so sure of a better place, you should not be afraid to leave.' "

Telasa interrupted. "And so, like us, they had to leave."

This time Kaina remained serious. "You may profit or not from the wisdom of my people, Telasa. But do not assume there is none."

The women sat quietly in the torchlight, Ana alert, ready to witness whatever conflict might break out.

But after a moment Telasa looked down into her lap. "I'm sorry." She brushed her cheek with the back of her thumb. "I'm just—. There's nothing we can do. I can't stand being so helpless." She gestured vaguely at the mangled vines and looked around at the scorchers who were sorting the property of the House of Jianin into carts.

"Not completely helpless," Kaina said, taking up another vine. "There is always something we can do. Now listen." The old Kainite resumed her tale, and she seemed to grind out each word even more slowly, demanding patience. "The immortals said, 'If you are so sure of a better place, you should not be afraid to leave.' But Svetlaba-

Hansha said, 'I am *not* afraid. For I have already been to the unseen world. And I have seen that it is good.' "

Kaina wiped her hands on her apron and selected another vine from the heap of mangled branches. "Well, this was a surprise, and the immortals asked him many questions. When had he gone? How could he have gone? Where was the unseen world? What was it like? Some, of course, did not believe him. But Svetlaba-Hansha answered all of their questions. He told them everything he had seen, and he revealed a world they had never imagined. He described lush jungles and dry deserts. Jagged mountains, vast oceans. He described all manner of animals they had no names for, and he said some were ferocious and some were friendly."

Kaina paused and looked around the courtyard.

"What else?" Sarana asked.

Kaina frowned slightly and stared at the carts lined up near the gate. "There won't be time to finish my story if I tell you everything he said. But Svetlaba-Hansha's tales filled the other immortals with wonder, and some with dread. And many of them felt a desire to see the unseen world."

"What filled them with dread?" Telasa asked. This time without disdain.

"Ah," Kaina said. "That is what I was about to tell you. Svetlaba-Hansha also told them if they wanted to see the unseen world they would have to experience things they had never known before—pain and fear and sadness. He told them about hunger; he told them about war. He told them about sickness and death. And when the immortals heard about these things, their hearts grew cold and turned to stone.

"But while Svetlaba-Hansha's stories were dreadful on the one hand, they were wonderful on the other. And the more his stories were told and retold, the more curious the immortals became. Many longed to see the unseen world. Many believed experiencing the wonders of the unseen world was worth any price. And so the conflict over Svetlaba-Hansha's words grew. It was a time of great tumult among the immortals."

Ana interjected. "I think he was telling the truth."

Telasa let out the slightest huff and shook her head, smiling wanly. "Many immortals agreed," Kaina said. "But Svetlaba-Hansha still had one more thing to tell them. And it was a thing he had waited to say, for he knew it would turn many of the immortals against him. He said, 'There is one more thing you must know. By traveling to the unseen world, I have brought about the end of Predan-shomo-telo.' The other immortals did not understand. But then he explained. He said, 'Already the peace of Predan-shomo-telo is gone. Knowledge has created conflict, and conflict has bred distrust and some enmity. And soon Predan-shomo-telo will pass away entirely.'"

"But why?" Sarana asked.

Kaina smiled, a sweet smile. "That is the very question they asked Svetlaba-Hansha. And he told them, 'By design.' So then Svetlaba-Hansha told them what they had to do. He called all of the immortals together. He said, 'I know you have been trying to determine what course you should follow. But in your hearts, you already know the choice that is before you and the course you will choose. You can choose to leave Predan-shomo-telo, or you can choose to be forced to leave. Those are your only choices.'"

Kaina paused.

"That's not much of a choice," Telasa said.

"What do you think they did?" Kaina asked.

Telasa shrugged. "I'm guessing they chose to leave."

"It seems like everyone would have chosen to leave," Sarana said.

"That's what almost everyone who hears this story says," Kaina said. "But not all of the immortals chose to leave. For some, the fear of experiencing every sort of pain, every sorrow, every hardship—the fear of losing each other—was too great to overcome their hope of happiness. Many did choose to leave, however, and they soon departed the place without days. Some wept, but they remembered the wonders of the unseen world Svetlaba-Hansha had described. And they left with hope in their hearts."

Kaina stopped and brushed her hands on her apron. Most of the *rebboth* had been harvested; the vines lay in curling heaps around the women. "There is more to the story," she said. "But it's almost time.

So let me ask you. Do you think you would have chosen to leave Predan-shomo-telo?"

"I would have," Sarana said.

"I suppose. But it wasn't much of a choice," Telasa said.

"Ana?" Kaina turned her dark eyes on the younger woman.

"I don't know. But I think I might have."

Kaina nodded. "I am certain you all would have. And here is the lesson you must learn from Svetlaba-Hansha's story." Kaina paused and looked at each of them. "I know you all would have chosen to leave. The fact is, you all *did*." She paused again. "You all did. You just don't remember it."

For a moment no one spoke; then Telasa asked, "What do you mean?"

"I mean that you were *there*. I mean that you lived there, in Predan-shomo-telo—that you were one of the immortals, and you chose to leave. You are one of the immortals. You chose to experience the sorrows and joys of the world."

"You're saying I lived somewhere else before I was born?" Telasa's disdain had returned.

"That's not true," Sarana said.

"You think you did not?" Kaina did not wait for a response. "Surely you believe your spirit will go somewhere else when you die. Where do you think it came from?"

"That's different," Telasa said. But her voice had moderated.

Kaina shrugged. "Perhaps. Perhaps not. But the story of Svetlaba-Hansha tells me something about myself. About who I am. It reminds me I am capable—that everyone in the world is capable—of great courage. That everyone has already *shown* great courage by choosing to live this life. And, so, when we face a difficult choice, or a harrowing confrontation, we know we have the strength to choose valor. Because we have all chosen valor before."

Telasa looked down into her lap. "That's a nice sentiment, Kaina. But we still can't do anything about all this."

Kaina produced a pruning knife from inside her robe and examined the vine in her lap. "We can't stop these men or change the will of the Council, but we might be able to save a part of our master's vineyard. We still have choices to make." She ran her fingers over the supple vine, pausing at points and bending the little leafy branches. Then, satisfied, she cut off a section and put it into the jar by her side.

"Scions," Telasa said softly; and then she looked over her shoulder toward the soldiers. But from where they stood they would discern nothing.

"Finish up with those vines there," Kaina said. "And let me know if any of them are suitable. I can save a dozen or more cuttings in my jar."

Telasa went back to work; she asked, "Will they survive?"

"I don't know. I hope some of them will. I don't have grandmother Jianin's skill, but I watched her work many times. There's a little water in my jar. And when I have a chance, I'll wrap them properly, bundle them up, and keep them safe until I can graft them into new plants."

Sarana looked at the pile of vines beside her, but she had never learned anything about grafting. The others would have to find the right vines.

Kaina glanced toward the scorchers. "I'm also going to demand payment from the scorchers for my labors here. And in payment I'm going to take a share of the seeds I harvested. As a free woman, I am entitled."

Sarana stared at the little baskets of seeds, her mind riven. *Why hadn't she thought of it?* If she could escape with a basket of Lord Jianin's *rebboth*, she could repay her master's kindness tenfold, a hundredfold. The vineyard could be replanted. And his goodness, his faith in her would be justified.

"You can't take payment from scorchers," Telasa said. "You'll be unclean."

"I know," Kaina said. "But I cannot think of another way to do more for our master. And it's my choice."

"The *rebboth* belongs to Gibson," Sarana said, whispering fiercely. "We should just take it."

"No," Kaina said. "Not anymore. It belongs to the scorchers, now."

"And besides," Telasa said. "What would you do with it? We won't be able to plant them in our new houses."

Sarana bit her lower lip. Assignment to another house had not yet taken hold in her mind. A new servitude in some other house, a servant to some new master—she had not let herself confront it. But when the soldiers took her from this place, everything would change. She thought about what it meant. To never be with Kaina again, or Ana, or even Telasa. And Pelem and Ganon. To never see her master again. To never learn the rest of the letters he had promised to teach her. Bleak paths of loss unfurled in her mind, and her sorrow and anger rekindled. Stealing a basket of *rebboth* would alter nothing. And Kaina's efforts were ridiculous.

She looked from one woman to the other, her grief and rage trembling in her eyes. But they had no comfort for her; they had seen the truth of it before she had. They knew the House of Jianin was gone, destroyed. Silent panic fluttered in her breast. She was helpless before the inevitability of her loss, the impossibility of avoiding what would happen.

"What do we do?"

Kaina smiled. "I already told you what I'm going to do."

"You can't do anything," Telasa said.

"But we—" Sarana stopped, suddenly aware. There was something she could do. There was a path still open to her. She had done it once before, if imperfectly, but this time she would not fail.

"I'm coming with you," Sarana said, turning to Kaina.

"Don't be a fool," Telasa said. "You can't just leave. They won't let you."

Sarana shook her head. "They won't have any choice. I'm going to renounce my servitude."

"You can't—" But then the older water woman halted.

Ana's mouth opened slowly in unbelieving surprise.

Telasa regained her voice. "You're more foolish than I thought, Sarana. How can you even consider it?"

Sarana did not immediately reply.

"Consider carefully," Kaina said.

Telasa leaned forward and said softly, fiercely, "You cannot abdicate your sacred vow, Sarana. It would be a grievous error. Gibson would not ask you to. You don't understand what you are saying."

"Yes I do," Sarana said. And she thought about the day she had left her jars and abandoned her servitude, if only temporarily.

"You think you know. You walked away from your duties a few days ago, but you didn't really renounce. Not really. If you do this, there's nothing to come back to."

Sarana recalled how she had crawled back, groveling. The sense of failure, of weakness, of spiritual poverty, had been overpowering.

"You won't survive among the *nebini*, Sarana," Telasa said. "It's not so simple as that. You'll have nothing."

Sarana hesitated, but her resolve hardened around a simple conviction. "I will find Gibson."

"You foolish girl," Telasa said. "Foolish, foolish girl. He could be anywhere. You won't—how will—" Telasa cut herself off. "You'll end up in a house of levity or worse, a whore, dancing for strangers and their filthy lucre. But maybe you won't mind that, after all."

Ana's mouth fell open.

"Sarana," Kaina said, ignoring Telasa's harsh words. "You do not know what Gibson would think if you renounced your vow. He is a man of the Lines. He might not lightly overlook it."

"I have to do something," Sarana said. "And I know you want to, too." Sarana looked at Telasa.

The older water woman clenched her jaw, but she did not deny the younger woman's charge. Her eyes dropped; she said, "I would do almost anything to put things back the way they were."

Sarana stood. She understood Telasa's fear; she did not know why she did not feel it as strongly. "If you can think of some other way to get out of this, tell me. But I won't be given to some other house." She looked over her shoulder toward the gate.

The captain had glanced over at her when she stood, and he raised his chin and looked at her. She took a step toward him, hesitated briefly, and then she strode across the yard to confront him.

Chapter Thirty.
Broken Vow.

"I want you to get them out if you can," Gibson said. "Any who wish to go."

Nef stood with his arms folded, one fist pressed against his lips. In the lamplight, his face looked softer, but the intensity of his gaze evinced the working of his mind as he considered Gibson's request.

The house in Gazelem was quiet, nearly empty.

Gibson did not know if the remaining members of his house in the Great City would want to abandon the city and flee to Shal-Gashun, but he was certain some would. And he wanted to give them the option. He could not just leave them behind.

"It will be difficult," Nef said.

"It might not be possible," Gibson said. "Not if they've already been taken to the temple compound. But if they are still at the house, you might be able to convince the soldiers there to let them go—that it is not worth their trouble to hold them. How many men can you take with you?"

"I don't know," Nef said. "A few. Most of our best men left with the van. Among those who remain—" He shrugged. "Most of them are regular day laborers and contract workers. A few men who have been on the road. Reliable enough. And decent fighters, some of them. But the problem is calling them up in time. I could buy all the loyalty I need with the money you've given me. There just isn't time."

Gibson rubbed his face and steepled his fingertips between his eyes. "Right." He turned to Pelem; the stable boy was sitting beside the hearth, listening carefully to the older men. "How many soldiers were there?"

"I don't know, my Lord."

"You didn't see them?"

"No. When Ganon saw them coming, he sent me to wake the women. He told me to climb over the back wall and come here as fast as I could. He said you needed to know."

"He did well." *Though he would have done better to tell you how many he saw.* But he knew Ganon had done the best he could with little time to act. And Ganon had stayed at his post. A good man.

"Probably at least a dozen soldiers," Nef said, following Gibson's thoughts. "Not to mention the scorchers."

"They won't interfere," Gibson said.

A sound at the door drew their attention. It was Lisana; her pale features looked like stone. "I heard something in the distance. Some sort of commotion. I think they must be coming."

"That's it, then." Gibson turned to Nef. "No more time. If you can get them out, do it—any who want to go. Use the money if you need to. Whatever is necessary. But do not tarry. You need to be out of the city before first light. If I am not at the meeting place when you arrive, leave without me and join up with Maran and the others. Do not delay. I may be gone ahead of you, depending on how things go here."

Nef clasped Gibson's outstretched hand. "Until we meet again."

"*Es-prida,*" Gibson said. "And to you, too, Pelem." He held out his hand to the boy. "You served me well tonight. *Es-prida.*"

When they had gone, Gibson turned to Lisana and gestured toward the front door. She adjusted her shawl on her shoulders, and Gibson followed after her into the vestibule.

"You don't have to stay," he said, facing the door. He had been surprised when she had sent her servant back to her parents' house and accompanied him to their home.

"I'm not going to run out the back door of my own home," she said. "And don't purport to advise me. This debacle is not my doing. I warned you long ago of the need to form alliances."

Gibson turned to look at his wife. She was looking toward the door expectantly, her face in profile, as if waiting to greet guests. His thoughts strayed, and he recalled the lazy, easy days of a brighter past, when their house had been open to friends and visitors. Time had been spent like money in those days, lavished simply on the excesses of wealth. His family's earlier struggles had passed away like a dream; his fortunes had proliferated. He never would have foreseen this moment then—standing on the cusp of destruction in an empty house with his estranged wife.

Perhaps that's why this day has come, he thought. *Because I did not plan for it and avert it. That's what she would say.*

He watched as her hands smoothed the front of her clothes, her adamancy seemingly revealed by her bodily form. His thoughts turned to admiration. *By the Wayfarer, I am glad she is by my side.* He turned and looked back at the open door, trying to think of something to say to her.

She spoke first. "You won't gain much advantage by staying for this."

"The longer I stay in the city, the less chance there is anyone starts looking for the vans. Any advantage is useful."

"Every bargain exists within limits," Lisana said.

He laughed briefly. And then he smiled at her use of his father's phrase. "So it does. But if you won't run out your own backdoor, I won't either. Besides, if Tendar shows up, I want to give him his gift." Gibson had left a finely crafted wooden bowl of *kivich* on the table in the guest hall.

A little smile showed on Lisana's face. "The brave fool." She seemed about to say something more, but she did not, and the little smile evaporated.

Gibson waited, but when she did not speak, he said, "You always forgave my foolishness, found it endearing."

"Not always."

They stood silently for a moment, expectantly. But no one came, and the distant sounds of commotion did not grow nearer. Gibson turned his attention outward, his eyes on the dark street beyond their little courtyard.

Then a scream sounded in the night, and Gibson tensed. And then distant sounds resolved in his ears. A fight had broken out. More than one. He smelled smoke then, and he heard someone running in the street.

"Fighting," he said.

Lisana looked at him.

"Listen." He stepped out into the courtyard and she followed. At the gate he leaned out carefully and looked up and down the street. Another scream erupted in the distance, followed by the sound of swords clashing. Toward the lower end of town and to the south, the sky glowed with fire.

For several seconds, Gibson stood still, immobilized by the unexpected sight. Then his mind unlocked, and blocks of thought shifted. Whatever the Council had planned for him this night, his house here in Gazelem would not be put in order just yet. He stood there for a moment longer; he needed to know what was happening. But the sounds of fighting were sporadic and brief, and there was shouting from more than one location.

And then he thought he understood. And dread—and anger—filled his bosom.

"Come!" He pulled on Lisana's sleeve and hurried back to the house. He ran to the storeroom and looked over the things Urudu had left behind. Not much remained, but his own arms were still there. He picked up his knife belt and tossed it to Lisana. She caught it and quickly secured it around her waist. She was not a trained fighting woman, but she was not inept.

"Take the knives," he said, gesturing toward a small shelf where they lay in a neat line. He picked up his short sword, pulled it halfway from its sheath, and snapped it back into place. He regretted Urudu's absence, but there was no use worrying about things he did not have.

"The horses are still in their stalls," Gibson said, thinking through options aloud.

"Who's doing this?"

"I can't be sure." He shook his head minutely. "But it's not the Council—though they are ultimately responsible for the hostilities with Hrusk." He looked into Lisana'a eyes. "I think it is the *hinavu.*"

She balked. "But the Hruskan army is still days away. The Daniti are holding them north of Noot, at Penuk."

Gibson acknowledged and dismissed her observation with a quick tilt of his head. "That may be," he said. "But the *hinavu* would operate separately from the main army, moving at their own speed. Single units could easily slip through—make their way across the countryside."

Lisana said nothing for a moment, considering his words. "If you're right, Kim will have her way with the Council," she said finally.

Gibson tensed, certain he had heard something from the front of the house. He held up a silencing hand, tingling on the edge of action. They stood motionless. But he heard nothing more.

After a few seconds of silence, he said, "We need to move." He looked around the storeroom, but there was nothing else useful. He regretted now leaving himself alone with Lisana; he doubted his ability to protect her. "Come. Let's go to Urudu's quarters. We can see the stables and the alley from the side room there."

The little room was mostly dark, but light from the hallway fanned back the gloom, revealing sparse furnishings. Gibson went to the window and parted the curtain with one hand. The yard and stables were quiet, but beyond them, the revelatory glow of fire suffused the sky. He let the curtain fall back into place.

"Fire to the west," he said, turning. "I hope Nef and Pelem are all right."

Lisana nodded slowly, but she was looking at the ground. She took two steps and turned, the fingers of her right hand clasped inside her left. For a moment she hesitated, her face stony. Then she said, "If it is the *hinavu,* Tendar will have to change his plans. He'll have larger problems to deal with."

Gibson frowned. "Tendar stands to benefit almost as much as Kim. An attack by the *hinavu* can only strengthen his push for unity."

"Yes, but he won't be coming for you. Not tonight."

"It hardly matters now," Gibson said. "The house has already been seized."

Lisana hesitated. Then she said, "It matters if his plan was to have you arrested."

Gibson felt his thoughts sharpen. "Was that his plan?"

"I don't know." Lisana met his gaze. "I don't. But that's why I came here tonight. That's why I got you out to the *hodari*."

"That doesn't—" He cut himself off. "If you were worried about that, why didn't you tell me?"

"Because my first concern was Maran. I knew he wasn't here—in Gazelem—but I didn't know where he was. If he had not been gone already, I would have told you my fears then. I would have warned you against returning home, and I would have told you to get him out immediately."

"But since he was already gone—" Gibson shrugged. "It didn't matter if I were arrested."

Lisana closed her eyes and shook her head. She turned away. "You saw the need to stay here yourself, to maintain appearances. Even if it gained Maran only a little time, it was better for you to stay." She looked back at him. "You were right about that, I admit. I almost told you to leave anyway, but instead I came here with you—to resist any attempt to arrest you."

Gibson considered her explanation. He wondered what she would have done, or said, to halt an attempted arrest. But he did not doubt her ability or resolve. The image of her standing by his side in the vestibule was still fresh in his mind.

"I'm sure you would have been persuasive," he said.

"They would not have wanted to force the issue with me," she said, dismissing his attempt at lightheartedness. "But now we have to think about something else. This attack may give you an opportunity. If Tendar has to change his plans or accelerate them, he may be willing to bargain more liberally."

Gibson demurred. "No," he said. "They have seized my house illegally. I won't bargain with Line breakers. Besides, I've already made my plans. In a few weeks I'll be in Shal-Gashun."

"You have other options," Lisana said.

The distant sounds of a fight drew their attention to the window, but the noise of conflict had diminished.

"The *hinavu* may be withdrawing," Gibson said. "But that won't be the end of it—they'll want to do as much damage as they can—create chaos and confusion—before the city tightens its defenses. This may be our best opportunity to get out."

Lisana stared. "Haven't you even wondered why Tendar has come after you?"

Gibson shrugged. "The merchant houses look to me. He has long wanted greater influence among them."

"It's more than that," Lisana said. "It must be." She paused again. "Why would he bring your house down if he wanted to peddle your influence? Why did he have your house seized?"

"My last meeting with him might have something to do with it."

Lisana stood still for several moments, and then she looked up. "You must have something he wants—something he knew you would not give up willingly."

"My support in the Council. He offered me my house and my seat if I would agree to give him my support."

"Did he ask for anything else?"

"No."

"Oh, Gibson." Lisana pressed her palms together and raised her fingers to her mouth. She closed her eyes. "Did he get your maps? Were they at the house when it was seized?"

Gibson's defenses rose up, and he looked instinctively toward the open door before responding. "Only three people know about those maps, Lis. You and Maran and I."

Lisana let her hands drop back to her sides. "You know I would never reveal the secrets of our family. But even the best-kept secrets have a way of escaping."

"Not this," Gibson said.

"Did he get them? Were they seized?"

Gibson considered her question for a long moment. But he had to trust her; he could not bring himself to do otherwise. "No," he said. "Maran has them."

Lisana let out a breath and bit her thumbnail, letting her thoughts continue to run their course. "It almost makes sense for Tendar to do this, if he somehow learned about them." She paced again, clutching the fingers of her left hand in her right. "But if he thought you had artifacts from the days of Yinock, he probably would have tried to buy them. Unless he didn't want you to know beforehand that he knew about them. In case you tried to conceal them."

"You really think he'd do all this to get my maps?" Gibson did not believe it.

"He holds the ancient office of Treasurer," Lisana said.

"Yes, and he won't let anyone forget it. But his proclamations about rebuilding the Great City of Old are little more than vain imaginings."

"He truly believes the city of old can be rebuilt. He's not merely posturing."

Gibson pushed aside the little curtain and looked outside again. "Tendar's vain ambitions don't concern me. The question I have is what you intend to do now." He turned back to her. "The fighting has stopped for now, I think. And as far as I'm concerned, this attack has provided an opportunity to get away sooner, with fewer complications."

Lisana was about to reply, but she stopped abruptly and held up a hand. Then she closed her eyes, made a loose fist and held up one finger. "Did Tendar propose a partnership with you? Did he suggest an expedition?"

"What? No." The question seemed odd, misplaced. "No. He wanted my support in the Council."

Lisana fixed her gaze on Gibson's eyes and said, "Think carefully. Did he say anything about the Wayfarer?"

"Yes, he thinks the Wayfarer's fall is some kind of sign."

"It's more than that." She started pacing again. "He believes it can be recovered."

"Recovered?"

"Yes. And he intends to find it." Lisana grimaced and almost growled her annoyance. "I should have thought of it sooner. Its seems so clear now—I see now why he might have seized your house."

Gibson frowned as he worked through the implications of her words. It did not seem clear to him. He said, "You think he intends to find the Wayfarer?"

"Yes. And I think he seeks to coerce your cooperation. No other house can match the House of Jianin in such an endeavor. He wants to control you." She paused and shook her head slightly. "Perhaps he thought he could find family records or journals to help him with his search."

Gibson recalled Tendar's cryptic words about the fallen Wayfarer. *It is a sign. And perhaps more.* Tendar had said something else, too—though Gibson had thought little of it at the time. *You and I could accomplish many things together.* It had seemed like an empty platitude at the time, a means of placating and persuading. But it fit with Lisana's suspicions. Perhaps Tendar had been hinting at an imagined venture to find the fallen Wayfarer. It seemed an incredible possibility. And, yet, his thoughts had briefly quickened when Tendar had said the city of old could be rebuilt.

"I should have thought of it sooner," Lisana said again.

Gibson shook his head. "It would have made no difference. Now that Hrusk has attacked the city, the rule of the Council will become even more peremptory, and any who fall out of favor will have no recourse. It's time for me to leave, and I think you should come with me." He gestured toward the yard. "This little skirmish was only the beginning, and the city is not ready for war. When the Hruskan army breaks through at Penuk—and I think it will—you do not want to be in Gazelem. The Daniti won't be able to defend it."

"You think the rumors are true? About the Daniti?"

"True or not, Gazelem is not defensible. You and your parents—everyone in Gazelem—will have to move into the city."

Lisana was silent. Finally, she said, "I can't just leave my family."

"If Hrusk prevails, your family will be small comfort."

She looked down, her eyes falling away from his, her shoulders falling slightly. "I cannot go to the South," she said.

Gibson clenched his teeth together, and his upper lip twitched. *By the Wayfarer, she is stubborn.*

Even facing the prospect of war and the threat of being trapped in a besieged city, she resisted his pleas. But she had no real fear; she did not believe the bin-Yinocki could be defeated by Hrusk.

He was about to argue with her, but he knew her defenses. He knew she would not yield. She would emerge triumphant, if only in her own mind, and a little part of him wanted her to be spectacularly wrong. And to suffer for it.

He swallowed his anger, his bitter anger. "We'd better go then," he said. "I can take you to your parents' house before I meet up with Nef and the others."

CHAPTER THIRTY-ONE.
SWORD OF HRUSK.

Sarana stopped in front of the captain. She saw his eyes appraise her, dropping from her face, flicking downward and back up. His eyes were dark, his cheeks narrow and stern.

"Have you finished with the *rebboth*?" he asked.

"No, not yet," she said. She glanced back over her shoulder, and her heartbeat strengthened in her chest. The other women were all staring at her, and Telasa shook her head. She quickly turned back. "But I—I have something else to say." She took a breath. "I am renouncing my servitude."

The words had no immediate effect. But then his eyes narrowed, and he shook his head. "What did you say?"

"I am renouncing my servitude." She said the words carefully, loudly.

A little pool of silence rippled outward from her as nearby soldiers and scorchers became alert. The captain paused. His brow furrowed, and he frowned slightly. "You can't be serious. You—" But he cut himself off. He reached up and rubbed the side of his neck. Then he made a dismissive gesture and said, "Whether you do or not does not concern me. Wait." He held up a hand when Sarana threatened to interrupt him. "You certainly have that right—however foolish it might be to exercise it—but it does not concern me, here. You can take that up with the temple stewards when you get to the complex.

We're nearly finished here." He started to turn away.

"No," Sarana said. "I won't go."

"You will," the captain said, turning back to her. And then he held up a placating hand, forestalling her again. "Wait a moment." He turned and called out to one of the nearby scorchers. "Have you completed the inventory? Is the manifest ready?"

"We're done," the scorcher said.

The captain turned back to her. "My orders are to bring the former servants of the House of Jianin to the temple complex. Your bonds have been reclaimed, so any renunciation will have to be dealt with there." He looked off to the side before continuing; he spoke more softly, leaning toward her slightly. "When you've returned to the temple complex, you can make your decision. You can renounce your servitude there. But trust me when I tell you—think about it carefully. Do not be hasty."

"I don't need more time," Sarana said.

"Do you even know—have you thought about what the Lines demand of those who renounce their servitude?"

Sarana thought back to her days in the courtyards of the temple complex; she knew. She recalled Abasha's kindly face and her soft but stern teachings. She was free to renounce or keep her servitude—all temple servants were—but choosing a life outside of her godly bonds was akin to choosing death. Those who chose to renounce received no tenth, no house, and no promise of labor or livelihood.

"I know what the Lines say," she said.

"But have you ever seen them carried out? Have you ever seen anyone stripped of the rights of servitude?" The captain shook his head. "It doesn't matter, anyway. I have my orders, and I won't let you go. It's not up to me."

"I know," Sarana said. She held up her hand and pulled back her robe, revealing the silver mark of the House of Jianin she wore on her wrist. "It's up to me."

Neturu moved slowly among the scorchers who were readying the last carts. He leaned heavily on his crutches, fatigued from the long labors of the night, and his broken leg complained with pain. He had scratched his hand while loading one of the carts, and it hurt.

Tension in the yard had dwindled slowly away. The servants of the house had settled near a tree in the center of the yard, and some of the women had offered to assist in harvesting the remnants of the vineyard. The destruction of the *rebboth*, the wanton ruination of so much wealth, had astonished him. He had not known the *Yinoi* were so unmitigable in dealing with their own. *Perhaps we are not so different.*

Neturu looked at the empty house, its dark windows. The house was not familiar to him, but he wondered what had become of Maran. He had known the heir of Jianin only briefly; they had been baptized on the same day. He shook his head. Both of them had abandoned the teachings of their youth to follow a rogue prophet of the bin-Yinocki. Now both of their houses had been destroyed—more or less. And their prophet languished in prison.

His wandering thoughts halted. Something was happening near the gates, and some of the scorchers and soldiers had stopped to stare. He stepped closer.

A young servant woman stood in front of the captain, her hand upraised. For a moment the image held. And then she lowered her hand and started to remove the little chain of servitude she wore on her wrist.

"Stop," the captain said loudly.

But the woman did not stop. Instead, when she had loosed the little chain, she held it up and said, "You can take this to the stewards, as proof that you did your duty here. You have witnesses." She held out the little chain, and the silver mark of her servitude hung in the light of the torches.

The captain clenched his jaw; he said, "By the Lines, woman, you cannot force this. I have my orders to take you in. All of you." He waved her off and turned away from her.

But the woman did not relent. "I have made my choice," she said loudly. "Please take it." The little silver mark hung from her clenched fist.

The captain ignored her, but when she did not move, he turned back. He started to say something, stopped himself, and frowned. He did not take the proffered chain.

Finally, he spoke. "You don't understand. You've only barely begun what the stewards will demand of you. As one of the *nebini* you have no right to any of your former master's belongings." He gestured in her direction. "You have nothing that is your own. Nothing. Not even the clothes you wear. Are you going to satisfy the Lines right here in the yard?" He gestured around at the assembled people.

For a moment, the woman stood rigid. She did not move; no one moved. The captain stared at her a moment longer, and then he turned and said to one of his men, "Get these people moving." He gestured with his head toward the woman, telling her go back to the other servants.

Neturu let out his breath; the confrontation had ended.

And then he blinked. The woman had tossed the little silver chain to the ground at the captain's feet. She was not done. Her hands reached up and, trembling a little, she removed the scarf from her head. She tossed the scarf to the ground.

As her hair fell loose, Neturu looked around at the various bystanders, certain someone would do something to stop her. Surely someone would prevent her from doing what she was about to do; surely the captain would stop her. But everyone stood rapt, including her sister servants who were huddled around the ruined remains of the vineyard. No one moved.

And then the young woman removed her robe, letting it fall to the ground around her ankles. The captain's eyes widened, and, finally, one of the women sitting beside the *rebboth* vines stood up. One of the former servants of the house—the man with the bloody lip—said something, but it was a powerless murmur. Still no one stepped forward.

The young woman's dark hair curled and fanned over the back of her neck and arms in beautiful disorder. A long shift still covered her body, but the thin fabric was a frail shield against greedy-eyed onlookers. Neturu saw one former servant of the house—a young man—shift slightly from behind a larger man to get a better look.

"Stop," the captain said. He held up both hands. "Stop now. Even if you do this, you will not go free. I have my orders, and I will make no exceptions. Every servant of the house must be delivered to the temple complex."

The woman hesitated. But then she took hold of the shift near her waist, grabbing handfuls of the fabric with both hands. Her shoulders lifted slightly; she was going to take it off. Neturu stared, unable to turn away. He did not want to turn away.

Sarana trembled. But not with fear.

Like the stones at the Well of Geb, she trembled with latent energy. The fabric in her hands felt insubstantial. Only the idea of renouncing her servitude, of pulling off her shift in front of this soldier—and everyone else—seemed real. It was a moment of coalescent power and weakness. A cusp. And her belly tingled with nervous energy. And perhaps a little fear, after all.

"Stop," the captain said again. "You will only shame yourself."

But his words were hollow and weak, prompted by fear. And she knew she had already prevailed over him. His threat was empty: she could not shame herself by fulfilling the Lines, and a part of her wanted to tear off her shift and throw it to the ground. A part of her wanted the narrow-faced soldier to know he had lost. And she knew she could do it. The vision of it blazed in her mind, like the image of Esana standing on the wall of the temple, framed by *kolobian* glory. It was the work of a moment. An everyday action. She had but to raise her clenched fists, to draw her shift up over her head.

But before she could resolve further, a cry pierced the quiet air of the yard. It was followed by shouting. Sounds of fighting. More cries.

The imagined world of possible futures evaporated, and Sarana found herself looking into the captain's eyes. Something had changed in his look, but she did not have time to divine what it was. He turned and jogged briskly toward the head of the line of scorcher carts. He called to his men and sent one of them running out the gate.

All around her, the flow of the world resumed. Some of the soldiers moved toward the gate and others stood their ground, waiting for further orders. The scorchers moved to their carts and wagons, and a few of the smaller carts started to roll out. But they did not get far; they stalled inside the gate where the captain and some of the soldiers had gathered.

Sarana looked around. Kaina was coming toward her. A hand touched her shoulder, and she flinched. But it was only Ganon, and he touched her tentatively. He had picked up her robe, and he held it out to her. Kaina picked up her discarded scarf.

"What's happening?" Sarana clutched her bundled robe against her chest.

"I don't know," Ganon said. "Come on." He urged the women back, away from the gate.

The yard grew darker as several soldiers dropped their torches and readied their small shields. Sarana and the other servants gathered in beneath the *hresta*. Another yell sounded in the distance. An alarm.

A moment later, more shouting erupted in the street, right outside the gate. A man was arguing with the captain, demanding entry. Their voices grew loud, and then Nef pushed his way in, with Pelem at his heels. Sarana felt a burst of relief, and her body tingled. Nef was close to Gibson; he would know their master's plans. Perhaps Gibson was with him. She stepped forward hopefully.

The captain trailed behind Nef, continuing their argument. "This is no longer your master's house."

Nef turned back and pointed at the captain. "Right now you need every man you can get."

The captain beckoned to one of his men. "Put him with the other servants of the house."

"Don't touch me," Nef said to the approaching soldier. His calm authority and menace were unmistakable. Then he said, "Captain, you need to listen to me."

"I do not—"

But Nef interrupted him. "Hruskan fighters have attacked the city. They're killing people and setting fires."

The captain hesitated. "The Hruskan army is still days away."

"No," Nef said. "The *hinavu* are already here. I was in Gazelem when it started. But I think that was just a diversion. You need to draw your men in. We should move inside and secure the house."

"You think they'll come?"

"And everyone here needs to be armed. Now." Nef gestured toward the waiting wagons. "There are a few weapons in those wagons, and we need anything else that can be used as a weapon."

"You—" But the captain suddenly choked. His hands clutched at the shaft of an arrow protruding from his throat. For a moment he struggled to speak, to breathe—*guk, guk, guk*—and then he yanked the arrow out reflexively. He fell unconscious to the ground; blood pooled and flowed outward.

Nef whirled around and drew his sword.

A second soldier staggered backward, an arrow protruding from his shoulder joint. He screamed shrilly.

Nef yelled, "The roof!" And then he ran toward the house.

Neturu saw the captain fall, and he watched as the other man drew his sword and ran toward the house. Caught unaware by the abrupt death of their leader, the remaining soldiers reacted slowly or not at all. But one finally understood, and he ran inside the house after the other man to find their attacker. He called out to the others, and several more followed behind him, swords drawn.

Neturu turned; Doman had stepped up beside him.

"We're leaving," Doman said. "We can't do anything here. It's not safe."

Even as he spoke, the scorcher carts and wagons started to roll out of the yard. Doman did not wait for a reply; he simply pointed and went back to directing the other scorchers.

Neturu nodded, but he turned back toward the house, unwilling to withdraw from the unfolding events.

They won't find him there, he thought, looking up toward the roof of the house. He knew how the *hinavu* operated. They moved swiftly, always seeking new targets, constantly sowing confusion. They killed indiscriminately, blazing multiple paths of chaos, and then they withdrew, only to return again hours or days later, until they were dead or until the war was finished.

A part of him felt a predatory satisfaction. *They deserve it.*

But he immediately regretted it. And, yet, he could not fully turn his thoughts away from it. *They do deserve it. For what they did to my father.*

Sorrow grew in Neturu's breast. He looked at the servants huddled beneath the tree in the middle of the yard. They did not know what to do; they argued and gestured, helpless. The soldiers at the gate had disappeared, and the scorchers were slowly trickling out. There was yelling inside the house; they could not find their attacker.

Neturu felt a grim smile, a prideful smile. He looked around. The yard had grown dark, and distant sounds of conflict rived the night. He leaned on his crutches and started to turn away, to join the departing scorchers.

But as he did, a dark-clad man emerged from the vineyard, running swiftly and silently across the yard. Neturu froze, fascinated. The man veered toward the servants standing beneath the *hresta*, his movements smooth. A thin, curved blade flashed upward, and for a moment, Neturu's enkindled mind saw—or maybe just imagined—the massacre unfolding before his eyes. The swordsman passed through the group like a wind of knives, a purveyor of death.

Then Neturu yelled. *"Tulu on-Damu! Tulu on-Damu Hruskai!"*

Only a few understood his words: Bow to the Sword. Bow to the Sword of Hrusk.

Sarana saw a black shape rush toward them. A man, an upraised sword. But he was among them even as she cried out a warning.

With a fluid motion, the attacker turned the blade of his sword outward as he ran past Pelem. At the last moment, Pelem perceived his peril and flinched backward. The blade cut across his forehead. Pelem screamed and clutched at his sundered face. Blood trickled from beneath his hands.

Sarana pushed Kaina to the side, and the old woman stumbled. Some of the others ducked and scattered outward. But it was too late. The upraised blade of their attacker flashed across his body.

The metal bit into Sarana's neck. And at the same moment, she heard someone yell.

But she did not understand the words. She did not understand anything. Her throat filled with fire, and she tried to speak. But no words would come. Her mouth gulped noiselessly, ineffectually, unable to release the fiery revelation. *I need some chalk, to write it down. I know the letters.* And then the waters of her mind overflowed. The well, the Line of *Es*, her jars. Innumerable drops of memory. The stony path of her servitude. It seemed nothing had been lost.

She tried to turn her head, to find Kaina. But she could not move. Distantly, she heard the old woman crying her name: "Sarana! Sarana! No. No!"

Her knees broke suddenly beneath the strain of standing, and she fell backward on the hard ground of the courtyard. A crack sounded in her ears.

At first she saw only darkness above her. But then the black, gnarled branches of the old *hresta*—adorned with their new leaves— resolved against the lightening sky. Dawn threatened at the edge of creation, but peeking through the gaps in the leaves, stars.

Worlds, she thought. And her mind flitted. *To some, we live in the heavens. And up there, among the stars, is Esana's homeland. My homeland.*

For a moment, her thoughts seemed to move outward, and then she felt the hard ground beneath her. The back of her head ached. She had dropped her clothing. She clutched at the ground by her side, fingers slowly scrabbling to find her things. She had dropped her clothes. She had dropped them. And she had left the mark of her servitude on the ground. *My hair is uncovered.*

Then she thought, *I am going to die.* And then, unexpectedly, *That soldier is dead.* She felt her eyes sting, and the light of distant worlds became distorted through the liquid crystal of her tears.

Something pressed down hard on her throat. But the pain seemed distant. She closed her eyes.

Neturu swung forward on his crutches, desperate. He nearly fell as his left crutch caught briefly on the ground. He caught himself.

But he was too slow. The young woman who had confronted the

captain was in the path of the *hinavu*, and the curved sword found its mark. Blood emerged in a line across her throat. She stood rigid, and then she fell. Her head smacked the ground.

"*Tulu on-Damu!*" he cried again.

The dark-clad *hinavu* stopped and turned toward him. He took two deliberate steps toward Neturu, and his sword moved slowly upward, preparing to strike.

"*Tulu on-Damu Hruskai*," Neturu said quietly, firmly. Bow to the Sword of Hrusk. He let go of his crutch and held out his right fist. The on-Dam's ring gleamed dully on his finger.

The *hinavu* took another step forward, paused, and dropped to one knee. He planted the tip of his sword on the ground and knelt with one hand on its hilt. "*Tulai on-Damu*," he said.

Neturu looked down at the young serving woman. Blood had flowed down over her shift; it looked black. An old woman knelt beside her, attempting to bandage her throat with something. She repeated the young woman's name, and she wept. "Sarana, oh, Sarana, Sarana." There was nothing to do for her, and Neturu stared helplessly.

A man stepped out of the house. "Neturu on-Dam," he said.

The *hinavu* stood and turned in a smooth motion, his sword raised to a defensive position. Neturu looked up. It was the man who had arrived before the attack—the man who had led the charge against the *hinavu* on the roof.

The man slowly laid his sword on the ground and held up his empty hands. "I wish you no harm. In fact, I am glad to see you alive. My master and I feared these past few days that you were dead."

"Who are you?" Neturu asked. The *hinavu* remained poised to fight.

"I am Nef. My master is Gibson bin Jianin."

Neturu did not know what to say. "Why would you be concerned about my death? What do you want?"

Nef paused before answering. "My master was a friend to your father, even if you—and he—did not know it. And I need your help."

Neturu shook his head. "I can do nothing for you."

"You stopped him," Nef said, gesturing with his head toward the *hinavu*. "And you can help us get out of the city."

"That was—" But Neturu did not finish his thought. He looked around. Then he said, "I just didn't want him to kill them—I didn't want . . ." He gestured vaguely toward the servants. "I didn't want them to die."

Nef nodded. "You are the on-Dam." He stared intently at him for a moment before continuing. "You *are* the on-Dam. And as the Sword, you will hold many lives in your hands. As you hold ours now."

The words sank in slowly, and Neturu realized this *Yinoi* was setting a course for him to follow. If he desired it. The same course Doman had suggested to him earlier. He looked around at the gathered people; he turned back to Nef. "What do you think I can do?" he asked.

Nef gestured toward the former servants of the house. "My master sent me here to gather any of his house who wished to remain with him. But the city gates are secured by now. There won't be an easy way for us to get away." He paused. "But you and your scorcher friends could take us out through Pekel."

A few of the servants muttered protests. They did not want to be unclean.

Nef turned and spoke to them, silencing them. "You have one chance to remain with the House of Jianin. One. You can come with me or not. Gibson has promised that any who come will be free—released from servitude but free to remain in his employ or go. If you stay, you can take what the Council gives you. A new home. New masters."

One of the former servants stepped forward. "I will come with you," he said.

Nef nodded. "What about you Telasa? Kaina?" He turned toward the old woman who was kneeling beside the young woman who had been cut down. "You all will have to decide quickly."

The old woman looked up. Her gnarled hands were covered with blood; she had wrapped the fallen woman's shawl around her neck to stanch the flow. Neturu looked down on her piteously, knowing there was no hope after such an injury.

"I know you loved her," Nef said. "But our master cares for you, too. He told me to bring you out." Nef stepped toward the old woman and held out his hand, urging her to stand.

Kaina shook her head. "I will go," she said. "But we cannot leave Sarana. She still lives."

"Impossible," Neturu said. And he stepped forward, drawn inexorably by the old woman's words.

"You do not know God's power," the old woman said.

But he did. Or at least he knew there were greater powers at work among the *Yinoi* than he once knew. He recalled the little burning stones driving back the darkness of Pekel, guiding the physician's hands.

Nef knelt beside Kaina and pulled back the bloody fabric. He pulled it slowly from her neck and tossed it to the side. He ran his fingers over her blood-smeared throat, probing gently. "There's no wound," he said.

Neturu shuffled forward and picked up the discarded shawl. It was covered with her blood and still damp. *How can there be no wound?* He felt a little shiver on his arms, a tingling that began in his hands, and a superstitious part of his mind reacted. He dropped the bloody shawl and took a step back.

Nef laid his head gently against the young woman's blood-stained chest. "By the Wayfarer," he said softly. "She's not dead."

CHAPTER THIRTY-TWO.
WAYFARERS.

Gibson lingered on the dark hillside as the sky lightened in the east. Nef had not come. Or if he had, he had already left, as Gibson had told him to do. It was time to follow his own admonition.

In the city—in the distance—fires burned, and smoke-woven darkness obscured the lights of the temple. The *hinavu* had wrought destruction, and Gibson wondered how many of the Great Houses had felt the wrath of Hrusk in the night. At least a dozen homes in Gazelem had burned, but the *hinavu* had already been withdrawing from the Jewel City—no doubt to converge on the Great City itself—when Gibson escorted Lisana home. Their last moments alone, in the mostly empty streets of Gazelem, still filled his mind with longing and anger.

Her own parents' home had not been scathed. Once again, she had not paid anything for her obstinance. And he had left her there without any ceremony, and without renewing his invitation to her. He had not even exchanged greetings—or farewells—with her parents.

Perhaps I was petulant. He criticized himself silently, but not harshly.

He knew what she would have said, and he had needed to move quickly. Even if she had indicating any willingness to go, she would not have gone immediately. She would have found ways to slow him, to impede him. All the way to her parents' home, she had urged him to bargain with Tendar. She was convinced he could still leverage the power of his House to form a partnership with Tendar, especially since his family's maps and journals were safe with Maran.

He wondered if she was right about that and about Tendar's design to find the fallen Wayfarer.

It was possible she was right. He had to admit that. She often was right. But he found it difficult to believe in this instance. It seemed more likely Tendar had decided to use the House of Jianin as an example, to show the other houses what happened to the prophet's followers and sympathizers.

And yet, if the Wayfarer could be found, the discovery would be far greater than anything the House of Jianin had done in days past. The discovery of the Oasis of Rume and establishment of the road through the *pustinya* was nothing compared to recovering the fallen Wayfarer.

Gibson felt a stirring in his chest, and a fierce sort of thought rose up. *If any house can lay claim to it, the House of Jianin should.*

And if any house could do it, no house was better suited than his own—even if his interests in the Great City had been taken from him. It was a long road to Shal-Gashun, but everything he needed was there. And perhaps, if he were successful, it would be enough to bring Lisana back to him.

He looked down the hillside, still hoping to see Nef and the others coming up the rocky incline. But he was alone.

He worried Nef and Pelem had not been able to get anyone out. Or perhaps they ran into trouble with the *hinavu*. He thought maybe he should have gone with them. But that was only hindsight. At the time he had sent them, his decision had been right.

And now it was time to go. *Every bargain exists within limits.*

He gathered up his pack and put his arms through the straps. It was strange to be alone, and to have so little, when setting out for Shal-Gashun. But he did not worry; he expected to join his people within days.

With a final glance toward the great city, he turned to the east and surveyed the hilly landscape, determined to keep his eyes forward.

Let him have it, he thought, thinking of Tendar. He smiled. The

thought of Tendar bin Amin finding the house in Gazelem empty—
except for a finely crafted bowl of *kivich* on the table—warmed his
heart.

And what if I did find the Wayfarer without him? He would not be pleased.
He chuckled and walked further up the rocky hillside, smiling.

Sarana opened her eyes and sat up suddenly. She gasped.

"Shh, child, be still." It was Kaina's raspy voice. The old woman
put a hand on her shoulder and eased her down. "You are safe."

Sarana settled back, only slowly realizing they had left the house.
They were in a scorcher wagon, riding among piles of clothing and
blankets. A scorcher walked along beside them, one hand resting on
the side of the wagon. Several more carts and wagons rolled slowly
down a narrow street, laden with the former belongings of the House
of Jianin. Sarana did not know where they were.

And then her breath caught, and she reached up and touched her
throat, jolted by the memory of the curved sword parting her flesh. A
man in the darkness, rushing toward them. And then the sword. She
had thought she was about to die.

She sat up again and ran her fingertips over her throat, searching.
But the reparative work of her blood was complete; no injury
remained. As always, she had been restored. Her heart calmed.

"It is a miracle you lived," Kaina said.

Sarana vaguely recalled the old woman's cries, the darkness, the
chaos of the moment before she fell. And then she remembered the
captain, and her confrontation with him. Dead. An arrow in his
throat. She touched her wrist. Her mark was gone. No one had
thought to pick it up.

Kaina spoke again. "You have been greatly blessed, child. The
blood of the ancient wayfarer surely flows in your veins." The old
woman paused. Then she chuckled warmly. "Perhaps all of your
looking at your beautiful hands was not in vain."

"What happened?" Sarana asked. "After I fell."

"The scorchers are taking us out of the city. Nef came back for us.
He convinced the scorchers to take us out through Pekel."

"Through Pekel?" Sarana looked around. The city looked empty and dim in the predawn gloom. "I remember Nef coming for us. And Pelem. Is this Pekel? Is everyone all right?" And then she remembered the blood running through Pelem's fingers. "Is Pelem all right?"

"He will be all right. He—his blood is not as strong as yours, but his injury was not as serious, either."

Sarana let out a breath, relieved. "Is this Pekel?"

"We're in the forsaken quarter."

The scorcher walking alongside their cart chuckled and said, "Where the unwanted dead are collected. One step up from Pekel."

"So they say," Kaina said.

"And so it is," the scorcher said. "For many."

"We'll be unclean," Sarana said. "We already are."

"As I said," the scorcher said.

"We don't have to go," Kaina said slowly. She gestured vaguely with a gnarled hand, and said, "This will eventually pass over us, like water over stones. My mother and my grandmother lived through the war that conquered my people. War does not seek to kill people like us."

"But you don't want to stay."

"There is little reason to kill women like us," Kaina said. "But no, child, I don't want to stay. And I knew you would not."

Sarana nodded, but exhaustion pulled at her. The labor of her body had emptied her, and the restorative power of her blood demanded its toll. She lay back on her makeshift bed and closed her eyes.

Kaina rested a hand on Sarana's shoulder and continued. "The scorchers will take us into Pekel, out of the city. From there, Nef will lead us to Gibson. The scorchers have agreed to sell him whatever provisions we need."

But only one thing mattered to Sarana. They would find Gibson.

Neturu stood at the eastern edge of Pekel, watching the remnants of the House of Jianin as they walked away. They were heading east, on foot, laden with what little they could carry on their backs. A pitiable group. But Nef, their leader, seemed capable. If it was possible to get them to safety, he might do it.

Neturu leaned on his crutches and rocked gently back and forth. The on-Dam of Hrusk. The Sword of Hrusk. It was a title he had lived near all his life, as his father's son, and a part of him had always assumed, at least vaguely, he would take his father's place. But then everything had changed; he had come to terms with the idea that he would not be the Sword.

And now the title was his to claim.

Perhaps.

He turned his head toward the burning city. His father's house lay in ruins. He despaired of it ever being rebuilt. He questioned if he was the one to do it.

My father has no other son.

The duty of a son of Hrusk was always to his fathers—both to the father who raised him, and to all of the fathers who came before. He touched the little bronze star beneath his shirt, and he remembered the face of his father.

What would he have me do?

He thought he knew. But he would not abandon his faith to do it.

Can the Sword of Hrusk bend the knee to Esana? It was a question his father had asked him.

Once, he had told himself he could. The reality seemed far more complicated. An army of Hrusk approached. War awaited, hungry for more blood. The assembled host would expect a resolute Sword; they would not accept a leader with riven loyalties. He shook his head and closed his eyes, a rueful huff escaping through his nose. Already he had held himself out to the *hinavu* as the Sword, and the tokens of his authority held them in sway. But that could change.

To the east, the escaped portion of the House of Jianin had disappeared among the hills in the pre-dawn gloom. Perhaps they would have it easier out there.

Neturu turned on his crutches and headed slowly back to Lihana's house. He had his own troubles to sort out.

It was several minutes before he realized he felt no more pain in his broken leg.

Epilogue.

The Line of Es.

A woman sits quietly beside a flickering fire. She runs her smooth, perfect fingers through her hair, reveling in the softness of the loose strands. Carefully, slowly, she ties her hair back with silky Hruskan ribbons, following a pattern shown to her by a hari-Hruskan woman.

As she works, she listens to the familiar voices ebbing and flowing around her in the semi-darkness. At her feet, in the flickering firelight, are wild flowers and grasses. And across from her is a man, her former master. Her teacher. He is writing letters on a slate, but she is watching his face.

The caravan is encamped beside a copse of *plesa* trees, and a little river flows nearby, burbling in the darkness. There is nothing but empty land in every direction, and each day the land grows more desolate.

"The last letter," Gibson says, and he draws the letter on the slate. "Some say it represents the world."

Sarana looks at the final letter, but she feels as if she is merely remembering a thing she once learned and forgot. Its sinuous lines follow the same hidden pattern her eyes have discerned as the letters and combinations have been revealed to her.

Gibson looks up. He sees her wide eyes, and he knows the woman who once cowered at his feet is gone.

He feels a little awe; he knows now she is a child of the ancient bloodline. The story of her resuscitation after being cut down by the *hinavu* would be difficult to believe, except Nef is not prone to exaggeration.

It is a wonder she ever became a part of his household.

He realizes she is waiting for him to continue. "The last letter. In the priestly Lines, it says that, in the beginning, Aram was alone in the world, and he was at peace with God. But he had not yet truly lived, and he had no knowledge of anything. And when he discovered he was in the world, he looked up to heaven and asked God what he should do.

"So God came down and stood on the ground beside Aram and said, 'You should stand up. There is a world prepared for you. A new world.' And when Aram stood, God walked with him through the world and showed him the forms of creation. There was much to see, and Aram listened carefully. But as time passed, he wondered what each thing was for. So he asked, 'What is the purpose of all these things?'

"But God said, 'In due time, Aram. You must first learn the forms of creation.' And so Aram learned what each thing was, but he did not know the purpose of any of them.

"One day they came to a place where four rivers flowed from the earth. And God said, 'From these three you may drink, but from the fourth you must never drink. You must never even touch it. For when you drink of that river, you shall always thirst, and you shall never be filled. It is the source of all that is good and evil.' "

Gibson pauses and looks at Sarana's face. Her dark eyes return his gaze.

"Did he drink from the fourth river?" Sarana asks.

He raises his eyebrows. "I think you know."

For a moment, Sarana says nothing. She does know. Or at least she thinks she knows. "*Che no peya, nikol ne bo zheya,*" she says. When he drinks, he will ever thirst.

"That's right." Gibson nods. "And if Aram had not drunk from the waters of the fourth river, he would not have become a true man, and the world would not be as it is. Or perhaps the world would be as it is, but we would not see it as it is." Gibson smiles and shakes his head. "The priests debate such things," he says. For a moment, he falls silent and broods upon the city he left behind.

"Why does the last letter represent the world?"

"Ah, well. That's just what some people say, priests mostly." Gibson makes an expansive gesture with his hand. "The world was the last thing Aram saw. He had seen all the forms of creation, but he finally saw the world as it is, when his eyes were finally opened."

Sarana considers the words, and her eyes stray toward the little burbling river. It flows in the darkness beyond their camp, its soft sounds evidencing its passage. She imagines God standing beside an ancient river in a shining white robe. He is gesturing toward the river, and his face is gentle, knowing.

She remembers then a thing Abasha once said about God: *He will gladly move a mountain for a man, but he is loath to move a man's hand.*

"What do you think you would have done?" Gibson asks. "Given the choice Aram was given?"

Sarana turns back to Gibson. "What?"

"If you had been given Aram's choice, what do you think you would have done?"

"Given the choice," Sarana says. "I think I'd drink."

Gibson looks at her with an amused smile and says, "Would you? Would you, like Aram, also steal from God?"

She laughs lightly and says, "I guess I would." And, then, touching her chest with her fingertips and caressing the little gold circle concealed beneath her clothes, she becomes thoughtful and says, "About that . . ."

THE END

Made in the USA
Monee, IL
02 November 2019

16230614R00173